The SAINT

Also by Tiffany Reisz

The Original Sinners: The Red Years

THE MISTRESS
THE PRINCE
THE ANGEL
THE SIREN

* * *

Ebook Novellas

THE LAST GOOD KNIGHT
THE MISTRESS FILES
THE GIFT (previously published as SEVEN DAY LOAN)
IMMERSED IN PLEASURE
SUBMIT TO DESIRE

* * *

Cosmo Red-Hot Reads from Harlequin

CAPTIVATED (coming soon)
SEIZE THE NIGHT (coming soon)
MISBEHAVING

There are more books in
The Original Sinners: The White Years series!
Watch for THE KING
coming soon from Harlequin MIRA

TIFFANY REISZ

The SAINT

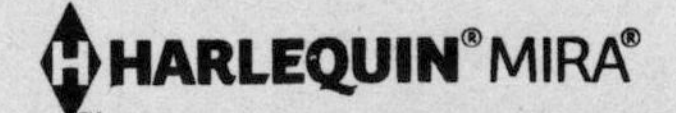

ISBN-13: 978-0-7783-1614-5

THE SAINT

For questions and comments about the quality of this book, please contact us at CustomerService@Harlequin.com.

HARLEQUIN®
www.Harlequin.com

Printed in U.S.A.

Dedicated to Saint Ignatius of Loyola
and all the good men who serve in God's Army—The Society of Jesus.

Dedicated to St. Ignatius of Loyola, His Holiness Pope Francis and all the soldiers of God who serve in The Society of Jesus.

"He was part of my dream, of course—but then I was part of his dream, too."

Through the Looking-Glass

Lewis Carroll

1

Nora

NORA SUTHERLIN WAS BEING FOLLOWED.

She didn't know she was being followed as she drove through Bavaria and into the heart of the Black Forest. Who would follow her, after all? And why? No one back home knew why she'd left, and no one at all knew where she'd gone. She kept her eyes on the road ahead and didn't once think to look behind her.

A vague uneasiness, a quiet sort of dread, had burrowed into her mind and made a home there. The sun, which had seen almost as much as she had in her lifetime, chased her car as she raced down a road shrouded in towering pine trees. Dark. Light. Dark. Light. Nora sensed the shadows wanted to catch her and keep her. She pushed the accelerator and fled deeper into the forest.

At last she came to the end of the road and spied a small thatched-roof cottage hidden among the pine and fir trees. Two stories and made all of stone, the little house seemed an exile from a fairy tale. A kindly woodcutter could live in that house—the sort who'd save a little girl from the jaws of a wolf. If the cottage were part of a fairy tale, who was she? The woodcutter? The girl?

Or the wolf?

She gathered her things from the car and strode toward the cottage. The owner had warned her there was no lock on the door but promised she would be safe. This part of the woods was on private land. No one would trouble her. No one at all.

Ivy covered the cottage from the ground to the chimney. She felt as if she'd stepped back four hundred years when she crossed the threshold. Gazing around the interior, she made her day's plan. She'd build a fire in that great gray stone hearth. She'd drink tea out of ruddy earthenware mugs. She'd sleep under heavy sheets in a rustic bed with posts of rough-hewn wood. In another time and under different circumstances, she would have loved it here. But grief clawed at her heart, and her task lay hard before her.

And it wasn't in Nora's nature to relish the prospect of sleeping alone.

She took her bags upstairs to the sole bedroom and knelt on the floor by the smaller of her two suitcases. She unzipped the bag carefully, slowly, reluctantly. From a bed of velvet she pulled out a silver box the size of a pew Bible and held it in her shaking hands.

As the cottage owner had promised, she found the cobblestone path that led to the lakeshore. The smell of pine surrounded her as she wandered down the path. It was April but the scent called Christmas to mind.... "O Holy Night" playing on the piano, red and green candles, silver bows, golden ornaments and Saint Nicholas coming to hide coins in the shoes of all the good little children. Idly she wished Saint Nicholas would see fit to visit her tonight. She'd welcome the company.

The path widened and ahead of her she saw the lake, its dark clear waters silver tipped in the sunlight that peeked through clouds. She stood on the stony shore at the water's edge.

She could do this. For days now she'd been preparing herself for this moment, preparing what she would say and how she would say it. She would be strong. For him, she would do this, could do this.

Nora swallowed hard and took a quick breath.

"Søren..." As soon as she spoke his name she stopped. She could get no more words out. They backed up in her throat and choked her like a hand around her neck. Turning her back on the water, she half walked, half ran to the house, the silver box clutched to her chest. She couldn't let it go yet. She couldn't say goodbye.

She set the silver box on the heavy wood fireplace mantel and turned her back to it. If she pretended it wasn't there, maybe she could believe it hadn't happened.

Outside the cottage, the wind picked up. The rickety, ivy-covered shutters rattled against the stone walls. Electricity brushed against her skin. Ozone scented the air. A storm was rising.

Nora started two fires—one in the great stone hearth and one in the smaller bedroom fireplace. The owner of the house had stocked the refrigerator and cabinets for her. An unnecessary kindness. She hadn't had much of an appetite for two weeks now, but she'd make herself eat if only to stave off the headaches hunger inflicted on her.

The day passed as she kept herself busy with small tasks. The cottage was clean but it gave her a sense of purpose to wash all the dishes in a large copper kettle and to sweep the hardwood floor with a witch's broom she found in the pantry. She worked until exhaustion overtook her and she lay down on top of the bed and napped.

Nora woke from a restive, dreamless sleep and ran water in the claw-foot porcelain bathtub. She sank into the heat, hoping it would seep into her skin and relax her. Yet when she emerged an hour later, pink and wrinkled, she still felt tight as a knot.

She dressed in a long white spaghetti-strap nightgown. The hemline tickled her ankles as she walked and brushed the tops of her bare feet. To distract herself, she stood in front of the mirror twisting and pinning her hair this way and that, taming the black waves into a low knot with loose tendrils that flowed over her neck and framed her face. When she finished, she almost laughed at the effect. In her white nightgown, with understated makeup and her hair coiffed in curls, she looked like a virgin bride on her wedding night. An older bride, of course—she'd turned thirty-six last month. But still the woman in the mirror looked demure, innocent, even scared. She thought grief aged people, but tonight she felt like a teenager again—restless and waiting, aching for something she couldn't name but that she knew she needed. But what was it? *Who* was it?

She wandered downstairs and considered eating. Instead of feeding herself, she fed the fire. As the wood crackled and burned, lightning split the sky outside the kitchen window. Thunder rumbled close behind. Nora stood at the window and watched the night rip itself open. Bursts of thunder rattled the forest again and again. Between rumbles, Nora heard a different sound. Louder. Clearer. Closer.

Footsteps on stone.

A knock on the door.

Then silence.

Nora froze. No one should be out here. No one but her.

The owner had promised her privacy. This cottage was the lone house for miles, he'd said. He owned all the land around it. She would be safe. She would be alone.

Another knock.

The cottage door had no lock. Whoever stood outside could walk in at any moment. For two weeks now the only emotions she'd felt were sorrow and grief. Now she felt something else—fear.

But Søren had trained her too well—Hebrews 13:2, "Do not neglect to show hospitality to strangers, for thereby some have entertained angels unawares." And such a night was fit for neither angel nor demon, saint or sinner.

She threw open the door. A man, not an angel, stood on the opposite side of the threshold.

"Sanctuary?"

Rain drenched his dark hair and beaded on his leather jacket.

"What the hell are you doing here?" she asked, crossing her arms over her chest, self-conscious about the low cut of her nightgown. She should have thrown on a robe.

"Begging for sanctuary. Should I do it again? Sanctuary?"

"Did you follow me?" she asked. She'd flown into Marseille last night and had dinner with him. She never dreamed he'd chase her all the way to Germany.

"I would have come sooner, but I took a wrong turn at Hansel and Gretel's. A girl in a red cloak gave me directions, and now I'm here, Snow White."

"You found your way here, Huntsman. You can find your way back," she said. "I can't give you sanctuary."

"Why not?"

"You know what will happen if I let you in."

"Exactly what we both want to happen."

"It can't happen—you and me. And you don't need me to tell you why."

The smile faded from his face.

"You need me," he said.

"It doesn't matter. I have to do this alone."

"You don't have to do it alone." He took an almost imperceptible step forward. The toes of his rain-soaked buff-colored boots touched but did not cross the threshold. "You do too much alone."

"I can't let you in," she said, and felt that fist in her throat again.

"Would he want you to face this alone?"

"No," she said. "He wouldn't."

"Let me in."

"That sounded like an order. I told you what I am. You know I give the orders."

She could already feel her resolve crumbling. Twenty-five years old, tall, deeply tanned, dark hair with the slightest wave to it that demanded a woman's fingers run through it again and again, clear celadon eyes—an inheritance from his Persian mother—and a face that someone should sculpt so it would endure even after both of them turned to dust and ashes… How could she turn him away? How could anyone?

"Then order me to come inside," he said.

She closed her eyes and held the door to steady herself. This was wrong. She knew it. She'd sworn before she'd even seen him that she wouldn't do this, not ever, not with him. But then she'd met him. And now, after all that had happened and the grief that threatened to overwhelm her, could anyone blame her for taking her comfort with him? One man would blame her. But was that enough to stop her?

"Order me in," he said again, and Nora opened her eyes. "Please."

She could never resist a beautiful man begging.

"Come in, Nico," she said to Kingsley's son. "That's an order."

2

Nora

SHE SHUT THE DOOR BEHIND NICO AND PULLED HIM to the fireplace. She helped him out of his jacket and boots. Battered and mud crusted, his shoes looked nothing like Kingsley's spit-shined riding boots. These were work boots, steel tipped and utilitarian.

"Do I want to know how you found me?" she asked as she brushed the mud off Nico's boots and set them to dry by the fireplace.

"I followed your trail of bread crumbs."

"Bread crumbs?"

"You might have accidentally left your bag open at the restaurant and I might have accidentally seen the address on your rental confirmation."

"Leaving my bag open *was* an accident," she said.

"Finding the address might not have been." He pulled off his socks and ran his hands through his hair, shaking the rain out of it.

"Like father, like son." She sighed. "You're as sneaky as Kingsley."

"Are you angry?"

"No, I'm not angry." She raised her hand to her forehead and rubbed at the tension headache lurking there. Nico pulled her hand down and looked at her with concern.

"Need food? Wine?" she asked before he could ask her how she was—a question she didn't want to answer. "Or did you bring your own?"

"There might be a bottle or two of Rosanella in the car."

"I won't make you bring them in," she said. Outside the storm still raged wild.

"I will later. First things first." Nico took her by the wrist and pulled her close.

"Nico..."

"Don't," he said. "Don't fight me. Let me help you."

Sighing, Nora rested her head against his chest and let him rub the knot of tension in her neck. When they'd met in December she'd had Zach with her, and Nico—only his mother called him Nicholas, he'd said—had shown her editor/friend/occasional lover all due deference. But when she visited again a month later, Nico did nothing to hide his delight at having her to himself. He was barely twenty-five. Handsome and young and French, what reason did he have for wanting her—nearly twelve years his senior and with a long history of sleeping with the man he'd learned was his biological father? She got her answer while they were out walking one day. Two women—a mother and daughter—had stopped them, asking for directions. The mother looked forty years old, the daughter around Nico's age. Both were well-dressed classic French beauties. Nico barely blinked at the daughter. To the mother he'd flashed a smile so flirtatious even his father would have been impressed. Kingsley's son had a fetish for older women.

Well...how nice.

"You're in pain," he said. "I can feel it all through you."

"I like pain," she reminded him.

"No one likes this kind of pain. I would know."

She lowered her eyes in sympathy. The man who'd raised Nico as his son had died five months ago. A month after that, she'd shown up and told him he had another father, which had torn the stitches on his still-healing grief. If anyone understood the pain she felt right now, it was Nico.

"Let me ease your pain tonight."

"How?" She looked up at him. "Can you bring people back to life?"

"I can bring *you* back to life."

She almost told him he was as arrogant as his father, but before she could speak, he kissed her.

Nervous as a virgin, her lips trembled under his. If it had been anyone but him, she would have wondered at this newfound shyness. She'd never been shy, never been demure, never been innocent. And yet, this was Kingsley's only son, and by sleeping with him she would lose something far more dear to her than her virginity had ever been.

"You're shaking," Nico said against her lips.

"I'm scared."

"Scared? Why?"

"I don't know."

"I'm here," he whispered. "You don't have to be afraid."

He was here. That was why she was afraid. But the fear didn't stop her from opening her mouth to receive his kiss. He kissed along her jawline to her ear, nipped at her earlobe. Over the pulse point in her neck, he pressed a long, languid kiss. The heat from his mouth seared her all the way to her spine. His kisses were neither tentative nor hurried. As he kissed her, her muscles slackened, her skin flushed with heat and the fear faded. For the first time in days, she felt human. Since meeting back in December, she and Nico had been in weekly contact. Emails, phone calls—he even wrote her letters by hand. Letters she read and reread and answered. Letters she burned before anyone found them.

Her head fell back as Nico kissed the hollow of her throat. He placed his hands on either side of her neck and rubbed his thumbs into the tendons of her shoulders.

"What's this?" he asked as he lifted the chain of her necklace.

Nora wrapped her hand around the pendant. She couldn't talk about it yet. It meant too much to her. Especially now.

"A saint medal. It's a Catholic thing."

"I know about saints. I am one, remember?"

"Saint Nicholas brought me Christmas early this year," she said, smiling as he kissed her throat. "Although sleeping with him will put me on the naughty list for eternity."

"It's my list. I'll be the judge of that." He slipped the strap of her nightgown off her shoulder and traced her bare shoulder with his fingertips. Her body shivered with the pleasure from the touch of his work-roughened skin.

"You're so beautiful in white." Nico whispered the words into her ear as he ran his hand down her back, caressing the silk of her gown.

Nora said nothing. She'd bought the white gown to wear for Søren on their anniversary, a celebration that wouldn't happen now.

She released the medal and it fell once more against her skin. She wrapped her arms around Nico's broad shoulders and pressed her breasts to his chest. He wore a basic black cotton T-shirt and work jeans. She wore a silk nightgown. He'd been working all day and had come to her with mud on his boots. She'd been mourning all week and came to him with sorrow in her heart.

"I want to spend all night inside you," Nico breathed against her neck.

She pulled away from his embrace, but only to take him by the hand.

"Come upstairs," she said. "We can sleep when we're dead."

She led him up to the bedroom. He released her hand to tend to the fading fire. He fed it with paper first, then kindling, then threw a log on top of the smoldering flames. The room warmed and glowed red from the heat and firelight.

"You're good at that," Nora said. "Do you have a fireplace at your house?"

"Two of them," he said. *Two of zem.* Nora bit the inside of her mouth to keep from laughing. She'd learned from Nico that he'd spent a year in California and another year in Australia in his teens. Even though he lived in France now, he'd mastered English to the point that his accent was faint. Still there, but certainly not as pronounced as Kingsley's deliberately exaggerated accent. But every now and then Nico's accent came out in full force. "You should come to my home. I'd like you to see it."

She'd refused all invitations to come to his home and instead met him in neutral locations—Arles, Marseille. She knew once they were alone together in his house or hers this would happen. And so it had.

"If I come to your house, will you put me to work?" she asked as she came to stand next to him. The fire crackled and a burning ash landed near her foot. Nico brushed it away with his bare hand.

"Everyone works at Rosanella."

"I still can't believe you are what you are."

"Why not?" He smiled up at her.

"Kingsley does not get his hands dirty. Not in the literal sense anyway."

"You think he's ashamed that I'm a farmer?"

"You make wine. He drinks wine. He's proud of you."

Whether he'd admit it or not, Kingsley had fallen in love with the idea of being Nico's father. "My son the vintner," he said sometimes, and Nora saw the pride in his eyes. It broke her heart that Nico had yet to feel any pride that Kingsley was his father.

"And you?" Nico looked up at her from where he knelt on the floor. "Are you proud of me?"

"Does it matter?"

"It matters more that you're proud of me than him."

She caressed his face with the back of her hand. The slight stubble on his chin chafed her skin. Once she'd asked him what he was looking for every time he went to bed with a woman ten, fifteen, twenty years older than he. A mother figure? A teacher? A trainer? "My Rosanella," Nico had answered, referring to the name of his vineyard's bestselling Syrah, "the one woman who is all women."

"Yes, my Nico. I'm proud of you."

They gazed at each other. The shutters were closed. Fire alone warmed and brightened the room. Outside, the wind and rain poured and howled so wildly she imagined everyone but she and Nico had been wiped off the face of the earth. Only they two remained, sole survivors.

Nico rose up on his knees, put his hands on her waist and kissed her stomach through the fabric of her gown. Slowly he slid his hands down the backs of her legs and grasped her ankles. Nora buried her fingers in his hair as he kissed her bare thigh where it peeked out of the hip-high slit in her nightgown. He ran his hands back up her legs. Everything he did, every way he touched her, set her nerves tingling and her stomach tightening. Now with his thumbs he parted the slit of her gown. Nora grasped the bedpost behind her as Nico pressed a kiss onto the apex of her thighs. She pushed her hips forward as Nico sought her clitoris with his tongue.

"What's this?" he asked, tickling the little metal hoop he'd found.

"Clit ring."

Nico raised an eyebrow.

"I'm going to play with that later."

"You can play with it now."

She opened her legs wider, and he slid one finger between her wet seam and inside her. He hooked his finger over her pubic bone and ground his fingertip into the soft indention he found there.

He teased her with his tongue before sucking on her clitoris in earnest. She leaned against the footboard behind her to steady herself. The room carried the heady scent of smoke. The heat from the fire stoked her own inner heat. She could hear Nico's ragged breaths as he licked and kissed her. He turned his hand and pushed a second finger inside her. He spread his fingers apart, opening her up for him. Her inner muscles twitched around his hand. It was too much. She couldn't wait anymore.

"Stop," she ordered. Nico obeyed and rested back on his hands. She grasped the fabric of his T-shirt and he raised his arms. He unbuttoned his jeans as she tossed his shirt to the floor. Hard muscles lurked under his clothes—muscles he'd earned working the vineyard and not at a gym. He put those muscles to use as he rose up and pulled her hard against him. She felt his erection pressing against her. She raised one leg and wrapped it around his back, opening herself up to him. The tip went in easily and Nico lifted her and brought her down onto him, impaling her. It was only a few steps to the bed and he carried her there, laying her on her back across the burgundy coverlet.

Nico covered her body with his and drove into her with a slow sensuous thrust that sent ecstasy radiating from her back to her fingers. He pulled out to the tip and pushed back in again, her wet body giving him no resistance. He showed total mastery of his desire as he moved in her, advancing, retreating, performing the ancient steps of this primal dance with powerful male grace. He seemed in no hurry to come, as if he fully intended to stay inside her all night. She ran her hands down the length of his torso and let them rest at the small of his back. She could feel his taut muscles working as his back bowed every time he entered her and arched with each retreat.

With every thrust, Nora raised her hips to meet his. The base of his penis grazed her clitoris, and she lifted her head to kiss and bite his shoulders. Fluid ran out of her, glazing her inner thighs. She lifted her knees to open herself even more to him. She breathed in and inhaled his scent—warm and alive, like the new spring that surrounded them in the forest.

He slipped his hand between their bodies. She shivered beneath him, her head falling back against the bed as he grasped her swollen clitoris between his fingertips and stroked it. He pushed forcefully into her, and Nora gasped as her inner muscles clenched around him.

The world went still and silent around them. Nora couldn't even hear the storm anymore, the crackling of the fireplace, the creaking of the bed. All she could hear was the quiet metallic jangling of Nico's belt, his ragged breaths and the sound of her wetness.

Every part of her body went tight as Nico bore down on her, and came inside her with a shudder. He pulled out and kissed a path down her chest and stomach. With his head between her thighs he lapped at her clitoris again. Her back tensed, her stomach quivered, and she inhaled and forgot to breathe out. He pushed his fingers into her dripping body and sent her over the edge. Every muscle inside her spasmed violently. She hadn't had sex in so long that it felt as though a week's worth of orgasms thundered through her all at once.

Nico's semen spilled out of her and onto the bed. Nora wrapped her arms around him as he relaxed on top of her, covering her neck and shoulders in carnal kisses.

"Thank you," she said. "I needed that."

"So did I. I've needed it for months."

He kissed her long and deep on the mouth before pulling himself up.

He crawled off the bed and grabbed his shirt off the floor. She watched him pull himself back together. She'd always loved this part, watching a man dress after sex. She loved the perfunctory way Nico pulled on his shirt as if it never occurred to him she would be watching him and enjoying the view.

"Where are you going?"

"You need to drink my wine. Want some?"

"Nico, if you came in a cup I would drink it."

He stared at her. Had she actually made the son of Kingsley Edge blush?

"We'll save that vintage for later." With a wide grin, he left her alone in the bedroom.

She pulled herself up slowly. She'd come so hard even her arms trembled. Was that from the sex? Possibly. She also hadn't eaten anything all day. She cleaned herself off in the bathroom and found Nico downstairs in the kitchen uncorking a bottle of red wine. He handed her a glass, and she raised it to her lips. It had a sweet pungent scent, and when she drank it, she could taste its potency. A virile wine, just like its maker.

"Parfait." She sighed as she lowered the glass. "But that will get me drunk in about two more sips if I don't eat something."

"Sit," he said and pointed at the large battered armchair by the fireplace. "If you please."

She laughed at his chivalry.

"I do please," she said, sitting and pulling her legs to her chest. She felt relaxed now, loose limbed and spent. She could almost make herself forget the box on the mantel. Almost. But not quite.

"What is it?" Nico asked.

"Nothing. Only wondering how much trouble I'm in for sleeping with you."

"Trouble with whom?"

"Kingsley."

"Is it his business?" From his tone, Nora could tell Nico had no plans to tell Kingsley anything about tonight.

"You're his son. He'll make it his business."

Nico brought her a plate of cheese, crackers and grapes.

"Don't worry about it," he said. "If he's angry, we'll tell him I took advantage of you in your grief."

"Oh, good idea. He might buy that except for the part where you took advantage of me." She took the plate from him and balanced it on her knee. "He does know me, after all."

"Being with you was my choice," Nico said. "My choice, my consequences. Not yours."

"Oui, monsieur. Merci beaucoup," she said in her best sultry French.

"You know I speak English," he reminded her as he took a grape off her plate.

"I know," she said. "But I speak French, too. Thank your father for that skill."

"He made you learn it?"

"He and Søren would speak it all the time around me while I stood there like an idiot not understanding a word. I had to learn it so I knew what they were saying about me."

Nico sat on the floor in front of her, his arms clasped around his knees. He looked young sitting there like that, but still undeniably strong and masculine. In the low firelight she could see the veins in his forearms, and the light dusting of dark hair on his skin.

"How do you know Kingsley?" he asked between sips of wine.

"How do I know Kingsley? That's a loaded question. You sure you want to know the answer?"

"I asked." He shrugged his shoulders and in that moment, in that shrug, she saw his father in him. So dismissive. So French. So Kingsley.

"Why do you want to know?"

"I don't understand him at all," Nico confessed, and she saw a flash of grief in his eyes. Grief to match her own. She crooked her finger and Nico moved closer, close enough to kiss her knee and rest his chin on her thigh.

"He's a hard man to like and a very easy man to love. But he's nearly impossible to understand," she said, caressing the back of his neck.

"But you understand him."

"I do. But he and I, we're the same in many ways."

"I want to know him. I want to know you even more."

"Unfortunately, there's no way to tell you the story of Kingsley and me without telling you the story of Søren and me," she said. "It's all one story, the three of us."

"Will it hurt to talk about it?"

"Yes," she said. "But a little pain never stopped me before."

"Will you tell me?" Nico asked. He took her hand in his, twining their fingers together. She looked down at their interlocked hands—his tanned, calloused hand dwarfed her paler, daintier fingers. Moments earlier he'd lain between her thighs, and only now did they hold hands for the first time. The day they'd met she'd told him who he was. Perhaps it was time to tell him who *she* was.

"Okay, story time, then. But I'll charge you. I get paid for my stories."

"I'll pay you in orgasms."

"It's a deal," Nora said and she and Nico laughed. God, it felt good to laugh like this again. A few days ago she would have bet she'd never laugh again. He turned his hand and sensuously rubbed the center of her palm with his thumb.

"Since this is the Black Forest, we should make it a fairy tale," she said.

"I like fairy tales."

"You'll like this one, too. It begins with a whimper but ends in a bang."

"Is it a real fairy tale? Are there witches and fairies in it?" he teased.

"Sort of."

"Kings, yes?" Nico grinned.

"Definitely," she said. "One king. One queen."

"What else?"

"Since we're in Grimm's territory, we're going to do this right," she said. "Ready?"

Nico kissed Nora's fingertips.

"Ready," he said, gazing up at her with heat in his eyes. She could still scarcely believe Nico was here. She'd idly wished for him earlier and behold—he'd come to her in a storm, begging sanctuary. What other magic might work itself tonight?

"All Grimm's fairy tales start and end the same way," she said.

She took a deep breath and began.

"Once there lived…" She paused and let the knife of grief stab her stomach again. She took the pain, breathed through it and let it out. "Once there lived…a priest."

3

Eleanor

SHE WAS EITHER DYING OR HAVING AN ORGASM. ELLE couldn't quite tell which.

"Something funny, Miss Schreiber?" her teacher demanded.

Elle glanced up and stared at Sister Margaret's forehead. Safer than looking her in the eyes.

"Nope. I… That's a great sculpture," Elle said, pointing at the image on the projector screen at the front of her Catholic studies class. "Is she getting, you know, murdered there? Or…something else?"

"Not murdered," Sister Margaret said with a smile. "Although I can understand why you might think that she was dying."

Sister Margaret turned back to the image of St. Teresa of Avila she'd projected onto the screen. Every Friday was Know Your Saints day at St. Xavier High School.

"This famous sculpture by Gian Lorenzo Bernini is called the *Ecstasy of St. Teresa*. Teresa of Avila was a mystic. Can anyone tell me what a mystic is? Mr. Keyes?"

She pointed to Jacob Keyes in the front row.

"Um..." he said. "People who had mystical experiences?"

Elle rolled her eyes. Didn't he know you weren't supposed to define a word with that same word?

"Close," Sister Margaret said. "Throughout our Catholic tradition, our clergy has acted as the intermediary between the faithful and God. Mystics are those rare souls who connect with God in a profound way without an intermediary. In the case of St. Teresa, an angel of the Lord came to her. Let's read her own words about it. Page three hundred seventy."

They all turned to the page and at the top in a box Elle read:

> I saw an angel near me, on the left side in bodily form. In this vision it pleased the Lord that I should see it thus. He was not tall, but short, marvelously beautiful with a face which shone as though he were one of the highest of angels.... One of the highest of angels who seemed to be all of fire. I saw in his hands a long golden spear, and at the point of the iron there seemed to be a little fire. This I thought that he thrust several times into my heart, and that it penetrated to my entrails.

"As you can see," Sister Margaret said, "the sculptor was attempting to show the profound and sudden closeness to God St. Teresa experienced when the angel came to her and struck her with the arrow, and, Miss Schreiber, you seem to be laughing again. Would you care to share with the class exactly what you find so funny?"

Elle sensed all eyes in the class on her. She really wished Sister Margaret would stop calling on her. Maybe if she told her the truth, Sister Margaret might learn her lesson.

"Nothing," Eleanor said. "Except St. Teresa's having an orgasm."

"Excuse me?" Sister Margaret sounded scandalized.

"Oh, come on. She's got her head back and her eyes are closed and her mouth's all open. And the angel is *thrusting* the arrow into her and she's all on fire. Seriously, *penetrated to the entrails?* Sign me up for that. I wanna be a saint if I can get some of that action."

The entire class burst into uproarious laughter. Only Sister Margaret didn't seem amused.

"Eleanor," Sister Margaret said and nothing more.

"I know. I know." Elle gathered up her books and headed to the vice principal's office.

Again.

Luckily V.P. Wells didn't have time for a theological argument today. He told her to stop talking about orgasms in her Catholic studies class and she promised to keep her commentary to herself from now on. He only threatened her life once before sending her out. After gathering her books from her locker, Elle left school and headed home.

As she turned a corner at Elm Street, Elle sensed something behind her. She glanced back and saw a car in her peripheral vision. Ignoring it, she started walking again. The car followed, going slow enough to stay behind her.

Finally the driver pulled up next to her and rolled down the window.

"I lost my new puppy," the man in the car said. "Will you come help me find him?"

"Oh, hell, no," she said, glaring into the car at the almost-handsome man sitting behind the wheel. "I saw that very special episode of *Diff'rent Strokes.*"

"Then will you come help me drive this Porsche into the ground?"

"Oh, hell, yes!"

Elle raced around to the passenger side, threw herself in the car and launched herself into the driver's arms.

"Dad, what are you doing here?" She clung to him tightly and pressed a kiss onto his cheek.

"I haven't seen my little girl in weeks. I thought you'd want to come on a test drive with me."

She slammed the door behind her.

"Then let's drive."

Her father put the car in gear and tore down the street. With her father at the wheel, the Porsche slunk through the narrow city streets with the lissome speed of a cheetah. Elle put on her seat belt without being told. Once they hit the highway her dad would rev the engine and swerve in and out of lanes. He knew where all the speed traps were and always had a radar detector with him.

"I love it." Elle rubbed her hands over the dash.

"That's real leather."

"Where'd you get it?"

"Borrowed it from a friend."

"Can I drive it?"

"You have a valid driver's license and proof of insurance?"

Elle glared at him.

"Dad."

"Fine."

He took the exit ramp and they changed seats in a gas station parking lot.

"Now go easy," he warned her as she put the car in gear. "It's got a featherlight touch. The space shuttle doesn't accelerate this fast."

"That's because the space shuttle doesn't have its engine up its ass."

Elle put her foot on the accelerator and gunned it. Gravity

introduced itself to her body, but she and her stomach ignored the pressure and didn't back off. Her dad was a good driver. She was better. He handled a car like a NASCAR driver. All power and speed. She drove like a Formula One driver—pure feminine finesse. Porsches required finesse. The engine sat in the back, not the front, and many a new Porsche owner had wrecked their baby on the way home from the car lot because they didn't know how to handle a rear engine.

She took the exit and soon they were careening down a scenic two-lane highway at eighty miles an hour.

Her dad sat back, looking utterly relaxed even as the trees raced by them in nothing but a brown blur.

"Keep it steady. Don't pump the accelerator."

"I'm not pumping. I'm pushing. I love this car."

"I'm not keeping you from something, am I?" her dad asked.

"Nah. Just a hot date with an extremely religious, much older guy."

"Anybody I need to kill?"

"Already been killed. I have to write a paper on Jesus."

"Okay, you can date Jesus. But nobody else."

"He's about the only guy I know of who doesn't piss me off constantly," she said.

"You're never going to get a boyfriend with an attitude like that so...keep that attitude."

"I don't want a boyfriend. Every guy at school is an asshole."

"I'm happy to hear I don't have to get the shotgun out yet. I kind of like the thought of you not having a boyfriend. Ever."

"Don't worry. No boys for me."

"Girls?" He gave her a steady, "is there something you need to tell me" stare.

She shook her head.

"No girls, either."

"Thank God."

"I want a man."

"Where's my shotgun?"

"Right here."

Elle gunned the engine.

"Mom said I'm not allowed to date. Ever, I think. She didn't give me an age."

"You know your mother. She doesn't want you getting in trouble like she did."

"You mean knocked up at seventeen? And whose fault is that?"

"Elle, shut up and drive."

"Sorry, Dad."

Elle shut her mouth and concentrated on the curves ahead. They could come out of nowhere on these back roads, but that was what made the drive so much fun. Whipping around curves, facing the unknown, looking death in the face. It was exactly like high school, except for the part about it being fun.

As they drove deeper into nowhere, Elle noticed her father studying her.

"What?" she asked. "Something wrong?"

"You look like your mother."

"You want me to let you out right here?" She pointed at the expanse of nothingness around them.

"Your mother is a very beautiful woman."

"She is a very crazy woman who is driving me crazy. Did I mention the crazy?"

"What's she doing that's so crazy these days?"

"Our priest, Father Greg, is sick. Mom worshipped him so she's real upset."

"Did you worship him?"

"He called me *Ellen*."

Elle turned around in a driveway.

"I have homework," she said. "I should get home."

"No problem. Glad I got to see my baby girl."

"Ugh. Don't call me that."

Her father laughed and ruffled her hair. Maybe she could crash the car in such a way it would only hit his side....

"Sorry, kid. You're growing up too fast."

"You know I'll be sixteen in less than three weeks."

"God, you make me feel old." He exhaled heavily. Her dad wasn't old at all. Only thirty-five. And he would have looked thirty-five if he didn't live so hard. He drank too much, did things he shouldn't, hung out with bad, scary people. But still, he didn't make her go to church or do her homework, so between him and her mom, she knew which parent she preferred to hang out with.

"I can't wait to get older. Trust me, I'm counting the minutes until my birthday. Driver's license, here I come."

Elle grinned at the prospect of finally being able to drive to school, drive to the city, drive anywhere she wanted, especially away from her mom and her house and her life.

"Elle?"

"What?"

"You know I can't buy you a car, right? And neither can your mom."

Her stomach knotted up.

"Dad, you promised me two years ago—"

"I had a lot more money two years ago than I do now."

"What happened?"

"Life's expensive. Business isn't great."

"Business isn't great," she repeated. "You mean the car-stealing, chop-shop business? Did that get hit by the recession, too?"

"You have a smart mouth," her father said, all affection gone from his voice.

"If you weren't going to buy me a car, you shouldn't have promised me one."

"You want to keep this one?"

"You're the car thief in the family, not me."

"Can you back off me for five fucking seconds, please?"

Elle pulled over a block from her house, where there would be no chance of her mom seeing her with her father.

She turned off the car and sat in silence.

"Elle...baby...I'm sorry. I wish I could buy you anything you wanted, but I can't right now. I owe some money. I have to pay it back."

"Whatever."

"Don't be like that. You know I love you, and I'd do anything for you."

"I know," she said, although she wasn't certain that she did. "I gotta go."

Her father grabbed her forearm, pulled her over and gave her a gruff kiss on the cheek.

"Don't be mad at your dad. He's doing the best he can."

"Tell my dad I'm not mad." Her shoulders sagged. Her heart sagged. Her hopes sagged. "I just wish things were different."

"Yeah, well...you and me both, kid."

She gave him a faint smile and got out of the car.

She shut the door behind her and said under her breath, "Don't call me *kid*."

As she walked the final block to her house she choked back tears of disappointment. Two years ago, on her fourteenth birthday, he'd promised her with all his heart and all his soul he would get her a car for her sixteenth birthday. And she'd believed him even though deep down she knew better. He made promises all the time and never kept them. *I promise I'll see you at Christmas. I promise I'll make the school play. I promise I'll get a new job so you won't have to worry about me.* Promises made, never kept. One day she'd learn.

Maybe it was her fault. Maybe nobody could be trusted to do what they said they'd do. Once in her life she'd love to have someone who gave enough of a shit about her to make her a promise and keep it. For once she wanted someone to treat her like she mattered.

Nice pipe dream there. That happening was about as likely as her getting banged by an angel like St. Teresa.

Eleanor unlocked the back door and walked into the kitchen. The car was in the driveway, but where was her mom? Her mom worked the night shift as a motel manager and did bookkeeping part-time for a small construction company. If she wasn't at work, she was either asleep or at the kitchen table with her ledgers and adding machine. Eleanor made herself dinner—a bowl of cereal—and went into the living room to eat.

She found her mom in her shabby bathrobe curled up on the frayed paisley couch, wiping her eyes.

"What's wrong?" Elle asked her mother. Her mom swiped at her face with a tissue. "Did Father Greg die?"

"No," her mother said, pushing a hank of black hair over her ear. "But he's probably not coming back. Not anytime soon."

"I'm sorry," Elle said, sitting cross-legged on the floor. Her mom never let her eat on the furniture, which made no sense. The furniture was old and threadbare and stained. Like a little cereal on the couch was going to make things any worse than they already were. "What's going to happen?"

"We're getting a new priest in the meantime," her mother said, entirely without enthusiasm.

"That's good, right?"

"No, it's not good."

"Why not?"

"The new priest is..."

"What?"

"He's a Jesuit."

"A what?"

"A Jesuit," her mother repeated. "They're an order of priests. They founded your high school, although I don't think any Jesuits teach there anymore."

"Are they bad priests?"

"They're scholars," she said. "Scientists. And very, very liberal."

"That's a bad thing?"

"Jesuits are... They can be... It might be fine. I would have preferred a loving shepherd to a scholar, though."

"Well," Elle said, taking a bite of her cereal, "maybe you'll get lucky. Maybe this new priest will really love sheep."

Her mother glared at her.

"I know. I know," she said for the second time today. She gathered her food and her books and went to her room. Did no one like having her around?

She finished up her cereal in her room and stared at her pile of homework. But how could she even think about doing homework with so much shit going on? Her dad wasn't getting her a car for her birthday like he promised. Her mom was having a nervous breakdown over the new priest. And she was turning sixteen in a couple of weeks and had no boyfriend, no money, no car forthcoming and no hope that things were going to get better, now or ever. Her stomach felt like someone had punched it. Her head ached and her throat itched. She didn't know if she wanted to scream or cry or both at the same time.

Instead she walked into the bathroom and locked the door behind her.

She turned on her curling iron and sat on the toilet while waiting for it to heat up.

Five minutes later she stood in front of the counter and rolled her left sleeve up. She picked up the curling iron and took a breath.

Easy. You can do this. She started the countdown.

Three.

Two.

One.

On the *one* Elle pushed the burning metal barrel against her left wrist. She whimpered as pain scalded her right to her soul. She lifted the curling iron off her arm, then pressed it back down again. After one full second she pulled it off and dropped the curling iron back onto the counter.

She panted through the pain, not fighting it, but accepting it, relishing it, letting it remind her she was alive and could feel everything she wanted to feel. There were boys at school who would have cried like little bitches if they'd gotten burned like that.

She rolled her sleeve down over the burns and turned off her curling iron. She went back to her room and sat on her bed, her hands still slightly shaking. She opened her math book and got out a pencil.

She felt much better now.

4

Eleanor

SUNDAY MORNING, ELLE DECIDED SHE WOULD NEVER go back to church again. She'd thought about this decision ever since she'd found her mother crying in the living room. All her life, her mother wanted to be a nun. She dreamed of the day she'd take her vows and put on her habit the way other girls dreamed about their wedding days. But at seventeen she'd fallen in love with a handsome charmer named Will and a few months later, she was married and pregnant, and not in that order.

And here her mother was, sixteen years later—divorced, working two jobs and going to church five days a week because it was the only thing that gave any meaning to her life. Well, it didn't give any meaning to Elle's life. She doubted God actually existed. She thought the Catholic Church was stupid to ban birth control and then tell priests they couldn't get married. Make up your damn mind. Either people should be fruitful and multiply or they should be celibate and childless. The church didn't get to have it both ways. The hypocrisy disgusted her. The Catholic Church was one big business and they all worked for it.

So she was quitting. Now how to tell her mother this?

Elle flinched as he mother banged on her door.

"What?" she yelled as she grabbed a pillow and slammed it down on her face.

"Eleanor Louise Schreiber! Get out of bed this instant."

Here we go. Now or never. She steeled herself and called out with more confidence than she felt…

"I'm not going."

"What?"

Elle lifted the pillow up.

"I'm not going to Mass this morning." She enunciated every word. "I'm a Buddhist!"

"Eleanor, get out of bed this instant and get ready for Mass."

"I'm an atheist. I'll incinerate the second I walk into church. It's for everyone's good I stay away from that place."

Her mother growled under her breath.

"I don't even know what that is, but I'm not having this argument with you."

"Then don't. I have civil rights. You can't force me to go to church against my will."

"As long as you're underage, and you're living in my house, I can."

Elle sat up completely and met her mom's eyes. Enough joking around. She meant it this time.

"Mom," she said, her voice as calm and as reasonable as possible, "I don't want to play this game anymore."

"Church isn't a game."

"It isn't real."

Her mother said nothing at first but she didn't leave, either.

Bad sign. Her mom wasn't giving up. Her mom was about to bring out the big gun—guilt.

"Father Greg is officially retiring soon. He's not coming back. Today is the day the new priest is starting. If the new priest hires someone else to the church's books, you don't get free tuition to St. Xavier anymore. I need you to help me make a good impression."

Elle shrugged. "Don't care. Send me to public school. No more uniforms." And no more fights on the bus. No more getting mocked because her dad had been in jail. No more getting teased for her breasts that didn't seem to want to stop growing. No more blood on her knees.

"Eleanor, I'm serious."

"Mom, *I'm* serious. You're going to have to give up trying to turn me into a junior version of you minus the kid you didn't want. Go without me. There's nothing at church for me. Not now. Not ever."

Elle threw herself back into bed. She knew she hadn't heard the last of this topic, but maybe winning the battle was the beginning of winning the war. Covering her face with her pillow again, Elle tried to will herself to fall back to sleep.

She waited to hear her mother's footsteps retreating. But instead of creaking floors, she heard whispered words. Eleanor peeked out at her mother from under her pillow. Too bad her mother hated men so much. Her dad was right. At thirty-three her mother was still young looking and beautiful. At least she could have been beautiful if she tried at all. No makeup. She never did anything with her hair. She wore clothes as baggy as a nun's habit. Elle might have liked a stepfather. It would be nice to have a man around who actually gave two shits about her.

"Mom? What are you doing?"

"Praying to Saint Monica." Her mother's eyes remained closed. She clutched her saint medal in her hand.

"Saint Monica? Was she a martyr or a mystic?"

"Neither. She was a mother."

"Good. Hate the martyrs." Stupid virgin martyrs. Between getting married and getting murdered they picked murder. She'd pick a dick over death any day. Why did no one ever offer her those sorts of choices?

"She was the mother of Saint Augustine. He, too, was a willful, disobedient child. He had a mistress and fathered a child out of wedlock. He partied and played and didn't care at all for the things of God. But his mother—Monica—was a Christian and she prayed and prayed for him. Prayed with all her might her child would see the truth of the Gospel and convert. God granted her prayer and Saint Augustine is one of the doctors of the church now."

"The church has doctors?"

"It does."

"Why is it still so sick, then? They must be really crappy doctors."

Her mother stopped talking again, stopped whispering, stopped praying. But still she didn't leave.

"Elle..." Her mother's tone was softer now, kinder, conversational. Not a good sign.

"What. Now. Mother?"

"Mary Rose told me the new priest is supposed to be very handsome."

"Mom, he's a priest. That's gross." The pillow was once more firmly planted on her face.

"And he rides a motorcycle."

Elle pushed the pillow off her face.

"A motorcycle?"

"Yes." Her mother smiled. "A motorcycle."

"What kind? Not some no-thrust piece-of-crap crotch rocket from Japan, is it?"

Her mother shook her head.

"Something Italian."

"A Vespa? Those are scooters, not motorcycles." Elle giggled at the image of a priest in a collar on the back of a little Vespa scooter.

"No. Something that started with a *D*. Du-something."

Elle's eyes widened.

"A Ducati?"

"That was it."

She knew about Ducatis but had never seen one up close. She'd kill to have a Ducati between her thighs. All that power. All that freedom. What she wouldn't give…

Would it kill her to go to church one more day? One more hour? One more Mass? She could see the bike, maybe touch it, then get out again.

"Okay." Elle threw off the covers. "I'm coming. But I'm doing it for the Ducati, not for God."

Her mother slammed the door behind her and Elle got out of bed. Grabbing her uniform skirt off the floor, she headed to the bathroom. Mass or not, she would have had to get out of bed anyway. Her bladder had been about to explode while arguing with her mom.

She pressed her hand to the bathroom window and felt nothing but room-temperature glass. Good. A warm morning. She wouldn't have to bother with tights under her skirt.

Her hair looked like it belonged on a crazy person since she'd fallen asleep with it wet. No amount of curling or brushing was going to tame it. She grabbed a bottle of tinted green hair gel and streaked it through her hair, taming the wild flyaways enough that she could pull it back into a high ponytail.

Elle shoved her feet into her black combat boots. Carefully

she applied a thick swipe of black eyeliner around her eyes. She was short and her boobs were too big but at least she could pull off the makeup component of heroin chic.

In her bedroom she found her thickest flannel shirt and pulled it on over her Pearl Jam T-shirt. She layered her green army jacket on top of her flannel.

Elle jumped in the backseat of their old Ford and her mom barely let her shut the door before backing out of the driveway.

"I want you to say hello to the new priest if you get a chance. Father Greg had me doing the books since he couldn't handle it. This younger priest might want to change things up."

"I'll say hi. And then I'll steal his Duck and ride away into the sunset."

"His what?"

"Ducks. Dukes. Ducatis. Never mind."

"I'm attempting to be open-minded about the new priest. You could at least give him a chance," her mother said.

"I'm going, right? But only for the motorcycle. I mentioned that part, right?"

Her mother gave a ragged sigh.

"You should be going to church for God, and no other reason."

"I told you, I don't even think I believe in God anymore."

"God is everywhere. He's in everyone. We're all created in His image."

"I haven't met anybody who looks like God yet."

"How many people would it take to get through to you? God told Abraham he would spare Sodom and Gomorrah if ten righteous men could be found in the city. Only ten."

Elle thought about it, thought about the boys at school who were dicks in sneakers, the teachers who did nothing but punish, her father who couldn't keep a promise to save his life, her mother who forced religion down her throat…

She saw God in none of them. Not even in herself.

"Ten? Mom, I swear I'd settle for one."

If she met one single person who seemed holy, righteous, kind, self-sacrificing, smart and wise who kept his promises and gave a flying fuck about her? Maybe she'd believe then.

"Only one?" Her mother sounded incredulous.

"Well, one person and a little 'St. Teresa and the angel' action wouldn't hurt, either." Eleanor grinned and her mother shook her head in disgust.

"You know, all I ever wanted was a daughter who loves God, goes to church, respects her priest and maybe even respects her mother a little. You think that's too much to ask?"

Elle thought about the question one whole entire second before answering.

"Yup."

Once her mother pulled into the Sacred Heart parking lot, Elle jumped out of the car. Her mom could make her go to church, but she wasn't about to sit with her at church.

Elle entered the sanctuary and took a seat on the Gospel side—the left side of the church facing the altar. A visiting priest had explained the difference between the Gospel side and the Epistle side, or right side, a long time ago. He was also the same priest who taught everyone that *Amen* was best translated as "so be it." That had surprised her. Until him she'd always thought *Amen* meant "over and out."

Her usual pew had already filled up by the time she got there so instead of sitting beneath her favorite stained-glass window, she had to sit on the aisle. That was okay. She'd be able to get a better look at the new priest from here. And if she didn't like the looks of him, she could "accidentally" step on the train of his vestments. Oops.

She wormed her way out of her jacket, picked up her missal and turned to the day's readings. From her backpack she pulled out her copy of *The Claiming of Sleeping Beauty* and slid it in between the pages. She'd heard some girls in her German class giggling over a copy of it. One of them had stolen it from her older sister. Gross, they said. Nasty, they said. So dirty. They couldn't believe people actually did this, they said. So of course Elle stole a copy of it from the public library. Now on her third reading, she still hadn't figured out why those girls in her class had called the book gross and nasty. Elle had fallen in love with the story of sexual slavery in a fairy-tale world of kings and queens. Even better, the main character—Beauty—was only fifteen, like her. Fifteen plus that one hundred years she'd been sleeping under the spell. Maybe Elle was also under a spell and didn't know it. Maybe she'd fallen asleep and everything happening was a dream, a bad dream where her father was a thief and her mother wished she'd never had her daughter. Maybe someday a prince would come along and kiss her and make love to her, and she'd wake up to discover she'd been a queen all along.

As Elle turned a page the bells rang. She closed her books and rose to her feet.

A hymn began.

Elle looked back to the door of the sanctuary, and saw the new priest.

The dream ended. The spell was broken.

Elle woke up.

5

Eleanor

STRIDING DOWN THE AISLE BEHIND THE CRUCIFER and the deacon was a man—a man with blond hair and a god's face. He looked forward with eyes so serious and solemn she followed his gaze to the altar to see if Jesus waited for him there.

As he stepped past her pew he turned his head and met her eyes for the briefest of eternities. The book within her missal fell from her hand and fluttered to the floor. She didn't bend to pick it up. It lay there, forgotten, as forgotten as everyone and everything else in this world. Everyone and everything else but this man who now mounted the steps to the altar and stood before the church.

Underneath the collar of his vestments she saw the hint of black with the white square.

This man, this most beautiful man she'd ever seen in her life, this man who was the incarnation of her every hunger, every desire and every secret midnight dream… This man was her new priest?

"Oh, my God..." she breathed, but whether she addressed the God in Heaven or the God before her, she didn't know.

She crossed herself when the church crossed themselves. She remained standing as they remained standing.

"In the name of the Father, and of the Son, and of the Holy Spirit," the new priest intoned, and together with the congregation Elle answered.

"Amen."

His voice, rich and resonant, echoed out to the very edges of the church and back again. His words wrapped around her like a golden cord binding her to him. The sanctuary brightened with each word he spoke as if the sun itself drew closer to hear his voice. Once in winter she'd seen a man on a street corner playing an old cello for coins. A cello on a winter night in the midst of a frozen city—that was what his voice sounded like.

She sat when the congregation sat and even as she sat down, her heart rose.

A woman read from the Old Testament.

A man read from the New Testament.

The priest read from the Gospels.

She heard none of the words. She heard only music. Even when the hymns had been sung and ended, she still heard music.

She knelt when the church knelt and prayed when the church prayed. And when it came time to rise for the Eucharist, she rose again.

On feet she could no longer feel she made her way inexorably toward the altar. Although she walked of her own volition, she felt drawn. That golden cord had wrapped itself around her heart and she would go wherever it led her. It led her to him.

With every step closer to him, the cord tightened, and yet the tighter it bound her, the greater her joy.

Visions flashed through her mind. A fluttering of white wings. A burning arrow. Stained glass under her feet. His hands on her face. His mouth on her mouth. His mouth on her breasts. His skin against her skin. His body inside her body. His heart in her heart in his hands…

From the deacon she took the wafer, said her Amen and swallowed it whole.

From the priest, she took the cup of wine. As she raised the cup to her lips, the sleeve of her shirt fell back, baring her arm and the two red burns on her wrist. She met his eyes and saw something flash in them, something she couldn't translate into words. It was as if he recognized her, as if he'd seen her before somewhere and now tried to remember where. She knew she'd never seen him before in her life. If she had, she would never have forgotten him.

The golden cord knotted itself tighter.

"The blood of Christ," he whispered, softer than he'd spoken it to anyone else, so softly she leaned in closer to hear him better.

"Amen."

Their fingers touched as she returned the cup to him, and she soared back to her seat. She picked her novel off the floor, closed it and stuffed it in her backpack.

The Mass ended. All were exhorted to go forth in peace. But Eleanor felt no peace and she would feel no peace until she'd spoken to him.

Him? Him who? When she reached the lobby of the church, Elle realized she had no idea what the new priest's name was. She had to know. Now.

She saw her mother whispering to a group of older women by the annex door. Probably talking about how the new priest was too young, too inexperienced, too handsome. As if there could be such a thing.

"It's a nice day. I'm walking home," she said to her mother and beat a hasty retreat before her mother could even say a word in argument.

The entire congregation surrounded their new priest. And yet she could still see him. He towered over most of them. He had to be six feet tall or more. Over the top of the crowd he met her eyes as if he'd been searching for her in the crowd. She mouthed, "I'll wait for you."

She slipped out the side door and watched the cars filing out. Soon nothing remained in the parking lot but a gleaming black motorcycle. Even on the opposite side of the parking lot she could make out the lines of it, the chrome detailing shining in the March sunlight. She'd never seen anything more beautiful in her life except for the man crossing the pavement toward it. Careful to make as little sound as possible, she stepped from the shadows and followed him to his motorcycle.

He'd abandoned the vestments for black clerics. Father Greg had always worn a plain black shirt and black jacket over it, usually without the white collar in place. But this priest had on a more formal looking and heavier black clerical shirt. It looked European to her. She'd never seen a priest who looked so… She couldn't find the right word. Elegant, maybe?

As he reached his motorcycle, he paused but didn't turn around.

"I was wondering where you went," he said, taking his helmet off the handlebars. He turned around and faced her. "You said you'd wait for me."

"You're kind of an idiot. You know that, right?" she asked.

He raised his eyebrow at her. Elle dug her hands in her pocket and stared at him.

"Am I?"

He sat astride his motorcycle, and she stepped in front of it.

"Do you have any idea what it is you have between your legs?" she demanded.

"I'm well aware of what is between my legs." He said the words without even breaking a smile. She narrowed her eyes at him and stepped closer, straddling the front wheel with her knees.

"Then you know that this is a Ducati. A 907 I.E.," she said.

"Is it?"

"It's in black. Never seen one in black before." She walked a circuit around the bike. "Do you have any idea how much this Duck is worth?"

"A small fortune, I'd imagine." He put the helmet back on the handlebars.

"Yeah. A small one. So where's your lock?"

"Pardon?"

"Your disc lock. You can't leave a Ducati sitting in a parking lot without a lock on it unless you're criminal stupid or you want it to get stolen. Which one is it?"

"Criminally stupid."

"So you admit it?"

"No, I'm correcting your grammar. And I didn't realize suburban Connecticut was such a high-crime district. Should I be afraid?" He asked the question in a tone that implied he knew what fear was, but only in theory, not practice.

"If I had something that valuable, I'd lock it up."

He smiled at her.

"I plan to."

"That's good. Okay, then." She stood there not knowing what else to say. The few things that leaped to mind were a little too forward. Like "I love you" and "will you marry me?"

"Tell me your name."

"Elle."

"Is that short for…?"

"Eleanor. Eleanor Louise Schreiber, at your service." She grasped the ends of her skirt and gave him her most sarcastic curtsy. "Now who the hell are you?"

"Try that again. More politely please."

She tapped the toe of her boot on the ground.

"Well?"

"Fine. What is your name, Father?"

He studied her face for a moment and didn't answer.

"Don't you know your own name?"

"I'm deciding how to answer the question. In the meantime, allow me to say this. It is a pleasure to finally meet you, Eleanor."

He reached out his left hand for her to shake. She had no choice but to give him her own left hand. As soon as her hand was in his, he gripped her fingers and pulled her toward him. He pushed at her sleeve and examined the two burns on her wrist.

"Hey, what the hell are you doing?" she demanded, trying to pull her arm back. He didn't give an inch, merely held her in place with his impossible strength.

"You have two second-degree burns on your arm and large scrapes on your knees. Care to tell me how those came about?"

"It's none of your business."

The priest studied her through narrowed steel-colored eyes. He didn't seem the least offended by her language.

"Eleanor," he said. "Tell me who hurt you. And tell me right now."

She felt the force of his will like a wall pressing against her.

"No. You won't even tell me your name."

"If I tell you my name, will you tell me about the burns?"

He let her hand go and she pulled her arm back and held it to her stomach. Her entire body fluttered from the touch of his hand on her hand, and the unrepentant way he studied her.

She stood still and silent while he stared at her face until she reluctantly met his eyes.

"Will you tell anybody what I tell you?" She wasn't wild about telling anyone something so private about herself, but for some reason, a reason she couldn't name, she trusted this man, this priest.

"Not a soul."

"Okay. Fine. Name?"

He reached into the black leather saddlebag on his motorcycle and pulled out what appeared to be a Bible in some foreign language. He flipped opened the well-worn cover to a page where he'd written his name in thick black ink with strong legible handwriting.

Søren Magnussen.

She reached out and with the tip of her finger traced the letters in the name.

"Søren... Did I say that right?"

"You say it like an American."

"How am I supposed to say it?"

"I like the way you say it. You should know, that's not the name anyone here will ever call me. That's what my mother named me. Unfortunately I'm forced to go by what my father named me—Marcus Stearns."

"So no one here knows your real name?" That he wrote Søren Magnussen in his Bible seemed to hint that he considered Søren his real name, not Marcus.

"Only you. And now that you know it, I believe you owe me an answer to my question."

"It's not a big deal."

"Eleanor—"

"I go by Elle, not Eleanor."

"Eleanor is the name of queens. Elle is merely a French pronoun that means *she* or *her.* I will call you Eleanor. And now, Eleanor, tell me how you arrived at the burns on your wrist. Then we'll discuss the knees."

"Curling iron."

"Self-inflicted or is someone in your home hurting you?"

"Self-inflicted."

"Why did you do it?"

"For fun."

"You enjoy hurting yourself?" He asked the question without shock or disgust. She heard nothing in his voice but curiosity.

She nodded.

"You think I'm crazy?"

"You seem quite sane to me. Apart from your clothes."

"What? Not down with grunge?"

"Your hair is also a cause for concern."

"What's wrong with my hair?"

"It's gone green."

"It's not moldy," she said, laughing at the playful look of disapproval on his face. "That's hair gel. I put green streaks in it."

"How old are you?"

"Fifteen. But I'll be sixteen in two weeks." She felt the need to add that part at the end. "My mom says you're too young to be a priest."

"I'm twenty-nine. But I'll try to age very quickly for her. I'm certain pastoring at a church you attend will age me considerably."

"I'll do my best." She grinned broadly at him as she toyed with the cuffs of her jacket. Once more she fell into an awkward silence. He didn't seem awkward at all. He seemed to be having the time of his life watching her be weird in front of him.

"Now for the knees. Those are impressive-looking wounds."

"I fell," she said. "Shit happens."

"You don't seem the clumsy sort. Perhaps I was mistaken."

She pursed her lips. Her? Clumsy?

"I'm not clumsy. Ever. My gym teacher said I move like a trained dancer."

"So then where did the injuries to your knees come from?"

"I got in a fight at school."

"I hope she looks worse than you do."

"He," she said with pride. "He looks fine. But he's still walking funny."

Søren's eyes widened slightly.

"You fought with a boy at your school?" He sounded mildly horrified.

"It's not my fault. There's this girl at school—Pepper Riley. And if her name wasn't bad enough, she has huge boobs. She's scared of her own shadow and won't fight back. So this guy, Trey, he was being a prick to her on the bus saying all kinds of gross shit about her body. So I told him to shut up. And then he starts saying gross shit to me. He was all, 'I want your body, Elle.' So I said he could have my body. Then I gave him my foot. Right in the nuts. It was kind of amazing. When we got off the bus he pushed me so hard I landed on my knees and ripped them open. Whatever. Typical Wednesday at your local Catholic high school. Your tax dollars not at work."

He continued to stare at her. His eyes had widened even farther.

"Father Stearns? Søren? Whoever you are?" She waved her hand.

"Forgive me. I was utterly riveted by your story. I might have entered a fugue state."

"Lucky for me, it all happened at the back of the bus and the driver didn't see it. Otherwise Vice Principal Wells would have my ass. He told me if I got sent to his office one more time I'd be publicly crucified as an example to the rest of the school. I think he was kidding?"

"Did you deserve such a threat?"

"Maybe. I said in class that St. Teresa didn't have a mystical experience but was, in fact, having an orgasm. It's not like I didn't prove it. She said the angel 'penetrated' her with his 'flaming arrow' right to her 'entrails' and that it gave her 'ecstasy.'" Elle used air quotes for emphasis. "That was not a mystical experience. That was a big O. V.P. Wells didn't appreciate my theology."

"I appreciate your theology."

Eleanor opened her mouth and then closed it again. She had zero words. None. Nothing. She had no idea what to say to that.

"I'm going to go away now," she said.

"Why?"

"You want me to stay?"

"I do."

She looked at him askance.

"No one ever wants me to stay. You know, after I start talking."

"I want you to stay," he said. "And I'd like you to keep talking."

"I'm not interrupting your golf game?"

"Golf?"

"All priests play golf, right?"

"Not this priest."

"What do you play?"

"Other games."

Something in the way he said the word *games* made Elle's toes curl up inside her combat boots.

"Then I should let you get back to your other games."

"Do one thing for me before I leave."

"What?"

"Take your hair down."

This time she didn't even argue or ask why. She simply pulled the elastic out of her hair, ran her fingers through the messy waves and dropped her hands to her side.

"Give me your right hand."

He held out his hand again and he took her unburned wrist in his fingers. From her left hand he took her ponytail holder and wrapped it around her wrist.

Slipping two fingers between the band and her wrist, he lifted it high and let it go, snapping the sensitive skin so hard she flinched.

"Fuck...Jesus, that hurt. What did you do that for?"

"Those burns on your wrist will take months to heal completely. There are other ways of inflicting pain on yourself that don't leave scars. You should learn them."

Elle looked down at her wrist. Her skin still reverberated with the pain of the vicious sting, but the redness had already started to fade.

"Did you... You just..."

"Your body is a temple, Eleanor. You should treat it like the priceless and holy vessel it is. I learned one thing and one thing only from watching my father's wife. If you're going to redecorate, either learn how to do it properly, or hire a professional."

He took his helmet off the handlebars and started the motorcycle. Its impressive engine roared to life and Eleanor felt the vibrations from the ground up to her stomach.

"You're not a normal priest, are you?"

He gave her a smile that hit her like a slap to the face and a kiss on the mouth all at once.

"My God, I hope not."

With those final words, he put on his helmet and kicked out the stand with his heel. Eleanor took three giant steps back. He rode out of the parking lot and left her standing there alone.

She watched him until he disappeared from view. And then she listened until the sound of his engine retreated into silence.

"I'm yours, Søren," she said to no one but God, and didn't know what she meant by it. She only knew it was true.

She was his whatever the consequences. She was his.

Amen. Amen.

So be it.

6

Eleanor

ON WEDNESDAY NIGHT, THE MIRACLE ELEANOR prayed for happened. Her mother had to go into work early. She'd be gone from five until midnight. Eleanor could leave the house for a couple of hours without anyone noticing.

She'd seen on the church bulletin that someone was holding a Lenten prayer service at six that night. Perfect excuse. For twenty minutes, she worked on her hair until it resembled human hair and not her usual lion's mane. She put on clean clothes—tight jeans and a V-neck sweater. In all her life she'd never walked so fast to church.

When she arrived at Sacred Heart, she didn't find anyone praying. She should probably ask someone where the service was. Maybe Søren would know?

Eleanor tiptoed up to the door and found it ajar. Inside the office she spied a lamp on the desk and shadows moving.

"Knock knock," she said without actually knocking. The door opened all the way, and Eleanor took a step back.

Søren stood in the doorway clad in his clerics and collar. He didn't seem displeased to see her.

"Hello, Eleanor. Nice to see you again." He crossed his arms and leaned against the door frame.

She peeked around his shoulder and peered inside. Books sat stacked on the desk and chairs.

"You're moving in?"

"Father Gregory's sister has asked for his things."

Eleanor took a step back. Standing so close to him meant she had to crane her neck to look up at him.

"He's really not coming back?"

Søren slowly shook his head.

"You have to understand that a stroke is a serious condition. Once he's out of the hospital he'll be staying with his sister and her husband."

"Are they nice people?"

He seemed momentarily taken aback by her question.

"His sister and her husband? I haven't met them, but she and I spoke on the phone. She seemed very kind and concerned."

"That's good."

Eleanor bit her bottom lip while trying to think of something else to say.

"What are you doing?" he asked.

"Oh, sorry. I was going to go to this prayer thing but I can't find it. I saw—"

"I mean with your lip."

"I don't know. I bite it sometimes. Habit."

"Stop it. The only girls I've ever seen doing that are either not very intelligent or are trying to look not very intelligent. I refuse to believe you're either."

"Really? You don't even know me."

He smiled and took a step back into the office.

"I know you."

Eleanor started to enter the office.

"What do you mean you know me?" she asked, but when she crossed the threshold, he held up a hand.

"Out."

"Out?"

"Out of my office."

"Why?"

"Because I said so."

Eleanor took a step back into the hallway.

"I'm not allowed in your office?"

"No one under the age of sixteen is allowed in my office without a parent present. No one over sixteen is allowed alone in my office unless the door is open. These are my rules."

"That's kind of strict."

"I'm strict."

He pulled a book off the shelf and added it to a pile on the desk.

"Why are you so strict?"

He paused while removing another book from the shelf and gave her a searching look.

"Can I talk to you like an adult?" he asked, shifting books on the shelf.

"I'd be pissed if you talked to me like a child."

He glanced at her as he put an empty file box on the desk and one by one started piling books inside.

"Last year an exposé was released regarding child sex abuse by Catholic priests and the churchwide cover-up by the bishops, the archbishops and even the Curia."

"Mom says those people, the victims, they're after the church's money."

"Your mother is wrong."

"So the sex abuse is as bad as they say?"

"Eleanor, do you know why I'm here?" Søren asked.

"I know Father Greg is retiring, and there's a priest shortage in the diocese so they had to call the Jesuits for a loaner. You're the loaner."

"It isn't as simple as that. Recently, I returned to my community after my ordination. Things were tense. A Jesuit in our province had recently been convicted on sex abuse charges stemming from his assignment at an inner-city school."

A chill passed through her body.

"He was messing with kids?"

"Rumors circulated that one of the school officials, another Jesuit, was attempting to hide documents from the plaintiff's attorney, who was suing the school and others in civil court."

"What happened?"

"I called the attorney and told them everything I knew, everything I'd heard and everything to ask for during the discovery process."

"You ratted out another Jesuit to lawyers? Jesus Christ, how big are your balls?" Her father had "friends" who got themselves killed talking to cops or lawyers.

Søren laughed softly.

"I believe those were the exact words my superior said to me. But he didn't smile when he said it like you did. I'm not telling you this story to impress you or shock you. I'm telling you this so you know why I'm here. I was to spend two weeks in New York visiting friends and family before being sent to India. Instead I'm here at this tiny parish in a tiny town in Connecticut."

"Oh, shit. You got in trouble."

"Me being here is the Catholic equivalent of 'go stand in the corner and think about what you've done.'"

"So you're not letting kids in your office because—"

"Of St. Paul and First Thessalonians 5:22. 'Abstain from every appearance of evil.'"

"I guess having kids in the office could look bad."

Søren rearranged some books in the box to make room for two more.

"It could. I'm afraid Father Gregory was slightly lax in those areas. Of course, from everything I've heard of him, he was a good and gentle man."

"He was."

"I'm an unknown integer here, however. Being alone with a seventy-year-old priest and a twenty-nine-year-old priest give two entirely different appearances."

"Doesn't help that you're like the hottest priest on the planet."

Søren looked up sharply at her. Eleanor went pale.

"I said that out loud."

"Should I pretend I didn't hear it?"

Eleanor thought about his offer as the blush stared to fade from her cheeks.

"I said it. I'll go say some Hail Marys."

"Finding another person attractive isn't a sin."

"It isn't?"

"Desire is not a sin," Søren said, sitting on his desk and facing her. "Fantasy is not a sin. Sins are acts of commission or omission. Either you do some act you're not supposed to do. For example, shooting someone. Or you fail to do an act you should do. For example, not giving alms to the poor. Finding someone attractive is no more a sin than standing on a balcony and enjoying a lovely view of the ocean."

"What's lust, then?"

"You ask excellent questions. These are the questions of a young woman who is not of the lip-biting variety."

"I'm going to bite my lip out of spite from now on."

"That is exactly what I knew you would do. Would you like me to answer your question?"

"About lust? Yeah."

"Let's go into the sanctuary. You can sit down there."

"I don't mind standing."

"You're wearing combat boots."

"They're comfy."

"Where does a young lady in Wakefield, Connecticut, purchase combat boots?"

"Goodwill," she said.

"You're wearing Goodwill combat boots?"

"Yes."

"Congratulations, Eleanor. Your footwear has achieved irony."

Before she could ask him what he meant by that, he stepped past her. She spun around on the heel of her Goodwill combat boots and followed Søren to the sanctuary. He opened the doors, putting the stoppers down to keep them open.

"You're really into this 'avoiding any appearance of evil' thing, aren't you?"

"I am. I wouldn't want either of us accused of anything we hadn't done."

"What if it's something we have done?" she asked, kneeling backward on one of the pews to face Søren, who was seated in the row behind her.

"That's an entirely different situation. But we're talking lust."

"I'm lusting for your answer."

"You aren't, actually." He gave her a steady gaze with his unyielding eyes. "You're simply desiring my answer. Lust is overwhelming or uncontrollable desire that leads to sin. A man might desire another man's wife. It happens. The question he has to ask himself is, given the chance, will he act on his desires? Will he try to seduce her the first time they're alone? Will he attack her? If she came on to him, would he give in? Or would he honor her marital state, politely tell her no and suggest she and her husband go to counseling?"

"So it's a matter of how much you want something that's the difference between love and lust?"

"Partly. But it's not only a question of degree of desire, but what you do with it. If I were to find a young woman stunningly attractive, intriguing and intelligent, then I will not have committed a sin. I could take that to my confessor, and he'd laugh and tell me not to come back and see him until I had something worth confessing. Now, if I acted on my attraction to this young woman, then we might have a problem."

"Or a really good evening." She grinned at him. Søren cocked an eyebrow at her. "I mean, a really sinful evening."

"Better."

"So it's okay to desire someone as long as you don't act on it?"

"There are many situations when acting on one's desires is not a sin."

"Married couples, right? They can have sex all they want."

"Married couples can certainly engage in sexual acts with each other."

"And..." Eleanor waved her hand, hoping for more to the answer. "Nobody else? The rest of us are screwed? I mean, not screwed?"

"I believe that is a question for your own conscience. I'm not dogmatic when it comes to sexual behavior in the modern world. The church can proscribe anything and everything it wants to, but the church is still made up entirely of human beings. Heaping rule upon rule on our congregations isn't going to make anyone holier. It'll serve only to add to the guilt that is endemic in our churches."

Eleanor pointed at the sanctuary doors.

"You said five minutes ago you were imposing new rules on the church."

"The rules are not for the church. They are for me. If I were to allow you and I to be alone together in my office, I would be breaking the rule, not you."

"So what are all these rules?"

"Nothing burdensome, I promise. Actually, you might be able to help me with one of them. I have a feeling it's not going to go over well."

"Oh, no. What are you doing?" Eleanor knew her church well enough to know any sort of big change would be met with fear, anger and confusion. She couldn't wait to see everyone freak out.

"The rectory. I'm closing it off to parishioners."

"Whoa. Wait. You're closing the rectory?"

"No church members will be allowed inside it."

Eleanor's eyes nearly fell out of her skull.

"I take it from you look of wild-eyed horror that such a declaration will ruffle a few feathers?" Søren asked, a slight smile on his lips. He didn't seem the least bothered by the prospect.

"If you turned the church into a McDonald's, that would ruffle some feathers. This is going to ruffle the whole fucking turkey. Pardon my French."

"Pardoned."

"Why close the rectory? The church uses it all the time."

"This church has a sanctuary, a chapel and a large annex. There's no need to use the rectory for church services. I, however, will need a home. I'll no more hear confessions in my bedroom than I'll take a bath in my office."

He said the words without a hint of flirtatiousness, but that didn't stop Eleanor from mentally conjuring the image of Søren lying wet and naked in a bathtub. Or was it laying wet and naked?

"Eleanor?"

"Sorry. I was trying to remember when you're supposed to use *lay* versus *lie,*" she lied.

"*Lay* requires a direct object and *lie* does not."

"Oh, that makes perfect sense. Thank you. Also, no. You can't close the rectory. You're going to piss off the entire church."

"I had a feeling. Your prayer service you're supposed to be at is meeting at the rectory right now. A sanctuary, a chapel, and for some reason neither of those will work."

"The rectory is cozier. Father Greg always had snacks."

Søren tapped his knee. "That's unfortunate, but I've made up my mind. It's important for a pastor to have strong boundaries with his church. I'll do my best to explain my logic to them."

"Logic? You're going to use logic on Catholics?"

"Do you have a better idea?" From anyone else, the question would have sounded sarcastic or like a challenge. But instead from Søren it sounded like a genuine question. If she had a better idea, he wanted to know it.

"Look, I know these people. I grew up with them. They don't really like outsiders. Everyone's already freaking out that you're a Jesuit instead of a regular priest."

"They're afraid of Jesuits?"

"They say Jesuits are really..." Eleanor waved her hand to beckon Søren forward. He leaned in and she put her mouth at his ear. "Liberal."

Søren pulled back and looked her in the eyes.

"I have to tell you a secret." She leaned in again toward Søren and inhaled. In that inhale she smelled winter, clean and cold, and briefly she wondered if someone had left a window open. "We are liberal."

He sat back in the pew again and brought a finger to his lips.

"But you didn't hear that from me," he said and gave her a wink. Eleanor's body temperature, already running a low-grade fever from being in the same room as him, shot up even higher. "But that's beside the point. You were going to give me a better idea than logic."

"Yeah…no. Logic won't work. What might work is if you trick the church into thinking closing off the rectory was their idea."

"How so?"

She shrugged and raised her hands. "I don't know. Tell them you heard from concerned members of the church who want more rules and safety procedures or whatever?" They were always talking about safety procedures at school. "And you can say you heard the cry of the people and have decided to take their advice and add some new rules so you can keep everyone safe and avoid all appearance of evil. Nobody wants to be in a church with a scandal, right? You're doing what they asked."

Søren raised his fingers to his mouth and slowly stroked his bottom lip. It seemed an unconscious gesture, as unconscious as her lip-biting. But whereas her lip-biting apparently made her look like an idiot, his lip-caressing made her want to straddle his lap, wrap her arms around him and put her tongue down his throat.

"So you're telling me I should manipulate the church into thinking that closing the rectory was a suggestion they made me?"

"Or just flat-out lie. Or lay. Whatever."

"I could lie. That would be a sin, but I appreciate that suggestion."

"You don't sin?"

"I try not to."

"I don't."

"You don't sin?" Søren sounded so skeptical she would have been insulted if he weren't entirely right to be that skeptical.

"No, I don't try to *not* sin."

Søren closed his eyes and shook his head.

"What?" she asked.

He held up his hand, indicating his need for silence.

"What?" she whispered.

"Do you hear that?"

She tilted her head and listened.

"No. I don't hear anything. Do you hear something?" she asked Søren.

"I do."

"What?"

"God laughing at me."

Eleanor rested her chin on her hand. "You hear God laughing at you?"

"Loudly. I'm quite surprised you can't hear it."

"He's laughing at you, not me," she said.

"Excellent point. And you made another excellent point about handling the church. I'll consider your suggestion."

"You will?"

"It's a wise and Machiavellian strategy."

"Is that bad?"

"No. It's biblical. Matthew 10:16. 'Behold, I send you forth as a sheep among wolves—be therefore wise as serpents, and harmless as doves.'"

"Sheep among wolves. That makes the church sound dangerous. You think we're dangerous."

"I think you're dangerous."

Eleanor sat back on her heels. They'd been joking the entire time they'd been in the sanctuary, but what he'd said and how he'd said it? That was no joke.

"Me? Dangerous?" she repeated.

"You. Very."

"Why?"

"Because you want to be. That's part of the reason."

"I also want to be six feet tall and have straight blond hair, but wanting something doesn't make it real. I'm not dangerous."

"I'd explain my reasons for saying you are, but I have to get back to packing. I promised Father Gregory's sister I would have all of his things ready to pick up tomorrow."

"You know there are like a million old ladies in this church who would have packed up the office for you."

"I know, but I said I would do it, and I feel only another priest should take care of his personal things for him."

"That's really nice of you." She winced. *Really nice of you?* Could she sound like a bigger suck-up or idiot? "I should go home, I guess. Mom might call and wonder where I am."

"Where is your mother?"

"Working." Eleanor followed him out of the sanctuary.

"She works this late often?"

"This early. She works the late shift a lot. It pays more."

"Does your father not help out financially?"

Eleanor stood in the doorway of the office again while Søren got back to work packing the boxes.

"Mom won't take a cent from him even if he offered, which I doubt he would. He says he's broke."

"I take it the divorce was not entirely amicable."

"She hates him."

"Do you?"

"Hate Dad? No way. I love him."

"Why does your mother hate him? If these questions are too personal you don't have to answer them."

"No, it's okay." She liked answering Søren's questions. They were personal but not embarrassing. "Mom and Dad got married when she was eight months pregnant with me."

"Eight? Talk about waiting until the last minute."

Eleanor tried to smile but couldn't.

"What is it?" Søren asked.

"She waited that long because she was hoping she'd have a miscarriage."

Søren dropped the book on the desk with a loud thud.

"Surely not."

"It's true. I overheard her talking to my grandmother one night about some guy named Thomas Martin. She said she felt bad about thinking it, but she had once wished God would handle the pregnancy the way he handled Thomas Martin, whoever that is."

"Thomas Merton," Søren corrected.

"You know him?"

"He was a Trappist monk at the Abbey of Gethsemani in Bardstown, Kentucky. He's arguably the most famous Catholic writer of the twentieth century. When he was a young man, he fathered a child out of wedlock, but the mother and child were both killed during an air raid in World War II, which allowed him to eventually become a monk without the familial obligations of fatherhood."

"Makes sense, I guess. She was hoping God would kill me so she could be a nun."

Søren gave her a look of such deep and profound sympathy she couldn't stand to look at it.

"Eleanor…I'm so—"

"Sorry. I know. Don't be. She loves me now. I think." Eleanor laughed. "Anyway, it was young lust with Dad. She was seventeen. A year after she had me, she found out what my dad does for a living. They got divorced. She didn't want any of his money because she said it's all dirty."

"Dirty money? What does your father do for a living?"

"He…" Eleanor paused and considered the best way to say it. "He's a mechanic, sort of. Works with cars."

"Nothing to be ashamed of."

"They're not always his cars."

Søren nodded. "I see."

"He's been in prison a couple times."

"Does that trouble you?"

"No," she said. "Not too much anyway."

They looked at each other a moment without speaking. It wasn't an awkward silence, but a meaningful silence.

"Anyway, I'll let you get back to packing." Eleanor wanted to stay and keep talking to him. But she didn't want to be a nuisance either, and wear out her welcome.

"I'll see you Sunday?" he asked.

"What's Sunday?"

"Mass? Church? Holy Day of Obligation?"

"Right. Sunday. I'll check with my secretary," she said. "You know, see if I'm free."

"Do you have the office number here?"

"It's on the fridge."

"Call my number when you get home. I want to know you've arrived safely."

She stared at him.

"Seriously?"

"How long does it take for you to walk home?"

"I don't know. Twenty minutes?"

"Then I'll expect to hear from you within the half hour. Please be safe."

She gave him a wave and took a step back. It hurt walking away from him. That cord she felt last Sunday, she felt it again now, felt it in his presence, felt it even more when she moved to leave him.

"Three more things, Eleanor, before you go."

"What?" She turned back to face him. Once more he stood in the doorway to his office.

"One." He held up one finger. "Earlier you said you wished you to be six feet tall and have long straight hair. Don't ever wish that again. God created you. Don't argue aesthetics with the Creator. Do you understand?"

"Sure, I guess," she said although she didn't.

"Two." He held up a second finger. "Don't be troubled I said were you dangerous. It wasn't an insult."

"If you say so."

"I do. And three." He took a step back into the office. "I've been at Sacred Heart four days and already half the parish has made it abundantly clear to me that I am not wanted here. Father Gregory is much beloved. The parish is not ready to let him go and accept a new pastor. You aren't the only one who knows what it's like to feel unwanted."

Eleanor felt something funny in her throat. It burned so she swallowed it. The burn remained.

"The church isn't your own mother."

"No, it isn't. And I won't minimize your pain by pretending the church's distrust of me compares at all to your pregnant, terrified seventeen-year-old mother making a desperate wish that her problems would magically disappear and the dream she lost would be hers again. But I will say that it doesn't matter anymore if your mother wanted you at the time or not. Nor does it matter if this church wants me here or not. We're here, you and I. We're not going away. We're here, if for no other reason than God wants us here, and He gets the final say."

"If it makes you feel any better, I want you here."

Søren picked up one of Father Gregory's books again.

"That does make me feel better."

"Thank you…Søren." She still couldn't believe she was calling a priest by his first name, no "Father" attached.

"Good night."

She turned and started to walk away from the office.

"Thirty minutes," Søren called out, and Eleanor allowed herself to give free rein to the ear-to-ear grin she'd been holding back for the past hour.

The second she entered her kitchen, Eleanor picked up the phone. She had to stretch the cord all the way to the fridge so she could read off the office number to Sacred Heart.

Søren answered on the first ring.

"I'm home safe," she said.

"Good."

"Thanks for talking to me tonight."

"I enjoyed our conversation, Eleanor."

She smiled at the phone. Usually she hated being called Eleanor. Why did it sound so right coming from him? Eleanor…sounded so classy the way he said it, so adult.

"Can I ask you a quick question?"

"Of course," Søren answered, and she heard the sound of books dropping into boxes.

"Are you dangerous, too?"

She held her breath waiting for his answer.

"Yes."

"Thought so," she said. Søren said no more.

"Good night, Søren. See you Sunday."

"Try to avoid doing anything to prove I'm right about you being dangerous between now and Sunday, please."

Eleanor would have laughed, but she knew he wasn't joking. She wasn't joking either, when she answered.

"No promises."

7

Eleanor

FRIDAY NIGHT CAME AND ELEANOR STAKED OUT THE bathroom. Ever since meeting Søren she'd thought about him nonstop. She woke to him, fell asleep to him, wrote his name on scraps of paper and whispered it under her breath when no one was listening. Tonight she had to deal with these feelings. Thankfully her mom had already gone to bed.

Elle cleaned the bathtub and pulled out two candles from her secret stash. They lived so close to the railroad tracks that the entire house shook when the train rumbled by. Her mother had banned candles after one near miss during Thanksgiving. Thank God turkeys weren't flammable. Unfortunately, the tablecloth was. At least the firemen had been nice to her. But the next train tonight wasn't due for an hour, so Elle lit the candles as she filled the bathtub with hot water. Once it was full and steaming, she stripped naked and sank into the bathwater. She needed her alone time in the water tonight. Over the past year her body had turned on her. Almost overnight she had developed breasts that felt huge to her and the spread of her hips made her feel fat most of the time. And she could have lived her entire life very happily without pubic hair. Floating in the bathtub made her feel weightless and buoyant. The water surrounded her body and cradled it like strong arms. Something about sinking into the water always turned her on. Being naked in the bath made her hyperaware of every inch of her body—what it did, what it could feel.

Elle lay back in the water and let it hold her up. The heat penetrated her skin, tickled her sensitive nipples and lapped between her legs. She let her mind wander to a thousand erotic fantasies. She'd love to take a bath with Søren. Maybe then it wouldn't be bathwater licking her breasts or slipping through the folds between her legs.

She opened her eyes and picked up the nearest candle. Sitting up in the water, she lifted her left arm into the flickering light. Holding the candle steady in her hand she tilted it and let the wax drip onto the inside of her wrist. Søren had told her to find a new way to hurt herself. Candle wax seemed to work. It hurt, it stung but it never scarred. The wax hit her flesh and she winced as the heat seared the delicate skin that covered her veins. Another dollop of melted wax fell onto her forearm. She'd be sixteen this month. In honor of her impending birthday she adorned herself with sixteen wax burns from her wrist to her inner elbow. With each burn she felt herself growing more and more aroused. The fire and the light and the heat seemed to come as much from within her as without. She breathed through the pain, conquering it, mastering it. Taking the pain made her feel stronger, powerful even.

After the final burn, she dipped her arm into the bathtub and rinsed off the solidified candle wax. She stared at her skin, now raw and bright red from the burns. Lying back in the water, she slipped her right hand between her legs and found the tight knot of her clitoris. *Clitoris.* She loved that word.

She'd been reading a magazine in the doctor's office waiting room the first time she'd discovered it. It wasn't a word she heard often or ever got to say out loud. Nobody used real words at school when talking about sex except during those embarrassing girls-only lectures in gym class. Even then it was *menstruation* and *uteruses*. No one ever talked about the clitoris, which seemed crazy to her. It was the most amazing thing. When hers got swollen like this she could rub it between her fingers and these incredible feelings would wash all over her. She couldn't believe her own body could make her feel this good. Every time she touched herself she became aware of an emptiness inside her, a hollowness in her hips. That hollowness ached to be opened up, explored and filled.

Carefully she eased two fingers inside herself. Going inside always made her nervous, which added to the excitement. She felt resistance against her fingers, like something would rip if she pushed in too hard. But she had to go inside. Her body wanted it. The heat inside her vagina surprised her. Was it from the hot water in the bathtub, or did that fire come from within her? Maybe it came from Søren. With her eyes closed she could easily imagine lying on a bed, naked and waiting. And in her mind, Søren crawled over her, kissing her stomach, her hips, her breasts. In her mind she reached for him, wrapping her arms around his shoulders, pulling him to her. Had he had sex before? Or was he a virgin like she was? What would he be like in bed? Gentle? Careful? Rough? Did he talk or stay silent? Would he tell her he loved her or simply show her all night long?

She felt the pressure building in her lower back and stomach as she rubbed her clitoris again with her thumb. Her body rose in the water as muscles deep in her hips and her bottom started to contract and flutter. She felt like a taut cello string had been plucked inside her. Everything hummed and vibrated. At last the pressure reached its peak. The orgasm sent her clitoris pulsing hard between her fingers as if it had a heartbeat of its own. And within her, her vagina clenched over and over again, pressing against itself. In that final moment of pleasure, Eleanor imagined the moment Søren entered her body and buried himself deep in her, penetrating her like Teresa's angel had, all the way into her entrails.

As the climax waned, Eleanor sat up in the water and washed her hands and arms with soap. She'd started sweating in the bath so she turned the tap on and ran cold water now, splashing her face with it.

Feeling relaxed and clean, Elle got out of the bath and wrapped a towel around herself. She drained the tub and hid the candles away. Friday night. Best night of the week.

Eleanor padded to her room and curled up in bed. She found her secret notebook she kept hidden behind her headboard. She had to write down all the thoughts she had about Søren. In her mind she could see his pulse throbbing in the hollow of his throat and his unusually dark eyelashes casting shadows on his face. She wanted to capture those images before they were gone. They lived and died quick deaths in her mind. Ink could preserve them long after her mind had moved onto new fantasies.

Søren thrust into her, she wrote. Thrust? She'd already used the word *thrust* twice in this scene. She got out her thesaurus and flipped to the entry for thrust.

"Ram, jab, prod, push, poke, drill," it read.

Drill? He drilled into her?

"He's fucking me, not installing new kitchen cabinets," she said to her useless thesaurus. Whatever. Back to writing. She'd fix her thrust issue later.

Lost as she was in her writing, she at first ignored the tapping on her window. A branch, a bird, a burglar coming to rob them—she couldn't give a damn about that now. Only when the tapping morphed into knocking did she turn her head toward the sound.

Eleanor peered through the dirty glass and spied a man's face. She flung the window open.

"Dad, what the hell?" she whispered.

"Long story. I need you to get your things and come with me." His face wore no smile. She saw fear in his dark green eyes.

"Dad, what's—"

"Get your stuff right now," he ordered.

"Okay, okay. I'll be right back." She started to pull away but her dad grabbed her hand.

"Put on your school uniform. I'll be waiting in the car."

He released her hand and stepped back into the darkness.

In the bathroom Eleanor stripped out of her pajama shorts and T-shirt and pulled on her abandoned school uniform—plaid skirt, white polo shirt, tights and boots. She'd put her hair in pigtails when she'd gotten home from school in a failed effort to tame the black waves. She looked like some kind of cartoon character with the pigtails, the combat boots and the Catholic-schoolgirl getup. But her dad had promised to explain so she grabbed her coat, grabbed her backpack and snuck out the window, shutting it behind her.

A beige Camry idled across the street. She'd never seen her father in a car so nondescript before. Bad sign.

"So what's up?" she asked as she threw herself in the passenger seat and her dad took off at twice the speed limit.

"I'm in trouble," he said.

"How bad?"

Her dad paused before answering.

"Bad."

"Oh, fuck."

"Yeah, I got into some money trouble a few months ago. I had to take out a loan. They called it in early. I either pay by morning or—"

Eleanor gripped her knees in fear. Her hands shook. Her stomach flip-flopped.

"Or I don't."

She leaned forward and breathed through her hands. "Or you don't..."

Her dad tried to shield her from what really happened at his shop. And when he talked about his *business partners,* he never used the words *mafia* or *mob*—because he didn't have to. She was young, not stupid. She'd seen enough gangster movies to know the score. If her father didn't pay back his loan by dawn, he was in trouble. Bad trouble.

"What do you want from me?" she asked.

"We need quick money. Manhattan. I have the crew out and working. We need more."

"Dad, I can't—"

"You can. You're faster than any of the guys on my crew."

"That's only in the garage. I've never done this on the street before."

"It'll be easy. No one will worry about a girl your age in a school uniform. They'll think you're some private-school snob wandering around after curfew."

"What if I get caught?"

"You're not going to get caught. It'll take two hours. You'll be in bed by morning."

"No way. This is crazy. Take me home." Eleanor shook her head and fought off a wave of nausea. Yeah, she knew how to steal a car. She'd known as long as she could remember. This way to bend the hanger. This wire to that wire. But that was a game she played in her dad's garage in Queens, something to do to impress her dad and the guys he worked with. *Look at me, I can do it faster than you.* They'd pat her on her head, applaud, tell her she needed to work for them instead of wasting her time in school. Those were jokes, funny cracks, playtime.

"Honey. I need your help here. I wouldn't ask if it wasn't life and death."

Life and death. She closed her eyes and tried to ignore the visions of her father lying in casket that danced through her head. Casket? Probably not. If he didn't pay off the mob, there wouldn't be enough left of him for a casket.

"Don't call me *honey*."

They drove in silence the rest of the way to the city. Friday night in Manhattan, all the money had come out to play. Up ahead on the left Eleanor spotted a black Jaguar trying to parallel park in front of a bar.

"Elle—" her father began but she didn't let him finish.

"How many?"

He shrugged. "Five?"

"Five. Fine. I'll see you at the shop." She opened the door and slammed it behind her.

Five cars. Home by dawn. No one would suspect her.

Eleanor walked down the sidewalk, not taking her eyes off the Jag. Finally the driver managed to worm the car into the spot. He opened the driver's side door and Eleanor stood on the passenger side.

"Sir, I think you hit that car behind you," she said over the roof.

"What?" He barely glanced at her. "No way."

"Looks like it to me. Check the bumper."

The driver, who looked half-drunk already, stumbled to the rear of the car and bent over.

"Nah, it's good. You scared me there." He pointed at her over the trunk and smiled.

"No problem. My mistake."

He walked into the bar, barely giving her a second look. He didn't seem to notice that while he'd examined the rear bumper, she'd unlatched the passenger side door. When she was certain no one on the street was paying her any attention, she dropped into the car and shut the door behind her.

Seconds later, she was on her way to Queens.

She'd snagged the Jag so fast she beat her father back to the garage.

Sitting on the hood of the car, she watched the shop at work. They'd known her since she was a baby; Jimmie, Jake, Levon and Kev had entertained her with card tricks and jokes and let her watch them working under the hoods of the cars anytime she'd come around. Now they barely glanced at her. In fact, in the past year whenever she'd stopped by they all treated her like a stranger.

"Nice Jag," Oz, the oldest guy on her dad's crew, said as he shuffled past her. He had so much grease and oil on his overalls she couldn't tell what color they were supposed to be. "Yours?"

"Mine. I'm keeping it."

"You got good taste, kiddo."

"In cars only. I suck at picking parents."

Oz raised his hands. "You know he wouldn't have asked if he wasn't desperate."

"How desperate?"

Oz glanced around. He looked back at her and dropped his voice to a whisper.

"Told me five hundred."

Eleanor couldn't wrap her mind around the number.

"Five hundred...*thousand?*"

Oz nodded. "Had to borrow to pay off an old debt. Swapped an old debt for a new one."

"Jesus H. Christ." Eleanor sighed. Someone had loaned her

dad five hundred thousand dollars? Wonder what he'd spent it on. She'd gotten nothing for Christmas from him.

Oz patted her knee and started to shuffle away again.

"Hey, Oz?"

"Yeah, toots?"

"Do Kev and Jake hate me for some reason?" Even now Kev and Jake eyed her from their various posts. Both of them were in their mid-twenties, her dad's two best guys.

Oz burst into peals of big-bellied laughter.

"Hate you, toots? Hell, no."

"Then what's their problem?"

"They don't wanna piss off your papa by getting caught staring at his baby. You're getting too pretty for your own good. Stop that, now. And get rid of those pigtails. That only makes it worse." He slapped the side of her leg in a fatherly sort of way and headed back to work. Eleanor couldn't believe these guys she'd known since she was a tiny seven-year-old, and they were zit-faced teenagers, now couldn't even talk to her because she had boobs. She yanked her ponytail holders out of her hair.

Eleanor glanced around the garage while she waited. Bad night. Everybody working like demons. She'd never seen the garage looking so dismal or so frenzied. A great furnace boiled with flames in one corner casting heat but no light. The whole place smelled of smoke and sulfur. She couldn't wait to get the hell out of here.

Finally her father pulled in the back entrance and got out of the Camry.

"One down," Eleanor said as he glanced first at the car and then at her. "Four to go."

A convertible driven by her dad's friend Tony pulled up outside the back entrance to the garage. Eleanor threw herself inside.

"Where to?" Tony asked as he peeled out and onto the street.

"Find me some rich bitches. They keep their cars cleaner."

"Gramercy Park it is then, ma'am."

On 23rd Street, she nabbed a Mercedes. Too easy. They hadn't even locked the fucking thing.

Canal Street netted them one BMW, silver. It handled like a dream. Such a pretty car it broke Eleanor's heart to scratch the window with the coat hanger. She didn't want to think about the thousand different parts it would be chopped up into by tomorrow morning.

On Union Street she spotted a high-end Acura, bright red, parked outside a restaurant. The owner had probably tipped the hostess to keep an eye on it. The hostess was probably off getting stoned in the kitchen.

"Four down, one to go," she said to her dad as she tossed him the Acura's spare keys. The genius owner had left the set in the visor. She didn't even have to wire this one.

"Be careful," he called out as she headed back to the street.

She flipped him off on her way out the door.

One more car and it would be done. One more and she could go home to bed. With all the adrenaline surging through her body, she knew she'd crash hard the second she got home and wouldn't wake up until noon.

As Tony drove her into SoHo, Eleanor kept her eye out for a nice American car. American manufacturers were arrogant, and that made them shit at security. No Ford or Dodge had ever put up much of a fight.

"Nice..." Tony purred as he spotted a car in tiny ten-space paid-parking lot.

She saw what he saw the second after he saw it. A Shelby Mustang. Looked like a 1966 to her, not that she'd bet her life on that. She knew make and model on sight, but she wasn't enough of a nerd to bother with all the years. She'd leave that to her dad.

"It's mine," she said. Tony wolf whistled his agreement.

"Go for it. See you back at the shop."

Eleanor hopped out of the car and sidled over to the lot. She saw a few people milling around but no one seemed to notice her. She probably looked like some drunk preppy waiting for her friends to come out of a bar.

Let them think that. Let them think anything they wanted as long as they didn't notice her standing with her back to the driver's side window, a bent coat hanger behind her back. She dug under the latch and lifted up, popping the lock with ease.

Ten seconds later she and her new friend Shelby were already on the street.

Done. She'd jacked five high-dollar cars in one night. One night? She'd done it in four hours. A sense of relief flooded her. In no time she'd be back in her bed at home dreaming of Søren. Good thing she'd finished her job early. The skies had opened up and rain exploded from the clouds. The temperature, unusually warm the past week, turned frigid in minutes. The rain fractured the city lights and set everything in her rearview mirror alight with a blue glow.

Blue?

"Fuck." In a panic Eleanor glanced behind her. A police car, blue lights ablaze, nestled in behind her. It hadn't turned on its sirens and the silence of the car menaced her far more than sound.

She knew she had about two seconds to decide what to do. She could gun it and run. The second she lost the cop car she could dump the Mustang and disappear. But this wasn't the highway or the interstate. This was Manhattan after midnight. Narrow streets. Pedestrians. Her foot hovered over the pedals. Accelerator on her right, brake on her left. Eleanor looked around for an escape route. She saw no alleys. No easy exits. And up on her right loomed a church, its ancient spire casting a cross-shaped shadow onto the shining streets.

Eleanor hit the brakes and prayed for a miracle.

8

Eleanor

FOR TWO HOURS THE COPS KEPT HER IN THE BACK of the squad car while they asked her questions and talked on their shoulder-mounted walkie-talkies. She did her best to stick to her story. *I'm sorry. I wanted to drive it around the block. You know—joyriding.* But for some reason the cops didn't quite buy it. Apparently joyriders usually borrowed cars they had the keys to, not cars that had to have their locks popped and their ignitions hot-wired.

The two cops—one white, one black, both young—seemed way too excited about having pulled her over. Mobsters and murderers and rapists were running all over town and Officer Ferrell and Officer Hampton couldn't stop patting themselves on the back for bringing down a fifteen-year-old car thief.

"We called your mom," Officer Hampton said, giving her a wink.

"Oh, no, not my mom."

"She'll meet us at the station," Officer Ferrell said.

"Station? We have to go to the station?"

"Sure we do." Officer Hampton waved his hand, motioning at her to stand up. She stepped out of the back of the squad car and into the driving rain. "That's where we take everybody we arrest."

"Arrest?"

Ferrell and Hampton laughed as they pulled her arms gently behind her back and placed handcuffs on her wrists. The cold metal bit into her skin. She'd never worn handcuffs before. The heft of them surprised her. She'd never dreamed they'd feel so heavy and cold.

The white cop, Ferrell, placed a hand on the back of her head as he maneuvered her into the back of the squad car.

"You, little girl," began Officer Hampton, "have the right to remain silent."

"Take that advice, little girl," Officer Ferrell said as she pulled her feet into the car.

Eleanor glared up at his wide, plain and arrogant face.

"Don't call me *little girl*."

Her bravado lasted until the door slammed behind her. Alone in the backseat of the squad car, she started to shake. The temperature had dropped. Rain had soaked her clothes and hair. Her skin felt clammy and cold. But that wasn't why she couldn't stop shaking.

Once at the station the two officers pulled around to the police entrance. Officer Ferrell opened the door and ordered her out. As they headed toward the door, she saw two figures ten yards away at the main entrance standing in the rain both holding umbrellas. One was her mother. She'd recognize that shabby pink umbrella with the ruffles anywhere. Her mother stood watching her, her face as wet with tears as Eleanor's was wet with rain. Behind her under a black umbrella loomed someone else. Tall, stern and watchful, he followed her every step with his eyes. She raised her head, not wanting him to see her fear and her shame. Something about the sight of her must have amused him because his gaze darted once to her handcuffed wrists before meeting her eyes with the subtlest of smiles on his lips. Officer Hampton ushered her inside and put her in a plastic chair.

"Can I see my mom?" she asked him as the officer at the desk took her mug shot, and another starting typing on a computer behind the high desk.

"Soon. We're gonna get you in a room. Somebody's coming to talk to you."

"Do I need a lawyer?" she asked, having learned long ago from her father that in their world the *L* word had magic powers.

"You can talk to your mom about that later," Officer Hampton said as he scribbled on a clipboard. She wondered if he was drawing dinosaur doodles the way his hand flew all over the page. All the files and the forms and the pictures were intimidation tactics. They'd asked her fifteen times in the car on the way over where she'd planned on taking the car. She knew they wanted her father and his shop, and they weren't about to get that information from her.

"How long do I have to keep wearing the handcuffs?" The metal cuffs kept hitting the back of her plastic chair and making a scraping sound like nails on a chalkboard.

"We'll get those off in a minute," Officer Ferrell said. "Once I remember where I put the keys."

"Come on, Speed Racer." Officer Hampton snapped his fingers in her face. "We got a room for you."

He took her gently by the upper arm and escorted her down a dingy beige hallway to a room with nothing but a table in the center and two chairs.

"You're going to interrogate me?" Eleanor asked as she sat down in the chair.

"Nothing but a friendly conversation. Someone will be in soon."

He shut the door and left her alone in the room with nothing but her fears. *Calm down,* she ordered herself. *It'll be okay. Dad will find out and he'll come straight down here and tell them it was his fault, his doing, that he asked me to help him because he owed the mob a lot of money.* He'd never let her take the fall for him. Not his own daughter, his only child. Right?

But deep down she knew he wasn't coming for her.

Time dripped by as slowly as frozen honey from a bottle. The adrenaline drained from her body and soon Eleanor felt the exhaustion under the fear. Her head throbbed; her arms ached. She'd give anything to get out of these handcuffs and stretch.

Eventually her chin dropped to her chest. For a few minutes she even slept.

The sound of a door opening alerted her to the presence of someone entering the room. She kept her head down, her eyes closed.

Something touched her cuffed hands behind her back. Fingers brushed her palm, caressed her wrists. She heard a click and the cuffs came off. In any other room under any other circumstances she might have enjoyed the sensation of large warm hands on her cold skin. Some cop touching her in such a personal way made her stomach turn.

She heard the rasp of a chair on the floor and the sound of the metal handcuffs landing on the table.

If she opened her eyes and raised her head, it would start. The whole ugly mess would start. Interrogation, investigation, accusations... Her eyelids were a wall, and until she opened them the world would stay behind that wall. But she couldn't hide forever.

She opened her eyes expecting to see a cop or a lawyer or maybe even her mom.

But no, it was her priest. He didn't speak, not a word. She brought her arms around in front of her and started to rub her wrists. It had been him touching her fingers and chafing her skin as he'd removed the handcuffs, not some creepy cop.

Eleanor hated that he'd been dragged into this mess. Her mother had probably called him in a panic the second after the cops had called her. Anytime anything bad ever happened, her mother's first call was to Father Greg. Had it been Father Greg she'd called, the old priest would have prayed on the phone with her, offered her words of advice and comfort. He never would have dragged himself out of bed in the middle of the night to go to a police station in the city. But Søren had. Why?

He continued to stare at her in silence and Eleanor felt like she'd unwittingly entered into a staring contest. Fine. Staring contest it was then. She knew how to get him to blink.

"So," she began, "since our last talk about rules and priests and sex and stuff, I've been meaning to ask you a question. Are you one of those priests who likes to fuck the kids in the congregation?"

She waited.

He didn't blink.

"No."

Okay, so he was good at this game. She was better.

She raised her chin and gave him the sort of smile she'd dreamed of giving a handsome older man but never had the guts or the chance to try it.

"Too bad."

"Eleanor, we need to discuss the predicament you're in at the moment."

She nodded her agreement.

"I'm in a real pickle."

Smile? Laugh? Withering glare? Nothing.

"You were arrested on suspicion of grand theft auto. Several luxury vehicles with a combined value of a quarter of a million dollars were stolen tonight. You wouldn't know anything about that, would you?"

"I take the Fifth," she said, proud of her legal knowledge. "That's what I'm supposed to say, right?"

Now she received the withering glare she'd been hoping for.

"To the courts, yes. To me, never. To me, you will tell the truth always."

"I don't think you want to know the truth about me, Søren." She dropped her voice to a whisper at the moment she said his name. It seemed like a magic word to her, his name. Like knowing his name meant something special like it did in fairy tales.

"Eleanor, there is nothing I don't want to know about you. Nothing you tell me will shock or disgust me. Nothing will cause me to change my mind about you."

"Change your mind? You've already made up your mind about me? What's the verdict?" She braced herself, not wanting the answer. They had nothing in common, she and her priest. He looked like money, talked like money. He had the whitest fingernails she'd ever seen on a man. White fingernails, perfect hands like a marble sculpture of a Greek god. And her? She was a fucking train wreck. Chipped black nail polish, soaked clothes, dripping wet hair and her entire life over in one night.

"The verdict is this—I am willing and capable of helping you out of this mess you've gotten yourself into tonight."

"Can we call it a *pickle? Pickle* sounds less scary than mess."

"It's a disaster, young lady. The car they caught you stealing belongs to a very powerful man. He's already demanding the police try you as an adult and put you away for the maximum sentence. You could spend years in juvenile detention, or worse—an adult facility. At the very least, this man doesn't want you seeing sunlight until you're twenty-one years old. Blessedly, I have some connections in this area. Or, more accurately, I have someone who has some connections in this area."

For the first time since they started speaking, he broke eye contact with her. He glanced away into the corner of the room. His face wore the strangest expression. Whoever this powerful person was, Søren didn't seem all that excited about asking him. In fact, if she had to guess, she'd say he was dreading it.

"You're going to go through all this trouble for me, why?"

Søren looked back at her and gave her a smile that stripped her soul naked and put it on its knees.

"Because there is nothing I wouldn't do to protect you, Eleanor. Nothing I wouldn't do to help you and nothing I wouldn't do to save you. Nothing."

The way he spoke the final "nothing" sent a chill through her body. It scared her instead of comforting her. He meant it. That was why it scared her.

"That's not an answer. You're saying you're helping me because you're helping me."

"I am."

"There's no other reason?"

"There is, but I can't tell what it is yet."

"But you will?"

"In time. But first, Eleanor, there is something you should know."

Eleanor sat up straight her in her chair and gave him her full attention.

"What?"

"There is a price you will have to pay."

"Oh, goodie," she said, and gave him a wide smile. "Now we get back to my first question about the fucking of the kids at church. Well, if you insist."

"Do you value your worth as a child of God so little that you presume I would only help in exchange for sex?"

He asked the question calmly and with only curiosity in his tone, but the words still hit as hard as a fist in her stomach.

"So that's a no?"

Søren raised an eyebrow at her and Eleanor was overcome with a fit of laughter. She was beginning to like this guy. She'd fallen in love with him the moment she first saw him, and she would love him now until the end of world. But she'd never dreamed she'd like him so much.

"That would be a no," he said. "I will, however, require something from you."

"Do you always talk like this?"

"You mean articulately?"

"Yes."

"Yes."

"Weird. So what am I paying you for your help? I hope it's not my firstborn child or anything. Don't want kids." She wasn't sure about that last part but it sounded kind of tough.

"My price is simply this—in exchange for my assistance, I ask that you do what I tell you to do from now on."

"Do what you tell me to do?"

"Yes. I want you to obey me."

"From now on?" She couldn't believe she'd heard him right. "Like, for how long?"

Søren looked at her again, looked at her without smiling, without blinking, without jesting, without joking. He looked at her like the next word he said would be the most important word he ever spoke and the most important word she ever heard.

"Forever."

The word hung in the air between them before falling into her lap and seeping into her skin.

"Forever," she repeated. "You want me to obey your every order forever?"

"Yes."

"What are you going to order me to do?"

"As soon as you agree to my terms, you will learn your first order."

"You know forever is a really long time. It's the longest time, actually. You don't get longer than forever."

"I am aware of this."

"I could be in juvie until I'm twenty-one. Forever's longer than six years."

"It is."

"I'll take juvie, then." A foolish boast, but one she meant.

"You would rather go to prison than obey me?" Søren sounded horrified. Maybe even scared. His fear made her afraid. But not so afraid she would give in, not yet.

"If I'm going to give you forever," she said, raising her chin higher, "I want something in return."

"I already offered to help you out of your mess. What else do you want?"

Eleanor considered her demands. He sounded open to suggestion, which was good because she had a suggestion.

"Everything."

"Everything?" he repeated. "As in…?"

"Every. Thing." She stared at him across the desk, and this time it was her turn not to blink. "I give you forever, the least you can give me is everything."

"I believe I know what you're asking, and you should know that's problematic where I'm concerned."

"Because you're a Catholic priest, and you're older than I am?"

"That would be two of the three reasons."

"What's the third?"

"I will tell you the third reason at the same time I tell you the second reason I'm offering to help you."

"Jesus H. Christ, so many questions. Do I need to write this shit down?"

Søren reached into his coat pocket and pulled out his battered leather-bound Bible, the one that had his real name in it. He flipped through the pages and glanced at the scraps of paper inside. They all appeared to have writing on them but not in English. Finally he flipped to the very back, ripped out a blank end page and slid it across the table to her. From inside his coat he produced a pen, a heavy black one.

"Write."

Eleanor eyed the pen and paper. She looked at Søren.

"I will answer your questions," he said. "Eventually. In the meantime I wouldn't want either of us to forget any of them."

On the end page she wrote *What's the third reason that being with me is problemmatic?* and *What's the second reason you're helping me?* She furrowed her brow as she studied the paper.

"Something wrong?" Søren asked.

"I think I misspelled *problematic*." She held up the note and Søren narrowed his eyes at it.

"One *m*."

"Can I answer your two objections?" she asked, rewriting the word *problematic* with only one *m* this time. "I don't care if you're a Catholic priest. Forcing priests to be celibate is the stupidest rule ever. Why would God invent sex and then tell people not to have it? And second, so what? You're older than I am. I'll be sixteen in a couple days."

"I can't believe I'm even discussing this with you, Eleanor," Søren said.

She smiled at him.

"I can."

Søren turned his head and stared at nothing for a moment. He smiled a little and turned back to her.

"Very well, then."

"Very well what?"

He held out his hand, waiting for her to shake it.

She stared at his hand, his perfect hand.

"You're kidding, right?"

"I want you to obey me forever. It is a high price, and I realize that. If we have to negotiate, then we have to negotiate. I accept your terms. Can you accept mine?"

Eleanor slowly raised her hand off the desk and put her fingers into his.

"Okay," she said. "You got me. I'm yours."

He wrapped his much larger hand around hers. She expected his hand to be cold for some reason. He had such cold eyes, such an icy demeanor, but no, his skin was warm and she couldn't help but imagine him touching her in far more intimate places than her hand.

"Forever," she said.

And he said, "Everything."

The deal was done. They released each other's hands and Søren stood up.

"I'll leave you now. Do not answer any questions until you speak to an attorney. The church will pay your legal fees. Rest assured you will pay us back for them in time."

"Okay." The fear had returned. She didn't want him to leave her. Not now. Not ever.

"When your lawyer arrives, tell her the entire truth and leave nothing out. Your father was involved, no doubt. You need to tell the lawyer the level of his involvement."

"Rat out my dad? No way."

"Eleanor, less than one minute ago you promised to obey me forever. These are your orders. Your father is the reason you are here in this police station in the middle of the night with your entire future hanging in the balance. You are here. He isn't. You will tell the lawyer and the court everything you know about your father and his illegal enterprises. You should be able to parlay that into a plea agreement or a very reduced sentence. In the meantime, I'll meet with my friend who has useful connections. I will leave nothing to chance where you are concerned."

He took two steps toward the door.

"Eleanor?"

"Yeah?"

He gave her a smile, this one showing his kindness and concern.

"I will take care of you. Forever."

She returned his smile as best she could.

"This friend of yours, he'll really help me?"

"He will."

"How come?"

"Add that question to your list."

Eleanor rolled her eyes and exhaled heavily as she wrote *Why will your friend help me?*

"I'm gonna need legal-size paper for this freaking list. Anything else?"

"Yes. You're missing a question on your list."

"I got them all. What am I missing?"

Søren returned to the table, took the pen and paper from

her and wrote nine words. And without a word, he slapped the cuffs back on her wrists and left her alone in the room.

Eleanor looked down at the paper and read the question he'd written in his elegant, masculine handwriting.

Why would a priest have his own handcuff key?

9

Nora

NICO DROPPED HIS HEAD AND LAUGHED, RUBBING the back of his neck in consternation and amusement. Nora put her toe under his chin and lifted it.

Nora put on her best dominant face.

"Young man, do you think it's hilarious that I stole cars for my father and got arrested? I promise you I didn't find it funny."

"That's not funny. You at fifteen forcing your priest to agree to sleep with you *is* funny."

"I admit I was pretty damn proud of myself for my negotiating skills."

"More like hostage taking. If you hadn't obeyed him..."

"Bye, bye, Catholic high school. Hello, juvie."

"Didn't he scare you? You were fifteen. He was twenty-nine."

"Had it been any other man it probably would have scared me. But with Søren, everything felt like destiny. When we met he said, 'It's a pleasure to *finally* meet you.' We'd both been waiting for each other, like it was meant to be that we would find and love each other. We belonged together—me, Søren, Kingsley. Getting arrested brought all three of us together."

"So it was Kingsley your priest was talking about?" Nico held out his hand to her and helped her out of the chair. She could have done it herself. But she wasn't about to turn down a chance to let Nico touch her any way he wanted.

"It was. The friend Søren said had connections and could help get my ass out of the hot seat? That was your father."

Nico grabbed their glasses and the wine bottle and led her up the stairs. Despite the fire, the downstairs had grown colder as midnight neared, and it was hard to think and speak of the past with the silver box on the fireplace mantel in front of her, its contents so precious and so terrifying.

"Kingsley has interesting friends," Nico said as they entered the bedroom. He set the wine and glasses down on the bedside table and went to work building the fire back up.

"And even more interesting enemies. Kingsley and I share something in common—we're both fascinated by other people," Nora said, pulling the covers back. "Where we differ is that when I'm fascinated by someone, I fuck him. When Kingsley is fascinated by someone, he fucks *with* him."

Nico laughed and walked back to the bed. He kissed her neck and nipped lightly at her shoulder.

"Is that why you let me inside you?" he whispered in her ear. "You're fascinated by me?"

"That's part of it, yes. You're my first farmer." She pulled away and smiled up at him.

"You're my first dominatrix."

"But not your first shamefully older woman?" she asked as she slid into bed and propped herself up on the pillows. Nico pulled off his shirt. Such an exquisite male form. Where was her camera when she needed it?

"My last girlfriend was forty-three," he said.

"Forty-three? Jesus, you do have a Mrs. Robinson complex, don't you?"

"It's a choice, not a complex," he said. "Life is short. I don't want to spend it with someone my age who doesn't know anything more about life than I do. I have a friend, she's my age. She's funny, beautiful, smart. Everyone thinks we should be together. But she always has money trouble, always has a crisis. She's forever calling her father for help. She doesn't know what to do with her life. I love her, but I couldn't be with someone like that. I own a successful vineyard. I have employees, people who depend on me. My last girlfriend owned a château and had a staff of ten people working for her. Even with the age difference we had more in common than my friend who's my age who changes jobs and boyfriends every six months."

"I don't have a château, only a house. A big damn house, but no one works for me. I did have an intern once, though. Unpaid." She conjured one little memory and held it in the palm of her hand. She smiled at it, loved it a moment and then let it go.

"Women and wine always get better with age," Nico said.

"I want to think that. I get richer with age anyway. I'm at the point where I have more money than I know what to do with."

"Buy more time to spend with me, maybe?"

Nora narrowed her eyes at him.

"Did an older woman teach you how to talk like that? Because, if so, I need her name and address to send her a thank-you note."

Nico grinned down at her.

"Every woman I've been with has taught me something about women. How to kiss, how to fuck, how to dress. My first lover told me women are always watching. If you're rude to the waiter, she sees and files that away." Nico tapped his temple.

"You had a good education."

"I want to learn everything from you, too. And everything about you."

"Everything?"

"Everything." He straddled her thighs and wrapped his hand around the back of her neck. "How you like being touched. How you like being fucked. How you like your eggs in the morning. How you like your tea at night. How you love to be kissed."

She raised her mouth to his, eager for more of his drugging kisses. When he kissed her and touched her, she could almost make herself believe he was the reason she'd run away to Europe and hidden herself in the middle of the Black Forest, where no one but Nico could find her.

"I like being touched the way you touch me," she said. "I like being fucked the way you fuck me. I like my eggs scrambled and covered in cheese. I like my tea like I like my men—hot, ready and in my hand. And I love the way you kiss me because it helps me forget why I'm here." Her voice broke at the final words and Nico took her by the shoulders.

"Can you forget?"

"No," she said, shivering. "I want to. I'm so angry it happened that I can't even… I can't breathe when I think about it."

"I was angry, too. Angry at everyone. Especially my mother. She moved to Paris five days after Papa's funeral. Then I realized she was grieving, too. Being near his vines, his life's work, reminded her too much of him. I never thought she really loved him. But then I knew. She couldn't breathe, either."

"Help me breathe," she said, feeling the anger like a vise around her lungs.

He pulled her close and put her head on his shoulder.

"Breathe with me," he said. "Do what I do."

He inhaled deeply and pushed on her back with both hands. She forced air into her nose and held the breath.

"Now push it out," Nico said. Nora forced herself to exhale. "Good. Again."

With his hands on her back, he guided her breathing. In and out. Deep and long. A push against her back meant "breathe in." A gentle slide of his fingers down her spine meant "breathe out." After a few minutes she felt the fury and the panic subsiding.

She felt dizzy with gratitude for Nico's presence. She clung to his arms as he held her and kissed his neck.

"Do you want me to make you come again?" he asked softly in her ear.

"Yes," she said without shame. "It will distract me, and that's as much as I can ask for now."

Nico pulled the straps of gown down again, lowered his head and took a nipple into his mouth. Nora sighed and relaxed into the pillow. His tongue circled her areola while his hands held and warmed both breasts. She reached down to stroke him but he grabbed her hand by the wrist and pressed her hand over her head into the pillow.

"My kind of game," she teased as he pressed her down into the bed.

"No games. I'm taking care of you tonight." Nico kissed along the edge of her collarbone. "All night if you'll let me."

"I'll let you." She sighed, surrendering to him. It felt good to let go, to relax a little, to let him pleasure her without needing to give him anything in return. He resumed kissing her breasts and she did nothing but lie there underneath him. He pinched her nipples and bit them gently until they were swollen and sore—the way she liked them.

Nico slipped his hand between her legs and found the ring that pierced her clitoral hood.

"Decoration?" Nico asked.

"Mostly," she admitted. "But it can be useful if you know what you're doing."

"I don't know what I'm doing, but you can teach me." Nico gave her a roguish grin.

With everything that had happened to her, with everything she'd been through and with everything she'd lost, she shouldn't even be in bed with Nico, much less loving every second of his company. Had what she'd lost created such a vacuum that she needed to fill it with Kingsley's son in her bed? Apparently so.

"There's a bag in the bathroom," she said. "Black silk."

Nico raised his eyebrow.

"Trust me," she said.

Nora straightened her gown and adjusted her pillows as Nico went into the bathroom to retrieve her bag. She gave him a wink before untying the cord and opening it. It contained nothing but a few pieces of jewelry she always traveled with—two pairs of earrings, a bracelet and the rings Søren had given her for Christmas. She'd taken the rings off two weeks ago, but she didn't leave them behind. She could never leave them behind.

From the bag she selected an eighteen-inch silver beaded chain. She removed the camphor glass fleur-de-lis pendant, a birthday gift from Kingsley, and laid the bag aside.

"Are you getting the idea?" she asked, holding up the chain and running it through her fingers.

Nico took the chain from her hand.

"Lie back," he said. "Open your legs."

"The five best words in the English language."

"Couche-toi. Écarte les cuisses," Nico said.

"The five best words in the French language."

Nora lay back as instructed and opened her legs wide for Nico. He tried and failed to unclasp the chain. She took it from him and opened it.

"Smaller fingers," she said. He took the chain from her and threaded it through the ring. This time he managed to lock the clasp. He pulled the chain taut, and Nora flinched with the pleasure of the gentle tugging.

"Now pull the chain through."

Nico did as instructed. The beads of the silver chain rattled the ring. Nora shivered at the sensation it created—like a vibrator but much more intimate and concentrated. She dug her fingers into the bed as Nico spun the chain through the ring over and over again, slowly at first and then faster as her breathing quickened.

With the chain in his left hand, he tugged and teased her clitoral ring. With his right hand, he pressed three and then four fingers into her. Nora spread wide for Nico as his hand explored her vagina. He massaged her G-spot, went deeper and pushed against the high back wall near her cervix. Her inner muscles twitched and tightened around his fingers. She gasped when he pushed into a soft corner of her, the pleasure so intense she flinched.

Nico laughed as he moved the chain back and forth. Her clitoris pulsed and her stomach tightened. Her hips rose of their own accord as she moved in time with the muscles clenching and releasing around Nico's fingers.

She came with a sudden shiver that she felt from her shoulders to her knees before collapsing back on the bed with a spent laugh.

"Now that," Nico said as he pulled out his hand and unclasped the chain, "is a good trick."

"One of many up my sleeve," Nora said, as she took the chain from him and put it back in her jewelry case. Nico ran his hand over her thighs and stomach.

"Where did you learn all these tricks?" he asked, kissing her mouth.

"You don't want to know."

"Kingsley?"

"And Søren. And my own wicked imagination."

She pulled back from the kiss to wink at him.

"You amaze me."

"That's your erection talking."

"And my heart," he said.

She laid her hand on the side of his face. Such a young, handsome face. But he didn't have an ounce of innocence in him. He worked too hard, lived too hard, had seen too much of the world to have stars in his eyes. Good. She liked his eyes the way they were right now—warm and hungry. He had none of his father's cynicism and all of his secrets. But Nico's secrets never scared her like Kingsley's did. She knew one secret he kept from her for her own sake.

"I know you're in love with me," she said, caressing the arch of his cheekbone with her fingertips.

"It doesn't matter," he said. "My feelings are my own. They shouldn't concern you."

"God, you're so French."

Nico laughed and buried his head against her chest.

"I can't help it," he said. "I get it from my father."

"Which father?" she asked.

"The one who raised me. My real father. Not Kingsley."

"Kingsley would have raised you and loved you if he'd known about you."

"Let me love you since I can't love him," Nico said.

She ran her fingers through the dark waves of his hair. In her younger days she would never have appreciated a man like Nico—quiet, industrious, low-key. He had presence and intelligence but he made no spectacle of himself. He didn't need to to own every room he walked into. He was so self-possessed he felt no need to possess anyone or anything else.

"Nico, look at me." He raised his head and gazed into her eyes, the smile long gone from his face. "I've known your father twenty years. Twenty. Think about that."

"If I can accept that, why can't you?"

"It's not that I've known him for a long time. It's how I know him, what we are to each other, what we've been through together."

"Then tell me. Please."

"Are you sure you want to hear this story?" Nora asked as she settled into the pillows. Nico lay next to her, his arm draped over her stomach.

"Yes, I want to hear the story. Kingsley might be my biological father, but he's not really my father. My father taught me how to plant vines and prune them, how to press wine and rack it. He's the one who sent me to Australia to learn the secrets of Shiraz. Kingsley seduced my mother while my father was in Paris going bank to bank begging for a loan to keep the vineyard in the family after a bad harvest."

"If you knew King like I did, you would find a way to love him."

"Help me find that way."

Nora took a deep breath.

"This might help you love him a little," she said as she took her jewelry bag back to the bathroom. She grabbed her hairbrush and retuned to the bedroom. "So I got arrested for stealing cars for my dad, right? And Søren promised to help me out of my little legal trouble. He knew he'd need Kingsley to call in some favors. Even back then Kingsley had a few prosecutors and judges in his pocket. But when Søren went to him and asked for help, that was the first time he and Kingsley had spoken to each other in over ten years. Still, Kingsley helped him and helped me, too. He didn't ask for anything in return except that Søren stay and be his friend."

"It's good he helped you. You're here now with me and not in prison."

"I'd do okay in prison. Helps that I love having sex with women."

"This isn't helping my erection," Nico said.

"I'd say I'm sorry, but you're too pretty to lie to."

Nora sat on the edge of the bed and pulled a pin from her now mussed mane of hair. Nico stopped her hand and with a spin of his finger indicated she should turn around. She raised an eyebrow and turned her back to him. One by one, Nico extracted the hairpins and unwound the low knot at the nape of her neck. Then he threaded his fingers through the waves, breaking them apart.

"You said getting arrested brought you and Kingsley and your priest together?" Nico asked as he took the hairbrush from her hand. Nora stiffened. The only man who had ever brushed her hair for her had been Søren. It seemed almost traitorous to let Nico do it. And yet, she couldn't stop him. She needed the comfort and the contact far too much. Nothing felt more exquisite than the gentle pull of the brush through her hair. If only untangling the knots in her stomach were this easy.

"Yes, it was Kingsley who helped keep me out of juvenile detention. I was sentenced to twelve hundred hours of community service, which I had to complete before I turned eighteen. And here's the fun part—Kingsley made sure the judge assigned Søren to monitor my community service. Soon I was feeding the hungry and hanging out with the homeless and scrubbing toilets and teaching poor kids how to make tassel bookmarks at summer camp."

"Better than prison?"

"It was. Until I fucked it up. But that was Kingsley's fault. He was getting me into trouble before we even met."

"He's talented."

"Tell me about it."

"What happened?"

Nora turned her head to the side so Nico could reach all her tangles.

"It was June. I was sixteen. And my lawyer had put me under house arrest. She told me I could go to school but nowhere else. Not even church. So the day my community service started was the first time I'd seen Søren in months. Things got weird. Fast."

Nico gave a low, warm laugh and kissed that sensitive spot on her back between her shoulder blades.

"How weird?"

"The story starts with a stick in the ground and ends with an orgy."

"As every story should."

10

Eleanor

AT 9:00 A.M. SHARP THE DAY AFTER SCHOOL ENDED for summer break, Eleanor walked into Sacred Heart Catholic Church for the first time since March. She knew she'd be working that day so she'd put on an old white T-shirt and cutoff denim shorts and pulled her hair back in a ponytail.

She went to Søren's office. Not Søren, she corrected herself. Father Stearns. She said it a few more times in her head. Father. Stearns. Other parishioners hung around the church, and the last thing she wanted to do was slip up and call him by his real first name. People were already going to be suspicious of a teenage girl at the beck and call of a handsome young priest. No reason to make things worse. Father. Stearns. Not. Søren. She could do this.

She knocked on his office door and took a step back. He opened the door.

"Hi, Søren," she said.

He arched an eyebrow at her.

"I mean, Father Stearns."

"This is going to be an issue for us, isn't it?"

"Probably."

He paused a moment before speaking again.

"Come with me. We need to talk."

She followed him out to the back of the church and onto the shaded lawn. She had to stretch her legs to keep up with his long stride. He led her to a path, which bordered a small public park.

"First, how are you, Eleanor? I haven't seen you in months."

"Sorry about that. House arrest. But I'm okay. I'm grounded for life."

"I can't blame your mother for that decision. But you will start attending church again."

"Your wish is my command," she said, stuffing her hands in the back pockets of her shorts.

"A good attitude to adopt. I heard your father was arrested."

She shrugged her shoulders. "Yeah, big shock there. He was eight states away by the time they caught that fucker. Sorry."

"You were arrested, and he ran. You have my permission to call him anything you like."

"Thank you. I'm sure he was scared, right? That's why he ran."

"You deserve better than someone who will abandon you in times of trouble."

"He's out on bail now. He's tried to call a few times."

"You will not speak to him."

She stopped and Søren stopped and looked at her.

"He's my father."

"The moment he chose to protect himself instead of protecting his daughter is the moment his rights to see you, speak to you or even be in the same room with you ceased to exist. We made a deal, Eleanor. You obey my orders. This is one of them. You understand this?"

She paused before answering. She'd hoped the whole "obeying" thing with Søren would involve orders like "take your clothes off" and "get into my bed." A deal was a deal, however.

"I understand."

"Good. Your well-being is my top priority. I'm supervising your community service, which puts you in my hands. I take this responsibility very seriously. There can be no part of your life you keep from me if I'm going to help you find the right path."

"My lawyer said I've got to be here about twenty hours a week. This is my life now."

"I want more of your time than twenty hours a week. Those hours are for community service. You also need to keep your grades up. When school starts again in the fall, I want you to do your homework here at church so I can help you if necessary."

"I'm good at school, it's okay. I'm smarter than I look."

"There's nothing unintelligent in your appearance," he said as they started walking again. Mothers pushing strollers walked past them. They barely noticed her, but every last one of them smiled at Søren. "One failed test, one missed assignment and your grades could drop. If you can't do the work and keep your grades up, the judge will send you to juvenile detention."

"I know. I promise I'll do my homework. These park women are totally checking you out."

"Eleanor."

"Sorry."

"In addition to your community service work, you'll receive spiritual counseling."

"Spiritual counseling? Do I even want to know what that is?"

"As a Jesuit, I went through years of spiritual counseling

with mentors. All of it was enlightening and edifying. Priests and laypeople alike can benefit from the teachings of Saint Ignatius. I'm certain you will, too."

Eleanor's stomach tightened at the prospect of spending so much time with Søren.

"Saint Ignatius? Okay. I can handle that. Anything else?"

"As for your community service, most of it will be performed here at Sacred Heart. As much as I respect Father Gregory, his ministry seemed to focus far more on the spiritual needs of the community rather than the material needs. The church has no food bank, no outreach missions."

"Is that bad?" As they passed a small tree, Eleanor grabbed the end of a branch and shook it like a hand.

"Prayer is all well and good, but Christ made it abundantly clear we'd be judged by our works far more than our prayers."

"You're about to quote a Bible verse at me, aren't you?"

"I am. Matthew 25: 31–46."

"The sheep and the goats." She almost yelled the words. Søren looked at her with his right eyebrow raised. "Sorry. I remembered that one. I got excited."

"Wonderful to hear such enthusiasm about the Bible. You remember the verses?" As they passed a bush bursting with roses, Søren reached out and stroked the pale pink petals.

"Yeah. Jesus says when he comes back he'll divide people into two groups—the sheep and the goats."

"Correct. The sheep, Jesus says, will inherit the kingdom of God because they clothed him when he was naked, fed him when he was hungry, gave him water when he was thirsty and visited him in prison. The sheep will say they do not remember ever doing such things for Jesus. And Jesus answers, 'Truly I tell you, just as you did it to one of the least of these who are members of my family, you did it to me.' The goats were the ones who never fed the hungry, gave water to the thirsty."

"I always liked those verses. We acted them out in Sunday school. We had little sheep ears and goat horns." She put her hands on her head and mimed horns with her fingers. Søren seemed to be biting back a smile.

"I want you to be counted among the sheep. As part of your community service, you'll start a food bank at the church. We have a massive kitchen that only seems to get used for wedding receptions or baptisms. You'll also work at church camp and visit the homeless at the shelter on Sixth Street."

"Visit the homeless shelter?" She couldn't quite keep the fear out of her voice. She'd heard bad stories from that shelter. Most of them involving drug addicts or alcoholics. Fights would break out. People would end up in the hospital.

"Don't be afraid. I'll make sure you're safe. Do you babysit?"

"Sometimes. Kids like me."

"I can't imagine anyone not liking you."

She tried not to smile. She failed.

"I've spoken several times with your mother. She'll keep you on your schedule and monitor your grades."

"You talked to my mom?"

"She loves you. We're going to work together to keep you out of trouble."

Eleanor grimaced.

"What was that expression for?" Søren demanded.

"Sorry." She sighed. "I like trouble."

They had made one complete loop around the park, a quarter mile according to the sign. Søren led her away from the path and back toward the church. He paused in a clearing about fifteen yards from the back of the church and picked a stick up off the ground. The stick was about two feet tall and two inches thick. Søren shoved it deep into the soft moist soil.

"Your first act of service is this..." Søren said as he stood back up. "Every day for the next six months come rain, shine, snow, sleet, hail or hurricane, you will water this stick."

Eleanor stared at the dead stick jutting up from the ground.

"It's a stick."

"I know it is."

"It's dead."

"I realize that."

"Watering it isn't going to bring it back to life."

"I realize that, as well."

"But I'm supposed to water it?"

"It's an order."

"I'll take that as a yes."

"It is."

"Are you going to tell me why I'm watering this stick?"

"I told you why. It's an order."

"No other reason?"

Søren stroked his bottom lip with his thumb. She never wanted to be a thumb so much in her life.

"That list of questions you wish to ask me that I can't answer yet..."

"Yeah, what about them?"

"If you water this stick every single day without fail for six months, I'll answer your questions."

"You will? All of them?"

"Any question you have for me, no matter how personal or intrusive, I will answer it in six months if you water the stick every single day."

Every single question? She couldn't believe it. If he'd offered her a million dollars or the answers to all her questions, she'd pick the answers, hands down.

"So six months is…"

"The day after Thanksgiving," Søren said. "Rather fitting. I'm sure you'll be thankful to have finished your task."

"Forget the stick, I want answers."

"You'll have them if you earn them," he said.

"How will you know if I watered it or not?"

"I'll know."

"When do you think you'll, you know, want to hold up your end of the bargain?" Eleanor tried to keep the nervousness from her voice. In exchange for her eternal obedience, Søren had promised her "everything." Two months had passed since she'd spoken to him that night at the police station. Did he remember what he'd promised her?

"We shall discuss that part of our agreement when you're finished watering the stick."

"Great. I'll water it right now."

"I meant when you're finished watering it…in six months."

Søren left her standing there staring at the stick as he walked back to the church.

"Hey!" she shouted after him. "Six months?"

"Do as you're told and we'll discuss it in six months."

Eleanor stared down at the stick and looked back up at Søren's retreating form.

"I hate you!" she yelled after him.

"That stick won't water itself," he called back.

She looked back down at the stick in the ground.

"I hate you, too," she said to the stick. And for good measure, kicked it.

After replanting and watering the now slightly shorter stick, she returned to the church, where Søren put her to work in the fellowship hall annex scrubbing the kitchen and cleaning out the pantries. He'd told her he would inspect her work when she'd finished. She wanted to make him proud of her.

By five o'clock she'd lost almost all the polish on her fingernails. Her hands were rough and chapped from all the scrubbing. Her back ached from sitting on the floor and bending over so much. Still the pantry did look pretty amazing when she'd finished with it. She stood in the middle of the room, admiring her work, when she heard footsteps behind her.

"Good work," Søren said as he stood in the doorway.

"I could live in this pantry. You could eat off the floor. Or you could if we had any food in it."

"That will be your next step. This Sunday at the end of Mass, you'll announce a food drive."

"I will?"

"You will."

"In front of the entire church?"

"You have a fear of public speaking?"

"No, I don't think so. But I'm sixteen and I'm only doing this because the court is making me. I don't think anyone is going to listen to me."

"They'll listen to you. You'll be speaking from my pulpit and with my permission and on my authority."

"I'll guilt-trip my heart out and their pantries."

"Good. Now you're done with work for the day. Let's go into the sanctuary. We'll start our Spiritual Exercises."

"Spiritual Exercises? Does my soul have to do push-ups?" she asked as they entered the sanctuary.

"Can it?"

"I don't know. Pretty sure it's never tried."

"The Spiritual Exercises from Saint Ignatius are something like push-ups. They were created to uplift the people doing the exercise, strengthen them and bring them closer to God."

"So who was Saint Ignatius? I know he founded the Jesuits, but that's all I know."

Søren slipped a finger into his collar and pulled out a silver chain. A saint medal hung from it. Eleanor stepped close to Søren and peered at the face on the medal.

"He's bald," she said.

"He shaved the top of his head because he felt his hair acted as a barrier between him and God."

"Wow. Really?"

"No."

"Can I punch you in the arm?"

"Yes."

Eleanor punched him in the upper arm. She hit him hard, but he didn't seem to feel it.

"Thank you." She shook her hand out. Did he have steel arms under his clerics? She couldn't wait to find out. "Now are you going to tell me something real about Saint Ignatius?"

"I will tell you the two most important things you need to know about Saint Ignatius. First, he was a saint."

"I never would have guessed."

Søren ignored her.

"And second, of all the saints, he alone has a verifiable criminal record."

"He does?"

"He does. As a young man, Saint Ignatius, then still Iñigo Lopez de Oñaz y Loyola, was arrested for brawling. A street fight apparently. He had a hot temper, a sword and wasn't afraid to use either."

"Sounds so punk."

"That would be one word for it. He was arrested *and* convicted. So you and the founder of my order have two things in common now. You both have police records. And you both received a second chance to do God's will."

Eleanor said nothing as Søren tucked the saint medal back under his collar.

"You know, no offense, but I'm not sure I believe in God."

Søren shrugged. "Least of our worries. His existence does not depend on your belief."

"Good news for Him, then."

"Quite. Now let's talk about the windows." He swept his arm to indicate the stained-glass windows that lined each side of the sanctuary.

"Are the windows part of the Spiritual Exercises?"

"Yes and no. I'm interested right now in getting a sense of what parts of the Bible speak to you. Saint Ignatius believed images are powerful tools that lead us to discover what God intends for us."

"You think God cares about what we want to do?"

"Of course. Desire is the most compelling of all human emotions. Desire prompts human beings to the heights of glory and drags us into the depths of Hell. Out of desire for Helen, Menelaus launched a thousand ships to win her back in a deadly war. Out of desire to save His people, Christ allowed Himself to be crucified. Desire is a God-given gift. Like any gift, we should use it to honor Him."

"Desire is from God?"

"It is. Like any tool, it can be used for good or for evil. We'll try to use your desire for good. Which leads me back to the question—of all these images in the windows, do any of them speak to you? And by that I mean, do any of them touch your heart or stir emotions or desires? Think about it. Study the windows. Take your time and—"

"That one." Eleanor didn't even have to look at the window. Without even taking her eyes off Søren she pointed.

Søren looked at the window she'd indicated and then back at her.

"Are you sure of that?"

She nodded. "Yeah, it's always been my favorite. I sit in the pew beneath it every time I come to church."

Søren walked to the window and stared up at it. Eleanor stood next to him.

"It's the story from Luke, right?" Eleanor asked. She'd looked up this story after she'd fallen in love with the window.

"Yes, Luke chapter seven. Christ was invited to dinner at the home of a Pharisee. A woman in the town who all knew to be a sinner came to Jesus and knelt at his feet. She anointed him with expensive oils. She bathed his feet with her tears, she dried them with her hair. An act of utter humility on her part. Humility and submission."

"It's so pretty," Eleanor whispered, not knowing quite why she felt the need to lower her voice. Something about this window always made her feel reverent. The woman was draped in a purple robe, Christ a red one. The sinful woman, kneeling before Jesus, focuses only on Christ's bare feet as she washes them. Two men sitting behind Jesus glare but Jesus looks at nothing and no one but the woman. "She looks so peaceful. You don't think she'd be peaceful, right? I mean, she's in public crying and sitting at this man's feet while other people talk about her. I remember reading that the Pharisee guy told Jesus she was a sinner. And Jesus told him off. I don't think she gives a fuck what that Pharisee said about her. Why should she care? Jesus was letting her wash his feet. I think that's why she was crying. She was happy to be so close to him."

"There's a tradition in the church," Søren began, his voice also low and reverent, "that it was Mary Magdalene who washed his feet with tears and dried his feet with her hair."

"The prostitute?"

"She may not have been. The Bible doesn't say, but church tradition has perpetuated that story."

"I hope she was a prostitute."

"Do you?" Søren sounded intrigued by her comment.

"It means more if she was a prostitute. I mean, this is Jesus, the guy who never committed any sins. He's never even had sex, right?"

"There is no evidence he ever married so no, following Jewish law he would have been chaste, a virgin most likely, although he may have married young and been widowed. There's little to no evidence of that, but it would account for why no one made any mention of his being unmarried, which in that day and age would have been considered highly bizarre for a Jewish man."

"Jesus a widower?" Eleanor had never even considered the possibility.

"It's one theory. Far more likely is that the miraculous circumstances of his birth led him to believe he would be called to perform a special mission for God. He remained unmarried for the same reason a soldier being sent into battle would remain unmarried. He knew one day he wouldn't be coming home."

"So Jesus was a virgin."

"That would be my guess."

"Poor guy."

"There are far worse things in life than living without sex."

"You know, I can't think of a single bigger fuck-you to all those judgmental assholes than perfect, virginal Jesus Christ having a prostitute at his feet. It's like saying 'you can't judge her without judging me. So judge me, I dare you.'"

"Safe to say our Lord was one of the first radical feminists. He constantly berated men who judged women. The woman with the alabaster jar. The woman with the issue of blood. The first person he spoke to after His resurrection was not Peter, but Mary Magdalene."

"Jesus loved the ladies. I like that."

"The more other men disparaged the woman, the more likely Jesus was to be kind to her."

"So what does it mean that this is my favorite image? God wants me sitting at Jesus's feet?"

"I think He wants you at someone's feet."

Søren turned his back to the window as if it hurt to look at it anymore. He wore a strange expression on his face, almost pained. He took a deep breath as if to steady himself, and soon he looked as peaceful as the woman in the window. Eleanor pulled a piece of paper from her back pocket.

"Got a pen?" she asked.

He took a pen from the missal holders at the back of the pew and handed it to her.

"Why do you need a pen?" he asked as she unfolded the paper.

"New question to ask you after Thanksgiving."

"What's the question?"

She wrote two words on the paper and held it up for him to read.

Søren read the words aloud.

"Whose feet?"

Eleanor shoved the paper in her pocket.

"One problem with that question, Eleanor."

"What?"

"Only you can answer that."

11

Eleanor

ONLY YOU CAN ANSWER THAT.

For days after her exchange with Søren about the stained-glass window, Eleanor pondered his words. They'd lodged themselves in her heart like a bullet and she couldn't dig them out with all the scalpels in the world.

It was late on Thursday night. Nothing going on. She walked to church in the hopes of finding Søren in his office. She wanted to talk to him about what he'd said, about how only she could answer that question—whose feet should she sit at? It felt like the answer to that question would determine the rest of her life. But she didn't understand why.

Once she stepped through the front door of Sacred Heart, she could tell from the hollow echoing sound of her footsteps she was alone. Søren's office door was closed. She knocked but heard nothing. With a shaking hand, she turned the doorknob and found the lights off, the office abandoned.

On nervous feet she stepped inside the office. She shouldn't be in here, but curiosity got the better of her. In the darkness she reached out and ran her fingertips across the books on Søren's shelves. Cloth. Leather. Paper. Cloth. She pressed her hands to the back of his chair—an old leather-and-wood number that had probably been here since the church was erected two hundred years ago. In the dark she traced the spiraling scrollwork of the chair's arm and ran her hands over the smooth leather of the chair.

Eleanor returned to the door, shut it and locked it. Light from a streetlamp shone through the stained-glass rose window and made a shadow of her body on Søren's desk. She eased into his chair and shivered as she sat where he sat. The desk in front of her had featured in so many of her fantasies since meeting Søren.

She sat up in the chair and pulled her tank top off. She stood and slipped out of her shorts. And when she closed her eyes again she heard the door opening. She didn't need light to tell her it was Søren in the office with her. She'd know his footsteps anywhere, his breathing, his scent. And now she knew his touch as his arms came around her and rested on her lower back. She turned her face up to his and his mouth came down to her mouth, his tongue sought her tongue. He didn't simply smell like winter, he tasted like it, too, like new fallen snow melting in her mouth.

His hands roamed up her back and unhooked her bra. He pulled it down her arms and let it fall to the floor. Was this right? Was this good? Should she stop him? Could she if she wanted to? Did she want to?

No.

He sat in the chair in front of her and slid her panties down her thighs. Without a word she stepped out of them and stood naked before him. She wasn't blushing, but the faint light from the window cast a pale rose-tinted glow over her body.

"Mine," he said as he gripped her by the hips.

"Yours," she replied, bending her head to kiss him.

He kissed her mouth and her neck. She shivered when his lips lightly danced across the sensitive flesh of her chest. He took a nipple in his mouth and she wrapped her arms around his neck, holding his head to her breast. She'd never dreamed anything could feel as good as his hands and mouth on her body.

Søren stood up and took her in his arms, lifting her like she weighed nothing and laying her back on his desk. The surface of the desk was cold and smooth against her bare back. A chill passed through her even as his every touch set her blood burning. Without being told to, she opened her legs for him. He gripped her thighs and pushed her legs apart even more. With his hands on her hips, he used his thumbs to part her inner lips. He spread her wide and slipped a finger into her wetness. Then a second one. She opened up as he moved his hand inside her, touching the deepest parts of her.

His fingers left her and she heard the sound of a zipper being lowered. She shut her eyes tight when he pulled her hips to the edge of the desk. Then he was entering her. She'd expected it to hurt but it didn't, and her body opened up to receive him as if she'd been created for him and him alone. He filled her until she could take no more of him. Now he moved inside her, thrusting in, pulling back and then thrusting in again. Her body enveloped his hardness, coating it with her wetness, coaxing it in farther as she raised her hips in her eagerness for more. He held her breasts while he moved in her. He restrained her against the desk with his hips and his hands, and she lay there helpless, naked and defenseless before and beneath him. This was what she'd wanted from the second she'd seen him, and now she would take everything he could give her.

He clasped her throat but didn't grip it. Instinctively she

understood why he made love to her with his hand on her neck. He owned her, possessed her. Her very life beat against the palm of his hand. She could feel her pulse pounding in her neck, pounding against his fingertips. *I own you,* that hand on her neck said. *Every part of you. The part I'm fucking. The part I'm touching. Even the air flowing in and out of your lungs is mine.*

Her breathing quickened as he increased the pace of his thrusts. Her back arched off the desk as an orgasm ripped through her. Her clitoris throbbed and her innermost muscles clenched tight as a fist. They released in wild flutters through her stomach, back and thighs....

Eleanor sat up on the desk, all alone, her head aching from the blinding intensity of her fantasy and the orgasm she'd given herself. She picked her clothes up off the floor and dressed quickly. She ran her hand over the top of the desk. She felt a few drops of fluid, her own, that had fallen there. With the bottom of her shirt, she wiped it off and prayed Søren wouldn't notice anything amiss the next time he sat at his desk. She couldn't believe she'd done what she'd done on his desk. What if he'd needed something in his office and found the door locked? Would he have heard the sounds of her breathing through the door, heard her coming as she imagined him taking her virginity on his desk with God and the portrait of Pope John Paul II hanging on the wall watching them?

She shoved her feet into her shoes, slipped out into the hall and carefully closed the door behind her.

And then she heard it.

Piano music.

She wasn't alone in the church, after all.

Eleanor knew she should run for it, head straight home and pretend nothing had happened. But the music called to her like a siren's song and drew her inexorably to it. It came from the sanctuary. The notes slid under the door and out into the hallway. They wrapped their fingers around her and drew her in. She slipped through the doors of the sanctuary and followed the music to its source.

Søren sat at the upright piano tucked to the right of the sacristy where he and the deacons changed in and out of their vestments.

She stood just feet away from him and watched as he played. No, that wasn't it. He didn't *play* the piano. He enslaved it. His fingers moved with shocking speed and agility across the keys. He seemed a being of pure concentration right now. Did he even know she was standing there listening and watching and wanting him? She didn't recognize the piece, but she wished she did. She wished she knew what he was playing and why he played it so intensely, as if he would die if he stopped.

Minutes passed. Maybe an hour. She never grew tired of watching him. The music pinned her to floor the way his hand had pinned her to the desk in her fantasy. She couldn't move if she tried. She didn't try.

Finally the piece ended and Søren lifted his hands off the keys. He kept his head bowed as if in prayer before lifting it. He didn't look at her.

"I can't talk to you right now, Eleanor," he said.

"Can you look at me?" she asked, and despite the echo in the nave, her voice sounded small and timid.

"No."

She stuffed her hands in her pockets.

"Are you mad at me?" she asked.

"No."

Eleanor let that "no" hang in the air between them. She wanted to believe him, but she sensed tension in him. His jaw was set tight and his posture stiff.

"Please talk to me," Eleanor begged.

"What would you like me to say?" His voice sounded stilted, as well.

"Anything. I don't know." She grasped for words. Something told her he knew exactly what she'd done in his office, but surely if he did he would say something to her about it, yell at her, punish her.

He looked up at the ceiling.

"They make a kind of goggles for horses. Blinders, they're called," Søren said. He raised his hand and put it to the side of his eyes. "They can only see forward when they wear them. No peripheral vision. I wish I had some."

"Are you sure you're not mad at me?"

"The opposite, I promise."

She searched for something to say and came up empty. So she asked the stupidest question she could think of.

"So…you play piano?"

"I do," he said.

"What were you playing?"

"Beethoven's Piano Concerto No. 4."

"Where did you learn to play like that?"

"My mother is a piano teacher."

"Weird," she said.

"Weird that my mother is a piano teacher?" He sounded almost amused now. Good. She feared what she'd done in his office had changed things between them irrevocably.

"Weird that you have a mother. I thought you fell from the sky. You know, like a meteor. Or an alien."

Or a god.

He smiled slightly but still didn't look at her.

"I have a mother and a father. I love my mother. I hate my father."

"You've got one up on me. I hate both my parents."

"You don't hate your mother."

"No. But I don't like her very much, either. I think the feeling's mutual."

"She loves you."

"Are you sure about that?"

"How could she not?" he asked, as if it were the most foolish idea in the world to consider for one second that anyone could not love her.

Eleanor fell silent again. She'd never had a more painful conversation in her life. Even her allocution before the judge when she'd pled guilty for the car thefts had been less awkward and uncomfortable than this nightmare chitchat.

"Why did you come here tonight?" Søren asked her, his eyes still on the wall in front of him.

"I wanted to talk to you," she said. "I had a question."

"What question?"

"I don't remember it now. Seemed important at the time."

Søren clasped his hands together and rested them in his lap. He wasn't praying now. At least it didn't seem like it. It looked more like he was trying to control himself, trying to hold his hands down to keep them from doing something. Doing what?

"This is going to be difficult for us," Søren said. "You and I working together. You understand this?"

"I..." She paused and thought about the question. "I think I do."

"I'm a priest. Do you also understand that?"

"No."

"No?"

"Of course I don't understand why you're a priest." The words she'd been holding back since the day she met him rushed out. "You're twenty-nine and you're the most beautiful man on earth. You could have any girl in the world you wanted. You're brilliant and you could do any job you wanted.

You could get married and have kids. Or you could have crazy sex with anyone you wanted whenever you wanted to. This is fucking Wakefield, Connecticut. You walk two miles south of here and you reach the end of the world. There's nothing here for you. You're wasted in this place. You could be running the world if you wanted and the world would probably be okay with that. I hate following the rules, but I would follow you into Hell and carry you back out again if I had to. Do I understand why you're a priest? No, and I don't think I ever will. Because if you weren't a priest…"

"If I weren't a priest," he repeated. "Do you know what would happen if I weren't a priest?"

"Yeah," she said. "You and I could—"

"You and I could do nothing," he said. "If I weren't a priest, Eleanor, you and I would never have met. If I weren't a priest, you would be in juvenile detention right now because Father Gregory wouldn't have been able to help you the way I did. If I weren't a priest, you would have a felony conviction on your permanent record. You would graduate from high school in detention and the likelihood of you getting into college would be practically nonexistent."

Eleanor felt the floor shiver under her feet. Her eyes filled with tears.

"Søren?"

"When I was fourteen I decided to become a priest," he said. "Once I made that decision, I felt peace in my heart for the first time in my life. And I didn't know why or from where that peace came. It should have scared me—a life of poverty, a life of celibacy and chastity, a life of obedience to a community that could and would send me all over the world. But I knew there was a reason I needed to be a priest. I was certain of it. And that certainty carried me all the way through seminary and all the way here. And now I know why

I needed to become a priest. Because God knew long before I did that I would need to be a priest to find you and help you and keep you on the right path. And I will keep you safe even if it kills me."

A lone tear traveled down her cheek and dropped onto the floor. Now she was grateful he wouldn't look at her so he wouldn't see her crying.

"And if I weren't a priest," Søren continued, "I would likely be dead. There were moments when I was your age and younger, foolish moments when I feared I didn't deserve to live. The things I'd done, the things I wanted to do, taunted me constantly. I worried God had made some terrible mistake when he'd made me, and perhaps the world would be better off if I wasn't in it."

"No..." She nearly choked on the word. The thought of Søren dead was an insult to everything she believed in, especially him because she believed in him the most.

"When I felt the first stirrings of the call to become a Jesuit, those feelings started to fade and new ones took their place. God had created me for a reason, made me like I was for a reason."

"Like what? You're—"

"My call to the priesthood saved me, Eleanor. Like it saved you. If I weren't a priest you wouldn't be in this sanctuary and neither would I. So please..." He stopped and raised his hand, holding it up almost in a posture of surrender. "Please don't make this any more difficult than it already is."

He lowered his hand again.

"I'm sorry," she whispered.

"There's nothing to be sorry for."

"Are you sure?"

"I am. I told you months ago that the new rules I created

were for my sake, because of my need for boundaries. I'm asking you to honor that."

"I can," she promised. "I will."

"Thank you," he said.

She wanted to say more, to say she would never go into his office again, not without permission anyway. He hadn't said anything about what she'd done on his desk but she was certain he knew, and it was because of that he couldn't look at her right now. She imagined he wasn't looking at her for her own sake—to protect her from the embarrassment. But strangely, she felt none. Only sadness that he was right. As much as she wished he wasn't a priest so they could be together, she knew that they would never have met if he wasn't a priest. What had brought them together was the very thing that kept them apart. She wanted to say all that to him but before she could open her mouth, the sound of a car horn discreetly honking interrupted their tense silence.

"That's for me," Søren said. "I have to go."

"Where are you going?"

"I can't answer that," he said.

"Can't or won't?"

Søren rose off the piano bench and walked past her, still without meeting her eyes. She followed behind him.

At the door to the sanctuary he paused.

"We won't ever have to have this talk again," Søren said. The sentence was phrased like a statement but she heard an order lurking under the words. She knew what he meant. They would never have to have this talk again because she was never going to sneak into his office and masturbate on his desk again. "And we'll pretend we didn't have to have this talk. By tomorrow we'll both feel better. In a week it will be a distant memory. Yes?"

"Okay," she said.

Søren nodded. He put his hand on the door handle but didn't push it open.

"Are you sure you don't remember what it is that you wanted to ask me?"

"I'm sure."

"If you think of it…"

"Doesn't matter," she said, remembering the question she'd wanted to ask him and deciding not to ask it. "Are you sure you can't tell me where you're going?"

"Quite sure. I will say this—I wish I could take you with me."

She smiled. Finally some of the tension started to leave her body.

"Me, too. I'd go anywhere with you."

Søren met her eyes for the first time that night and gave her the faintest of smiles.

"Don't worry. Someday you will."

And with that, he pushed open the door and strode into the night. In front of the church in a shadowy patch of street sat a car, but not any old car. Søren entered the back passenger side and the car drove away.

Eleanor couldn't believe what she'd seen. But she had seen it. She knew cars. She knew all cars, all makes, all models. But it made no sense what she'd seen. Whose was it? Where had it come from? Where was it going?

Maybe someday she would get her answers to those questions. But tonight she had to content herself with the answer to one question. *Only you know the answer to that,* Søren had said when she'd asked him whose feet she should sit at.

Now she knew what he meant. It was her decision whose feet she sat at. Only she knew the answer to that question because only she could make that choice. Søren couldn't tell her, her mom couldn't tell her, God couldn't tell her. It was her choice alone. Whose feet? She already knew the answer.

And the answer was being driven away right now in a gleaming, glorious, pristine, worth-a-fortune 1953 Silver Wraith limousine-style…

Rolls. Fucking. Royce.

12

Eleanor

AFTER THAT NIGHT OF THE ROLLS-ROYCE, AS ELEAnor had dubbed it, things between her and Søren went back to normal. Or as close to normal as things ever were. Summer passed so quickly that the days blurred like scenes outside the window of a moving car. She almost grieved when the time came to start her junior year of high school. She'd practically lived at church for the past three months and saw Søren nearly every day. Each week she logged almost forty hours of community service. Søren gave her reading assignments from her Bible and made her meditate on them. Even those couple of weeks she worked at a day camp for underprivileged kids she still saw him in the evenings. She'd even made him an embroidered bookmark.

But time wouldn't be denied. September came and she survived the first day of school without incident. No fights. No arguing with teachers. No accusing beloved saints of having unnatural relations with seraphim. Fuck, she was a saint these days. She didn't run away to the city to hang out at her dad's shop anymore. She didn't sneak out to her friend Jordan's anymore. She didn't stay up until 3:00 a.m. reading dirty books with a hand down her panties anymore. Well, she still did that, but only on the weekends. Before Søren, Elle had wanted school to end so she could go home, sleep and read. But now she counted the hours until she could get out of school only so she could go to church.

When she arrived at Sacred Heart after her first day back to school, she changed clothes and got her watering can. Søren's office door was shut, and she could hear voices inside. Curious, she pressed her ear to the door and tried to make out the words. Søren spoke clearly and loudly enough that she could hear him, but none of the words made any sense. In fact, it sounded like he was speaking a different language. Definitely not German. No, it sounded kind of sexy and romantic. Hearing him talk like that made her thighs quiver. It must be French.

French? Who the hell was he talking to in French?

Next time he was on the phone while she stood outside his office eavesdropping, he should have the human decency to at least speak in English.

Frustrated, Eleanor started toward the fellowship hall when she heard the door open. She turned around and saw Søren's arm extending from inside the office like some kind of sideways periscope. He crooked his finger at her and Eleanor walked back to him.

"Are you trapped inside your office?" she whispered as she pressed her back flat against the wall by the door. "Some kind of force field and only your arm can escape it?"

"Yes," he said as his arm disappeared back inside his office. She faced him from across the threshold. "It's called a dissertation."

"A who a what?"

"A dissertation." He sat back behind his desk. Two piles of books flanked him. "I'm finishing my Ph.D. work. I have ordered myself not to leave my office until I have made significant progress on it this evening."

"What's a dissertation?"

"If Satan gave you instructions for writing the book report from Hell, it would closely resemble those of a Ph.D. dissertation."

She scrunched up her face in sympathetic disgust.

"I wrote the book report from Hell last year on *Jane Eyre* and the wife in the attic. I called it 'Jane Versus One Crazy Bitch.'"

"An interesting topic."

"What's your topic?"

"'The theology of pain and suffering in the letters of Saint Ignatius.'"

"Is that as boring as it sounds?"

"More."

"It needs a better title."

"Better than 'The theology of pain and suffering in the letters of Saint Ignatius'?"

"How about 'Hurts So God.' It's a riff on that John Cougar song 'Hurts So Good.'"

Søren rested his chin on top of the nearest pile of books and narrowed his eyes at her.

"Your mind must be the most marvelous playground."

"I think my mental swing sets are rusty."

"We should fix that." He got up from behind his desk, grabbed his Bible and left the office.

"Hey, whoa there, big papa." She followed him as he strode toward the sanctuary. "You aren't supposed to leave your office."

"I made the rule. I can break it."

"Can I break your rules?" she asked.

"No." He stared down at her. "Come with me. Bring your Bible."

She grabbed her Bible from her backpack and made her way to the choir loft in the sanctuary.

"What are we doing today?" she asked once she reached the loft. "Are you going to make me meditate on Jesus again?"

"You don't want to? Meditating on the life of Christ is a vital part of the Spiritual Exercises."

"I know," she said as she threw herself down in a pew and stretched out long ways. "But Jesus always looks like Eddie Vedder in my meditations, and I don't like finding Jesus sexy. It's uncomfortable, like seeing a picture of your grandfather when he was eighteen and thinking he was a babe."

"I'm sure Jesus would be honored that you picture him as attractive. There is no sin in finding someone attractive."

"You said that before, but I don't think that rule applies to Jesus."

"Well, do you have any questions you want answered?" Søren asked, slapping her thigh with a Bible to make her sit up. "Meaning of original sin? The prophecies regarding Christ found in Isaiah? Anything?"

"Yes, I have a question." She looked up at him.

"Ask."

"Why are you so damn tall? You're what? Six foot something?"

"Six foot four."

"That's ridiculous. Is it necessary you're this tall or are you doing it for attention?"

"This is your theological inquiry?"

"God created you. He created you tall. This is my theological inquiry."

"Very well, then. Tall people are closer to God. Since I'm tall I can hear Him better, which is why you should always listen to me when I tell you something."

She glared at him.

"That is the biggest pile of bullshit anyone has ever dumped on me."

"Prove me wrong, then. Using the Bible."

"This is my assignment? I have to prove to you that you're full of shit?"

"Yes."

"You can't give me a good Bible assignment? Like read all the sexy parts?"

"You can do that, too, if you wish."

"Song of Songs it is, then. I like that he describes her tits as being like antelopes."

"I prefer the Book of Esther. More plot. Fewer bizarre metaphors involving ruminant mammals."

"Esther's a sex book?"

"It is if you can use your imagination. Which I'm certain you can."

Eleanor blushed. She had a feeling he referred to that little incident on his desk.

"What do I get if I prove you're full of shit?" she asked, desperately wanting to change the subject.

"Enlightenment."

Søren left her alone in the choir loft with her Bible and her assignment to prove him wrong. That shouldn't be too hard. She doubted there was a single verse in the Bible that said God preferred tall people. Of course, she'd have to read the entire Bible to make sure there wasn't. That would take a while. Easier to prove God liked short people. Wasn't there something Jesus said about suffering the little children? She flipped to the back of her Bible and found the concordance. Little...little...little children...little ones.

Little ones? She flipped to Psalms and found the verse.

> The Lord is the keeper of the little ones; I was little and he delivered me.

Bam. Perfect. Easy enough.

God liked little people. She won. Søren lost. Now what?

She flipped a few more pages in the Bible to the Book of Esther. She'd heard about Esther but she didn't remember ever hearing any homilies about the book. They hadn't covered it in her religion class at school yet, either. All she remembered about Esther was that she was a queen and there was something about a beauty pageant? Didn't sound sexy to her. But Søren said he preferred Esther to the Song of Songs, so...

> In the days of Xerxes, who reigned from India to Ethiopia over a hundred and twenty-seven provinces...

This was supposed to be a sexy book?

Eleanor kept reading. She read it all, beginning to end. There was something odd about the story, something not quite right. Esther...and the king...did they really...? No way. But maybe?

She closed her Bible, and found Søren again in his office.

"Did I just read what I think I just read?" Eleanor asked without preamble.

"What do you think you read?" Søren asked as he closed a book and gave her his full attention.

"King Xerxes fired his queen and then needed a new queen."

"Yes."

"And he auditioned for a new queen."

"That he did."

"Am I reading it wrong or did King Xerxes audition for virgin queen candidates by fucking them?"

"That would be one rather graphic, albeit accurate, way of putting it."

"So he did?"

"Yes."

"So King Xerxes had virgins brought in from all over the Empire. He gave them a year to pretty themselves up for him, and then they had a one-night audition with him in his bedroom to become queen."

"Is there a question in there somewhere, Eleanor?"

"Yes. What did Esther do?"

"I don't follow."

"To the king to get him to pick her, I mean," Eleanor explained. "What did she do that the other girls didn't do so she could be queen?"

"I assume she was better in bed than the rest of them."

Eleanor gaped at Søren.

"What?" he asked.

"The reason she was the person chosen to save the Jewish people was because she was good in the sack?"

"The Lord works in mysterious ways."

"The Lord works through sex?"

"All the time. Saints were babies once. They had to be conceived through sexual intercourse. There's nothing unbiblical about that."

"But Esther wasn't married to the king. She was part of a harem. She had premarital sex. Catholics aren't allowed to have premarital sex."

"Esther wasn't Catholic. Catholicism hadn't been invented yet."

She glowered at him.

"You know what I mean. It's in the Bible."

"Shocking, isn't it?" He didn't sound the least shocked, only amused.

"I'm speechless."

"Then why are you still talking?"

"Because I found a biblical heroine who is a biblical heroine because she spread for a king. It's seriously sexy but seems like a piss-poor way to choose a world leader. Or not. Maybe that's how we got President Clinton."

"In all fairness to Esther, she was a prisoner and didn't have much choice in the matter—the sex or becoming queen."

"She was amazing in bed and that helped her save her people."

"I knew you'd like her."

"I want to be her. I wonder if Xerxes was hot."

"Perhaps he looked like Eddie Vedder."

"Do you even know who that is?"

"No."

"I didn't think so. I wonder what Esther did to impress the king so much in one night."

Søren picked up his pen and tapped it on the desk.

"She was beautiful, according to the author of the book," Søren said. "And clearly intelligent. The women of the harem were allowed to take anything they wanted with them for their night with the king. But Esther takes only what the harem guard Hegai says she should take. Smart of her to ask someone in the know what he would suggest."

"Maybe she didn't ask him because he knew the king. Maybe she asked him because he was a man."

"That's one possibility." Søren flipped through his Bible.

"What would you have told Esther to do?"

"Pardon?" Søren arched an eyebrow at her.

"If this virgin girl came to you and said that she was going to spend a night with the king, what advice would you give her?"

"Interesting question. Priests aren't often asked for sex advice. Then again, Hegai was a eunuch. I doubt they're often asked for sex advice, either."

"What's a eunuch?"

"A castrated man."

"Ow."

"Exactly."

"Well, a priest is better than a eunuch for advice, then. I'm guessing you still have all your original parts."

"Warranty included," he said.

Eleanor crossed her arms and leaned against the door frame. "So what would you tell Esther to do?"

"I was hoping you'd forgotten that question."

She heard a tense note in his voice.

"Oh, sorry," she said. "We're not supposed to be talking about S-E-X, are we?"

"We can talk about sex in a biblical context."

"Does it embarrass you, talking about sex?"

"*Embarrass* wouldn't be the word," he said. "I'm disconcerted, perhaps."

"Disconcerted?" she repeated. "Talking about sex disconcerts you."

"No, talking about sex *with you* disconcerts me."

"So you don't like it?"

"I like it far too much. And I think you know that."

Eleanor's hands trembled slightly. The world around them had gone quiet, as if even the walls were listening in on their conversation.

"What advice would you have given Esther?" Eleanor asked again, refusing to back down. He never answered her important questions. She wouldn't give up until he answered this one.

Søren leaned back in his chair and steepled his fingers. As he thought about her question, her mind started to wander. She could easily imagine herself as Esther. Girls in that day married young, Søren had said. She and Esther were probably about the same age. If she lived back then, would she have been one of the virgins brought in to audition for the role of queen? What would she have done in that situation? Esther asked the guard for advice, and according to the Bible Esther took only what Hegai told her to take. She took less than the other women. But what was it? What did he tell her to take? And what did she do when she was alone with the king?

"I think if I had to give Esther advice as a man and not a priest—" Søren leaned forward to rest his elbows on the desk "—I would tell her to go to him without fear and with total trust. She should offer herself to him in a spirit of submission. After all, it was Queen Vashti's refusal to submit that infuriated the king. Clearly he prized submission highly. She should tell the king she was his to do with as he pleased, that she would obey his every whim and submit to his every desire. I would tell her to let him bare his most secret self to her and accept it without question and to show her most secret self to him. She should submit to him in love and without fear, giving her body to him like a holy offering and making their bed an altar."

Eleanor's knees trembled at Søren's words. She couldn't help but picture herself in a silken gown being escorted to the bedroom of the king, a king who bore a strong resemblance to the priest in front of her.

"Eleanor?" Søren prompted.

"What?"

"You whimpered."

"Did I?" She had. She knew she had. "Sorry about that."

He leaned back in his chair again and looked at her without a smile on his face but with a dark and amused gleam in his eyes. Right there—she saw it. That look. Those eyes. He knew he'd turned her on with his words and was congratulating himself for it. The expression on his face was arrogant, patronizing and imperious. She wanted him so much it hurt.

"Who's disconcerted now?" he asked.

She narrowed her eyes at him. Without a doubt, he was the only man who'd ever lived who could make the word *disconcerted* sound sexy.

"Whatever this game is we're playing," she finally said, "I'm going to win it."

If she expected him to be thrown off or confused by that statement, she was sorely disappointed.

"If you trust me and obey me," he said, "we might both win."

Trust him. Obey him... She could do that. And out of nowhere came the answer. Eleanor knew exactly what Esther had taken with her.

"I know what Esther took with her to the king," she said, looking up at him with a smile.

"You do?"

"When I know I'm going to ace a test, I go to class with nothing but my pencil," Eleanor said. "If Esther knew she was going to ace her audition, she wouldn't have taken anything with her at all."

"You might be right."

"Might? I'm sure of it. But I wish the Bible writers hadn't skipped all the good details."

"I told you it had sex in it if you used your imagination."

"Oh, I'm using it. I'm using it hard."

"Go use it to do your homework."

"First day of school. I don't have any homework."

"Did you do your other homework I gave you?"

"Oh, yeah. You're totally full of shit. Psalm 116. And I quote, 'The Lord is the keeper of the little ones, I was little and he delivered me.' God loves little people, He keeps them and He delivers them. I'm short so God is going to keep me and deliver me because I am a little one. Considering He sent you to keep me out of prison, I think I have all the proof I need."

"Very good, Little One." He smiled broadly and for a moment she was nearly blinded by it.

"Don't call me *Little One*."

"Do you hate it?"

"Totally."

"Good. Now go find something to do, Little One. I'm working on my dissertation and you are detrimental to my powers of concentration."

"What am I supposed to do?"

"You could use your impressive powers of imagination and your newfound prowess as a Bible scholar to formulate a theory on what Esther did to earn the king's favor."

"So I'm supposed to figure out what made her better in bed than anyone else?"

"Precisely."

"My kind of homework."

Eleanor left Søren in his office with his eight billion books and his dissertation. She hid out in the food bank pantry and rearranged the cans of green beans on the floor into columns like she'd seen in pictures of exotic palaces.

As she stared at her green bean palace in front of her, Eleanor picked up a pen. On the top of a clean sheet of notebook paper she wrote:

One Night with the King.

For the fun of it she wrote underneath, *By Eleanor Schreiber.* And then she wrote for four straight hours.

13

Eleanor

One Night with the King
By Eleanor Schreiber

Tonight was my night.

For a year now I'd been going through the training—how to curtsy, how to simper, how to dance, how to whimper. They dressed me and pressed me and made me beautiful. For twelve months I had to listen to the girls talking all around me, deciding what gift they'd give the king, what they'd do to impress him.

"I have composed him a hymn," one girl said.

"I have written him a poem," another announced.

"I have knitted him a cardigan," said another girl.

Everyone had looked at that girl like she was an idiot. She was an idiot. It was ancient Persia. Kings didn't wear cardigans. Cardigans hadn't even been invented yet.

I spent most of the day in the bathroom getting ready. By evening I smelled like orchids, looked like a princess and had no unwanted body hair.

Then Hegai came for me.

"Are you ready?" he asked.

"I think so."

"Are you taking anything with you for the king?"

"I have a hymn."

"You're going to sing?"

"No. Sorry. I have a hymen. I get them mixed up."

Hegai left me at the door to the king's chamber.

I opened the door.

At first I didn't see anybody. All I saw was chamber stuff—big sexy-looking couches, tall sexy plants with big sexy flowers blooming on them, a long sexy gold mirror for checking out how sexy you look in it. And it had the biggest, sexiest bed I'd ever seen in my life. Red silk sheets, red-and-gold pillows and those fancy bed curtains only people in the past had before central heating existed. It's good to live in the past. It's sexier here.

The big door to the balcony was open so I stuck my head out the door and saw a man standing by the ledge staring out on the kingdom.

Before I saw the man I thought the palace was beautiful, I thought the kingdom was beautiful, I thought jewels were beautiful. But they were nothing compared to the king.

He had blond hair and was so tall I knew he was probably doing it for attention. He wore jeans and a white T-shirt. I thought jeans hadn't been invented yet but then I realized they had been invented because they looked so good on him.

And if anyone had put a gun to my head and told me I had to say who the most handsome man in the kingdom was, I would first remind that person guns hadn't been invented yet.

And then I'd point at the king.

"Him."

"Him, who?" asked the king as he turned around to look at me.

"Oh. Sorry. Did I say that out loud? I was having this bizarre fantasy about a guy holding a gun to my head."

"Guns haven't been invented yet."

"That's exactly what I told him." I took a step forward and held out my hand. The king shook it. "I'm Esther. I'll be your entertainment this evening."

"Oh, God, did you bring a poem?"

"I don't write that shit."

"Hymn?"

"No."

"Please tell me you didn't knit me anything. I don't need sweaters. This is Persia. It doesn't even get cold here. Except in the winter."

"I don't knit."

"Do you know any good jokes?"

"A hymen walks into a bar. Well, that took care of that."

The king didn't laugh. But I think he wanted to.

"What else do you do?"

I stepped up to the king and rose high on my tiptoes.

"Whatever you tell me to."

And then we kissed.

And what a kiss it was. It took my breath away, that kiss did. I forgot my name and my age and my phone number. I even forgot that phones hadn't been invented yet. He kissed me with his mouth on my mouth but it felt like his soul kissed my soul and all I wanted was to never ever stop kissing this king who tasted like melting snow on my lips and smelled of winter in a magic world where no one aged, no one died and once people fell in love they never fell out of it again.

"You didn't bring anything with you?" the king said, pausing from their perfect kiss.

"I only brought me."

"Good. That's all I want right now."

"What do I call you? Your Majesty?"

"Call me Xerxes. That's my name."

"No one calls you by your first name."

"You do."

"Why me?"

"Because," he whispered against my lips, "when I'm inside you, I want you to say it and know you're talking to me and not some other king somewhere. Got that?"

"Yes, Your Maj…Xerxes."

He picked me up in his arms.

The king carried me into the bedroom and laid me on the bed. It felt like floating in sea of red silk. Xerxes sat next to me on the bed and kissed me again.

"You're really good at that," I said. He kissed my mouth and my neck for a long time.

"I practice a lot."

"On all of us?"

"Anything to keep from hearing more bad poetry." He smiled at me and kissed me again. His tongue in my mouth would definitely keep me from reciting poetry.

"Do you like being with all these girls?" I asked as he kissed my chest. I felt weird about wearing such a low-cut dress but now I decided it had been a good idea. His lips tickled my skin and his light touches gave me goose bumps. I imagined him kissing other parts of my body. Then he pulled my dress down to bare my shoulder and kissed me from my neck to my upper arm. Those parts, for example.

"I don't dislike it," he said. "It gets a little boring with the same thing night after night. Different girl. Same thing. No offense."

"It's okay. I'd probably get bored, too. You know, Xerxes," I said, trying his name on for size. It fit my tongue well. "If you want, we can do something different than you usually do with the other girls."

"Like what?"

"I don't know. You're the king, so you can decide."

"You aren't afraid?"

"I was before, but I'm not now."

"Are you sure you want to do something different than I do with the other girls?"

"I've met the other girls. Yes."

My dress tied at the front with a single ribbon. I started to get nervous again when he untied the bow and my gown loosened. But I knew this would happen and I wasn't afraid. I refused to be afraid.

He slid the dress off me. I lay naked on the bed now. He looked at me like I was some kind of prize he'd won. I never wanted him to stop looking at me like that.

He didn't touch me, which made me more nervous. Instead he left me laying/lying on the bed while he walked over to a big brass box. The box had a lock on it and the king took out a key. He opened the lid, took something out of it, locked it back up and came back to the bed.

While he was at the box I pulled the covers on the bed down and slid underneath them.

"Are you cold?" the king asked. He held something behind his back.

"I'm naked."

"Are you embarrassed about being naked?"

"I'm not embarrassed. I'm…disconcerted."

"Do you want me to take my clothes off?"

"I hope yes is the right answer."

"It's the right answer. I'll take my clothes off if you take the sheets off."

I threw the covers off and the king sat next to me on the bed again.

"Now I'm going to tie you to the bed," the king said.

"How come?"

"You said I could do anything I wanted."

I couldn't argue with that, so I held up my hands and he held out a golden rope.

It didn't take long for him to tie my wrists to the big sexy headboard of his bed. The ropes felt tight but not too tight on me. I could wiggle my fingers and move my hands. But I couldn't touch him, which made me want to touch him even more.

He took another rope and tied my ankles down to the bed. Once he finished I realized I couldn't close my legs. This king knew what he was doing.

Xerxes took off his jeans and I tried not to watch. Well, I didn't try very hard not to watch.

"Oh, wow," I said once he was naked. I looked back up at the ceiling.

"Just wow?"

"Holy wow?"

"Much better."

I moaned a little when the king stretched out on top of me. His skin felt so warm next to mine. His body was strong and muscular, and I felt safe underneath him. Who could ever hurt me now with the king like a shield over me? Who could steal me now that I was tied to his bed? No one.

The king kissed my mouth again and my neck. He rubbed my breasts, which felt better than I ever dreamed it would. He kissed them, which was embarrassing at first until I realized that it was the best thing anyone had ever done to me. He put his hand between my legs and pushed a finger inside me. I wanted to close my legs, but the ropes stopped me. But he moved his finger in and out of me and I tensed up and relaxed at the same time. He touched me for a long time until I thought I would die from wanting him so much. I couldn't touch him because he'd tied my hands. I couldn't close my legs because he'd tied my ankles. I couldn't kiss him because I couldn't rise up. All I could do was lie there and want him and want him and want him.

Then he was inside me.

"Xerxes," I said as he pushed all the way into me.

"Good girl," he said. He'd told me to say his name while he was inside me. I wanted to obey him. Obeying him was the most important thing.

He moved inside me and it hurt. I didn't care that it hurt, though, and I didn't want it to ever end even if it did hurt. The pain stopped but the pleasure stayed behind. I felt a storm in my stomach like lightning and thunder were throwing down inside me. My whole body crackled with electricity. I wasn't sure if electricity had been invented yet but I didn't care anymore. I only cared about Xerxes, about my king.

Xerxes lowered his head and bit my chest over my heart. I flinched from the pain.

"Why did you do that?"

"You're beautiful, and if another man sees that bruise he'll know you belong to me."

"I belong to you," I said. I loved those words. I loved belonging to the king. I loved it so much I said it again. "I belong to you."

"You're mine."

The ceiling had lied to me. It wasn't over soon. We slept a little bit, but then we woke up and he made me his again.

At dawn I woke up in his arms. Even while I was sleeping he'd kept one of my ankles tied to the bed. I liked that he wanted to keep me in his bed, in his arms.

Then morning came, and I was mad at it for coming so soon.

Xerxes untied my ankle from the bed and helped me put my dress back on.

"I'll miss you, Xerxes."

"I'll miss you, too, Esther. Last night was better than any song or any poem."

"Or cardigan," she said.

"In fact, it was so good, I think we should have a thousand more nights like that."

"I'll be in the harem if you want me."

"Or…"

"Or what?"

"You could be my queen."

Eleanor waited in the hallway outside of Søren's office. He'd told her that if she figured out what happened between Xerxes and Esther on her audition night, she should tell him. So she rewrote her story by hand as neatly as she could, put it in a nice new folder and gave it to him. It seemed like such a great idea right up until the moment he opened the folder, started reading and shut his office door in her face.

Why had she given it to him? That whole story was ridiculous. She had Esther talking like she lived in 1993 instead of in ancient Persia, and she put the king in jeans and made him kind of funny and goofy instead of kingly. Regal. Kings were supposed to be regal. And the story… Oh, God, she had a whole sex thing going on in the story with Esther being tied to a bed while the king fucked her.

And now her priest was reading it.

Eleanor went back to the fellowship hall food pantry and sorted through the donations. Why did no one ever donate Oreos? All she wanted was to eat an entire bag of Oreos and cry for a few hours while listening to Whitney Houston sing "I Will Always Love You" on repeat. Instead she went to the bathroom and discovered she'd started her period. That explained the tears and the Oreo obsessing. Maybe it even explained her sudden moment of temporary insanity when she decided to let Søren read her stupid Esther story.

She grabbed her backpack and sat down on the bench outside Søren's office. If he was in there calling the men in white coats to come get her, she wanted to be on standby to knock the phone out of his hand and plead her case.

To kill time, she pulled her new math textbook out and flipped through it.

"What the holy fuck is this bullshit?" she yelled as she tried to decipher the precalculus before her.

Søren's office door swung open.

"Eleanor. Inside voice."

"Sorry," she said. "Math."

"Forgiven."

She looked up at him. He held her story in his hand.

"You're excommunicating me, aren't you?"

"Why did you write this story?" he asked.

"I don't know. We were talking about Esther and what happened that night and I...I thought it would be fun to write. And then I started writing it, and I couldn't stop."

"You couldn't stop?"

"I couldn't. It was like some demon had my hand and was racing it all over the paper." She grabbed her right wrist like a neck and pretended to choke it until it went limp. "Anyway, sorry. I won't make you read my weird stories anymore."

"I will read anything you write. You are a better writer than I am."

"Really? I thought it was kind of stupid."

"Stupid?"

"Yeah, goofy. Childish. I made hymen jokes."

"It's satire," Søren said.

"Satire? I wasn't going for satire. I just wanted to make the story funny to show how ridiculous it is to choose a country's leader by how good in bed she is."

"Using humor to hold human foibles—usually of a political nature—up to ridicule *is* satire, Eleanor. It's a difficult and sophisticated form of humor that very few adult authors have mastered."

"Oh," she said. "Cool."

"If you're not careful, I'll put you to work on my dissertation."

Eleanor blushed. Søren didn't seem to be joking.

"Don't you think I'd give those old priests who read your dissertation heart attacks?"

"You nearly gave me one," he said. He stared down at her story and shook his head. She felt inordinately proud of herself. One little short story and she'd gotten to Søren with it. She felt something, something she hadn't ever felt before. Powerful. She could put words onto paper and make a grown man think wicked things like how fun it would be to tie a virgin to a bed and fuck her until dawn. She could get used to this feeling.

"May I keep this?" Søren asked.

"You want to keep my story?"

"I think I should confiscate it. You're too young to be reading such things."

"I think you're forgetting something—I wrote it."

"I'm keeping it," he said.

"Okay. But you have to give me something in return."

"What would you like? And please keep your requests above the neck."

Eleanor sighed in acquiescence. No asking him to bend her over a pew, then. Fine. If she was smart she might get something out of this deal. She'd given him a sexy story she'd written—something private, personal, secret. Secret?

"Tell me a secret," she said. "Any secret. Then you can have the story."

Søren exhaled heavily.

"Something tells me I'm going to regret telling you this, but it's perhaps for the best that you know."

"Know what?"

"I have a friend," Søren said at last.

"A friend? That's the big secret?"

"You didn't ask for a *big* secret. Only *a* secret."

"Why is your friend a secret?"

"That's a secret."

Eleanor opened her mouth and then promptly shut it.

"Here," Søren said. "I've been intending to do this for some time now." He reached into his pocket and pulled out a silver case. He opened the case and extracted a business card. Black paper. Silver ink. He held out the card and she reached for it. Søren pulled the card two inches out of her reach.

"Before I give you this card, you must make me a promise," he said. "You will show it to no one. You will keep it to yourself. You will not call the number on the card. You will never go to that address except in the direst of emergencies. And by direst I'm referring to such events one would describe as apocalyptic. You can make this promise?"

"I promise," she said.

Søren stared at her another moment and then let her have the card.

"I'm trading you a King for a king," Søren said, holding up her story.

Eleanor read the card.

Kingsley Edge, Edge Enterprises, it read. *152 Riverside Drive.*

The card contained no other information but a phone number.

"Kingsley Edge. He lives on Riverside Drive? That's where all the rich people live, right?"

Søren inclined his head.

"Kingsley is not without means."

"So he's rich?"

"Filthy," Søren said.

"Does he own a Rolls-Royce?"

"Two of them."

Eleanor pondered that. So now she knew whose Rolls that Søren had driven off in that night.

"He's also dangerous, Little One, and I don't use the word lightly."

She suppressed a smile. When he called her *Little One,* her fingers trembled and her feet itched and her thighs tightened.

"I like him already. He's your friend?"

"Yes. Now put the card away. Keep it safe. Emergency use only. Understood?"

"Understood."

She slipped the card into her back pocket.

"Okay, now you can have my story."

"Thank you." Søren stuck the folder under his arm. "Before I take full possession of this fine piece of erotic satire, might I ask you one question?"

"I really wish you wouldn't."

"Why does the king tie Esther to the bed?"

Eleanor cocked her head to the side. That wasn't the question she'd expected him to ask.

"I don't know. I've been reading these books by Anne Rice and there's a lot of stuff like that in them."

"I think you do know why he did it, and it isn't because you read about it in a book. Tell me the truth."

She pondered the question a moment.

"I think he tied her to the bed for the same reason a smart man who is not an idiot would put a lock on his Ducati."

"Because he doesn't want it stolen?"

"No," she said, and knew she had the right answer. If this was a test she'd show up to take it with nothing but a pencil.

"Then why?"

"Because he loves it."

14

Eleanor

THANKSGIVING BREAK ARRIVED AND ELEANOR nearly cried with relief. Finally she would have her answers from Søren. She'd watered that goddamn stick in the ground for six straight months without missing a single day. She'd been sick in bed, and she'd gone to water it. It had stormed, and she'd watered it. It had even snowed last week, and she'd trudged through six inches of white powder in her beat-up combat boots and watered it. That day, it had been so unnaturally cold the water had turned to ice the moment it touched the ground. The day after Thanksgiving equaled exactly six months from the day she'd begun. She had twelve questions ready for Søren. He'd better be ready to answer them.

1. What's the second reason you're helping me?
2. What's the third reason being with me is problematic?
3. Why will your friend help me?
4. Why does a priest have his own handcuff key?
5. Whose feet should I be sitting at?

6. Why does everyone at church think your name is Marcus Stearns and your Bible says your name is Søren Magnussen?
7. Why do you want me to obey you forever?
8. Are you a virgin?
9. I'm a virgin. Are you okay with that?
10. When will you keep your end of the deal?
11. Who are you?
12. Are you in love with me?

If she had the answers to all these questions, she knew she would know everything she needed to know about Søren.

She spent Thanksgiving Day alone with her mom. They had turkey and mashed potatoes and a chocolate pie Eleanor had begged her mother to make. Eleanor slept for four straight hours after their dinner. She blamed the turkey for her coma but she knew it was simple exhaustion. Going to school five days a week and then spending seven days a week at church had worn her out. She couldn't complain, though. Better than juvie.

The day after Thanksgiving dawned bright and cold and painfully beautiful. She had to squint to see the sky for all the light shining down and reflecting off the snow. Her mother had to work that day, so Eleanor had the house to herself. Bliss. Utter bliss. She ate leftovers, wrote, read and tried not to obsess over the answers Søren would have to her questions. She would go to Sacred Heart this evening on the pretense of working on something. She'd water that fucking stick for the final time, go to Søren's office and hand him her list of questions. And then she'd have something truly to be grateful for.

She lay down to take a nap. What if their conversation went late into the night? She needed to be ready for that. But as soon as she lay down on her bed, the phone rang.

With a curse and a groan, she dragged herself to the phone.

"Hello?" she said, trying not to sound 100 percent irritated.

"Happy Thanksgiving, baby girl."

"Dad?" Eleanor's heart dropped.

"Of course it's your dad." He laughed, but Eleanor couldn't.

"Why are you calling me?"

"Oh, I don't know. Maybe because I love my daughter and miss her? Maybe because I haven't heard her voice in months and I knew her mom would be working today."

"Dad, we're not allowed to talk to each other."

"Who said?"

"Mom. My lawyer. My... Everybody." Her father definitely didn't need to know about Søren.

"We're not breaking any laws. A man has a right to see his own child."

"What do you mean, *see?*"

"I want you to come see me, Elle. Please? I'm going to be sentenced soon," he said, his voice now devoid of all levity. "I'd love to see you one more time before I have to go away."

"Where are you?" she asked.

"I have a little place in Washington Heights. You can be here in, what, an hour and a half? We'll have dinner and talk a little. You'll be back long before your mom gets home. How about it?"

"That's not a good idea," she said, even as her heart broke at the thought of her father going to prison. She'd never forgiven him for abandoning her the night she got arrested. But the truth was, she never really expected him to come in like a white knight and save her. That wasn't his style. He was still her father, though, and she knew how brutal a real prison could be.

"Baby, it might our last chance to see each other for years. You know that, right? Years. Your mom will never let you come visit me once I'm in. She always works Friday nights, right?"

She did. Eleanor was alone. And her father was right—her own lawyer had said her father would probably be imprisoned in another state hours away.

"I don't know…."

"It's okay. I understand." She could tell from his tone how hurt and disappointed he was. "But write down my address anyway? In case you change your mind?"

"Okay, fine. Give it to me." She figured it wouldn't hurt for her to have it. She scribbled the address down on a scrap of paper.

"I hope you change your mind. I've missed you so much. You doing okay?"

"Good," she said. "I'm really good."

"That's good, baby," he said softly, with such tenderness in his voice she found her eyes filling with tears and her throat closing up. "I want you to be happy."

"I am. Promise."

"Good. And you know I'm sorry I got you mixed up in my mess."

"I know. I know you're sorry."

"Miss you. I'm home all day if you change your mind."

"All right. Happy Thanksgiving." She didn't know what else to say.

"I love you, Elle. Always have, always will."

Eleanor could barely swallow for the pain in her throat.

"Love you, too," she whispered.

And then he hung up.

It wouldn't hurt, would it? Seeing him for an hour? Except Søren had told her never to speak to or see her father again. Maybe he'd let her if she asked permission? Maybe he'd understand that she wouldn't see her dad again for years and this might her last chance.

She picked up the phone again and called Sacred Heart. She had the number that rang directly into Søren's office. But it wasn't Søren who answered.

"Sacred Heart Catholic Church," a woman's voice answered over the line.

"Hi, Diane, it's Elle," she said to Søren's secretary. "Is Father S. in? I have a question for him about my hours."

"No, hon. He's out of town with family for the holiday. Father Jim O'Neil from Immaculate is handling the masses until he gets back. Can I help you?"

Eleanor couldn't answer at first. Søren was out of town for the holiday? But they had plans. He'd promised to answer her questions as soon as she finished watering the stick. That would be today. He hadn't even told her he was leaving.

"Elle?"

"No, it's cool. It wasn't important."

A sense of betrayal seared her. How could Søren have forgotten about her? Forgotten to even tell her he was leaving for four days? He would have been furious at her if she disappeared without telling him where she'd gone. And he'd done it like it was nothing, like her feelings and their plans didn't matter at all.

She looked down at the scrap of paper and the address on it.

If Søren couldn't be bothered to keep up his end of the bargain, why should she?

She took a quick shower and put on her best clothes—a new pair of jeans and a low-cut black sweater with a label from some fancy boutique she'd found at Goodwill, the original tags still on it. Washington Heights wasn't the greatest neighborhood, but she wanted to look good for the city. She shoved her feet into her boots and grabbed her coat. She had about a hundred dollars saved in ones and fives rubber banded around the business card for Edge Enterprises tucked in her dresser. That was more than enough to get her to the city and back.

She took a bus to Westport, where she caught the train to Manhattan and then the subway to Washington Heights. She'd been running on pure anger for the past three hours but now that she'd arrived at her father's building, a new feeling of dread threatened to take its place. The building looked one step above condemned. People on the street passed her, shooting her suspicious looks. But she wouldn't give in to her fears. She buzzed her father's apartment. When he heard her voice he almost sounded smug.

He buzzed her in and she climbed four foul-smelling sets of stairs to his apartment. He opened the door, and before she could say hello, he'd grabbed her and smothered her in a bear hug.

"Good to see you, too, Dad," she said, nearly struggling for air.

"God damn, I can't believe you're here." He pulled back and looked at her. "Who are you? And what have you done to my daughter?"

"I am your daughter."

"Don't look it. You look twenty years old now. When did that happen?"

"It's the clothes and the makeup."

"Supermodel."

"Stop it." She rolled her eyes. "I'm too short."

"And too pretty. You don't get that from me." He let her go at last and she glanced around his apartment. A small studio, it might have been nice if someone cleaned it up, put some decent furniture in it. Her father clearly didn't have the decorating gene.

"I know it's not much to look at," he said, walking into

the tiny kitchen. "I knew I wasn't going to be here long. But while you're here, take your coat off. Get comfortable."

She doubted she could ever feel comfortable in this place. Dirty dishes sat in haphazard stacks all over the apartment; clothes littered the floor. The whole place reeked of stale cigarette smoke and rotting food. She took off her coat and laid it over the back of the one chair that had the least amount of garbage on and around it.

"So...do you know what's going to happen?" she asked.

"I'm going to prison," he said and took a beer out of the refrigerator. "Want one?"

"You know I'm sixteen, right?"

"You're not driving, are you?"

"No," she said and took the beer from him. She'd had alcohol before but never in front of either of her parents. Communion wine didn't count. She took a sip and found it equal parts disgusting and wonderful.

"So how's community service treating you?" her dad asked, and she heard a note of bitterness in his voice.

"It's not bad. I do a lot of office work for charities. I hang out at the homeless shelter and help out. Did a day-camp thing this summer. That was fun."

"Nice work if you can get it. Sounds better than prison."

She winced. "I'm sorry, Dad. I wish..."

"What? What do you wish?"

"I wish you didn't have to go."

"Yeah, well, that makes two of us."

He drank his beer hard and fast. The man had an unnatural tolerance for alcohol, something he called "the Catholic effect."

"Still trying to figure out how you got off so easy. I mean, thrilled you did. Don't want my baby girl in juvie or anything, but still. Community service for five felony counts?"

"I had a nice judge. A good lawyer."

"Where'd the lawyer come from?"

"The church paid for her. I do some work at the church to pay them back."

"That's good for you, then. Real good for you."

"So...you said you wanted to go to dinner?" She desperately wanted to change the subject. She could tell talk of her light sentence didn't sit with her father.

"Yeah, sure. But let me ask you something first."

"Sure. What?"

"I have a new lawyer, too. Smart guy. Tough guy. Not a shark you want to meet in the ocean. Anyway, he's thinking he can maybe get me a new trial."

"New trial? Why?"

"Some fuckup with the evidence. Some dumb cop mislabeled a file or something, I don't know. But if he can swing it and I get a new trial, there's a chance I won't have to go to prison."

"You don't think there's enough evidence against you?"

"If I had a witness who'd maybe recant some of her statements she made to the police, then there's a chance."

Eleanor could only stare at her father in silence. He opened another beer. She'd barely made a dent in hers.

"You want me to lie on a witness stand for you? I gave an allocution. I'd go to juvie in a heartbeat if I start telling people I lied to the police. I'm on probation and I think I've seen enough TV to know perjury is a crime. A big one."

"Baby, you're sixteen. Even if you did end up in juvie, you'll be out by the time you're eighteen. That's a year and a half. I'm looking at ten or more years, Elle."

"I'm not going to lie for you."

"Ten years. Fifteen years. You don't care about that? You don't care about your own father?"

"And it's not just a year and a half for me. This could fuck up my whole life. Am I supposed to send in college applications with a juvenile detention facility as my current address? I don't think NYU lets in criminals."

"NYU?" He laughed. "You seriously think you're going to get into a school like that?"

"I'm smart, Dad, if you haven't noticed. I'm in college-prep classes. I get good grades. I score crazy high on those stupid IQ tests they make us take."

"How are you planning on paying for it? Turning tricks?"

"Ever hear of scholarships?"

"Don't kid yourself. You go to a Podunk high school and no preppy school is ever going to let you in."

"I don't believe that. My priest says I'm smart, and he's the smartest person I've ever met."

"If he's so smart why's he a fucking priest?"

"You're an asshole."

"I'm not the one who rolled on her father to save her own ass."

"That's your own fucking fault," she shot back. "Nobody asked you to be a criminal. Mom's got two real jobs. Why couldn't you get a real job?"

"You want me to work two jobs like your mom and be a frigid miserable bitch like her?"

"Better than being a piece-of-shit lowlife who let his own daughter take the heat for him, right?"

Her father's hand whipped out and slapped her with such speed she flinched far more from the shock than the pain.

She stared at him, wide-eyed and dazed.

"I hope you rot in jail," she said. Her father raised his hand to slap her again. She ducked and tried to push past him. He grabbed her and shoved her bodily against the refrigerator.

She pushed him back with all her strength and managed to get around him, even as he tried to grab her.

She raced to the door and ran down the four flights of steps as fast as she could and even then she heard her father's footsteps chasing right behind her. She hit the street and started running again. She turned a corner and found a subway entrance. When she went for her money she realized the horrible fact that she'd left her coat in her dad's apartment. And it had all her money in it.

"Fuck..." she breathed. She had nothing. Nothing but that stupid list of questions for Søren. No money. No keys. No train ticket. Everything that mattered was in her coat.

In desperation she studied the subway map of the city, hoping she'd think of someone—anyone—she knew in the city who could help her. One street name jumped out at her. Riverside Drive wasn't that far away from the looks of it. Three miles maybe? She could get there in forty-five minutes if she booked it. Søren had given her that card, that fucking card that was trapped in her coat, for his friend who lived on Riverside Drive. He said to go there in case of emergency. Getting stuck in the city without any money sounded like an emergency to her.

She got her bearings and emerged streetside again, glancing around to make sure her father wasn't anywhere watching or following her. It seemed safe, so she started out, walking as fast as she could in her boots. She shoved her hands into her jeans' pockets for warmth and tried not to cry. In her heart, she'd always known her father was exactly what she'd called him—a piece-of-shit lowlife criminal. But she'd wanted to believe so badly that he cared about her, that he'd missed her, that he loved her. She berated herself block after block for believing all that shit he'd shoveled on her. All he wanted was to suck up to her, get her in a good mood, make her think he gave a damn about her, and then get her to lie for him.

The temperature dropped and the air burned her lungs and nose. Tears streamed from her eyes as she walked. She prayed hard that this friend of Søren's would take pity on her and help her get home. If not, she'd grab a paper cup from a store and beg for change like the homeless people she passed huddled under the dingy blankets.

Finally she reached the address she remembered from the business card. The house—white stone with black iron trim—shone like the sun under the streetlamps.

"God damn…" she breathed. House? This was no house. This was a New York palace. She studied it for a good five minutes trying to memorize all the details. Three stories tall or maybe more. From where she stood she thought she spied glass on the roof—maybe one of those fancy greenhouses or conservatories or whatever they were called. The front of the house was white, but all the trim on the arched windows was black. The second story had a black iron balcony and people in party clothes—dresses and suits—came in and out of the door. She moved in closer as she worked up the courage to knock on the door. Then she saw it. In the shadows at the side of the house she spotted a black Ducati motorcycle.

Søren? She couldn't believe he was here. Diane had said he was with family for Thanksgiving and wouldn't be back until Sunday. What was he doing here at a party on Riverside Drive? She didn't know, but she sure as hell intended to find out. A limousine pulled up and a group of girls in short stylish coats and stiletto heels emerged and headed straight for the front door. Eleanor followed them and when the person at the door let them in en masse, she slipped in behind them.

For five solid minutes Eleanor did nothing but stand in the luxurious marble foyer and stare. To her left in the front room of the house, she saw a woman in a silver dress standing in front of a man wearing a suit. He threw a wad of cash onto a low coffee table. A dozen people around them threw down money, as well. The woman slipped the dress off her shoulders, and it cascaded to the floor. She wore nothing underneath. The man in the suit pulled her down into his lap and dug his fingers between her legs as he bit her neck and shoulders. Eleanor tried not to watch but she couldn't turn away from the scene. He pushed her onto her hands and knees, opened his pants and started stroking himself. Something started to tighten up in her stomach as he thrust into the naked woman from behind.

No one noticed her watching from the entryway. Why would they? The people fucking were rather occupied with the fucking. And the dozen people in the room with them did nothing but cheer them on and throw more cash on the table. People checked their watches, but not out of boredom. There seemed to be some kind of bet going on about how long the guy could last. Eleanor watched the girl. Her face was passive, as though she couldn't care less that she was completely naked in the middle of a room full of people getting pounded from behind. Eleanor had never seen anyone having sex before. She'd read about it in her books, saw pictures of it in magazines. But never had she seen it like this—live and in living color and so close she could see the woman had blue eyes.

The man grunted and pulled out of her. The woman laughed as she swept the money off the table. Still naked and wearing only her black high heels, she stood up and grabbed a glass of something—wine probably—and drank it while she casually wiped the wetness out of her with a linen napkin. She seemed in no hurry to put her dress back on.

Another woman in a red dress yelled that it was her turn.

She lay back on the coffee table, hiked her skirt to her waist and lifted her knees to her chest. Another man opened his pants and mounted her right on the table. Once again, all bets were on.

Eleanor heard footsteps behind her and spun around. A couple—two men this time—came laughing and kissing into the foyer, tumblers of something in their hands. They paid her no attention as they headed down the hallway past the grand main staircase. She followed behind them, staying out of their line of sight as they entered the kitchen. While shadowing the men, she peeked into the cavernous dining room. A naked man lay facedown on a huge ornate table. A woman dressed head to toe in leather stalked around the table periodically whacking the man on his back with some kind of long thin cane. He winced and she laughed. He cried out in pain and she laughed louder. She ordered him onto his back and when he turned over, he had already come all over himself. The woman in leather climbed onto the table between his thighs and began to lick the semen off his stomach and thighs with the prissy precision of a cat lapping at a saucer of milk.

"Oh, holy fuck," she whispered to herself. "Toto, we are not in Kansas anymore…"

15

Eleanor

ELEANOR CREPT BACK DOWN THE HALL TOWARD THE main staircase. In another room, one that held a piano, a woman stood with one leg over the back of a leather chair. A man knelt between her legs and pressed his face into her vulva while another man, standing behind her, played with her breasts and nipples. All the while she carried on a conversation with another equally well-dressed woman sitting on an elegant black-and-white striped couch. In every single room of this house, someone was having sex with someone else. Eleanor could hardly breathe. Heat pooled in her stomach and dripped down her legs. Even as aroused as she was by the sights and sounds and smells, Eleanor didn't forget her mission. She'd come here to find Søren. She'd seen his motorcycle, but where was he? And what the hell was a Catholic priest doing at a party like this? And why didn't she get invited?

She marched up the stairs trying to act like she knew where she was going. No one questioned her presence in the house.

No one stopped her or asked to see her ID or an invitation. At the top of the first flight of stairs, Eleanor found even more people in various stages of undress engaged in various acts of debauchery. A woman sitting in a leather chair with one leg draped over each arm was allowing a man at least twenty years older than her to slowly work his entire hand into her body. The woman giggled and wiggled and lifted her hips to help him with the whole process. Two men wearing nothing but pants around their ankles engaged in some kind of mutual dick-sucking that required both of them to lie on the floor on their sides. They blocked the entire hallway, so Eleanor had to step over them. They didn't seem to notice or care.

Finally, Eleanor found an empty bedroom. Ducking inside, she pressed her hand into her stomach, closed her eyes and breathed through her nose. She'd been in the house almost twenty minutes according to her watch, and she'd yet to see Søren. Her heart pounded so hard it threatened to burst out of her chest. She'd never been so aroused and so scared in her life. She couldn't tell the difference between the two anymore. Was it fear that made her heart beat like this or desire? She wanted to shut the door, lock it, lie in bed and give herself the orgasm her body demanded.

A door inside the bedroom opened. A man emerged from the en suite bathroom wearing nothing but a white towel around his waist and water on his skin.

"Hello there," he said, a wide smile crossing his face. He spoke with an accent, Australian maybe, and didn't seem the least bothered to find a strange, panting girl standing in his room.

"Sorry. I didn't mean—"

"It's all right, love. What's your name?" He shut the door and locked it.

"Um. Elle."

"Elle. Pretty name. Pretty girl. I'm Lachlan. Everyone calls me Lockie. Everyone but you. You call me *sir.*" He winked at her and Eleanor nearly hit her knees from the erotic power of that wink.

"Sure. I mean, yes, sir."

"Did King send you?"

She didn't know the right answer to that so she lied and said, "Yes."

"God, I love that man. What are you into, gorgeous?"

Eleanor had no idea what that question meant.

"Everything?" she answered. Seemed a safe bet.

He laughed and the rich, warm sound sent something like hunger pains rolling through her stomach. He had a rugged handsomeness to him and nothing but muscle on his nearly naked body. He looked about twenty-eight years old. Her mouth had gone dry talking to him, so she licked her lips in nervousness.

"Very good answer."

He put his hands against the wall on either side of her and brought his mouth down on hers. Eleanor froze as he kissed her. The potency of the kiss soon overpowered her fear and she found herself kissing him back. She'd had a boyfriend in the eighth grade for all of two weeks. They'd done nothing but make out every chance they got at school. Nothing like this. A grown man kissed her now. A man old enough he could have dated her mom without raising anybody's eyebrows. He slid his hand under her sweater and cupped her breast. He rubbed her nipple with his thumb, and Eleanor nearly climaxed from that touch alone. She melted against his hard, warm body as the kiss deepened further.

With one hand he cupped her bottom while his other hand unhooked her bra in the back. He pinched her right nipple hard enough that she gasped. Unthinkingly, she rubbed her hips into his, seeking something more from him.

"I'm going to beat you until midnight and fuck you until dawn," he whispered against her lips.

"Beat me?" she asked and his only response was to laugh again.

He took both her breasts in his hands and squeezed them almost to the point of pain. She closed her eyes tight, loving the pain as much as the pleasure. His thumbs flicked across her nipples as his erection twitched against her stomach. In her mind she saw him stripping her naked and nailing her to the wall with that thing. Jesus, where had that thought come from?

"You have perfect tits," he said, pinching and rolling her nipples. "Perfect size."

"Really?"

"Absolutely." He growled the word into her ear. "And a perfect ass, perfect curves. I like little things like you. Bite-size."

He punctuated the words by biting hard at her neck, hard enough she knew she'd have a real bruise tomorrow. When he unbuttoned her jeans and eased her zipper down, she inhaled and forgot to exhale.

Stop. That was what she needed to say. Stop. She could do that. One little word.

Stop.

She didn't say it.

He slipped his hand into her panties and pressed the tip of his finger against her clitoris.

"That's a good girl," Lockie breathed in her ear. Good girl? They'd met one minute ago, and she'd let him stick his hand down her pants, and he was calling her a good girl? She liked his definition of *good* so much better than the dictionary's. "I want you to come for me. You'll be nice and relaxed when I flog you then. Can you do that, bite-size?"

"Standing up?"

"I got you." He spoke in a low voice, his words soft and heated. And he did feel so good to her. She wanted this for so long, being touched this intimately by an older man. It wasn't the older man she wanted, but she'd take what she could get.

Lockie's finger gently worked her clitoris, teasing it, massaging it, stroking it until she went limp his arms. But she didn't fall. He held her safe and secure between the wall and his own muscular body.

"That's it, bite-size. Almost there..."

He coaxed her with kisses and whispered encouragements. Any second now she would tell him to stop, tell him to let her go. Any second now...

She panted from pleasure, shivered from need. Everything from her toes to her teeth seemed to clench and tighten. All she had to do was say "stop" and this incredibly gorgeous Australian guy would stop. And she wanted him to stop.

"Don't stop," she gasped as she felt a hard muscle contraction inside her.

"Never ever." He laughed against her skin.

His finger made tight circles against her. Tight...tighter... until finally Eleanor went stiff in his arms as an orgasm stronger than she'd ever experienced before shook her to the very core of her being.

"That's my girl," he said and kissed her again.

Lockie pulled his hand out of her panties.

"Take your clothes off. Get on the bed. I want to see all of you." Those words sounded like an order, an order she desperately wanted to obey.

He pulled away from her and yanked off the towel. She stared at the sight of him completely naked and fully erect.

She'd never seen a naked man this close-up before. She almost started to obey his orders when she remembered that she'd come here to see Søren, not have sex with a total stranger. She was a virgin. She wasn't on birth control. And she was in love with someone else.

"Um...Cockie. Lockie, whatever. I have to go to the bathroom."

"Diaphragm?" He nodded sagely. "Bathroom's over there, bite-size. Don't be too long."

"My, um, stuff's downstairs." She pulled her jeans up and zipped them. "I'll be right back. Hold that cock. I mean, hold that thought."

She unlocked the door and slipped out into the hall. She allowed herself all of three seconds to hook her bra and silently freak out before taking off toward the steps. In that three seconds she almost considered turning around and walking back in that room. If Søren wasn't going to fuck her, maybe she should find someone who would.

A door opened next to her and a woman stepped into the hallway. She was easily the most beautiful woman in the house—luxurious red-black hair, brilliant blue eyes. She wore an elegant black cocktail dress and everything about her screamed money and privilege. And yet for all of that she wore a subdued expression, almost submissive, even as her flushed faced seemed alight with some secret sort of pleasure.

The woman nearly bumped into Eleanor. She said a hurried "So sorry" and neatly skipped down the stairs. Eleanor saw movement and turned her head. And there stood Søren in the same room the woman had emerged from.

He noticed her the second after she noticed him. They stared at each other in silence. Søren held something in his hands, a black cloth that looked like nothing more than a silk handkerchief. And yet somehow she knew it was something so much more than that.

From the bedroom she'd escaped came Lachlan wearing nothing but a pair of jeans, only halfway buttoned.

"Bite-size?" Lachlan asked.

Lachlan looked at Søren. Søren glanced at Lachlan before looking at her.

"Eleanor?" Søren asked.

"Fuck you..." she breathed. And before Søren or Lachlan could say another word, she ran from them. She flew down the stairs and stopped abruptly when a man appeared in front of her. He blocked her path and for a moment she could only stare at him. He had dark eyes, olive skin and shoulder-length black hair with a roguish wave. In another time and place she would have stared at him for an hour he was that handsome.

He gave her a smile, but not a friendly one. A slow, cold, dangerous smile.

He raised one finger and shook it in a classic tsk-tsk motion.

"No children allowed." He practically purred the words, but she heard the underlying threat. For one brief moment she envisioned clawing his beautiful face off. Instead she pushed past him, fleeing the house like it was burning to ashes behind her. She was awash with grief and shame and embarrassment and fury—utter aching, biting fury. She'd never felt like a bigger idiot in her life. All this time she'd worshipped the ground Søren walked on. She'd offered him her body and he'd turned her down because of that collar around his neck. And it was all a lie. He wasn't some sort of saint. He was another sinner like everybody else. And he'd fucked that beautiful woman because why not? Who wouldn't? Eleanor felt so stupid she could almost believe her father had been right about her.

Although she didn't know what to do or where to go, Eleanor kept walking. She might freeze to death between here and Wakefield but what did it matter? She almost didn't care if she froze. Her father had hit her, slapped her right in the face. And then she'd seen the one man on earth she trusted with her life in a bedroom with a beautiful woman in a house that hosted an orgy.

She wanted to cry, needed to cry, but she was too cold. Her body shook so hard she thought she'd chip a tooth from how brutally hard her teeth chattered. Maybe she could find a police station and some cop would take pity on her and help her get home. She almost laughed at the thought. Nine months ago she hated the very sight of cops. Now she'd hug one if he so much as stopped and asked her if she was okay. The temperature had dropped in the past hour sending everyone fleeing indoors. She had the street to herself.

"Eleanor?" She heard her name but ignored it. Then she heard it again and didn't. She stopped and turned around. A silver Rolls-Royce had pulled to the curb, and next to it stood Søren.

"What do you want?" she demanded from fifteen feet away. She refused to take a step toward him, was too cold and too scared to take a step back.

"Get in the car. We'll talk about this."

"Go away."

"I'll take you home. You don't even have a coat on and it's twenty degrees out."

"I'm fine."

"You're not fine, Eleanor. You're risking hypothermia and whatever you think of me right now, I'm not worth hurting yourself over."

He opened the back door and waited. She took a step toward him and stopped. Her pride and anger wouldn't allow her to take another step forward.

Søren came to her, shedding his coat as he walked. When he wrapped it around her, she didn't even acknowledge him. With his arm around her shoulders, he guided her to the car.

"Hypothermia?" she said. "You're not worth getting a tan over."

She got in the car and refused to look at him, even when he sat opposite her on the bench seat.

He leaned forward and dug through the folds of his coat until he found her hands. He took them into his and chafed them, warming her skin with his own.

"Stop," she said. "I don't want you to touch me."

"I'll stop when you're warm. Your teeth are still chattering."

He pulled the coat tighter. All she wanted to do was close her eyes, fall asleep and never wake up again.

"Can you tell me what you were doing at Kingsley's house tonight?" Søren asked.

"I went to see Dad," she confessed. "He called me and said he was going to be sentenced and he'd be in prison for years. This was my last chance to see him."

"I see," Søren said.

She took a shuddering breath. Her whole body hurt.

"But he was lying," she said. "He doesn't love me, and he's not going to miss me. He was trying to get me to recant what I said. He said he might get a new trial and if I lied for him…"

"What did you tell him?"

"I told him he was an asshole. We fought and I ran for it," she said, leaving out the part about the slap for some reason. It was too embarrassing to admit her own father had hit her like they were some family on Jerry Springer. "But I left my coat in his apartment and it had my money in it."

"I'm sorry your father did this to you. I ordered you not to see him or speak to him."

"I tried to call you." Eleanor felt her body warming and relaxing. She pulled her hands away from Søren's and tucked them against her stomach. "I called the church. You were supposed to answer my questions tonight. But Diane said you were gone until Sunday. You forgot about me."

"I did not and will not ever forget about you. I was coming back to Wakefield tonight and leaving to visit my sister tomorrow morning. I know your mother works late on Friday nights. I thought we'd have more than enough time to talk."

"I don't want to talk to you anymore."

Søren sighed and sat back on the bench seat. He turned his head and stared at the frozen city that surrounded them.

"What you saw tonight—" he began.

"Stop," she said. "I told you I'd be pissed if you ever talked to me like I was a child. If you're going to pull that 'ignore the man behind the curtain' bullshit, let me out of the car right now."

"I would never speak to you like a child. Even when you're acting like one."

Eleanor couldn't meet his eyes when she asked the question she didn't want to ask.

"Did you have sex with her?"

"Did you have sex with Lachlan?"

"That's none of your business. I'm not your daughter, and I'm not your girlfriend."

"But it's your concern what I did tonight?"

"You're a priest. You have vows—"

"Vows you've been trying to get me to break with you for months."

"That's different."

"How so?"

"Because it's me," she said, anguished. "Because you promised."

Tears ran down her face, tears of jealousy and shame and fury.

She wanted to argue with him, but couldn't. So instead she pulled off his coat, threw it at him and curled up in the seat, her arms around her legs for warmth. Søren sighed as he folded his coat and placed it on the seat next to him.

They left the city and she recognized they were on the road back to Wakefield. She wanted to ask him why they were in a Rolls-Royce, who was driving, what would happen to his Ducati back at that house and a million other questions. But instead she punished him with her silence. Half an hour passed without them saying a word to each other. She could tell he waited for her to speak. Fine. He could wait all damn night if he wanted. She wasn't going to say another word to him.

Søren reached out and took her hand again. She felt her resolve to hate him melting.

"Little One, I didn't have sex with her," he said softly. "And you have a very large bite mark on your neck. If he hurt you in a way you didn't like, I need you to tell me."

"No," she whispered and met his eyes for one second. "I liked it."

"I see," he said and she thought she heard something strange his voice. Something like pain.

"Jealous?" she asked.

"Yes."

She hadn't expected that answer and her astonishment must have shown.

"Don't look so surprised," Søren said. "I wish I could give you everything you wanted. But even a good gift is a bad gift if given at the wrong time."

"What does that even mean?"

"It means one wouldn't buy a new car for an eight-year-old."

"Nice," she said, and nodded. "Now I'm an eight-year-old. What's the car? Sex with you? You're saying I'm too young to drive your ride?"

"Age is only a number. Maturity—or a striking lack thereof—is your issue," Søren added, seemingly oblivious to how much his words hurt her. "You're not ready to have an adult relationship. No amount of wishing on either of our parts will make it so. And I care about you too much to take you anywhere you're not yet ready to go."

"Do you have any idea how condescending that sounds? I want you. You promised—"

"I will not fuck a teenage girl in my congregation, Eleanor."

Eleanor gaped at him.

"Did you say *fuck?* You never swear."

"I needed your attention. I'm pleased to see I have it now."

"You were supposed to answer my questions tonight," she finally said.

"Do you have your list?"

"Never leave home without it," she said, and pulled the folded sheet of paper from her back pocket.

Søren tilted the list toward the light. As he read, she heard nothing but the sound of her own breathing.

"We need to work on your question-asking skills," Søren finally said.

"What do you mean?"

"You're hamstringing yourself with some of the wording. Never ask a yes or no question when you can asked an open-ended one. Your question 'why will your friend help me?' is a good question—it will lead to a long answer. Your question 'are you a virgin?' can be answered with a simple yes or no. I'm assuming you want a more thorough answer than that."

"What should I ask?"

"You could ask 'when was the last time you had sex?' which would reveal not only whether or not I've had it, but also when the last occasion of it took place. A far better question than that would be 'what is your sexual history?' A bit clinical, but it would do the trick."

"I can rewrite my list."

"Too late. It's in my hands now. Did you water the stick today?"

"No. I was going to do it when I got home."

"Look at your watch."

She pulled back her sleeve. It was 12:07 a.m. She'd missed the last day of watering.

"Fuck," she breathed, and buried her head in her arms.

"I didn't want to do this, Eleanor. I never wanted to do this. Not like this anyway. But perhaps the Bible was right in this instance—spare the rod, spoil the child."

She looked up at him with tears in her eyes.

"You going to hit me?"

"Not tonight," he said simply. "The night we made our little bargain, I told you there was nothing I wouldn't do to protect you. I meant it. Which is why you'll have to forgive me doing this now."

"Doing what?"

"Raro solus, nunquam duo, semper tres." Søren sounded as if he were quoting something.

"What does that mean?"

"It's an old Jesuit rule they beat into us. Figuratively, of course. It means 'rarely alone, never two, always three.' The Jesuits have rules against what they call *particular friendships.* In seminary we were to talk in groups of three or more. It's considered dangerous to be alone with another person, even another priest."

"Why? They thought you'd start having crazy gay sex the minute you were alone together?"

"Yes."

"Did you?"

"No. Although I was propositioned more than once."

"Color me surprised."

"But still, I thought it a pointless rule. I understand it now. You and I have a particular friendship. And it has to end."

"End?" Her voice broke on the word.

"I told you if you watered that stick every day for six months, I'd answer your questions. You failed in this task. You will not be rewarded. I told you that you had to obey me forever, and I would give you everything. You disobeyed me and went to your father and now you're suffering the consequences. For the foreseeable future, Diane will monitor your community service. This particular friendship of ours will cease until that day comes that I'm certain you are mature enough to be in an adult relationship. And by adult I do not mean sexual. I mean a relationship between equal partners."

"What do you mean? We can't be friends anymore?"

"Unfortunately, yes, that is what I mean. Of course, I'll still be your priest. And if and when you need a priest, I'll be here for you, but only in that capacity. Go, Eleanor. Go be a normal teenager for a year or two. Go grow up."

"A year or two?" It sounded like the worst prison sentence imaginable. No more long talks in the choir loft? No more help with her homework? No more cocoa when she was fighting with her math homework?

"I'm your priest, not your babysitter."

Eleanor only looked at him. Even in the faint light of a passing streetlamp, she could see how hard his eyes had turned. His face was as cold and stony as granite. All affection, all concern, all mercy had drained from his expression.

"You're a cold bastard," she said, refusing to let another tear fall. "You know that, right?"

"I do. And it is for the best you know it now, as well."

The Rolls-Royce pulled up at the end of her street, far enough away her mother wouldn't see where she'd come from, close enough she'd only have to be in the cold a minute or two.

She wanted to say something more to him, wanted to beg him to change his mind, wanted to tell him how much she hated him. Instead she simply opened the door.

"Eleanor," Søren said before she left the car.

She looked at him and saw the faintest look of anguish in his eyes.

"What?"

"This will hurt me more than it hurts you."

"Good."

She left him alone in the back of the Rolls.

As quietly as she could, she took the spare key from under the mat and unlocked the back door. She locked the door behind her and started when she heard a voice in the dark.

"Do I even want to know where you've been?" her mother asked.

Eleanor slowly turned to face her mother, who flipped on the kitchen light. Once more Eleanor was bathed in the fluorescent lights of an interrogation.

"I'm sorry, Mom. I didn't mean to stay out so late."

Her mother stood in the doorway wearing her dingy white bathroom and slippers. Disappointment lined her mouth.

"That's not an answer."

Eleanor weighed her words and decided to try the truth, at least half of the truth.

"Dad called. He said he was about to get sentenced. This might be my last chance to see him."

"You went to see your father? Oh, Elle."

"Yeah, Mom. I'm sorry. I missed him. But it was stupid. He didn't want to see me. He wanted me to lie for him. I ran out and left my coat behind."

"I could have believed that once. But this doesn't really help your case."

She pointed to the side of Eleanor's neck, where Lachlan had bitten her earlier. She must have a hickey the size of Delaware from how hard he'd bitten and kissed her.

Fuck.

"Mom, nothing happened. I swear I didn't—"

"I don't care." Her mother raised her hand. "I don't care anymore. I told you the night you got arrested that if you pulled something like that again I was done with you. Now I come home from work and you're gone. No note. Nothing. I call Jordan's and you're not there. School. Church. Gone."

"I got lost in the city. It took me a while to figure out how to get home."

"I don't know why you came home. You obviously can't stand it here. Not if you're running off to see your father, whom I forbade you from having any contact with."

"He said I might not see him again for years."

"That's a bad thing?"

"I thought it was. Now I know...I never want to see him again. I'm sorry. Nothing happened—"

"Save it. No matter how much I care you go off and you do whatever you want with whomever you want anyway. So I'm going to stop caring. I'm not even going to punish you. That's how little I care right now."

"No, Mom, don't be like that. Please don't..." Tears burst from her eyes. "Don't give up on me, too."

"Too? Who else is giving up on you?"

"I did something stupid, and now Father Stearns isn't even going to monitor my community service anymore."

"Then he's smart. You'd run right over him and his feelings like you do with everyone else who tries to care about you and help you."

"Mom…" Eleanor took a step forward but her mother stepped back and away from her.

Her mother stared straight into her eyes.

"When you were little, you always called me Momma. And you smiled when you said it. Now it's Mom. And you never smile at me."

"Please…" Eleanor didn't even know what she was begging for.

"Go to bed," her mother said, sounding tired. "Or not. Do whatever you want. You will anyway."

Her mother turned her back on Eleanor and flipped the light off as if Eleanor weren't still standing there in the middle of the kitchen.

She merely stood there in shock and sorrow, not sure what to do. She'd lost her priest, her father and her mother all in the same night. Who did she even have left? Anyone? Anything?

In the dark she found her way to her bed and without taking her clothes off, she slid under her covers. She pulled the blanket up to her chin and closed her eyes.

"Are You up there?" she whispered to God and waited, hoping, praying that someone somewhere was out there who hadn't given up on her.

But God didn't answer.

16

Nora

"WHAT VINTAGE OF TEAR IS THIS?" NICO ASKED, touching her wet face. "A 1993? Or something more recent?"

Nora smiled shyly at him.

"You're the vintner. What do you think?"

Nico brought his wet fingertip to his mouth and licked it.

"Whatever vintage this is, I can taste that it was a hard year."

"It was a hard year," she agreed. "Like this week. A lot of second-guessing myself, wondering if I could have prevented it. A lot of begging God to undo what happened. Even now I feel that same awful desperation—that, 'God, I would give anything, trade anything, to feel something other than this pain.'"

She closed her eyes and breathed deep again. God help her, she would do anything to not have to spread those ashes tomorrow.

"But," she continued, coming back to the present, "even

that night alone in my bed, I knew I'd brought it on myself. And maybe knowing that was the one sign of hope for me."

"How long did he punish you for seeing your father?" Nico asked.

"A long time." Nora sat up while Nico rolled onto his back. She still had her gown on but Nico lay naked in bed, the sheets pulled up to his hips, his chest bare and inviting. "When you're a teenager, every day without getting what you want feels like an eternity. Your heart's under a magnifying glass at that age—everything is blown out of proportion."

"How long before you and he spoke after that night?"

Nora cast her mind to that awful time. She remembered it as a particularly dark, cold and snowy winter. Streets turned gray with slush and treacherous with ice. But there, in her box of black memories, lay one shining star.

"Christmas," she said. "A few weeks later I went to midnight Mass, and Søren and I declared a Christmas truce for an hour. I think my mother had told him my father had been sentenced—fifteen years hard time. He knew I needed something to help me get through it. We talked. He gave me a Christmas gift."

"What did he give you?"

"A St. Louise medal," Nora said, smiling at the memory. "My middle name is Louise. And her Feast Day is March 15th—my birthday."

"A good gift."

"He let me cry on his shoulder a little. That was an even better gift. After that it was March before we spoke again."

"What happened in March?"

"Nothing," Nora said. "And everything. I skipped school and went for a walk. For some reason my wandering feet led me right to Sacred Heart. I didn't think I'd see Søren that day, but there he was at the rectory…in his backyard…planting trees…and wearing jeans and a white T-shirt."

"You remember his clothes from that day?"

"I remember everything. I'd never seen Søren in anything but his clerics and collar before. I had convinced myself he even slept in his clerics. But damn…" She smiled down at Nico. "He had dirt under his nails. Like you did the day we met."

"I'd been working that day. I work every day."

"I liked it. I like a man who's not afraid to get his hands dirty."

"Was he angry at you for coming to his house?"

Nora shook her head. "I can count on one hand the number of times Søren's been actually angry at me. And then it's usually because I've done something dangerously stupid or stupidly dangerous. No, that day he was… Well, he wasn't angry. By March it had been four months since he told me to back off, go away, grow up. Everything that had happened the year before already felt like a dream, like I couldn't be sure it had happened."

She remembered standing outside the fence and Søren on the inside. They talked for a few minutes, and from the way he spoke, the way he looked at her, she knew she wasn't the only one who remembered the dream.

"After that day, however…" Nora's chest heaved slightly. "Nothing. Nothing for months and months and months. No talking, no touching, no nothing. Søren and I became strangers to each other again. It wasn't awful. I didn't sit in my room and stare out the window for a year or anything. I went to school, got good grades, worked my ass off to finish my community service. I wasn't allowed to get a driver's license until I turned eighteen, but Søren's secretary, Diane, gave me rides places. I did okay. It wasn't fun, but I survived it."

Nico rolled up and moved closer to her. He took her knees in his hands and pulled her legs around his waist to bring them face-to-face. She relaxed into the circle of his strong arms and rested her chin on his shoulder.

"I'm glad you survived it," he said. "Otherwise you wouldn't be here."

"Oh, I survived it. And what's funny is that later on, after I became a novelist, I understood what Søren had done and why."

"And what was that?"

"It's a trick of the fiction writer," she explained. "You figure out what your main character is most afraid of, and then you make her face that fear."

"Is that what he made you do?"

"Losing him, losing his love, was my greatest fear. And he made me face it. I faced it, I survived it. And ultimately..."

Nora paused to kiss Nico's neck for no other reason than it wanted kissing.

"Ultimately, that time on my own turned me into what Søren said I was all along."

"What was that?"

Nora pulled back and gave Nico her wickedest grin. She raised one finger to indicate he should wait. Nico arched an eyebrow. She slipped out of his arms, out of bed and took something from her suitcase.

Her red riding crop.

She held it in front of her, the tip pointed at the center of Nico's chest.

"Dangerous," she said.

Nico smiled, his lips slightly parted, his breath quickening.

"You see," she said, letting the tip of the crop rest at the hollow of his throat, "when you face your greatest fear and you survive, what's left to be afraid of?"

Nico licked his lips. His chest rose and fell.

"Answer me." Nora slid the crop under his chin and forced him to raise his head an inch.

"Nothing," Nico said.

"My greatest fear was to live without Søren and I did. I wasn't afraid of that anymore, and I didn't need anyone anymore. I wanted him, but I didn't need him. But he needed me."

"I believe it," he said.

Nora looked down at him.

"Now, Nicholas Delacroix, tell me your fear."

"My fear is that this will be our only night together, and I will live the rest of my life never meeting another woman like you."

"I can't promise we'll have another night together, but I can guarantee this—you'll never meet another woman like me."

She didn't add that never meeting another woman like her was most likely a good thing.

He didn't seem to think so, however. A smile, sexy and suggestive, crossed his lips.

"Prove it."

Prove it?

Well, if he insisted…

Nora grabbed the back of Nico's neck and turned his face up to hers.

"Are you going to hurt me?" he asked, his voice equal parts fear and anticipation.

"Not tonight," she said, remembering the night she'd asked almost the same question of Søren and he'd given her that exact answer. "Tonight is only for pleasure."

She kissed Nico then with all the fierce passion only someone wounded and desperate to heal possessed. She kissed him like the meaning of life lay in his mouth and if she kissed him hard enough, sweet enough and long enough, it would brush her lips and she could catch it in her teeth and swallow it whole.

Nora pressed Nico onto his back, not once breaking the kiss. He moved to put his arms around her, but she grabbed his wrists and pushed them into the bed over his head.

"Lie there," she ordered. "Don't move. I want to make you come."

"I'm all yours, Nora."

She loved the way he said her name.

"I should make you call me *mistress*."

"Do you want to be my mistress?"

"Would you like that?"

"It would be a dream come true to belong to you, to be your property. But since I don't belong to you, Nora it is."

It embarrassed her how much Nico's words affected her.

"Nora it is, then," she repeated. "Now be good and don't come until I tell you that you can."

He nodded and fixed his eyes on the ceiling as Nora pressed his knees apart and settled between them. She licked her fingertip and slowly pushed it inside him. She went in deep but not too deep. She stopped when Nico gasped in pleasure.

"Good?"

"Parfait." He kept his eyes on the ceiling as if too embarrassed to look at her while she touched him so intimately.

"Good." She pulled her finger out of his tight passage and grabbed her riding crop. She twirled it once before catching it in the middle. Carefully she eased the narrow shaft of the handle a few inches inside him.

"See?" she said as she massaged a spot inside him. "Crops aren't made *only* for pain."

Nico said nothing. He had apparently lost all powers of speech. Nora took him in her hand and stroked his incredible hardness. Then she dipped her head and licked him from base to tip and then back down the full length of the shaft again.

Nico groaned and grasped at the sheets. She loved nothing more than making a beautiful man writhe.

"Have you ever been with a woman who fucked your ass and sucked your cock at the same time?" she paused to ask.

"Yes, if you count fingers."

"I do. But don't worry. I'm not done proving myself yet."

She sucked him deep into her mouth again. Hard, harder, so hard he gasped.

"Are you ready to come for me?" she asked in French. It had been one of the first sentences Kingsley had taught her.

"Oui."

"Not yet," she said, purring the words. "Not…quite… yet…."

She licked him a few more times for her own pleasure, relishing the velvet skin, the earthy taste, the fullness of him in her mouth. Gently she pulled the riding crop handle out of him.

Rising up, she clasped him in her hand and massaged him with long, thorough strokes.

"Get there for me," she ordered. "Get right to the edge of your orgasm and stay there. Are you there?"

Nico nodded and closed his eyes tight.

"Stay there at the edge, feel how sharp that edge is, Nico."

"It hurts," he gasped through clenched teeth.

"I know. Pleasure can hurt worse than pain sometimes. In three seconds, I'll let you come."

She reached out and took the empty wineglass off the bedside table.

"Un…deux…trois," she said, and brought the wineglass over the tip. He spurted into it, coating the sides with his semen as he winced from the intensity of his release.

After she'd collected every drop of him, Nora held the glass up in the light of the fireplace.

Nico opened his eyes and propped himself on his elbows, watching her.

She took the uncorked bottle of Rosanella Syrah and poured an inch of wine into the glass. She swirled the wine, letting it lap the sides.

"The two fruits of your labors in one glass," she said. *"Santé."*

She raised the glass to her lips.

"Nora..." Nico panted her name.

In three deep swallows she drank the wine down.

"My favorite vintage," she said.

Nico sat up and looked at her as his chest rose and fell rapidly.

"You win," he said.

"Thought so," she said and sat the glass aside. "I also have a fun trick with whiskey, but I don't drink hard liquor anymore. Zach won't let me."

Without a word, Nico pushed her onto her back and kissed her with shocking, breathtaking passion. His tongue delved into her mouth as if seeking the taste of himself on her tongue.

"You are dangerous," Nico whispered against her lips. "You can make a man want things he can't have."

Nico took a shuddering breath as if trying to calm himself. He eased away from her and stretched out once more on his side in bed.

"Talk to me before I tie you to the bed and never let either of us leave it," Nico said.

Nora laughed and lay on her side to face him.

"I should tell you about the first time I met your father," she said. "Really met him."

"What was he like?"

"Nothing like you," she said.

"Is that bad?"

"Not at all. That house I wandered into with the wild orgy going on—that was your father's house."

"I can truthfully say I've never been to an orgy. Although the days we harvest and stomp the grapes come close."

Nora grinned. She'd love to be with Nico at the grape harvest. Maybe she could sneak back for it. If her conscience would let her.

"You'll be glad to hear that a bottle or two or possibly even three of Syrah was involved when I met your father finally."

"He has good taste in wine and women." Nico grinned at her. "Where were you?"

"You'll never guess, considering your father was there. But the first time Kingsley and I talked, it was, of all places, at church."

17

Eleanor

ELEANOR ADJUSTED HER DRESS ONE FINAL TIME, straightened the baby's breath the stylist had woven through her hair and picked up her bouquet of bloodred roses. Bach's Minuet in G Major began and after one steadying breath, she stepped onto the red carpet and headed down the aisle toward Søren.

She'd practiced her walk last night at the rehearsal. Right foot forward, step together, stop. Left foot forward, step together, stop. She repeated those instructions in her mind over and over. The words forced her to walk slowly when all she wanted to do was run down the aisle and fly into Søren's arms.

At the altar she met Søren's eyes only briefly before taking her place at the far left facing the congregation. The other four bridesmaids joined her in a line.

The entire church rose when Diane appeared in the doorway resplendent in her white dress and veil. Eleanor stared over Diane's shoulder at the back wall of Sacred Heart. She didn't want to look at Diane, the bride, and didn't want to look at James, the groom. She wanted to look at Søren, the priest, but if she were to make it through the entire ceremony without turning into a basket case, she had to keep her eyes anywhere but on him. Since she couldn't will herself to disappear, she ignored the wedding happening around her entirely.

She felt like the butt of a joke today. Nearly one year ago Søren had dismissed her from his life, erected a wall around himself and ordered her to stay behind it. Go be a normal teenager, he'd said. So she'd left him. They hadn't spoken one word to each other in months. And now she stood at the altar as he performed a wedding ceremony for someone else.

She had no one to blame but herself for this pain she felt watching Søren perform his secretary's wedding. Diane needed a fifth bridesmaid to even out the numbers with the groomsmen. Eleanor had told her no at first, knowing how painful it would be, but Diane had begged and cajoled and since she'd given Eleanor rides for the past year, Eleanor felt like she owed her something. She couldn't give her gas money so she put on the damn dress, pasted on a fake smile and walked down a church aisle toward the man she loved more than life itself, knowing with every step that she would never have her own wedding with him.

Walking on broken glass would hurt less than walking down that aisle.

As Søren began the ceremony, quoting Bible verses of love and devotion that caused everyone in the church to sigh and weep, Eleanor tuned him out. She'd gotten good at that in the past year.

During the reception, Eleanor sat with the youngest two groomsmen, drank champagne and pretended to flirt. Søren stayed for an hour and talked to people. He ignored her, of course. Ignored her as much as she ignored him. She knew he ignored her because she watched him ignore her for the entire hour he ignored her.

"I need another drink," Eleanor said, and the bride's younger brother, who had apparently fallen in love with her cleavage, hurried to fetch her another glass of champagne.

Søren left the reception and Eleanor danced with the groomsman. She wanted to go home and sleep, but she promised to stay to the bitter end.

The party finally broke up at one in the morning. Diane and James ran through a hail of birdseed on their way to the waiting limousine. Ten minutes later the fellowship hall had turned into a ghost town. About goddamn time.

Eleanor went into the pantry of the food bank she'd set up last year and dug through the bag of clothes she'd stashed there. She yanked the flowers out of her hair and tossed them in the trash before shimmying out of the skirt of her two-piece bridesmaid's dress. She pulled on her jeans and slammed her feet into tennis shoes, sighing with relief at getting rid of her high heels. The bodice of her sleeveless dress proved a bit trickier. She couldn't get the zipper unstuck. Damn Diane and her "two-piece A-line dress with Empire waist—oh, my God, it'll look so good on you, Elle" bullshit. They should have all worn jeans and T-shirts.

She growled loudly, swore violently. And in the silence that followed, she heard a man laughing.

"Do you need some help in there, Eleanor?"

Søren? What the hell? She rolled her eyes and made another failed attempt to get the zipper down.

"I'm stuck in my dress. Do you have scissors or knives or guns or anything?"

"You need a gun to remove your dress?"

"Once I get it off, I'm putting it out of its misery."

"Is it that serious?" Søren came back to the pantry. She

glanced at him over her shoulder. He'd already beaten her to the jeans-and-T-shirt punch. In all the time he'd served as pastor at Sacred Heart she'd only seen him out of his clerics twice before. If the pope ever saw Søren in a pair of jeans His Holiness would probably order all the clergy to switch to that new uniform. Church attendance would skyrocket.

"I'm trapped."

Søren cocked his eyebrow at her. "Turn around."

"Are you going to cut it off? Do we need to call an ambulance?"

"Lift your hair up and hold still."

She dug her fingers into her hair and held it while Søren gripped the fabric of the dress and pulled it out from her skin. After a few seconds of tugging, the zipper finally budged.

Eleanor tried to take over for him, but he seemed intent on pulling it all the way down. Who was she to argue with him, especially when his fingertips brushed the bare skin of her lower back?

"Better?" he asked.

"Thank God. I thought I'd die in this stupid dress." Søren turned his back to her while she pulled the rest of her dress off, put on a bra and slithered into her white T-shirt.

"It's not a stupid dress. You looked lovely in it."

"Lovely? That bustier top pushed my tits up to my neck."

"But in such a lovely way."

Eleanor stuffed the dress into her bag and pulled her hair up into a ponytail all while glaring at him. She wanted to be happy he was here talking to her but she couldn't get over her anger. Over a year of the cold shoulder could not be forgiven with one compliment on her tits.

"What are you doing over here? Shouldn't you be all snuggled up in bed with Jesus?"

Søren watched her as she pulled out garbage bags from under the sink.

"I have company. I noticed the lights were still on. What are you doing here?"

"Cleaning."

"Cleaning?"

Eleanor took the bags into the fellowship hall and started dumping plastic plates and paper cups into the trash bag.

"Diane's been nice to me," Eleanor began. "She's sweet. Drives me places since I can't get my license until I'm off probation. I couldn't afford to get her a real wedding gift so I said I'd clean the hall up so her family wouldn't have to."

She balled up a paper tablecloth.

"What?" she demanded.

"I didn't say anything," he said.

"You're staring at me, *Father* Stearns," she said with sarcastic emphasis on his title.

"I am."

"Why?"

"I'm staring at you because entirely without intending to you've become a very kind and generous person."

"You can shove kind and generous up your ass."

"And I'm staring at you because you are stunningly beautiful."

Eleanor dropped the bag on the floor.

"Søren. Seriously." Her stomach churned. She wanted to cry and scream and kiss him and kill him all at once.

"When you aren't trying to look beautiful, you look beautiful. When you are trying to look beautiful, you are stunning."

"I hate you."

"No, you don't."

"Maybe not, but I'm trying to."

"I don't blame you, Little One." He stepped closer and Eleanor fought the urge to retreat.

"So we're back to this now?" she asked, sitting on the edge of a table and crossing her arms over her stomach.

"Back to what?"

"Back to us being honest with each other? You snap your fingers and the past year goes away just like that?"

Søren held out his hand and snapped his fingers by her ear. She flinched at the sound.

"Just like that," he said.

"You've been acting like I don't exist for months. Why tonight?"

"Two reasons," he said. "First, there is something you need to know. Second, I have an entire bottle of wine in me."

Eleanor gaped at him.

"You're drunk?"

Søren raised his hand. An inch separated his thumb from his index finger.

"That much?"

Søren slightly widened the gap.

"That would be slightly more accurate," he said.

"Great. It'll be easier to seduce you, then," Eleanor said, seeing how much she could push him.

"Later. We should talk first."

"You talk while I clean." So what if he was drunk and here and gorgeous and she'd missed him so much her hands were shaking from simply speaking to him again? She had a job to do.

"Can I help you?"

She picked up her bag.

"This is my gift to Diane, not yours. I have to do this myself or it's cheating."

"I feel useless simply standing here."

"You are useless."

"Is there anything I can do to be less useless to you?"

"Fuck me on the gift table?"

Søren glowered at her so hard she laughed.

"Fine." She pointed to the corner of the room. "You can put on some music."

"This is a job I can do." The DJ, otherwise known as the bride's cousin Tommy, had left all the equipment and music behind. He'd come by in the morning to haul it all away. "Or not."

Eleanor watched him as he flipped through stacks of CDs.

"What's wrong?"

"The music selection is shameful. What is this?" Søren held up a CD with a familiar-looking cover.

"Dr. Dre."

"Is he a licensed medical professional?"

"He's a rapper."

"And this?" he asked.

"4 Non Blondes. Obviously you would not be allowed in that band."

"I didn't want to join their band anyway," he said in a tone so dry her face hurt from swallowing her laughter.

Søren dug through a few more CDs.

"How does anyone dance to any of this music?" He sounded horrified.

"It's drunken reception dancing, not waltzing." She knew it was a weak defense, but she didn't have it in her to defend modern music tonight. Not when she'd been listening to the classical station every night in bed trying to learn something about the music Søren played so lovingly on piano. The last CD she bought had been a collection of baroque pieces.

He held up a CD.

"Finally," he said. "Decent music."

"What did you find? Bach? Beethoven? Vivaldi?"

"Sting."

Eleanor burst out laughing.

"You like Sting?"

"Who doesn't? He's a musician's musician."

"I can't believe you've even heard of him."

"I spent ten years of my life in seminary, Eleanor, not in a cave."

The music started and filled the room with cool blue sounds and Sting's arching voice that always managed to speed up her pulse and lower her blood pressure simultaneously.

"Music," Søren said as he walked to her, "has melodies and themes. It's not simply a collection of profanities and noise set to a bass line."

"God, you're a snob."

"Guilty. Now stop cleaning."

"Why?"

"Because I said so, and I never once said you were freed from your vow to obey me. So obey me."

"Can you please order me to punch your face? I'll obey that order."

"Later, perhaps. I have nothing but respect for your sadistic side."

With a growl Eleanor dropped the bag on the ground and put her hands on her hips. She hated how much she loved his orders, how much she'd missed them.

He took her wrist gently in his hand and placed her hand on his shoulder.

"What are you doing to me?"

"Dancing with you. Not drunken reception dancing, real dancing."

He took her other hand and led her in the first steps of something like a waltz. He took her on one turn around the dance floor before stopping midstep. He studied her face, his gaze penetrating and intimate.

"She's gone," Søren said, his voice soft with wonder.

"Who?" Eleanor asked.

"The girl. All of her is gone. Where did she go?"

Eleanor gave a tired half laugh.

"I killed her," she said without apology. "You said grow up. I grew up. She's gone. I'm here."

She held out her hand for Søren to shake. Instead he raised her hand to his lips and kissed the back of it before turning it over and pressing a kiss into the center of her palm. She felt the impact of that kiss all the way to her toes.

"A pleasure," he said, seemingly amazed by the change he saw in her.

Eleanor pulled her hand away. Not because she wanted to but because she didn't want him to know how much it affected her.

"So...you know how to dance?" Eleanor asked as Søren led her on another slow turn.

"I do."

"Is this something they teach in seminary?"

"No."

He gave her a subtle smile as he let go of her hand and spun her gracefully.

"You know this song is about adultery, right? You shouldn't be dancing to it," she teased, trying to hide how much she relished the touch of his hands on her.

"Eleanor, I've committed adultery. Safe to say I can handle a song about it."

Eleanor stopped dancing.

"Wait. You committed adultery? When?"

Søren said nothing for a moment. He lowered his hands to his sides as Eleanor pulled away from him.

"When I was eighteen, Eleanor. When I was married."

Eleanor lost all powers of speech. She took a step back from him, and Søren turned the music off.

"You were married?"

"Yes. Briefly and unhappily."

Eleanor's knees went weak on her. She pulled a chair out and sat down.

"Tell me everything," she ordered.

Søren pulled another chair out and sat a foot across from her.

"The first thing I'll tell you is that my marriage, such as it was, should never concern or trouble you. It's simply a fact of my past. I have no reason to hide it and several good reasons to reveal it. This is what I wanted to tell you."

Eleanor didn't have to ask what reasons he meant. Søren telling the church he'd been married to an adult woman would be like holding up a big sign that said I'm a Red-blooded Straight Male. As suspicious as people were of the Catholic clergy these days, she couldn't blame him for wanting to spill those particular beans.

"My marriage will be common knowledge in time, and I wanted you to hear about it from me and no one else."

"Go on."

"It's a long and fairly sordid story, so forgive me for giving you the bowdlerized version. My best friend in school was half French. His parents had died in an accident outside Paris when he was fourteen. He came to Maine to live with his grandparents. They sent him to the school I attended—a Jesuit boarding school. His older sister, Marie-Laure, was a ballet dancer in Paris. Brother and sister missed each other terribly. Neither of them had any money between them. She couldn't come to America. He couldn't go live in Paris again.

This might come as a shock to you, but my father had a great deal of money."

"Shocked. Stunned. Flabbergasted."

"I had a sizable trust fund I'd inherit when I married. I wanted my friend to be able to see his sister again. She wanted to live in America. Marrying her meant I would receive my trust fund, which I planned to give to them. Money and citizenship—I thought that would be enough for her. Everyone would win."

"What happened?"

Søren's lips formed a tight line. A shadow passed over his eyes.

"Nobody won. Money and American citizenship weren't enough for her. I had warned Marie-Laure in advance that ours would be a marriage in name only. I had no romantic interest in her whatsoever."

"Why not?"

Søren sighed and gave a low mirthless laugh.

"Let's save that answer for another time. Suffice it to say she wasn't my type. And I won't speak ill of the dead."

"She's dead?"

"She is. She said she was in love with me. I don't think she was. I think she considered my lack of interest in her a challenge. She pursued me obsessively and failed in her pursuit. She saw me kiss someone else and ran away in anger. She tripped and fell and died. Her brother thinks she committed suicide. I don't believe she had it in her to destroy herself. She loved herself far too much. Either way, she was gone, and I was a widower mere weeks after marrying. Her brother took her body back to Paris to bury her near their parents and never returned to school. I traveled Europe the summer of my eighteenth year and in the autumn I started seminary. That is the story—as much of it as I can tell you tonight."

Eleanor leaned into her hands and breathed. She had no idea how to react to this news.

"So you know how to waltz because of her?"

"I tried to distract her from her painful attempts at seducing me by asking her about ballet, about dance, about anything that interested her."

"You never had sex with her?"

"The marriage was unconsummated."

"Your own wife."

"I barely knew her when we married. And she was the sister of my closest friend."

"Still, it was legal Catholic fucking. And you said she was beautiful, right?"

"When I realized how strong her feelings were for me, I considered it. I didn't want to, but she was my wife for better or worse. I felt duty bound to make her happy. I failed. And it's for the best. I'm not the sort of person who can engage in sex simply to pass the time. The one person I was intimate with as a teenager loved me deeply and made sacrifices to be with me. I exact a certain toll on a person."

"I'm almost eighteen, Søren. You got married at eighteen. Stop acting like I'm too young for you."

"My reticence has little to do with your age and everything to do with me being a priest who has no desire to drag you into a relationship that will dangerously complicate your life."

"I want you so much."

"Eleanor, I could barely breathe watching you walk down the aisle today. Do you know how much it hurt knowing you will never walk down that aisle to me?"

Tears burned her eyes.

"It hurt me, too," she confessed, and blinked the tears away.

He took her chin in his hand and tilted her face up to meet

his eyes. When she looked in them she saw no mercy, no compassion, no love, no kindness—only the cold, bitter truth.

"Little One, to be with me is to hurt."

"To be without you would hurt more. It did hurt more. You won't scare me off. I'm not afraid of you."

He released her chin and Eleanor took a deep breath. Learning the truth about Søren was like fighting the Hydra. Every question he answered spawned three more questions. The more she learned the less she understood, the harder she had to fight.

"I'll let you get back to your cleaning." He stood up and Eleanor, still sitting, reached for his hand.

"Don't go," she said. "Please. We don't have to talk. Stay a while. It's been so long and I missed you so much...."

He threaded his fingers through her hair and she rested her head against his stomach.

"I missed you, too. Every day. But I can't stay, Little One." He caressed the back of her neck. "I have company."

She turned her face up to him and tried to smile.

"Hot date waiting for you?"

"He wishes."

"Don't we all?"

"We'll talk again soon. Once I've sobered up and recovered enough self-control to be alone in a room with you without thinking the things I'm thinking."

"Do they involve us breaking the gift table?"

"It never stood a chance."

Eleanor heaved a melodramatic sigh and stood on top of a chair.

"What are you doing, Eleanor?"

"I wanted to look down on you. This works." She slid her hands over his broad back and wrapped her arms around him. She rested her chin against his shoulder and closed her eyes.

"You owe me this," she said. "You dumped me. Now you owe me."

"I'll make it up to you in time," he promised. His arms tightened around her, tight enough she knew he meant it.

She started to release him, but he wouldn't let her go. Smiling, she clung to him even harder, relishing the feel of his large, strong hands on her back and his arms holding her so close to him not even God could slide between the cracks. Her body temperature spiked from the heat of him against her. A thousand dark and beautiful images flashed through her mind—him pressing her against the wall, capturing her mouth in a kiss, clothes coming off seemingly of their own will and him on top of her, inside her, claiming her as his own all night long.

"Why are you a priest?" She dug her hands in the back of his hair. Such soft hair and pale as spun gold.

"I love being a priest. It's who I am. And it's who I am because God wants me to be a priest."

"Are you sure?"

"If I had any doubt in my mind, do you think you'd still be a virgin?"

"Who said I was?"

Søren pulled back long enough to give her a dirty look.

"Oh, stop glaring and hug me, Blondie."

Laughing, he pulled her close again.

"You promised me everything," she whispered.

"And I will keep my promise. But not yet."

"Don't worry about it. I told you I can wait, and I'll wait. I know this is a big deal."

"What you want from me, what we want from each other… it's forbidden, Little One. If I'm caught, if we're caught…."

The warning tone in his voice gave her a chill.

"How bad would it be?" she asked.

"Best-case scenario? A transfer, therapy, public ridicule, private ridicule. Worst-case scenario? Laicization. Most people would consider me a sexual predator if you and I were found to be involved."

"That's ridiculous. I'm the one trying to get you into bed. And I'm seventeen. I can donate blood and get the death penalty if I murder someone, but I'm not allowed to have sex at seventeen? Jesus, it's my body," she said. "Mine, not theirs. And it's your body. Why do they get to tell us what we can do with our bodies?"

"Eleanor, are you trying to use logic on Catholics?"

She tried to laugh but the sound didn't come out quite right.

"I think someone smart once said that was a pointless strategy." She smiled at him.

"The whole world is a courtroom. And everyone loves to play judge, jury and executioner. A Catholic priest sexually involved with a teenage member of his congregation? I will be crucified. I've seen this happen over and over again. And the only people who won't hate me will be the people who hate you instead."

"Is this my fault?" she asked, afraid of the answer. She had pursued him, hadn't she?

"No. It's destiny. Or doom, perhaps. Hard to tell the difference sometimes."

"Maybe they're the same thing."

"Perhaps they are." He looked into her eyes and she saw her doom and destiny waiting in them. One kiss. Surely one kiss wouldn't kill them. She leaned in. She knew Søren would let her kiss him. She knew he would kiss her back.

But then she heard something. Whistling. Somewhere in the building someone whistled. She'd heard the song before but couldn't name it or place it. Hurriedly she pulled back from the embrace and put two feet between her and Søren.

"I'm changing my answer," Søren said. "It's his fault."

"Who is that?" she whispered in a panic. Søren did something she'd never dreamed she'd see him do. He rolled his eyes.

"*'La Marseillaise'*—the French national anthem."

"Who's in the building?"

Søren sighed heavily and rubbed his forehead.

"I suppose tonight's as good a night as any," Søren said.

"For what?"

"For you to meet the in-law."

18

Eleanor

THE WHISTLING SOUND GREW CLOSER. SØREN TOOK her hand in his.

"Eleanor, allow me to apologize in advance."

"Apologize? For what?"

"For him."

"Who? *Moi?*" asked the man who strolled through the nearest door and right up to them. "I hope I'm interrupting something."

Eleanor's eyes widened at the sight of the man.

"I love that reaction." He pointed at Eleanor's face. "That is the 'you didn't tell me how pretty he was' look, *oui?*"

"Didn't I almost punch you on a set of stairs once?" she asked him.

"You broke into my house. What do you have to say for yourself?"

"You have Eddie Vedder hair," Eleanor said, which was the only thing she had to say for herself. She was still trying to recover from the shock of the man. He wore the most amazing suit she'd ever seen in her life. Black trousers, riding boots, long black jacket, black-and-silver embroidered vest. He had dark shoulder-length hair and a face that belonged on a male model. And to make matters even worse, he was French. So this was the brother-in-law? The best friend? The Kingsley?

He picked up her hand as if to kiss the back of it, but at the last second he raised her fingertips to his nose and sniffed them. She pulled her hand back.

"So this is *elle?*"

"This is she. Eleanor, this is Kingsley. Kingsley, Eleanor. Now please go back to the rectory, Kingsley, before Eleanor starts liking you."

"Liking me more than you, you mean. Too late. Isn't it?"

"You are seriously French," she said.

"Would you like to see how French I am?" He imposed himself between her and Søren and stared down at her with the most seductive expression she'd ever seen on the face of a man with all his clothes on.

"Kingsley, please," Søren said.

"I'm not talking to you. I'm talking to her."

Kingsley stepped even closer.

"How old are you?" he asked her.

"Seventeen. How old are you?"

"Thirty. Is your hymen intact?"

Eleanor stood up straighter.

"Is your brain intact?"

"I ask for a reason." He shook his finger in her face to hush her. "I fucked a virgin last week. I didn't mean to."

"What happened? You trip and fall into her hymen?"

"You jest, but do you know how hard it is to get blood off raw silk upholstery?" Kingsley asked, sounding positively perturbed. "She could have told me before I fucked her. I would have put a towel down first. But *c'est la guerre.* What's the etiquette for accidentally fucking a virgin? Should I send flowers? If I fucked you and broke your hymen, what would you want from me after?"

"Hair of the dog that bit me?" Eleanor suggested her father's favorite hangover cure. "Fuck me again?"

Kingsley looked her up and down. He seemed to like what he saw.

"Would you like to play a round of Justine and the naughty monk with me?"

"Never heard of it."

"I swear I will have you arrested," Søren said to Kingsley. He sounded stern but Eleanor saw amusement in his eyes.

"Have you ever read *Justine* by Le Marquis de Sade? Wonderful book. Little twelve-year-old Justine runs away to a monastery and the monks rape her and subject her to orgies and beatings over and over again. So that's how you play the game. Shall we?"

"How do we know who wins?"

"Whoever has lost the least blood by the end of the game wins."

"Sounds fun," Eleanor said. "I'll play the monk. You play Justine."

"Why, Kingsley," Søren said in a taunting tone, "it's like she knows you already."

Kingsley only gazed at her a moment and she sensed him taking stock of her. The smile left his face; the amusement disappeared from his eyes. In a warning tone, the man addressed Søren.

"You are asking for so much trouble with this one, *mon ami*."

"He didn't ask for trouble," Eleanor interjected. "I offered."

Kingsley nodded his approval.

"You weren't exaggerating," he said to Søren.

Søren put his mouth near Kingsley's ear.

"I told you so," Søren said in a stage whisper.

"Can I have her?" Kingsley asked. Søren replied something in French, something that made Kingsley grin even more broadly.

"What did he say?" she asked Kingsley.

"He said, 'wait your turn.'"

She glared at Søren, who only shrugged as if Kingsley had lied to her. She knew he hadn't.

"She doesn't like my translation."

"She should learn French," Søren said. Kingsley nodded his agreement.

"Hello!" Eleanor waved her hands. "I'm still here. I can hear you both talking about me. And you, I can see you giggling." She stabbed the center of Søren's chest with her finger.

He gave her an affronted look.

"Priests don't giggle."

"What are you looking at?" she demanded of Kingsley, who seemed to be undressing her with his eyes.

"She's spirited, this one," Kingsley said to Søren.

"Unholy spirited," Søren agreed.

Kingsley turned his attention back to her.

"Why do you have your clothes on?"

"Was I supposed to take them off?"

"I've never heard a stupider question in my life," he said with a very French, very disgusted sigh. "You weren't supposed to have them on to start with."

"I get it," Eleanor said to Kingsley. "I do. You're Prince Charming if Prince Charming wasn't charming."

"And wasn't a prince but a king." Kingsley raked her body with his eyes. She might have been embarrassed by his nakedly hungry stare but he had a French accent, Eddie Vedder hair and the power to annoy Søren. The man got a free pass to make a pass.

"I could lose my watch inside you," Kingsley finally said to her.

"And good night." Søren grabbed the Frenchman by the back of the neck. Kingsley shivered as if the viselike grip Søren put on him seemed to have the opposite effect of the one Søren intended. "I can't take you anywhere. Go back to the rectory. I will be there soon."

"I have to go?"

"He really doesn't," Eleanor said.

"He really does." Søren released Kingsley, who gave her an apologetic smile.

"*Je suis désolé, ma belle.* I must leave you. I will be inside the priest's rectory tonight if you need me, want me or desire me. You know where to find me."

"In his rectory."

"Firmly ensconced. If I'm not there, I'll be inside a bottle of Syrah. I'm getting the priest very drunk tonight."

"I think he's already there," Eleanor said. She'd never seen Søren so playful before. They should get him drunk more often.

"Merely warming up." Kingsley took her hand, and this time he kissed the back of it instead of sniffing her fingertips. "Rest assured I leave you entirely against my will and with the firmest of convictions that we shall meet again someday."

"Nice to meet you," she said, fairly certain that *nice* was the least correct word she could have used in that sentence.

"And a pleasure to meet you at last," he said. "I look forward to you making the acquaintance of my ceiling."

He turned on his booted heel and, whistling the French national anthem, again headed to the door.

"I want to be his best friend." She grinned broadly at Kingsley's retreating back.

"Don't let your guard down yet. He's not finished," Søren said.

Søren was right. At the door Kingsley turned on his boot heel and strode back to her. He looked down into her eyes. A moment before he'd worn the air of a dashing rogue like something out of a romance novel. No more. Now he seemed dangerously sober to her.

"A word of warning." Kingsley looked at her and only her. "Your shepherd is a wolf. You will learn that eventually and you will learn it the way I learned it."

"How?"

"The hard way."

"Kingsley, that's enough." Søren wasn't joking anymore. Neither was Kingsley.

"Tell her what you are, *mon ami*," Kingsley said to Søren, his eyes never leaving her face.

"You've either had too much to drink tonight, or not enough."

Kingsley smiled broadly, but Eleanor saw no amusement in his eyes.

"Never enough." He bowed his head at her, turned on his heel again and left the room, this time without whistling. As he walked away she heard the sound of his military-style boots echoing off the floor.

Søren exhaled as if he'd been holding his breath for the entire exchange.

"Eleanor, allow me to finish apologizing—"

"What did he mean my shepherd is a wolf?" She turned her eyes to Søren. He didn't blink, blush, laugh or demure. But he didn't answer the question, either.

"The wolf eats the sheep," she said. "Should we, the sheep of Sacred Heart, be scared of you?"

"No."

"No?"

"I only eat other wolves."

"That's a comfort, I guess."

"It shouldn't be," he said.

"Why not?"

Søren gave her a look so dangerously hungry she'd almost describe it as wolfish.

"Because, my Little One, you aren't a sheep."

After that, Søren bid her the most perfunctory of goodbyes. She didn't blame him for leaving so abruptly. If that Kingsley person were in her house, she wouldn't want to leave him unsupervised, either. No telling what, or whom, he would get into. So that was the brother of Søren's dead wife? She had to sit down again while the reality of Søren's revelations sunk in. It didn't matter really, did it? Didn't matter that he'd been married once twelve years ago? No, it didn't. The dead wife was a dead issue. Buried. Gone. Eleanor shoved her out of her mind and resolved never to think of her again.

But Kingsley—now, he interested her. Søren had admitted to jealousy over her and that Lachlan guy getting to third base. But Kingsley had stood six inches in front of her and joked about beating her, raping her, fucking her, losing his watch inside her, which she didn't even understand.... Oh, fuck. Yes, she did.

Ow.

Kingsley had eye-fucked her, word-fucked her, teased and taunted her, and all the while Søren had stood by doing nothing except trying not to laugh.

And what had Kingsley meant when he called Søren a

wolf? What had Søren meant when he admitted to being one? Too many questions. Not enough answers.

Eleanor finished cleaning up. It didn't take long, as Diane and James had a small wedding with fewer than a hundred guests. They couldn't afford much more than that, but neither of them seemed to mind. They'd both smiled so much today Eleanor's cheeks had sympathy pains. It had caused some controversy when Søren had hired twenty-five-year-old Diane. She was black, for starters, and Wakefield was a lily-white town. Black and very pretty, which also raised eyebrows. Even more shocking, she'd been divorced. A divorced woman working for a Catholic priest. Søren had helped her get her first marriage annulled so she and James could marry in the church.

If only all priests were as rational and open-minded as Søren. Never once in his year and a half at Sacred Heart had she heard him give a homily condemning homosexuality, premarital sex or abortion. Instead he focused his attention on social justice issues—feeding the hungry, helping the needy, visiting the sick and the dying and those in prison. He was a good priest, the best priest. No matter what his secrets, no matter that he desired her as much as she desired him, he was still the best priest on earth.

A little after 3:00 a.m. Eleanor finally made it home. Mom had no doubt been in bed asleep for hours. Alone in her room, Eleanor stripped out of her shoes and jeans. In her T-shirt and panties she sat on her bed, the radio tuned to the classical station. She wanted to sleep, needed to sleep, but her mind wouldn't let her. She wanted to talk to someone, but there was no one to talk to. No one but God. Might as well give it a go.

When Søren had been taking her through the Spiritual Exercises, he'd taught her a specifically Jesuit way of praying. Søren said most people couldn't concentrate during silent prayer. The mind wandered here and there. Speaking prayers out loud helped with the focus. But Jesuits didn't stop there. One technique, Søren told her, involved standing before an image of God or Christ and speaking the prayer aloud to it. Some Jesuits even sat empty chairs in front of them and spoke to the chair as if God sat there.

"And this really helps them get through to God?" Eleanor had asked with more than the usual level of skepticism.

"No. It helps God get through to us. To quote my grandfather's namesake, Søren Kierkegaard, 'Prayer does not change God, but it changes him who prays.' All these tricks and techniques are for our benefit, not God's. God's a parent. Call Him, send Him a letter, go to His house, it doesn't matter how you reach out to Him, He wants to hear from His children."

Tonight Eleanor wanted to hear from God. She didn't expect an answer, but those few minutes she'd spent in Søren's arms had been like a gift. The embrace, the words of comfort, they'd come from nowhere. She hadn't asked for them or expected them. When given a gift, she'd been taught to say thank you. She didn't know who to thank for the gift of comfort she'd received today so she thought she'd give thanking God a try. She put a chair in the middle of her room and sat on the edge of her bed staring at it.

"I feel like an idiot," she said to the empty room.

The empty room didn't answer.

"Something's not right here. Søren's getting drunk tonight with the second-hottest guy on the planet, and I'm home alone praying. I think we accidentally switched our to-do lists."

Still silence.

"Tough crowd," she said and pulled a pillow over her lap, squeezing it for comfort.

She considered giving up and crashing, but her heart hadn't stopped racing since the moment she'd stepped foot onto that rose-petal–strewn carpet today. And today, after a year of ignoring each other to the point of pain, she and Søren had finally had a real conversation. She'd been living with a question mark for a year now wondering what, if anything, would happen with Søren. And tonight with a hug and a few words he'd proved himself worthy of her devotion again. She couldn't loiter in limbo anymore. She had to make a decision.

"Look," she said, once more addressing the nobody in the chair, "I know he's a good priest. Fuck that, he's an amazing priest. Have you seen how many people show up at church now? It's like twice as many as when Father Greg was here. And you and I both know it's not just because he's pretty. Although he is pretty. God damn, is he pretty. I mean…You damn."

She glanced up at the ceiling. "Sorry," she mouthed.

"Anyway, thank You for tonight."

She took a deep breath.

"So he says You want him to be a priest. He says he didn't really feel like himself until he became a priest. I can't ask him to give that up. Not for me or anyone else. I can't. I won't." She felt immediately better once she'd made that part of her decision. She loved him and he was a priest. She wouldn't ask him to change for her. What if it was the priest in him who cared for her? If he left the priesthood for her, maybe he wouldn't care about her anymore?

"About the priesthood thing…be straight with me here. Celibacy? You and I both know it's made-up bullshit, right? We Catholics want to be special, want to be different. God forbid we're too much like Protestants with their married pastors. The entire church harps constantly on how important the Catholic family is, Catholic marriage, Catholic babies and then we don't let our own priests have Catholic marriages, Catholic families? We're making it up. There's nothing in the Bible about this, right? I've read it. You've seen me." She held up the red leather Bible. For the past year she'd immersed herself in the Bible, reading from it every night. She zoned out through a lot of the begetting, but she'd more or less conquered a big chunk of the Old Testament and had worked her way through all the Gospels.

"Jesus didn't say anything about how people shouldn't get married or why it's better to be celibate. Yeah, there's a lot of stuff in there about not fornicating, but there's also a lot of stuff in there about not eating shellfish or having poly-blend fibers. Seriously? What's Your problem with spandex?"

She raised her hands in surrender.

"I know, I know. It's not You. This was our baggage and we put Your name on it and we blamed You. Our bad. Søren said to treat the Bible not as a work of history or a science textbook and to treat it instead like Communion. Communion is a spiritual meal, not a physical meal. So the Bible's the same thing—it feeds our soul. It's not a how-to manual."

Eleanor realized she'd gotten off topic. She'd never talked to a chair before and rather enjoyed having a captive audience. She should do this more often. Maybe she'd stick a real person in the chair next time. She could gag him and get the same sort of undivided attention.

"So to my point, God. I have one. I love Søren. I love him, and I'm in love with him. I love everything about him, even the stuff I don't know about him. He's proved to me that he's a good person no matter what it is that he's scared to tell me. I don't care if he's a wolf. He says I'm not a sheep, which is either a compliment or a threat. Both, probably."

As soon as she said "both" she knew that was the right answer.

"In Hebrews...I think. I think it's Hebrews, it says that 'faith is the assurance of things hoped for, a conviction of things not seen.' Something like that. So I'm saying now that I have faith in Søren. And he has faith in You. It's the best I can give You right now so I hope it's enough. I know he has secrets, stuff he's not ready or willing to tell me. It's okay. I still believe in him. He believed in me, so the least I can do is return the favor, right?"

Eleanor took another deep breath as she came to the conclusion of her rambling, barely coherent prayer.

"So here's the deal. I promise that if You let me have him, even in a small way, if You let us be together like we want to be…" She decided to not go into excruciating detail about exactly how she wanted to be with him. Surely God, if He existed, was well aware of the sexual fantasies she entertained on a nightly basis about Søren. "If You do that, let us be together, then I promise You I will never let him leave the priesthood for me. I don't need to get married. I don't need to have kids. I don't even need him. But please, God, let us be together."

The words hurt coming out. And because they hurt she knew she meant them.

In her mind she wore a wedding dress—white and made of silk—and held two pairs of baby shoes in the palm of her hand. She kissed the toes of the tiny shoes and sat them gently inside a large wooden trunk. Then she took off the wedding dress and carefully folded it, laying it over the baby shoes. She closed the trunk and locked it with a key. With all her might she tossed the key into the sky, flinging it a thousand miles away so it landed into the center of the ocean and sunk into the black waters of night. And on the off chance someone found that key and brought it back to her, she doused the trunk with gasoline, struck a match, set it on fire and watched it burn.

The tears came in silent waves as inside the privacy of her own mind, she burned her dreams to ashes. What would rise from those ashes she didn't know—she only knew something would be born from them, something she'd never seen before.

A new dream. A better dream.

A wind rustled the ashes at her feet. She opened her eyes and stared again at the empty chair.

"Deal?" she asked God. "Let's shake on it."

She held out her hand as a whistle blasted and a train barreled past her house, shaking the walls, the floors, the ceilings, everything to the very foundation.

Eleanor glanced at the clock—3:26 a.m. She stared at the clock in confusion. For seventeen years that train had rattled by the house at the same time every time—12:59, 6:16, 3:38, and 7:02. Never in all the years she'd lived in this house had the train rattled by this late at night.

Never once. Never ever.

Turning back to the chair she lowered her hand.

"Okay, then," she said. "It's a deal."

19

Eleanor

FOR THE THIRD TIME IN TWO HOURS, ELEANOR REfilled her bucket with cold water and poured in a cup of wood soap. She lugged the heavy bucket back to the sanctuary and sat it on the floor next to the center section of pews. For the past three weeks, she'd been washing the woodwork in the church in an attempt to pay Sacred Heart back for her legal fees. Maybe her dad was right. Turning tricks would be much a much easier way to make money.

As she washed the wood on her hands and knees, she let herself fantasize about her future. Søren had ordered her to apply to five colleges and she had. Now she couldn't stop dreaming of a life at NYU. She'd been in love with the Village and the NYU buildings since she'd first seen them as a little girl walking through the city with her grandparents. Still she knew it was a waste of a dream. She had good grades but not good enough to get a scholarship. Student loans would only cover a fraction of what she'd need to pay for NYU.

Maybe she could find a hot dean or something and trade her body for tuition money.

Eleanor couldn't believe how hot it was in the sanctuary. Sweat beaded on her forehead and spilled onto the floor. She'd already soaked through her shirt.

For another hour she washed the pews until she could hardly see straight. Her mascara burned her eyes. What the hell was going on?

Eleanor dragged herself off the floor and stretched her back. She shouldn't be this hot. She'd changed into a sleeveless T-shirt, her cutoff denim shorts, and other than a pair of kneepads, she didn't have anything else on except for sneakers. She walked over to the wall and squatted down by the vent. Boiling hot air poured from it into the sanctuary.

That wasn't good. Was the heat broken? She stepped out into the foyer and found the heating controls. Someone had jacked up the temperature to ninety degrees. Ninety. Fucking. Degrees.

Her priest was a dead man.

She stalked down the hall to Søren's office. Luckily they were alone in the church this fine Thursday evening so she could kill him without anyone trying to stop her.

She found him in his office sipping from a dainty teacup.

"Are you some kind of sadist?" she demanded.

He made a notation onto a piece of paper.

"Yes."

"You turned the heat up in the sanctuary?"

"I didn't want you getting chilly."

"You turned it up to ninety."

Søren looked up from his notes.

"Did I? My apologies."

"That was the least sincere apology in the history of the universe."

"Possibly."

"I'm working my ass off in the sanctuary scrubbing two hundreds years of farts off the pews and you're sitting in your seventy-degree office drinking tea and writing homilies. It's hot as Satan's balls in there, and I'm sweating like a whore in church. Do you have anything to say to that?"

Eleanor crossed her arms over her chest and stared daggers into the office.

Søren looked her up and down before turning his attention back to his Bible.

"I like the kneepads."

"I hate you."

"Forty-two," he said, as he pulled a file folder from his desk drawer.

"Forty-two what?"

"I've been keeping track of how many times you've declared your hatred of me. That was forty-two." He opened the file folder and scanned something inside. "No, forty-three."

He make a tick mark on the page.

"Forty-four. I hate you. Why the fuck did you turn the heat up to ninety?"

"You stole five cars. Instead of going into prison or juvenile detention, you endured nothing more than volunteer work. Now that you are paying back your legal fees, which were not inconsiderable, perhaps you need to suffer more in your service. It's good for the soul."

"Suffering is good for the soul? You're sitting in your cute little office drinking your gross-ass tea that smells like bacon—"

"It's Lapsang souchong."

"It's disgusting. You're drinking disgusting tea and writing homilies in your room-temperature office while I'm dying in there. I don't see you suffering."

"I have suffered. My suffering has ended."

"Did you find Jesus?"

"No, I found you." Søren closed his file folder and slipped it back into the drawer. He sipped his tea again, sat the cup down and returned to his work.

Eleanor pressed her hand into her fluttering stomach.

"How would you feel if I stood on top of your desk and screamed my head off?" she asked.

"To be perfectly honest, I'm surprised you haven't done it already."

To be perfectly honest, it surprised her, too.

"Now that I've suffered, can I turn the heat back down to a low boil? More first circle of hell than eighth circle?"

"If you insist. But while cleaning the pews, I want you to think about your sins."

"I will. Especially the ones I plan on committing with you someday."

"Good girl."

Eleanor started to turn around, but Søren said her name.

"Yes, your blondness. What?"

"Did you mail off all your applications?"

"I did as ordered, Your Majesty."

"Are you going to tell me where you applied?"

"University of None Ya. University of Mind Your Own. University of Not-tellin'. Big Secret College. And St. Stay-out-of-it Technical College."

"Interesting choices."

"The University of Not-tellin' is my safety school."

"Is there any particular reason you're being so secretive?"

"You got me out of going to prison. You have secret ninjas everywhere who get stuff done for you. I don't want you making phone calls on my behalf trying to pull strings for me."

"I would never do such a thing."

"Liar."

Eleanor loitered in his doorway for the sole purpose of cooling off in the draft. That and staring at Søren, who'd actually stepped foot into Sacred Heart tonight without his collar on. Dual purpose, then.

"Eleanor?"

"What?"

"You're staring at me."

"You're gorgeous. Of course I'm staring. How's the dissertation going?"

"Can't we discuss more pleasant topics? Like my summers spent in leper colonies?"

"Big baby."

"Go back to work."

"Yes, Father Stearns."

"I'd prefer you didn't call me that," he said.

"How about Mother Stearns?"

"How about *sir?*"

He raised an eyebrow at her. Eleanor's stomach tightened in a surprisingly pleasant way.

"Yes, sir," she whispered.

Søren gave her a look that set her fingers to tingling.

"Good girl. Now shoo. I don't have time for distractions today—even pleasant ones."

She left him in his office and headed toward the sanctuary. A shadow flickered at the end of the hallway, a shadow in the shape of a person. Had someone been here the whole time listening to her and Søren? In a panic Eleanor raced through the conversation in her mind. Did they say anything that could get them into trouble? Søren flirtatiously complimented her on her kneepads. That wasn't good but could be explained away as sarcasm. She told him his Lapsang souchong was disgusting, which it was. No one could argue with that.

Oh, fuck. She'd asked him why he no longer suffered. *Because I found you....*

Fuck.

Eleanor half walked, half ran down the hall toward the shadow. But when she reached the end, she saw no one and nothing. Being in love with a priest had made her paranoid. Who would give a damn about her enough to follow her around anyway? No one.

She thought about telling Søren she'd seen a shadow if only for the excuse to talk to him again. Through his office door, she heard his phone ring, heard him answer it. He spoke too quietly for her to make out the words, however, so she returned to the sanctuary.

Eleanor opened the doors and put the stoppers down in the hope that cooler air would start to circulate.

She found her bucket again and got on her knees as she dipped the rag into the pine-scented water. She'd only done about two square feet of cleaning when she heard footsteps echoing off the floor. Søren had apparently not tortured her enough for the day. Fine. Round two.

"If you come in here I'm going to make you clean," she said, glaring at him. She expected a smile or a laugh but no. Søren wore the strangest expression on his face.

He sat down in the pew behind her and gazed upon the crucifix behind the altar.

"Søren?" Eleanor knelt backward on the pew in front of him. "What's wrong?"

"Nothing's wrong. My father is dead."

Eleanor's hands went numb.

"Oh, my God. What happened?"

Søren shook his head. "I don't know. My sister Elizabeth is coming here tonight to talk."

"Are you okay?" She wanted to take his hand but although he sat only inches from her, he seemed too far away to reach.

"I am..." He paused for a long time. "I am *ashamed* of how happy I am that man is dead."

Eleanor didn't know what to say so she said the only thing she hadn't said to him yet.

"I love you."

Søren tore his gaze from the crucifix to her.

"Thank you," he said. "I needed to hear that."

Thank you? Better than "no, you don't," but not quite as good as "I love you, too." Still, she was glad she'd said something right for once.

"There is a visitation Saturday, the funeral on Sunday. You'll come with me, won't you?"

"I'll come with you?" she repeated, not sure she'd heard him correctly.

"Can you? Please?"

Søren sounded so humble with his quiet "please" that she would have handed him her own heart if he'd asked for it.

"I will. Yes. Definitely."

"Good. We'll leave tomorrow evening once you're out of school. Kingsley can send a car. Pack for two nights."

"Where are we going?"

"New Hampshire, to my father's house."

"That's not going to seem sort of suspicious? A priest bringing a date to the funeral?"

"My youngest sister is about your age. I'm sure she'll come. You can stay with her."

"Sure. Of course." Eleanor's head spun. She and Søren were going away to New Hampshire for the entire weekend. He wanted her to meet his little sister and attend his father's funeral with him. When she woke up this morning she hadn't suspected her entire life would change by the end of the day.

Apparently God didn't like to give out any warnings on that sort of thing.

"You can go home. You need to pack. And I need to make some phone calls."

"Can I do anything for you? Help with anything?"

"You help me by existing. And I promise, I'm fine. In some shock, but I assure you, this is good news."

If anyone else had heard him call his father's death "good news" they might have balked. But Eleanor wouldn't mind if her own father fell off the face of the earth. She could hardly blame Søren.

"So what do we do?"

"Come by the rectory tomorrow. We'll leave from there."

"You mean I'm allowed in the rectory tomorrow?"

"Eleanor, the reason I made you stay away from me for so long is so you could grow up and be ready for the things I need to tell you. Are you ready now?"

"I've been ready for you since the day we met."

Søren took her hand in his and pressed the back of it first to his heart and then to his naked throat, before kissing her knuckles.

A man had died.

She smiled all the way home.

Eleanor packed that night as ordered. She'd been to a few funerals in her day. Grandparents, one random great-uncle she didn't remember. She'd gone with Jordan to her aunt's funeral. But this was different. She had no right, no business going to Søren's father's funeral. She couldn't begin to think of a single rational way to explain her presence at her priest's dad's house. She would have to get creative.

First of all, she had to think of a way to explain her absence to her mother. Easy enough. One phone call to her friend Jordan took care of it. She told her mother she'd be accompanying Jordan on her college visits this weekend. Done.

As for everyone else? She'd have to wing it.

School dragged by the next day. She couldn't think about anything but the prospect of being in a car for four straight hours with Søren. In a car for four straight hours? Eleanor stopped drinking water at noon. Last thing she wanted to do was interrupt Søren to tell him she had to pee.

She stopped at her house after school and picked up her duffel bag. She left her mother a note reminding her she'd be gone all weekend. Hopefully she'd be able to use a phone at the house in New Hampshire to call her mother on Saturday night. As long as she checked in once during the weekend, her mother wouldn't get suspicious. Then again, it wasn't like her mother gave a damn what she did anymore.

As she neared the church Eleanor realized it might raise a few eyebrows if someone saw her trekking over to the rectory, overnight bag slung across her back. She walked around the block and found a path to the rectory through a back driveway. She'd have to remember this trick. If life proceeded as she wanted it to, this wouldn't be her last time sneaking over to Søren's.

Outside the house she paused. To knock or not to knock… While she debated those choices, she studied the house. She'd always loved the rectory at Sacred Heart. A beautiful Gothic cottage, the rectory had been around even longer than the church. She'd heard the church had practically arm-wrestled with the original owners to get the land and the house. She didn't blame them. As a little girl she'd thought of the house as magical, enchanted. It looked like the houses in her fairy-tale books—the steeply pitched roof, the gable dormer windows, the stone chimney, the cobblestone path, the trees that encircled it, hiding it from prying eyes.

It still enchanted her now, although for different reasons. No longer did she see the two-story cottage as something from a fairy tale. It had taken on much more potent significance. Søren lived in this house. He ate here, drank here, dressed here, bathed here and slept here. Someday, she knew, she would sleep here, too.

She knocked on the door.

Søren opened it without a word. He didn't speak to her, because he had a phone held to his ear.

"Leaving now," he said into the phone. "It's all saber rattling. They're trying to scare you. I know this trick. Don't fall for it."

A pause followed and in that pause Søren took her duffel bag off her shoulder and sat it on the kitchen table. She took comfort in how casually he'd welcomed her into his home, acting as if she'd been here a thousand times before. She checked out the kitchen while she waited for him to get off the phone. Pretty kitchen, clean and quaint and homey, like something out of a movie that takes place in turn-of-the-century New England. They would fuck in this kitchen someday. On that very table.

"Have you spoken to Claire?" he asked the person on the other end. Another pause, and then... "You know more about teenage girls than I do," he said and winked at Eleanor, who had to cover her mouth not to laugh. "It's fine. I'll talk to her. You have enough on your mind."

The hint of a smile faded from his face.

"Take heart," Søren said. "We'll talk more tomorrow."

Søren hung up the phone.

"Girlfriend?" she asked.

"That was my sister Elizabeth. Half sister. You'll meet her at some point this weekend."

"How many brothers and sisters do you have? And why are you dressed like that?"

"I have three sisters," he said, sitting on the kitchen table. "And this is a suit. Do you not approve?"

"You look amazing. I didn't expect you in, like, a business suit." She grabbed the lapels of his jacket as she pretended to examine his neck. "No collar. Weird. No tie. Even weirder."

"I have the tie. I haven't put it on yet."

"Leave it off. You look good in normal-person clothes."

"Thank you. I am attempting to stay incognito this weekend. A priest at a funeral and everyone wants to talk about God and the afterlife with you."

"Can't imagine why they'd think a priest would want to talk about God."

"Ridiculous, isn't it?" He grinned at her. "Car's on the way. Would you like to see the house?"

"No."

"No?"

"Well, yes. I do. But I don't."

"Why not?"

"I'm not ready to know that my fantasy of your bedroom doesn't match the reality. I'm guessing there's no hot tub in there."

She expected Søren to laugh but instead he took her by the wrist and pulled her closer to him. He put his hands on each side of her neck and caressed her jawline with his thumbs.

"Little One, there is something you'll have to understand. Your fantasies about us and the reality will not match."

She raised her chin.

"You don't know what I fantasize about. How do you know?"

He dropped a kiss on her forehead and she closed her eyes, relishing the touch of his lips on her skin.

"A fair point," he said, brushing her hair off her shoulder. Outside the house she heard an engine. "Our chariot awaits us."

Eleanor heard a car door open and close. Søren walked into the next room and came back with a small suitcase and a black garment bag over his shoulder. Meanwhile she had an army green duffel bag with a large yellow pin on it that read Jesus Loves You. Everyone Else Thinks You're an Asshole.

Søren started to pick up her duffel bag, but she took it from him. He had enough burdens to bear this weekend. She could carry her own damn luggage.

Outside in the back of the rectory sat a black BMW M3.

"Nice," she said, running her fingers over the still warm hood. A woman got out of the driver's seat and shut the door behind her.

"Sam?" Søren asked, raising an eyebrow at the driver—an incredibly beautiful woman with a shaggy pixie cut wearing a thick leather jacket and black jeans.

"This is as understated as Kingsley gets and you know it."

"Eleanor, this is Sam—Kingsley's second-in-command."

"Oh, I'm so sorry," Eleanor said.

"You and me both, beautiful," Sam said with a wink. She held out the keys to Søren.

"She's the driver," Søren said.

Sam looked at Eleanor.

"It's a stick."

"I love a stick."

"Then here you go," Sam said and tossed Eleanor the keys.

Eleanor caught the keys in midair. "You're not kidding? I'm driving?"

"Of course you are." Søren opened the back and put his luggage in. "My first car was a motorcycle."

"You don't know how to drive a car?" She would have been more shocked if he'd confessed to not knowing how to read.

"Never took the time to learn," he said without apology. "Are you comfortable driving?"

"Of course I am. My first bike was a car."

"Good," he said. He opened the passenger-side door.

"Not good. Community service? Probation? No getting a license until I'm eighteen? Remember all that?"

"Taken care of." Sam pulled a manila envelope out of her jacket pocket and handed to her.

Eleanor opened the envelope and found a driver's license with her picture on it, a high school ID card to some school in Long Island and an insurance card for the BMW.

"What the hell?" Eleanor asked.

"In case you get pulled over," Sam said. "But try not to do that."

"Who's Claire Haywood?" Eleanor glanced back down at the driver's license and noticed the name and birth date. "And why did Kingsley make me a year younger?"

"Because he made you my sister," Søren said in a tone of abject disgust.

"What?" She looked at Søren and then Sam again.

"King said you'd be pissed," Sam said to Søren, a wide grin on her face. "He told me to remind you that Claire is the only teenage girl in the world you could be alone with in a car without raising eyebrows."

"He might be right. Doesn't mean I have to like it," Søren said, almost smiling, but not quite. "Tell him I get the joke. And tell him I don't find him amusing."

"I will pass that right along, *Padre,*" Sam said.

"I don't care who the hell she is. I have a fake driver's license. If you both don't get out of the way, I'm taking off on my own."

"I'm out of here." Sam gave them both a salaam-style bow. "You two kids have fun at the funeral."

"Keys are in the ignition," he said and Sam walked over to his Ducati.

Eleanor threw her duffel bag in the trunk and got behind the wheel.

"So we're doing this?" she asked as Søren got into the passenger side.

"We are."

"We're going to your father's house in New Hampshire. This is a real thing. This is not a joke. And I am driving."

"All of that is correct. Are you nervous?"

Eleanor didn't answer. Instead she watched Sam rev up his Ducati and head out to the street. The woman handled the bike like a pro. How was it that Søren had all these amazing friends she knew nothing about?

She started the car and closed her eyes as the engine purred to life.

"Eleanor? Do you and the car need a moment alone together?"

"I came already. Let's go."

She drove out of the wooded back driveway. With the new trees he'd planted in early spring, the rectory now stayed hidden almost completely from the church. People could get in and out without anyone noticing. Wasn't that convenient?

"I have no idea where I'm going," Eleanor said as she turned onto Oak Street.

"I know where we're going."

"I also have no idea what you and I are going to talk about for the next four hours."

"We can talk about whatever you like."

"Can we talk about your father?"

"I wouldn't advise it."

"Can we talk about Kingsley and what his deal is?"

"That's a more complicated question than four hours could cover."

"So the whole 'we can talk about whatever I want to talk about' was..."

"Not an accurate statement."

"I give up."

"Don't give up, Little One."

"Fine. So...hobbies?"

"Piano playing."

"Phobias?"

"All my fears are rational."

"Pet peeves?"

"Calvinism."

Eleanor glowered at him.

"What?"

"Calvinism? Your pet peeve is Calvinism?"

"Yes."

Eleanor sighed as she turned onto the highway.

"This is gonna be a long drive."

Luckily Søren came to her rescue. More accurately, his little sister did.

"We should talk about Claire since she is your new identity."

"Claire's your younger sister, I guess."

"One of two. Freyja lives in Denmark. We have the same mother."

"And Claire?"

"Claire is the daughter of my father's second wife. She was born when I was fifteen, although I didn't know she existed until my older sister—Elizabeth—found out and told me about her. I met her for the first time when she was three."

"So Claire's a year younger than me, then?"

"Yes. Does that bother you?"

"No. Does it bother you?"

"I'll admit I'm trying not to think about it."

"Because, you know, it would be like Kingsley and Claire together."

"Eleanor, are you trying to make me carsick?"

She laughed openly, easily. It felt so good to be alone with him, teasing him, being near him.

"Sorry. I promise Claire and I will be cool."

"Good. I've been worried about her lately."

"What's wrong?"

"I don't know." Søren adjusted the seat to give himself more legroom. This was not an issue she ever had. "Claire has been a marvelous correspondent. I have almost a thousand letters from her. She's been writing me since she first learned how. I receive at least one a week. Or did until two months ago, when she stopped writing. I've spoken to her on the phone a few times and planned to talk with her at Thanksgiving. She's been secretive, unusually so. I'm hoping she'll talk to you since she won't talk to me."

"I'm not going to spy on your sister and report back to you. That is a violation of the Girl Code."

"The Girl Code? Is this something you've invented or is it actually codified somewhere?"

"It's a real thing. You can't write the rules down because that's also a violation of the Girl Code. Boys might find a written copy, and then they'd know the secrets."

"Are you violating the code by telling me about the code?"

"Yes, but the Girl Code is really fucking stupid, and I only follow it when I feel like it."

"And I assume you feel like following it now?"

"Right."

All the way to New Hampshire, she and Søren talked. They

started with music. She confessed that for the past year she'd been trying to learn about classical music. He confessed he'd borrowed Sam's copy of Pearl Jam's *Ten* so he'd know about this mysterious band she adored.

"So Sam's a Pearl Jam fan, too?" Eleanor asked.

"She is."

"Can I ask a theological question?"

"I have no idea why you think I would be interested in theology, but ask anyway."

"If I were to fool around with a woman, would it count as sex?"

"If the rumors about Sam are even half true, I can guarantee she would make it count."

"You have the coolest friends."

The four hours passed in what felt like minutes. She'd been worried the trip would be weird or awkward, but instead she discovered Søren, despite being a pompous, pretentious, arrogant, overeducated snob, was the easiest person in the world to talk to. As they neared the house, Eleanor almost regretted the end of the trip. She could talk to him forever.

"Is that it?" she asked, stopping the car at the end of a long driveway.

The sun had set two hours ago, but a spotlight shone on the house ahead. Søren had called it a "Federal" style mansion, whatever that meant. He said his father had married into money and gutted his first wife's family home, remodeling it to his exact specifications. It had two stories, two wings, twelve bedrooms, fourteen bathrooms and six thousand square feet. Søren also added that he'd rather be back in the leper colony than back at his childhood home.

"That's it."

She saw his jaw clench and his eyes narrow.

"What's wrong?"

"Nothing, Little One. Only bad memories from that house."

She reached over and covered his hand with hers.

"I'm here. I don't know if that helps any."

Søren raised her hand and kissed the back of it.

"It helps more than you can imagine."

She eased the car down the driveway and at Søren's instructions followed the winding path to the back of the house, where they parked. She turned off the car, got out and stretched a few seconds before pulling her bag from the trunk.

"Oh, another thing, Eleanor, before we go in the house."

"Is it the body? Is the body in the house?" She tried not to make a face. "No offense but dead bodies creep me out."

"No body at the house, I promise."

"Then what's up?"

"You're here with Claire, not with me."

She knew she was here with him, for him. Still, she nodded.

A light on the back porch flipped on.

"Here we go," Søren sighed. "Brace yourself."

"What's wrong?"

"Hurricane Claire is about to hit."

20

Eleanor

A DOOR SLAMMED, A LOUD SOUND THAT WAS FOLlowed by an even louder sound—a squeal and a laugh and then a blur of arms and legs racing toward the car.

A girl launched herself into Søren's arms and wrapped herself bodily around him.

"I'm so glad you're here," she said, burying her head against his shoulder.

"I would never have guessed," Søren said, breathless. The girl must have knocked the wind out of him with the force of her attack hug.

He put her down and leaned back against the car.

"I missed you, Frater," the girl said, grinning broadly.

"Missed you, too, Soror."

"I didn't miss either of you," Eleanor said, deciding to interrupt if only to get the awkward introductions out of the way.

"Claire, this is Eleanor." He crooked his finger and Eleanor stepped out of the shadows. At one glance Eleanor could see

Claire and Søren were related. She had his mouth and nose, his pale complexion and long dark eyelashes. She didn't have his height, however, or his blond hair. And although very pretty, she wasn't nearly as striking as Søren. "Eleanor is a friend from church. I didn't want you alone here at the house."

Claire looked up at Søren.

"Sure," Claire said, glancing at Eleanor and then back at her brother. "She's here for me. Got ya." Claire gave him an exaggerated wink. Eleanor liked this girl already.

"Hi. Call me Elle. He only calls me Eleanor because he has a stick up his ass."

"You noticed that, too?" Claire asked.

Eleanor turned to Søren.

"Oh, yeah, she and I are gonna get along fine."

"If I had a white flag," Søren said, "I'd wave it first to surrender and hang myself with it after."

The three of them walked into the house together. With that auspicious start, Eleanor expected a pleasant evening of hanging around the house and chatting. But as soon as they entered through the back door, Søren lost his smile and his sense of humor.

"Is Elizabeth here?" he asked Claire. Søren had his sister's hand in his and seemed unwilling or unable to let it go.

"She said she'd be back soon."

"Did anyone give you a room yet?"

"I'm upstairs in the red room. I took the one with the big bed."

"Good. I want you in your room now. You and Eleanor."

"It's only ten-thirty," Claire protested. If she hadn't argued the point, Eleanor would have.

"I don't care. I need to talk to Elizabeth, so I can't keep an eye on you two. It's late, we all have a big day tomorrow and I can't have either of you roaming around the house by yourselves at night. If you leave the room, you two leave together. And you lock the door and don't let anyone in the room but me. You understand?"

"Fine. Fine. If you insist. He's so bossy." Claire said the last sentence to her and Eleanor started to agree, but Søren shot her a "don't you dare" look. Claire stood on a step so she could face her brother eye to eye. "Good night, Frater. Tomorrow you're going to play with me, though."

"Have you been practicing?"

"Yes, and I'm awesome."

"Then we'll play. Tonight you sleep."

Claire kissed Søren on the cheek and grabbed Eleanor by the arm.

"Let's go," Claire said, dragging Eleanor up the steps. "We can talk about him behind his back, and then he'll regret introducing us."

"I already do," Søren said from behind them.

Eleanor followed Claire to the red room and found that the girl had damn good taste. Giant four-poster bed, huge couches, portrait art on the walls—it looked like a room from an English estate rather than an American mansion.

"Nice." Eleanor nodded her approval.

"It's okay. Old-fashioned. Are you in love with my brother?"

Eleanor dropped her bag on the floor.

"Can you tell me the right answer to that question before I answer it?"

Claire grinned ear to ear. With that big smile she came darn close to being as striking as her older brother.

"If I wasn't his sister I'd be in love with him. I am in love with him, but not that way."

"He's worried about you." Eleanor hoped a careful change

of subject would work. "He wants to know why you stopped writing him letters."

Claire groaned and threw herself onto the bed. She buried her face against a pillow and laughed.

This seemed like entirely inappropriate behavior for a girl whose father died that week. Eleanor decided to roll with it.

Claire flipped onto her back and smiled up at the ceiling. Eleanor dug through her duffel bag for the boxer shorts and Pearl Jam T-shirt she'd packed as pajamas.

"It's very weird having a brother for a priest."

"You mean, a priest for a brother?"

"Right." Claire nodded.

"I don't have any brothers or sisters, so having a brother would be weird enough to start with. But the priest thing, yeah, that's gotta be weird."

"It's beyond weird. Plus he's thirty and I'm sixteen so he should be the one out there doing stuff, dating, getting married, whatever, and I should be the innocent virginal one, right? Instead he hasn't dated anybody since he was a teenager and I'm..."

"You have a boyfriend." Eleanor stripped out of her shirt and unhooked her bra.

"I do."

"And you two are..."

"Yeah." Claire winced.

Eleanor glared at her.

"You lucky bitch."

Claire laughed again and pulled the covers down on the bed. They spent the next two hours talking about Claire's boyfriend, Ike, and their sex life, which didn't amount to much more than a dozen encounters in his bedroom or the basement after school while his parents were still at work. Claire had decided sex was the greatest thing ever and Ike agreed with her. They'd do it more often but he came from conservative Jewish parents who didn't like him dating a Gentile and would have been furious to find out they were having sex.

"I'd sell my soul to get laid," Eleanor sighed.

"You're gorgeous, Elle. You can get any guy you want. Why are you still a virgin?"

"Ask your brother that question."

"Oh, just do what I did with Ike."

"What is that?"

Claire grinned devilishly.

"Jump him."

By midnight Eleanor had extracted a promise from Claire that she'd tell Søren she had a boyfriend and that was why she'd been too busy to write lately. Mission accomplished, Eleanor fell asleep without giving a second thought to the fact that she slept in a bed in the house Søren had grown up in and that in bed with her was his baby sister. She was in love with a Catholic priest who acted liked he owned her. Weird was her new normal.

Eleanor woke up the next morning and she and Claire had breakfast in their pajamas. She couldn't believe Søren hated this place so much. She'd never been in a big old mansion like this before. This sort of country living suited her fine.

After breakfast she hid out in the bedroom while Claire went downstairs with Søren. The wake would last all day and the funeral and burial would take place tomorrow morning. She'd packed books and homework to occupy her while all the family stuff happened.

"Let no one in the door," Søren ordered, "except for—"

"Except for you and Claire. I know, I know. Am I going to get raped in the night if I leave the door unlocked?"

Søren had given her the most earnest of stares as Claire tucked herself under his arm and rested her head on his chest.

"You wouldn't be the first person that has happened to in this house."

Eleanor locked the door.

At about two in the afternoon, Claire returned to the bedroom carrying a plate of food for her. At six in the evening she brought another plate.

"Are you trying to get me fat, or are you looking for an excuse to get out of there?" Eleanor asked as she dived into her food.

"Mostly the second one. I hate stuff like this. I'm supposed to be sad and miserable. I'm not that good of an actress."

"No offense, but why aren't you sad? I mean, your dad died." Eleanor hoped she didn't sound judgmental. She wouldn't be all that sad if her own father died.

Claire threw herself down on the couch next to Eleanor.

"I barely knew him. I'm glad I barely knew him."

"Was he that bad?"

Claire sighed and grabbed a strawberry off Eleanor's plate. Eleanor pretended to stab her hand with the fork.

"You want to know how bad he was?" Claire asked.

"Probably not, but tell me anyway."

"Frater won't tell me much, so I got all this from Mom."

"Wait, stop right there. Explain the *Frater* thing to me."

"It's Latin for brother. Soror is Latin for sister. That's what he and I call each other—Frater and Soror. He says he hates the name Marcus."

"That was your dad's name?"

"Right. And this is why he hates the name, and this is why I'm not sad my father's dead."

Claire took a deep breath, kicked off her black ballet flats and curled up against the back of the couch.

"My father is...was a very bad person. My mom says he abused Elizabeth when she was a little girl."

"He hit her?"

"Worse."

Eleanor's heart stopped beating for a few seconds.

"Oh, fuck."

"Elizabeth's mom and my father got divorced over that. They got married in the sixties, divorced in the seventies. Everyone kept stuff like that a secret. Then he met my mom and married her. They had me. Elizabeth found out from her mom that our father had gotten remarried and had me. She didn't know what to do so she wrote a letter to Frater."

"What did he do?" Eleanor was careful to not call Søren "Søren." Apparently Claire didn't know his real name. Interesting that Søren thought her more worthy of knowing his real name than his own baby sister.

"This is what Mom told me. She said it was late November. I was three years old. My father was gone on one of his business trips. Mom said the doorbell rang one afternoon and she answered it. And standing on the front porch was, and these are her words, 'a blond angel.'"

"A blond angel?"

"That's what she said. He introduced himself as the son of her husband, which was a huge shock since she didn't even know my father had a son. He told her that she didn't have to let him in the house. He only wanted five minutes of her time."

"What happened?"

"Ten minutes later, Mom was packing our stuff, calling her parents and getting us out of the house—this house. My 'blond angel' brother told my mom she'd married a child-raping monster and if she loved her daughter she would never let her spend a single second in their father's company ever again. He had a friend with him, my mom said."

"A friend? Who?"

"Some French guy about his age. They both helped her carry the stuff to Mom's car. She said she offered to let him hold his baby sister. Me, that is. He said he didn't know anything about children and was worried he'd hurt me. Apparently his friend held me instead while she packed up the car. He said he liked kids. Now I make Frater hug me all the time to make up for that day he wouldn't do it."

"That is crazy." So a teenage Kingsley had gone with Søren to his father's house. She couldn't imagine Kingsley holding a kid. "So your brother left school to warn your mom about who she'd married?"

"He did. And guess what, Elle?"

"What?"

"Because of him coming to my mother that day, I lost my virginity at age sixteen to my boyfriend. Not at age eight to my father like Elizabeth did. So that's why I'm totally in love with my brother. Not that way, though." Claire grinned, a slight blush suffusing her cheeks.

"Yeah, not that way. I get it." Eleanor stared across the room and into the empty fireplace. "It doesn't surprise me, you know? I mean, it's horrible and it makes me sick to think about your dad and what he did to your sister. I have this friend at school—Jordan. Her mom won't let us hang out much anymore because of some trouble I got into once. But last year I could tell something was really wrong with her. I made her tell me. A teacher had felt her up."

"What a sick fucker."

"I know," Eleanor said. "I told your brother about it. He put the fear of God into that asshole teacher. That guy packed up his shit and left town. Your brother has this really strong protective streak toward girls."

"Elizabeth is the reason," Claire said. "He's so protective I didn't even want to tell him about Ike."

"He's protective of me, too," Eleanor said. "Except with me, he's protecting me from him, and I wish he'd stop."

"You *are* in love with him." Claire studied her with Søren's steel-colored eyes. They must have inherited that steely stare from their father.

"Yeah," she admitted, not looking Claire in the eyes.

"Does he know?"

"He does. Does that freak you out?"

"I don't want him getting in trouble, that's for sure. But I don't want him to be a priest, either. When he was in seminary, I'd cut out pictures of sexy women in magazines and send them to him in my letters. I wrote on the pictures 'see what you're missing?'"

"And you say I'm evil?"

"I know. He thought it was hilarious. He said mine were the most popular letters at his seminary. It was a joke at first. But then a few years ago when that thing happened in El Salvador, I called him and begged him to quit school and come home."

"What thing in El Salvador?"

"There was a war," Claire began, her face wearing an inscrutable expression. "The Jesuits had a school there. They weren't part of the war. But that didn't stop the military from killing them."

"Killing who?"

Claire looked Eleanor straight in the eyes.

"The Jesuit priests. Six of them." Claire wiped a tear off her cheek. "Elle, they killed them all. The priests, the housekeeper, the housekeeper's daughter… Mom bought the *News-*

week that had a story on it. I still have the article—'Bloodbath in El Salvador.' November 16, 1989."

Eleanor couldn't speak, couldn't think. All she could do was stare into the vision of Søren on his knees, a man standing behind him with a gun pointed at the back of his head.

"They call the Jesuits 'God's Army,' 'God's Marines,' 'God's Soldiers.' And the Jesuits take that seriously. They go to work in the most dangerous parts of the world, and sometimes they die there. I begged Frater to quit. He said God wanted him to be a priest. That was the end of that."

"He's in Connecticut now. He should be safe there."

"Yeah, if they let him stay there. They can send him anywhere anytime they want to, though. I can't get him to quit. Maybe you can."

Eleanor didn't have the heart to tell Claire not only couldn't she make Søren leave the priesthood, but she'd also promised God she'd never ask him to.

By eight o'clock that evening the guests had left and most of the other relations had gone to their bedrooms. Eleanor finally felt comfortable escaping the bedroom. Claire and Søren staked out the music room and Eleanor ate ice cream while Frater and Soror worked out a sonata on the grand piano.

"It's in C," Søren instructed Claire, and played a few notes for her.

"I don't like C. Everything's in C."

"It doesn't matter if you like C or not, the piece is in C."

"Can we do it in A?"

"Is your first name Ludwig? Is your last name Beethoven?"

"My first name is Claire, and my last name is Awesome-at-piano."

"Then it's in C."

Eleanor watched Søren and Claire on the piano bench playfully bickering. How normal it all seemed. How comfortable.

She wished she had a brother, too, someone to joke around with, to hang out with, to annoy and tease. Her parents had divorced when she was a baby. No siblings for her. Mom got full custody and two jobs. It would have been nice to not be alone so much growing up. Good thing she had her books to keep her company. No wonder Claire said she was in love with Søren. It wasn't anything weird or creepy, only hero worship and the joy of having a man in her life she could trust completely. Eleanor also trusted Søren completely. She owed him so much for everything he'd done for her. And yet he asked nothing of her. Nothing but eternal obedience. In light of all he'd done for her and how little he asked, paying him back in eternal obedience seemed like a steal.

They stayed up until about eleven when Søren ordered them both to bed again. Claire snuck off to call her boyfriend from the phone in the kitchen. Eleanor went to the bedroom and changed into her pajamas.

Claire came back, crawled into bed and fell asleep in the middle of telling Eleanor how much Ike missed her.

Eleanor curled up on her side, thinking of everything Claire had told her today. Søren's father had been a child molester, had raped his own daughter. She knew Søren and Elizabeth were only a year apart. Had he known this was happening as a kid? Had he tried to protect Elizabeth like he protected Claire? Or had it been happening to him, too? God, just the idea of anyone hurting Søren as a child inspired thoughts of vengeance and wrath that scared even her. It was a good thing his father was dead. If he'd even looked at Søren the wrong way, Eleanor would have killed the man herself.

Unable to sleep, Eleanor slipped out of bed and snuck into the hallway. She didn't know what to do or where to go. She only knew she wanted to talk to Søren a few minutes if only to make sure he was okay.

Behind a few doors she heard voices but none were Søren's. She would know his voice in the dark with her eyes blindfolded and a thousand other voices around her calling her name. Everyone staying overnight at the house had crowded into the west wing, as Claire called it. Søren had told her once that he valued his privacy above anything, so perhaps he'd found a room in the east wing of the house. Following only her feet and her instincts, Eleanor passed into the older part of the house that lay behind a set of double doors on the second floor. As soon as she entered that hallway a draft tickled her bare legs. The air smelled of dust-covered memories. She peeked into a few rooms and found the furniture covered in white sheets tinged yellow with time.

At the end of the long hallway Eleanor found a room with the door ajar. She looked in and saw Søren sitting in armchair with his eyes closed. The chair sat a few feet from the window and moonlight surrounded him like a halo. For a long time she did nothing but look at him, at his hands that lay on the arms of the chair, at his face so peaceful in repose, at his eyelashes—unusually long and dark for someone so blond—resting on his cheeks. Looking at Søren it was easy now to believe man was created in God's image. If God looked like Søren there would be no atheists.

"Eleanor, I told you not to leave your room alone."

She winced.

"I'm sorry. I'll go back."

"No, you can come in. Shut the door behind you."

She stepped into the room, shut the door and locked it.

Søren started to speak as she proceeded on nervous feet from the door to his chair. She found nowhere to sit but on the floor, so she sat at his feet and found herself at home there. He laid his hand on the back of her neck and twined his fingers in her hair. His fingertips traced circles on the nape of her neck. For a long time she did nothing but rest her head on his knee. She could live at his feet. She could die at his feet. If she'd had more courage, she would have told him that.

Eleanor looked up at him. He raised an arm and crooked a finger at her. She rose off the floor and sank into his lap, into his arms. His mouth found hers and in the dark and the moonlight they kissed for the first time.

The kiss surrounded her like air, held her up like water, supported her like the earth and burned her like fire. She'd read about passion, about hunger, about desire, and had felt them herself. But never had she tasted them in her own mouth.

Søren slid a hand under the back of her shirt and caressed her lower back as he feasted on her mouth. She relaxed into his arms, surrendering herself to him and the kiss. He wore his suit pants and a white shirt unbuttoned at the neck and Eleanor could finally touch his neck that forever seemed to be covered by his Roman collar. She pressed her fingers into his throat, felt his pulse beating against her hand, hard but steady.

He pulled away and they gazed at each other.

"You can say it now," she said, her voice low and reverent.

"I love you, Little One."

She relaxed into his arms and closed her eyes. He held her close, held her tight. She could have died in that moment and regretted nothing.

"What now?" she asked.

"There are things you need to know."

"Are you going to tell me?"

Søren laid a hand on her knee and slid it up her leg, stopping only when he encountered her hip.

"Eleanor, you have to understand that what I need to tell you will change everything. This is not some sort of melodramatic exaggeration on my part. It will change how you see me, perhaps even how you see the world. Once you learn the truth it can't be unlearned, can't be unheard. Please do not make this decision lightly."

Eleanor raised her hand to Søren's face and touched his lips. The kiss had torn down whatever was left of the wall he'd tried to build up between them. From his lips she moved her hand to his cheek dusted with the slightest stubble, to his forehead, where she ran her thumb softly over the tips of his eyelashes. She lowered her hand and spoke two words—not a question but a command.

"Tell me."

21

Eleanor

ELEANOR WAITED BUT SØREN DIDN'T SPEAK. NOT AT first. He stared out the window into the moonlight as if trying to find comfort in that white light.

"You asked me questions," he finally said. "I'll answer them now."

"About goddamn time."

"Eleanor."

"Sorry."

"We'll start at the end of your questions. Those are easier," he said.

"You remember all of them?"

He nodded. "All of them."

She didn't quite believe he had all her questions memorized. She didn't even remember them all. Once again he proved himself when he raised his hand and with one finger drew a number twelve in the air.

"Number twelve. Am I in love with you? I already answered that question tonight. If you need to hear it again, then yes, I am in love with you, Little One, and have been since the day we met."

"Since we met?"

"It would almost be accurate to say I loved you before we met. But that's another story for another night."

Eleanor took a few breaths.

"I thought..." She stopped and shrugged. "I fell in love with you the second I saw you. Glad I'm not the only one."

"No. You're certainly not the only one. Now question eleven—who am I? By the time I'm finished answering all these questions, you'll know."

He drew a ten in the air.

"When will I keep my end of the deal?" he said, reciting her question. "The deal that I'll give you everything, including but not limited to sex, I assume."

"Sex specifically, but I'll take what you've got."

"Not tonight," he said. "I know it seems parochial to you, but I would prefer we wait as long as possible. There's so much you still need to experience, so many decisions you need to make. I'll try to make the waiting as easy as possible. But you're not even out of high school yet. You should focus on graduating, getting into college. Once you're on that path, we'll talk about this again."

Eleanor sighed heavily. Disappointment warred with the joy of finally getting her answers.

"Fair enough. I can't say I want to wait. I've wanted to be with you from the beginning. But I'm not surprised, either. I know that it's not easy—you're a priest and I'm a—"

"Constant temptation."

"I'll take that as a compliment."

"It is. Also, there's a very good reason for waiting. We'll come to that with questions four and two. But now question nine, where you confess you're a virgin and ask me if I'm, and I quote, 'okay with that'?"

"Are you? I mean, I still am."

"Yes, Little One. Your virginity is no impediment and if you'd been sexually active before we met it would also be no impediment. I feel possessive of you now, however."

"I don't want to be with anyone but you."

"Are you certain of that?"

"Entirely," she said. "And maybe Sam. She is seriously..."

"Eleanor."

"Sorry. Continue."

"Your eighth question—am I a virgin?"

"You said you were with someone when you were a teenager so I'm guessing no," she said, not sure how she felt about that no. She wanted one of them to have some experience, but then again, being his first would have been something special.

"You would guess correctly. Many priests are. Most are not. We weren't born priests, after all."

"How old were you your first time? Or am I not allowed to ask extra questions?"

"I promise we'll get to that. But now onto question seven. Why do I want you to obey me forever?" He paused and seemed to weigh his words. "Let me give you the simple answer. In your Esther story, the king tied Esther to the bed. Is that something you think you would enjoy?"

She hoped the dim light masked her blush.

"I think so. It seems really sexy being tied up during sex. Is that weird?"

"Not at all. Many people, men and women, enjoy giving up control during sexual encounters and putting their bodies and even their lives in the hands of their partners. It's called sexual submission. Others, like me, enjoy the opposite. Taking total control of someone and dominating them."

Eleanor shivered at Søren's words. She didn't expect such a personal revelation from him about his sexual desires—he wanted to take control of her? To dominate her?

"Makes sense," she said, trying to keep her voice neutral.

"I enjoy your obedience to me much the same way you feel certain you would enjoy being tied up during sex."

"It turns you on?"

Søren met her eyes and in them she saw the world set itself alight and burn to ashes.

"More than you can possibly imagine."

Eleanor pressed her hand to his chest and felt his heart rushing under her fingers.

"Which," he began again after taking a ragged breath, "answers question number five—whose feet should you be sitting at? I don't know whose feet you should sit at. But I know whose feet I want you to sit at."

He wasn't hinting. She knew that. She knew he'd simply answered her question. Entirely of her own volition she pulled away from him, slid to the floor and knelt at his feet. With her head on his knee and his hand in her hair, she felt what Søren must have felt the first time he put on his priest's collar. She *found herself* at his feet. This was where she belonged. This was who she was. She would never look further to find herself than his feet.

"I wish you'd let go and be with me," she whispered against the fingers that brushed against her lips. "You wouldn't have to worry about self-control then."

"Eleanor, the first night we make love will be the greatest test of my self-control."

She wanted to speak, to protest, but he'd said *make love* and the beauty of those words rendered her mute.

"Now to question six. Why does everyone think my name is Marcus Stearns, but my Bible says Søren Magnussen? This is a complex question and it will require a long answer. Get comfortable," he said and forced a smile.

"I'm sitting in a bedroom at your feet. This is the most comfortable I've ever been in my life. I never want to leave."

"I never want you to. But you may change your mind after I answer the rest of your questions."

"Never. Trust me with the truth. Please."

"As you wish. This answer to the question begins before I was born. My father was Lord Marcus Stearns, Sixth Baron Stearns."

"The what?"

"A baron, and a minor one at that. My father was impoverished English aristocracy. His father squandered the last of the family fortune, leaving my father with nothing but a name and title."

"Your dad was a baron?"

"Madness, isn't it? Somewhere in Northern England there's a moldering estate called Edenfell I could claim if I desired. I have no desire."

"Your father's dead. So you're..."

"Surrender the tiara, milady. I am a priest. That's all I am."

"But you could be a baron if you wanted?"

"My father legitimized me. I suppose I could, although I have no interest in it."

"So weird. Your father was a baron, and he left all that behind?"

"He had to. You see, my father did what generations of noblemen had done when faced with poverty. He joined the army and became an officer. He quickly rose in the ranks. Intelligent, cunning, deadly... In Northern Ireland they called my father the Red Baron for all the blood he left in his wake. When he left the army, he fled England. He'd made so many enemies in the IRA he feared for his life. He came to America, ingratiated himself into New England society and married a wealthy young woman, an heir to a great fortune."

"I thought your mother was Danish."

"She is. My father's wife was not my mother. My mother—her name is Gisela—was an eighteen-year-old Danish pianist who came to New Hampshire to attend a music conservatory on scholarship. Her scholarship covered only tuition. She needed a place to stay. She was hired as my sister's nanny. My father's wife nearly died giving birth to Elizabeth, and only an emergency hysterectomy saved her life. It left her barren. My father wanted a son. He got a daughter and no chance for more offspring. He was a cruel man before that incident. After, he became a monster."

"What did he do?"

"He raped my mother."

Eleanor gasped. She pulled back and looked at Søren but found his face was blank, his eyes empty of emotion.

"She had you."

"Yes. I don't know if it was intentional, raping my mother so she could give him the son his wife couldn't. Deliberate or not, that's what happened. She had me and named me Søren, a family name. My father named me Marcus after himself."

"That's why you hate the name Marcus?"

"For many reasons. My mother wanted to flee, and would have, except she loved Elizabeth like her own child and couldn't leave her with my father, couldn't leave her unprotected. So we stayed in that house. My father pretended I didn't exist. It was the only way to keep peace between him and his wife, jealous of the beautiful Danish girl who cared for her child. I think my father was waiting for something, waiting to see something in me. And he did see it."

"See what?"

"I spoke my first words six months earlier than my sister

had. I started playing piano at age two. I mastered new skills quickly. My father decided I showed enough signs of high intelligence that I deserved to be acknowledged as his son. I pleased him enough that he paid the necessary bribes, had paperwork altered. His wife became my 'mother' and he my father."

"And here I thought my parents had a rough marriage. What happened to your mom?"

"I was shunted off to boarding school in England when I was five, and my mother summarily dismissed and returned to Denmark. We didn't see each again, not for a long time."

"How long?"

"Thirteen years."

Eleanor's eyes filled with tears at the sorrow in Søren's voice.

"Thirteen years…"

"School was difficult for me. I knew there was something different about me. My father had seen it. I saw it."

"Saw what?"

"Like father like son, Eleanor. I was…I am a sadist. I take the greatest of pleasures in inflicting the gravest of pains."

He stopped speaking long enough for the words to sink into Eleanor. She felt them settling into her body, into her blood, like some sort of magic incantation meant to change her from a girl into another being. She let them change her.

"Go on."

"The boys at school, I scared them. Even the simplest football game could turn bloody if I lost control. I pulled away, far into myself. I learned to keep my distance. I wanted to hurt them, but I didn't want to hurt them. I was a wolf on a leash, a leash that I held. And one night, when I was ten, the wolf broke the leash."

Eleanor shivered at his words.

"What happened?"

Søren smiled slightly.

"Have you read *Lord of the Flies?*"

"Yeah, freshman year."

"That book is a fair representation of what the boys at my school were like. Simply take them off the island, put them back in school."

"Were you Jack?" she asked, remembering the cruelest of the boys.

"No. Nor Ralph. I was almost Simon."

"Simon was the one who was murdered, right? You're not dead."

"Because I fought back. I started at a new school when I was ten. Most of the student leaders of the school, the prefects, were predators—sexual predators. A cycle of abuse had started years earlier and it was forever perpetuating itself. When the boys were first-year students, they were used by the older boys. When it was their turn at the top of the hierarchy, they meted out their vengeance on the younger boys. You were predator or prey at the school. The most notorious of the prefects came after me. He didn't live to regret that decision."

"Didn't live? You mean—"

"In the middle of the night he came to my bed in the dorm room I shared with three other boys. He pulled the sheets down and covered my mouth with his hand. Ten minutes later, his blood was staining the floor."

Eleanor went numb. She couldn't even speak to ask him to stop or go on.

"He died six weeks later. He never awoke from the coma I put him in."

"You killed him."

"I did."

"Did you get in any trouble?"

"It was considered self-defense by the law and the school. Everyone knew he was the worst of the offenders at the school. He was also fifteen and I was ten. He was one hundred and sixty pounds and I was one hundred and ten at the time."

"You beat to death a kid five years older than you and fifty pounds heavier?"

"It took six weeks for him to die of infection. But yes, I caused his death. I had no regrets, only shame."

"Shame? Why?"

"Because I had my first orgasm while I was beating him to death."

Eleanor stopped breathing. Søren looked away from her as if he couldn't bear to meet her eyes.

"What happened next?" She forced the question out.

"Some students were terrified of me. Some of his victims wanted to canonize me. Instead I was sent back home to America. My punishment of the boy had been so savage, and I so remorseless, no other school would have me."

"You came back here?"

"I turned eleven in England over the Christmas holiday and came home in January. Father said he would find a school in America that would take me. Until then doctors told him it would be best that I was kept away from other children."

"What was that like, coming home finally?"

"Difficult. I hadn't been here in five years. I'd only seen my father four or five times since being sent to England. I hadn't seen Elizabeth at all."

"Claire said your dad abused Elizabeth."

"Abuse is an understatement. He raped her the first time when she was eight years old. Not a week passed without him sneaking in her bedroom at night. My father had threatened to kill her mother if she told anyone. So she stopped speaking altogether."

"How did her mom not know all this was happening?"

Søren turned his head and gazed into a dark corner of the room. He seemed to be remembering something, something bad.

"The power of self-delusion is one of the greatest forces of the universe. My father's wife worshipped respectability and status. My father was a respected, even feared, businessman with an impressive pedigree. Divorce was not an option, so instead she convinced herself that the marriage was perfect. Eventually even she couldn't deny the cracks in the facade."

"What happened? Or do I not want to know?" For the first time she realized how right Søren had been. For over two years she'd begged to know the truth about him and he'd put her off. Now she understood why he'd kept his secrets.

"You don't want to know. But you need to know. You see, I hadn't seen Elizabeth in five years. We were strangers to each other. I tried to befriend her and after a few months back in this house, she started to speak to me a little."

He paused and closed his eyes. Eleanor feared what he would say next but she knew she had to hear it.

"My father had to leave the country on an extended business trip. His wife decided to go with him—a second honeymoon. She demanded the children be left behind. I think she sensed his unnatural interest in their daughter. Whatever the reason, it set a series of events in motion that have brought me to this place. And that brings us back to question eight. No, I'm not a virgin."

"When was your first time?"

"I'll tell you, and I only hope you can stomach the answer. At some point Elizabeth had overheard my father telling her mother about what happened when I was at school—about the boy who'd touched me in my sleep and how I'd killed him. Elizabeth wanted to die. You can't blame her. I certainly never have blamed her for what she did. Our parents left us alone in the house with only a few servants, and on the first night they were gone, Elizabeth came into my room. I was asleep, sound asleep. I didn't hear her open the door. I didn't hear her close it. I didn't feel her pulling the sheets down. I didn't even wake up until it was too late. When I did wake up, I was already inside her."

Eleanor clapped a hand over her mouth.

"It happens, you see. Boys get erections in their sleep. I can't blame her...." he said again. "She wanted me to kill her. She wanted to instigate an attack like what happened at my school. But she wasn't an older boy I already loathed. She was my own sister, and I loved her."

He closed his eyes as if to hide from something.

"So I didn't kill her. Sometimes I wonder if she still wishes I had. I don't remember much from that night. I know she ended up on her back. I know I left bruises on her. And I know..."

"What?" Eleanor barely heard herself asking the question.

"I know we liked it. Because the next night and every night after that for two months, we did it again."

She didn't know what to do, what to say, how to react. All she could do was take his hand in hers and twine their fingers together. His past reared up before them like a beast or demon. She wouldn't turn away from it, wouldn't run. They would face it and they would face it together.

"Eleanor, you cannot imagine what I did to my sister, or what she did to me. It's beyond what even your powers of imagination can conjure. I never want you to imagine. Know only this—there is no act of depravity we did not try at least once that long summer. It's a miracle we both survived each other. Please never imagine it."

"I won't. I promise." She made the promise easily and knew

she would keep it. She shoved away the images that attempted to enter her mind. Shoved them away, pushed them down and stabbed them through the heart.

"There is no room in this house we did not defile. But our favorite room to play in was the library."

"Why the library?"

"Sometimes we would read to each other. It made us feel normal, I suppose." Søren smiled then, a smile so pained it hurt to even see. She closed her eyes and buried her face against his leg. Every muscle in his body had gone tense. "But all horrible things must come to an end. At the end of the summer, we knew our father would be returning again. Elizabeth sometimes shook in my arms from the terror of knowing what would happen to her once Father returned. I told her we had to leave the house. We had to run away. I ordered her to pack, to call her grandparents, to find all the money she could so we could get as far away from this house as possible. She didn't obey me. She thought he would find us wherever we went. She should have..." Søren's voice trailed off a moment. "She should have obeyed me."

"Why?"

"Because our father came home early. And he found us together."

"Jesus Christ..." Eleanor breathed.

"We were lost children by then," Søren said. "We knew what we did was wrong but were powerless to stop ourselves. Despair brought us to depravity and we couldn't find a way out again."

"How did it stop?"

"Our father stopped it for us."

Eleanor pulled back and raised her hand.

"I need a minute."

"I warned you."

"I know you did. But I didn't know."

She leaned forward and rested both arms in his lap. He ran his hand over her back as if to comfort her when all she wanted was to comfort him.

"If God was in the world that day, He wasn't in that room when my father came home. He saw us together and he threw me against the wall. I remember the blood on the golden wallpaper—red on yellow. And he started to rape Elizabeth, to re-mark his territory. I found the fireplace poker and struck him with it. He moved. I missed his head. But it got him off Elizabeth. He came after me instead. He hit me, breaking my arm. I don't remember much from that day, but I do remember him tying me to a chair and telling me he would kill me. 'You're dead,' he said, and I knew he meant it. Then he was down, unconscious. Elizabeth had struck him over the head with the poker to save my life. I passed out to the sound of her laughter. I woke up in the hospital."

Eleanor tasted copper in her mouth. If she wasn't careful she would vomit from her horror at what Søren had suffered so young.

"What happened to Elizabeth?"

"Her mother heard her laughing and came to investigate. When she saw the scene before her, she could no longer deny the truth of who and what her husband was. She took me to the hospital and took Elizabeth away. She and my father divorced quietly and split all assets equally. Better to pay him off and keep things quiet than go through a messy public court battle.

"Question six was why does everyone think my name is Marcus Stearns and I told you my name is Søren? Søren is what my mother named me. Magnussen is her last name. I've tried for years to reject my father, his money and his world as much as I can. So I reject his name—at least in private. I wanted you to know the real me. To know the story of my name is to know me. There are few people who I want to know me."

"I want to know you."

"Now you do."

"Is what happened between you and your sister why you became Catholic?"

"Yes. My father came to his senses a few days after the incident. He remembered I was his only son, but he didn't want me in the house. I think he feared my retribution. I wanted to kill him, so I can't blame him for sending me away to a Jesuit boarding school in rural Maine. I felt polluted by what had happened between my sister and me. When Father Henry taught us about confession and reconciliation, about forgiveness...I knew I needed that. I converted to Catholicism and started studying to join the Jesuits."

"That's where you met Kingsley, right?"

"Kingsley... He was a gift from God. I kept away from everyone but the priests at Saint Ignatius. I didn't want to hurt anyone. I did...but I didn't. I wanted to but I didn't want to want to. When I lose control, it's not a pleasant sight."

"I trust you."

"You're in love with me. Of course you trust me. I hope I never betray that trust. I cannot promise you I never will. And now after all that, I can answer your remaining questions quickly. Question five—you asked whose feet should you sit at. I hope the answer is mine. Question four, you asked me why does a priest have his own handcuff key. Eleanor, I'm a sadist and for the sake of my own sanity I must inflict pain on someone every now and then. It's a powerful need and it grows maddening if I deny myself too long. You saw at Kingsley's house the sort of parties he has, the company he keeps.

I haven't had sexual intercourse since I was eighteen. I do beat someone at least once a month, sometimes once a week."

Eleanor's eyes widened in shock.

"That night at Kingsley's…?"

Søren nodded.

"That woman you saw me with is a friend of Kingsley's. She's a trained masochist who enjoys receiving pain as much as I enjoy inflicting it. Bondage is part of the sessions. A person tied up is defenseless. I'm less likely to overstep my bounds with a defenseless person. Question three—you asked why my friend would help you. That is a question only Kingsley can answer, and that is all I will say. The answer to your second question—what's the third reason being with you is problematic—is what I told you. I am a sadist and I can't get aroused unless I hurt you in some way first. I wish it could be otherwise, of course."

"Of course," she repeated, not even hearing herself. "So you…you can't—"

"Eleanor, you joked about us breaking the table during sex. I don't break furniture during sex. I break people."

"I see."

"As for question number one—what's the other reason I helped you the night you were arrested? The answer to question one is the same as the answer to question twelve. Because I'm in love with you and always will be. So there you have it. The whole sordid truth of me."

Søren fell silent and Eleanor let his words settle into the room. She knew he waited for her to speak, to pass some judgment, to make some declaration. He'd bared his very soul to her, laid out the humiliations and horrors of his past and confessed how they tormented him even to this day. She had no idea what to say to comfort him, or if she even could. But first she had one question.

"Is that all?"

He narrowed his eyes at her.

"Is what I told you not enough for you?"

"No, the sadism thing is plenty. I was worried it was something really serious."

"You have a different definition of *serious* than the rest of the English-speaking world."

She shrugged. "I don't know. Like *serious* serious. Like if you were a criminal on the run or you had terminal cancer. Or worse, you could be impotent. I mean actually impotent. Sounds like you just have a different definition of foreplay."

"My definition of foreplay is usually classified as assault."

"Obviously you and I are reading different dictionaries."

"You don't seem to understand the gravity of this situation. I am a sadist. I cannot escape that. I'm like my father."

"How badly do you hurt the people you play with? Like do they have to go to the hospital after or anything?"

"As a teenager I lost control once. It was consensual, but I crossed a line. Since then, no. I had a teacher in Rome who taught me ways of inflicting enormous amounts of pain without causing harm. At worst the person will have bruises for a few weeks. Bruises and welts. The masochists I play with are as well trained as I am. They trust me and do as I tell them to do. They put their lives in my hands, and I honor that trust."

"Your father hurt people against their will. You don't do that, right?"

"Never. I only hurt those who wish to be hurt, who enjoy it."

"So you're the opposite of your father, then. Right?"

"It's not that simple."

"If you stick your dick in a woman who wants it, it's sex. If you stick your dick in a woman who doesn't, it's rape. It's the same act but totally different, right? If this is why you're holding back from me, you can stop that right now."

"Something broke in me a long time ago, Eleanor. Or perhaps I was born broken. But yes, when the time comes for us to make love, I will have to hurt you."

Eleanor's hands shook as the words *make love* escaped Søren's lips again. She tucked her toes under her and rolled back. She rose up in front of him.

"Eleanor?"

She pushed her shorts down and pulled off her T-shirt. Naked and unashamed, she stood before him in the moonlight.

"Then hurt me."

22

Eleanor

SØREN GAZED UPON HER NAKED BODY WITH REVERent eyes. Still, he made no move to touch her. She took his right wrist in her hand and pressed his palm flat against her bare stomach. His hand slid to her back and he pulled her into his lap.

She straddled his thighs in the chair as he scored her back with his fingers. Her head fell back as he kissed her neck, her throat. His teeth found the tendon where her shoulder met her neck. He bit down hard, hard enough she gasped, and he shuddered in her arms.

"More," she whispered.

The world around her drained of color. Flesh and fire turned to black-and-white. Music thrummed in the back of her mind. For no reason and every reason, she felt like laughing.

Søren lifted her easily and carried her to the bed, throwing her down onto the sheets. She lay there, still, as he unbuttoned his shirt. With his knees he pushed her thighs apart.

When she raised her hands to touch his naked chest, he captured them and pinned them above her head. He put his full weight into holding her down. The muscles in her forearms contracted in agony, and she cried out in real pain.

"This is how it is," Søren rasped into her ear. "Do you still want this?"

"I want more." She turned her head and kissed his collarbone where it met his shoulder. "Hurt me."

He scoured her skin as he dragged his fingers down her body. Pushing his thumbs into the hollow of her hipbones, he pressed down hard. She cried out in the back of her throat as she felt a deep wrenching in her legs. Panting through the pain, she looked up at Søren. Søren…her Søren, he was the one inflicting this pain on her. What did she have to fear? Nothing.

He released her hips and brought his mouth down onto her lips. Panting had left her parched as the desert and his kiss was the only sea that could quench her thirst. He cupped the back of her neck with one hand and held her head, cradling it like a father holding an infant.

"I love you." She fought the pain, the fear, to release the words. He let her go and rose up over her. In the moonlight she watched as he pulled off his shirt and let it fall to the floor. She had never desired anyone as she desired him and knew she never would.

"Your eyes change color," he said, gazing down at her. "I noticed it the day we met. Green one moment, black the next. I've never seen anything like it."

"You've never seen anything like me." She smiled up at him.

"Have you ever had a dream feel so real that upon waking you thought you were still asleep?" He took her hand in his.

"Once or twice."

"I felt like that the moment I saw you, Little One. I dreamed you once. I think I'm still dreaming."

Eleanor kissed his hand. He cupped the side of her face.

"Call me *sir,*" he ordered.

"Yes, sir."

"Tell me I own you."

"You own me, sir."

"Say I am the only Father you will ever obey."

"I will obey you only, sir."

They spoke the words—call and response—like the most sacred of liturgies.

"Do you like the pain?" Søren gripped her thighs.

"Yes, sir."

"Even now?"

His impossibly strong hands pressed deep into her skin. She arched against the sheets, her body awash with pain. Søren covered her mouth with one hand and she screamed against it. How could bare hands hurt so much? How could she want more of it? Because it was him, the pain. Søren and pain became one in her mind and her body. She could never get enough of either.

At last he released her and she sank into the sheets. He traced a path down her neck with his hand, sliding his palm over her breasts. Her nipples hardened in response to his touch.

"Tell me to stop."

"Is that an order?" she asked.

"No."

"Then don't stop, sir."

In the next breath Søren slammed her flat on her stomach, grasped her arm and pinned it behind her back.

She felt teeth at the nape of her neck, teeth in the center of her back, teeth in the small of her back. All the while her shoulder burned like fire as the muscles strained to hold it in the socket. The pain threatened to overwhelm her.

The pain ceased as he released her arm. In that moment when the pain stopped, a relief far greater than pleasure suffused her.

Søren stretched out on top of her. He covered her hands with his hands, twined her fingers in his fingers, buried his face into her hair. The full weight of his body on top of hers, the feel of his bare chest against her naked back, caused her stomach to knot up and blood to rush to her hips.

His hand traveled between their bodies. She heard a zipper open and felt his erection pressing against the back of her thigh.

She loved him. He would never take her anywhere she wasn't ready to go.

She trusted him. He pushed up and pressed her into the bed, his hand on the back of her neck, his hips riding against her.

She needed him. He inhaled softly and liquid heat rained on her back.

A sigh escaped his lips—or was the sigh hers? She lay beneath him, warm and naked, and welcomed his semen on her body.

Eleanor wanted to roll onto her back, but she waited, sensing an order would come. How simple it seemed, obedience did, when she loved the man she obeyed so completely. There was nothing he could order her to do that she wouldn't do, because she knew he would never order her to do anything she didn't want.

She waited in silence and listened as he cleaned himself off and righted his clothes.

Søren slid a hand under her hip and turned her over onto

her back. His mouth captured hers again. She breathed in and inhaled that winter's scent on his skin.

"Is that what it will always be like?" she asked as his right hand cupped her breast.

"No. Some nights it will be much worse."

"Worse?"

"More pain."

"I can take it." She smiled at him through the dark and he raised his eyebrow at her.

"But do you want to take it? Will you always?"

"From you? Yes, always."

He brought his mouth down onto her breast. She arched into his mouth as pleasure spiked deep into her belly. More, more, more, she wanted to beg. His tongue teased her nipple. His fingers toyed with her other breast. He kissed his way back to her mouth.

"For you, pain is the prelude," he said into her lips.

"Prelude to what?"

"The reward."

"What is the pain to you?"

"Its own reward," he said, and she saw a shadow cross his face.

Søren slipped a hand between her legs and found her clitoris. Her body twitched from the shock of the touch, so intimate and unexpected. She spread her legs for him, wanting to offer all of herself to him. She met his eyes in the dark and he pushed one finger inside her.

Eleanor nearly came right then simply from him penetrating her so suddenly. She gripped the sheets as he explored inside her. He pushed in deep and slid out slowly before pushing in again.

"It's been so long..." He breathed the words, his eyes closed.

"Since you've been inside someone?"

He nodded and inhaled sharply as she raised her hips into his hand.

"Does it feel..." She paused and asked the question she really wanted to ask. "How do I feel?"

"There's not a word that's been invented to describe how you feel inside, Little One." He sat up and wrapped her leg around his back so he sat between her open thighs. He pressed his finger into a spot deep within her and sank into her softness. He seemed to be so far inside her she could feel him in the pit of her stomach. "Has anyone ever been inside you?"

"No one but me." She flinched with pleasure as he scraped the front wall of her vagina. He hit a spot inside her that made her shoulders come off the bed.

"I can feel your hymen," he said, turning his hand and pressing down. She winced at the sudden burning pain and he inhaled as if suddenly aroused.

"Feel free to get rid of it."

"That would be a terrible idea."

"You don't want to take my virginity?"

"No, I want it too much. I'm not entirely sure I could control myself to keep from truly hurting you."

"Is your... I mean, are you—"

Søren pulled his hand out of her and started to open his pants.

"Wait, I'm not on—"

But before she could finish protesting, Søren had taken her hand and wrapped it around him.

"Oh, fuck," she said.

"Does that answer your question?"

Even after coming a few minutes earlier, he was hard again, incredibly so. She stroked him from the base to the still-wet tip of his erection. He was big—big enough it made her nervous. When they had sex the first time it would hurt and hurt badly. That didn't stop her from wanting it.

"You're gonna kill me with that, aren't you?"

"Very likely."

"I can think of worse ways to die."

He removed her hand from him and she whimpered in protest. Laughing, he settled next to her on the bed again.

Once more he slipped his hand between her legs.

"I want you to come for me. Will you do that?" he asked her.

"Hell, yes, sir."

Even in the dark she could see Søren arching his eyebrow at her.

"I mean, yes, sir."

"Better. Now show me how you need to be touched."

Covering his hand with hers, she guided his fingers to her clitoris. Once they'd made their deal, she'd begun learning her own body and its responses. She'd snuck into the adult sections of the library and read every sex manual she could find, hiding them behind books on fall foliage and European architecture. She considered herself the only virgin sex expert in the world. She should win some sort of prize for that. This—Søren's fingers on her clitoris—must be that prize.

With her fingers over his, she showed him how to rub her in the way she knew would bring her to orgasm. Her hand fell from his as the pleasure built hard and high in her back. She'd been teetering on the brink of orgasm simply from lying naked in a bed with him for the first time. All her senses were on highest alert. Her entire body buzzed with desire. Wetness stained her thighs and the sheets beneath her. Looking down, she watched his fingers on the most private part of her body. Blood pounded in her ears. Her heart slammed against her ribcage. Muscles deep inside her started to clench and release. She closed her eyes and felt her body rising off the bed.

"Come for me, Little One," Søren ordered, and her body obeyed before her mind even registered the command.

She climaxed hard, gasping aloud as Søren pushed a finger into her and pressed it against the contracting muscles. It trebled her pleasure as she felt herself spasming around him over and over again.

Søren stayed inside her as she came down from the high. They kissed again, and the kiss stoked the fire still smoldering inside her. Søren kneaded her clitoris again and she came a second time, nearly as hard as the first time. She collapsed onto the sheets, limp and spent.

"Stay here." Søren slid off the bed and left the room for a minute. When he came back in, he locked the door behind him once more and sat on the edge of the bed. He ordered her to sit up with her back to him.

"How are you feeling?" he asked her as he started to wash the slight residue of semen off her back with a warm, wet cloth.

"I think my brain exploded."

He paused to kiss her naked shoulder.

"You'll have bruises tomorrow. On your thighs, on your back," he said, retracing the path of the pain he'd given her with his fingertips. "They'll start out pale and turn black soon after."

"I can handle bruises. I won't wear short skirts and backless dresses."

"Kingsley recommends his masochists take zinc. It helps the bruises heal faster."

"Is Kingsley like you?" She turned around and faced him, her knees pulled to her chest to cover her nakedness.

"A sadist, you mean?"

"Yes."

"He enjoys pain play enormously, although he can and does have sex without it often. It's safe to say Kingsley enjoys… everything."

"My kind of guy."

"There is something else you need to learn about Kingsley."

"What?" She wrapped her arms around her legs, suddenly chilly.

"There is God, there is you and there is Kingsley. Those are my three nonnegotiables. You understand?"

She nodded solemnly, wondering why Kingsley meant so much to Søren, but decided not to ask. Kingsley had been his best friend in school and their friendship had survived the death of Kingsley's sister. Søren called Kingsley a non-negotiable. She needed to know nothing more.

"I may have Kingsley instruct you about our world, the rules."

"It is that complicated?"

"It is. This world of ours is structured, hierarchical and ritualistic."

"Sounds like church."

Søren smiled broadly.

"Perhaps that's part of the appeal for me. It takes eroticism seriously, treats it as the sacred thing it is, that it should be."

"This feels sacred to me. It didn't feel like a sin. Was it?"

Søren turned her to face him. She should have felt embarrassed being naked with him like this, especially since he still had his trousers on, but instead she felt pride in her naked body, pleased she could finally display it for him. He took her breasts in his hands and held them while he kissed her.

"Did it feel like a sin?" Søren asked when he pulled back from the kiss and released her breasts.

"No. It felt like love," she said.

"Your friend St. Teresa of Avila who had the erotic encounter with the angel might have agreed with you."

"Really?"

"She said, 'It is here that love is to be found—not hidden away in corners but in the midst of occasions of sin.' Perhaps she was right."

"I think she was," Eleanor said. "I liked this, what we did. Loved it."

"I won't lie to you, Eleanor. It's been several weeks since I've hurt anyone. When you're starving nearly any food will do. When you're sated it takes much more to tempt you."

"Is that a fancy way of saying I got off easy tonight?"

"I'm saying I got off easy tonight."

Eleanor laughed. God, this felt good, being intimate with him. Naked. Talking. Laughing. Perfect.

Søren dropped a kiss on her sore shoulder.

"Tonight I gave you bruises, Little One. Someday it will be welts. It will be cuts and burns. I would never do anything to you that you did not want to do. Unfortunately, you may not know you dislike a certain act until you've tried it."

"Eventually you're going to have to realize I'm not scared of you."

"Eventually you'll have to realize that you need to be for both our sakes. Say 'yes, sir' if you understand."

"Yes, sir."

"Now put your clothes on before I change my mind."

"Change your mind about what?" She slid off the bed and found her pajamas. It amazed her how comfortable she felt being naked around Søren. She didn't even like taking her shirt off at the doctor's office.

"About not taking your virginity in the bed where I lost mine without having any say in the matter."

Eleanor's heart plummeted at his words, spoken so simply

and without any hint of the sorrow and shame she knew he must have felt that night. She came to him and wrapped her arms around him. He sat on the bed. She stood in front of him. Finally they were the same height.

"I want our first time in your bed at the rectory. Can we do that?" she asked.

"Yes. But it won't be any time soon. You may feel ready for it, but I know I'm not. Tonight shouldn't have happened. I don't regret it and I certainly don't want you to feel upset or ashamed about anything we did together. But the consequences for what we did could be enormous."

"We'll wait, then, as long as you think we should, until you feel safe."

"I'll feel more safe when you start feeling less safe."

"I'll work on that," she promised, kissing his neck.

"This is why I want you to let Kingsley show you a few things. You might understand the risk involved better."

"He won't try to lose his watch inside me, will he?"

"I'm not entirely certain he wears a wristwatch."

"That's a relief."

Søren raised a hand to her hair and brushed it off her face.

"You are too young for what I'll ask of you. The pain is one thing, but the time, the intense commitment to me I'll ask of you, is another. I love you too much to steal your youth from you no matter how much I want it for myself. You need to focus on your life. You need to go to college. You need to have a life outside of the church and away from me. You need to meet people…."

He paused then and let those words hover in the air between them. Meet people? What people? Before she could ask, he continued.

"The stronger and smarter and more independent the person, the better he or she is at submitting without losing themselves. I was with someone once a long time ago who would have died at my command. It terrified me to be loved that much. I'll need you to help me stay in control."

"I can do that. Order me to die for you."

"Eleanor."

"Try me," she said, digging her fingers into the back of his hair. She had no idea when she'd get the chance to be alone with him like this again, to touch him so intimately again. She wanted to drink in every precious second of him.

"Die for me," he ordered, his face a mask of seriousness.

"Go fuck yourself," she replied, and kissed the tip of his nose.

He laughed and pulled her close to him.

"Was that the right answer?"

"It was."

Eleanor relaxed into the embrace, tears ready to fall from her eyes. "I'm so sorry," she began. "I mean, I'm sorry about what happened to you when you were a kid."

"Don't be sorry. I'm not. I'm sorry for what happened to Elizabeth but not sorry for me. It took years to come to a sense of peace about it, but that I am here with you in my arms means I can repent of nothing in my past that brought me to this moment."

"Thank you. I guess I should say the same. We might not be here if I hadn't stolen those cars."

"Don't let that be an excuse to ever do it again."

"I promise. I'm a saint from now on."

"I don't believe a word of that."

She laughed softly and held him even closer.

"I'm glad you finally told me what you are," she said. "I like knowing I'm not the only one with a fucked-up family and some embarrassing stuff in my past."

Søren tucked a strand of hair behind her ear and kissed her forehead.

"When I was eighteen," Søren began, "I left the Jesuit school that had been my home for eight years. I was leaving for Europe, to seminary in the fall. Before I left, I came here one more time."

"Here? This house?"

"This house. I knew I would be gone for ten years. I didn't want my father beguiling another young woman into marrying him. I…"

"What? Tell me. You can tell me anything."

"I came here at night. I knocked my father unconscious and castrated him. I couldn't bring myself to kill him, but I could prevent him from remarrying and having more children that he would damage. He never knew it was me. I was on my way to Europe by the time he woke up."

"Why are you telling me this?" she asked.

"You wanted to know who I was. That I have the capacity to cause that sort of harm is part of who I am. To my everlasting shame, I don't regret it."

She laid both hands on each side of his face and looked him in the eyes.

"I'm proud of you," she said. "If I were you, I would have done the same thing."

"Thank you for loving me, Little One. You restore my faith."

She pushed close to him again but she could sense him pulling back from her, and she wasn't ready to let him go yet.

"Go to bed, Eleanor. You need sleep. So do I."

"Can I sleep with you? Just sleep, I mean?"

"Not tonight. Not in this house."

"But someday?"

He slapped her hard on the bottom, hard enough she

yelped. The yelp turned into a laugh. He pulled her even tighter to him.

"If you choose, Little One, I can own you. You would be my property, mine alone."

"Of course you can own me. You always have. You always will." She made the pledge without thinking. She no more needed to think about her words than she did about breathing. Yes, he could own her. Breathe in. Breathe out. He always had.

"But not yet," she said.

"I'll leave first." Søren released her from his arms. "Wait a few minutes and then go straight to bed."

He kissed her quick on the lips and walked to the door.

At the door he paused with his hand on the knob.

"Little One, you should know something else."

She sat back on the bed and pulled her knees to her chest.

"What is it?"

"What you know of me, what you've seen, this is only one small part of me. There are far less likable aspects to my character than what I've allowed you to see. If you don't believe me, you can ask Kingsley."

"What should I ask him?"

"Ask him to tell you why you should be afraid of me."

"What will he tell me?"

"Nothing. But ask him anyway."

She nodded although she didn't understand.

"Try to sleep. I'd like you to come to the funeral tomorrow. You'll meet Elizabeth, so prepare yourself."

"Is she okay? I mean, after all that happened to her."

Søren crossed his arms over his chest.

"She wants to have children," he said. "More than anything. I doubt she'll ever date or marry, but she does want to be a mother desperately. She was doing well until recently.

Medical tests revealed she can't have children. What our father did to her, it had consequences."

"She can't have kids?"

Søren shook his head.

"She did not take the news well," he said and she heard a deeper meaning in his words. "But I have faith in her. Try to have compassion for her."

"I do. I will."

"Good girl. Go to sleep."

"Yes, sir. Sir?"

"Yes, Little One?"

"Will you say it again? Please?"

He smiled at her. "In Danish or English?"

"You already said it in English. Let's go for Danish."

Søren walked back to where she sat on the bed. He took her face in his hands and kissed her long and deep.

"Jeg elsker dig, min lille en."

He kissed her again, told her good-night and slipped into the hallway.

Eleanor collapsed back onto the bed. Staring up at the ceiling she ran her hands over her upper thighs, feeling the new tenderness in them. Touching the bruises left on her by Søren and lying in the bed where he'd penetrated her with his finger was like lying in a bed of fire. She slid her hand into her shorts and started to tease her clitoris again. Søren told her to wait a few minutes before returning to bed. Getting herself off while imagining Søren fucking her would certainly take a minute or two. She came again quickly, quietly, trying not to moan aloud as her cervix bucked inside her and her vaginal muscles contracted onto themselves.

She dragged herself off the bed and left the room as quietly as she could. In the doorway she glanced back at the bed and had a vision of it burning. That was what she'd felt lying on it—fire. She shut the door behind her and crept down the hallway.

Careful of the darkness, she headed toward her room. As she passed into the main hallway, she heard voices. Next to a window, she made out the outline of two people. Hiding in the shadows she moved in closer. She saw Søren and a woman speaking softly, their heads bowed as if in prayer.

"I'm not sorry," the woman whispered. "I know that isn't much of a confession, but I'm not. At most I'm sorry I'm not sorry."

Søren crossed his arms over his chest as if wanting to hide behind them like a shield. He looked up into the woman's eyes.

"I'm not sorry, either."

Eleanor didn't know what she heard, only that she shouldn't have heard it. She turned back and retreated into her room. She slid into bed, where Claire lay sound asleep. Her entire body trembled as visceral memories of her time with Søren in his bedroom flashed across her mind's eye.

He'd ordered her to go to bed and she had. But she didn't sleep, not until dawn.

Groggy and sore, she reluctantly threw the covers off her when Claire nudged her awake.

"I'm up, I'm up," she said and started to stand up.

"Holy crap, what happened to your legs?" Claire asked, staring wide-eyed at her. Eleanor glanced down and saw the bruises Søren had left on her were already turning purple.

"Um…I was walking in the hall last night and ran into something. Some table or something. It was dark," she lied and disappeared into the bathroom.

Once in the bathroom she splashed water on her face and stripped naked. Before stepping into the shower, she gazed at herself in the mirror.

"Oh, my God..."

With his bare hands and nothing else, Søren had turned her upper thighs black. She turned around and lifted her hair. On her back were four black bruises about the size of her palm. She had bruises on her right breast and one on her shoulder. She counted two more on her upper arms, one on her forearms and four finger-mark bruises on the side of each hip and a black thumbprint on the top. If she had seen a naked woman with the identical bruises, she would have assumed she'd been raped.

Eleanor leaned back into the wall and put one leg up on the bathroom counter. While looking at her bruises, she brought herself to orgasm. She couldn't help herself. She'd never seen anything more erotic in her life than the marks Søren had left on her.

Luckily she'd packed a long-sleeved wrap dress for the funeral that covered both her back and her legs down to her knees. She and Claire ate a quick breakfast before the guests started to arrive at the home. They entered some sort of dining room—Claire called it the morning room. About forty people were packed into the room, drinking tea and coffee and whispering to each other. Still, the effect of forty people whispering all in one room sounded almost deafening to Eleanor's ringing head. She'd slept only two hours the night before. She'd never felt better about feeling shitty her entire life. Funeral, she reminded herself. No shit-eating grins allowed.

She spotted Søren across the room in a black suit, white shirt and black tie. A woman—young and lovely—stood next to him. Claire took her hand and dragged her over to them.

"Who is this?" the woman asked, giving Søren a fragile smile.

"This is Eleanor. She's a friend of Claire's."

"Hi." Eleanor sat her cup on a table and shook the woman's hand.

"Eleanor, this is my sister, Elizabeth," Søren said.

It was a good thing she had sat her coffee cup down, otherwise she would have dropped it. It took all her willpower not to gasp or gape as she looked at her. A beautiful woman with auburn hair and violet eyes, she could have been anyone's lovely older sister. She and Søren, despite having the same father, looked nothing alike. She must have taken after her mother. As much as Eleanor wanted to see Elizabeth with eyes of compassion only, she couldn't help but recall that this woman had done terrible things to Søren when they were children. But he didn't blame her, only their father, so Eleanor tried not to blame her, either. Eleanor looked in her eyes, trying to find the human being behind the mask of good daughter in mourning, but Eleanor saw nothing—only a blank, as if she stared into a body without a soul.

"The cars are here," Elizabeth said to Søren with no emotion in her voice. "Time to go."

Søren put an arm around Claire, who looked up at him and smiled.

"Good," Søren said, dropping a quick kiss onto Claire's forehead. "Let's go and bury the bastard."

23

Eleanor

IF ELEANOR HAD BELIEVED ALL THE LIES TOLD TO HER in her Catholic high school's sex-ed classes, she would have thought her life would enter a terrible and tragic downward spiral after daring to spread her legs for a man before marriage. Her Ursuline teacher had stressed that any sort of sexual behavior would lead to pregnancy, poverty, raging venereal diseases and death. Poor Jordan had bought into the lies hook, line and sinker. She'd not only decided she wouldn't have sex until she was married, but she also wouldn't even kiss a man until they were engaged. Better safe than sorry. But when Eleanor walked out the front steps of her school two days after Søren's father's funeral and saw a silver Rolls-Royce waiting for her, she decided that stripping naked for a priest was about the best idea she'd ever had.

"Holy crap," Jordan said, noticing the Rolls-Royce at the same time Eleanor did. "What is that?"

Eleanor tried not to burst into laughter at the sight of the

Rolls-Royce idling in the car pickup lane with the minivans and the beige Camrys.

"That would be my ride."

"Holy crap," Jordan said again. The Rolls inched up until it waited at the bottom of the front stairs. The driver door opened and a man in a chauffeur's uniform stepped out. He opened the passenger door, and none other than Kingsley Edge himself stepped out. He walked around the car, leaned back on the door, raised his hand and crooked his finger at her.

He wore riding boots, some sort of long frock coat and sleek modern sunglasses. He looked positively punk with his long dark hair loose down to his shoulders and a little smile on his lips.

"Holy..." Jordan breathed, apparently forgetting the "crap." "Who is that?"

"Told you. He's my ride."

"Can he be my ride?"

Eleanor wrapped an arm around Jordan and patted her on the back.

"Jordan, there might be hope for you yet."

Eleanor skipped down the steps to the Rolls and Kingsley opened the door for her.

"You're picking me up from school?" she asked before getting into the car.

"You're a member of the tribe now. Membership has its privileges. *Allons-y.*"

She had no idea what *allons-y* meant, but the hand on her lower back guiding her into the backseat gave her a good idea it meant something like "get in the damn car already." She happily obliged.

Kingsley got in after her and sat on the bench seat opposite her. The car headed away from the school at a brisk clip.

"So I'm a member now?" Eleanor asked as she settled into the luxurious dark gray leather seats.

He smiled at her as he pushed his sunglasses on top of his head and looked at her with his darkly twinkling eyes.

"You're his, aren't you? He's told you all?"

"Does this answer your question?" She pulled the collar down on her shirt to display the purple bruise on her neck. Kingsley raised an eyebrow. "How do you do that?"

"What?" he asked.

"Arch your eyebrow that high."

"It's a French thing."

"Are you really French or are you doing it for attention?"

"Both."

"Thought so. I love your accent."

"Do you love this one more?" he asked, the French accent completely disappearing from his voice. He sounded entirely 100 percent American. Eleanor gaped at him.

"No, it's horrible. Stop that. How do you do that?"

"My mother was American," he said, reverting back to his natural voice, complete with sexy-as-hell French accent. "I can speak English without the accent. I have to concentrate, however, and it gives me a headache."

"Plus it's not nearly as sexy."

"Exactement."

"So what are these membership privileges I get? I mean, other than being picked up from school in a Rolls."

"I'll tell you, but first, let's see the damage."

Eleanor attempted to raise her eyebrow as high as he did. She gave up and used her finger to push it up like Kingsley did.

"You want to see my bruises?"

"Bien sûr."

She pushed her eyebrow even higher.

"That's French for 'of course.'"

"I'd have to take my clothes off."

"I'm not hearing an objection."

She lowered her eyebrow. She wondered how Søren would feel about her showing off her bruises to Kingsley. Only one way to find out.

She threw her backpack on the floor and shrugged out of her coat.

"On the way back from the funeral, Søren told me you used to be in the French Foreign Legion."

"I was a captain, *oui*."

"So maybe you can answer a question for me."

"What's the question?"

She unlaced her boots and kicked them off. He wanted to see the bruises on her thighs, so she'd have to take her shoes and tights off under her skirt. Luckily the cold weather gave her an excuse to keep every bruise covered and then some. So if Kingsley wanted to see her bruises, she'd have to strip. She yanked off her tights and stuck her foot in Kingsley's lap.

"Do I have trench foot?"

Kingsley grabbed her leg by the ankle and raised her foot off his lap. He ran a finger down the arch of her foot.

"You have one blister, not trench foot. Stop wearing combat boots without socks."

"Thank you. I was worried we might have to amputate."

She placed her bare feet back on the floor, grateful Kingsley kept the Rolls warm and toasty. He must be feeling overly warm in his suit as he, too, started to remove his jacket.

"I can't believe I'm doing this," she said.

"Taking your clothes off for me in the back of my Rolls-Royce?"

"That." She unbuttoned her shirt.

"Get used to it."

She turned her back to him and lowered her shirt. Kingsley moved to sit behind her on her seat. His surprisingly gentle fingers traced the outline of the bruises that dotted her skin. His touch on her body made her feel treacherous sorts of things in her stomach and a little lower.

"Where else?" he asked.

She pulled her shirt back up and turned around. Feeling obnoxious, she threw her leg over his thighs and raised her skirt.

"Glad I shaved my legs this morning," she said as she displayed the bruises on her upper thighs.

"So am I."

"So you shaved your legs, too?" She pushed her skirt back down and put her feet on the floor once more.

He narrowed his eyes at her as she buttoned her shirt back up.

"You're intelligent."

"You say that like it's a bad thing." She put her boots back on and left her tights off. She'd worry about her trench foot later.

"Intelligence is dangerous in a woman. Next thing we know you'll say that marriage is a trap that tricks women into becoming unpaid cooks and housekeepers."

"Even if I were stupid I'd be smart enough to know that."

She turned to face him, pulling her legs into the seat cross-legged. She had a feeling he could see her underwear from this angle but for some reason she really didn't care. If Søren trusted Kingsley, she would, too.

"You're an interesting young woman. I thought he was out of his mind when he first told me about you."

"What did he tell you about me?"

"Nothing I'll tell you. What is important is that you're here now, and there are things you should know."

"I want to know everything."

"As soon as you turn eighteen, I'll take you to a club."

"Why eighteen?"

"Because you have to be eighteen to enter BDSM clubs in this state."

"Yes, I can see you're a law-abiding citizen. I've been in your house, remember?"

"You came uninvited."

"You were having an orgy that involved people betting money on sex."

"A friendly gentleman's wager. I never play, though."

"Why not?"

"No fun in it. I always win."

"I heard some rumors you were good in bed."

Kingsley plucked a nonexistent thread off his trousers and smiled at something out the window.

"If I were you, I would believe them."

The casual confidence in Kingsley's tone made something twitch inside Eleanor.

"I want to believe them."

"I would take you to a club right now and prove it to you if I could. I am under orders at the moment. *Je suis désolé.*"

"Blondie won't let me play yet?"

"Not at a club."

She heard something in his voice—a hint.

"Søren said you weren't allowed to take me a kink club."

"He did. But he didn't say I couldn't take you to my house."

Kingsley grinned and for a beautiful, terrifying moment Eleanor wanted to kiss Kingsley as much as she'd ever wanted to kiss Søren.

"What are we doing at your house?"

"A little demonstration of BDSM in action."

"BDSM?"

"Bondage. Domination or discipline. Sadomasochism. Or what I like to call 'my favorite hobbies.'"

"Can you pick me up from school every day?"

Kingsley laughed and pulled her into his lap. He gave her a quick kiss on both cheeks, going nowhere near her lips. Then he sat her bodily onto the bench seat before moving to sit across from her.

"Enough playing," he said with a more serious expression on his face. "I believe you have a question for me?"

Eleanor straightened her skirt, flattening it against her thighs.

"Søren told me to ask you why I should be afraid of him. Do I want the answer?"

"Only you can tell me that."

Eleanor glanced down at her boots, her Goodwill combat boots.

"I want to know. But Søren said you wouldn't answer."

"I won't answer. Not the truth anyway. But I can tell you a useful lie."

"That'll work, I guess."

Kingsley shrugged, sat back in the seat and smiled at her.

"He's a sadist, *chérie.* The most brutal sadist I've ever known. There are four women in the city who he plays with on a rotating basis. Once a week if he has time. It can take well over two weeks for them to heal entirely from a few hours with him."

"Jesus. What does he do?"

"Flogging, whipping, caning, cutting, candle-wax burns, bastinado…" He ticked the terms off on his fingers. "I'm forgetting something. What is it?"

He tapped his forehead.

"Oh, humiliation." Kingsley snapped his fingers. "I always forget that one. I don't do humiliation play so I forget it."

"What do you do?"

"Everything else. My specialty is rape."

Eleanor gaped at him.

"Rape?"

"Rape play. It's a game. There are women who love to be overpowered and treated like sexual property. It's their fantasy to be raped by a man they desire. I make the fantasy come true. It's all in good fun. Want to try?"

"How does it work?"

"Something like this." He grabbed her calf and yanked her so hard she ended up flat on her back. Before she realized what was happening, Kingsley hovered over her, his hands on her wrists, his body weight holding her immobile beneath him.

"Get off me," she said, grunting at the shock of his weight on her. "You're wrinkling my skirt."

"It's pleated."

"Oh. Good point. Then stay there." Obviously he was trying to scare her. She grew up with a dad in the mob. She didn't scare that easy.

"You take all the fun out of it." He still held her down, his hands on her forearms. It hurt, but she refused to let him see her in pain.

"Why? Because I'm not scared of you, either?"

"I have you pinned underneath me, and you aren't even nervous?"

"Sorry." She smiled up at him and batted her eyelashes. In all honesty, fear was last on the list of feelings she was experiencing at the moment. Ahead of fear were the following: first, enjoyment; second, desire; followed by curiosity third with embarrassment coming in a close fourth. The embarrassment ranked fourth only because she felt feelings one through three.

"Have you ever had sex in the back of a Rolls-Royce?" he asked her as he pushed his hips meaningfully into hers. What she felt pressing against her caused fear to jump ahead a few places on her emotions-currently-experiencing list. Fear and desire both shot right up her list.

"I've never had sex, you know, ever."

"Poor girl. Would you like me to take care of that little problem for you?"

"I'm Catholic, so I'm waiting."

"Until marriage?"

"No. I'm waiting for my priest to fuck me."

"Are you tired of waiting?"

"Yes. There's no reason to wait. He's being overprotective."

"He cares about you."

"Wish he cared less and fucked more."

Kingsley laughed as he sat up and let her go.

"He said you and I would be friends. I didn't believe him at first. I think he might be right."

Eleanor moved to the seat across from Kingsley and smoothed her skirt down over her knees. A little distance between her and him would be a good idea.

"I hope we can be friends. He said you and me, we were his nonnegotiables. Oh, and God. Can't forget Him."

"We will be, *j'espère.* I want you to trust me. There are things you need to hear that you would not hear if he said them to you."

"What do you mean?"

"You have fallen in love with the king of all the mind-fuckers."

"Mind-fucking? Is that when you stick it in her ear?"

"Not quite. It's when I stick it in her brain. The mind-fuck is one of many games the dominant plays. I might tie up a girl, blindfold her and then run my fingers so lightly across her stomach..." He raised his hand and tickled the air. Something inside Eleanor clenched at the erotic image. She couldn't help but imagine Kingsley doing such a thing to her. "And then casually mention the word *snake* or *spider.* Watch her tense. Hear her laugh nervously. She knows it's my fingers on her. Not a snake. Not a spider. But now the doubt is there…one sliver of a doubt in her brain."

"That is so evil." Eleanor grinned broadly. "But you don't ever actually put snakes and spiders on people, do you?"

"*Non*. Of course not. Unless…"

"Unless what?"

"Unless she asks for it."

Eleanor's eyes widened. Kingsley only smiled.

"You see, the mind-fuck is simply this—I take your mind, I play with it, I make you think things you didn't think you would think and then suddenly…you're thinking them."

"You can't pull that stuff on me."

"*Non? Le prêtre* is pulling a mind-fuck on you."

"How?"

"By making you wait for him. You don't want to wait for him, do you? You want to be his lover right now. Today even."

"No. Not today. I wanted to be his lover yesterday. There's no reason to wait."

"I know the reason for it."

"You do?"

"Oh, *oui*. He's manipulating you. Here you are. So young. So beautiful. So ripe for the plucking. And yet you sit there… unplucked. This is how he proves he owns you like a dog on a leash. Heel. Sit. Roll over. Play dead. You're not his lover. You're his puppy and you follow him anywhere. He feeds you crumbs and you lap them out of his hand."

Eleanor sat up straighter.

"He's not manipulating me by making us wait, okay? I'm seventeen and he's almost thirty-one. He's a priest and I'm in high school. I'm not even on birth control yet, and if I was and my mom found it, I'd be dead. If he gets caught fooling around with a high school student, he'll be dead. On top of all that, he's a sadist. He cares about me so much he wants me to know what I'm getting into before I get into it. So fine. We'll wait. I'll learn what I need to learn. We'll start having sex when he's ready and he knows I'm ready. That's not manipulation. That's good sense. And you could learn a little something from him about good sense."

"Moi?" Kingsley sounded positively scandalized at her insinuation.

"You. You picked me up from school in a Rolls-Royce? Do you know how much attention that's going to get me? You and Søren are related—sort of. You have to be careful. We have to be careful. We can't get him into trouble."

"I'll be more careful," he pledged.

"Good."

"I enjoyed your impassioned defense of your own lingering virginity."

"I don't want you thinking Søren is manipulating me when he's not."

"He's not."

"No, he isn't."

"But I am." Kingsley put his feet in the seat next to her and smirked.

"You…you got me to argue why Søren and I should wait when I said five minutes ago I didn't want to and there was no reason to."

"It was almost too easy."

"You mind-fucked me."

"Does your brain hurt? I tried to be gentle since it was your first time."

Eleanor picked up her combat boot and tossed it at Kingsley's head. He caught it and rolled down the window.

"Don't you dare. I love those damn boots."

"You promise you will not throw them at me again?"

"I promise. I swear."

"You promise you will be a good girl for me all evening?"

"The best girl."

"Will you let me fuck you right now if I give you the boot back?"

Eleanor opened her mouth and then closed it again. Was Kingsley serious? Serious or not…

"Not for all the combat boots in the world."

Kingsley held her boot at the window and waited.

"Toss it," she said. "It's fucking freezing in here."

Kingsley rolled up the window and handed her the boot back.

"You're giving it back?" She stuffed her feet into her boots before Kingsley changed his mind. In the future she would have to be smarter, stay on her toes.

"You passed the test."

"What test?"

"I like to test new people who come to our world. I get them into my Rolls and try to seduce them. The winners say no. The losers say yes. But since I still fuck them everyone wins."

"Why is it losing to say yes?"

"Because if you say yes to being fucked by a stranger without any discussion of limits, wants, protection and safety, you are very likely not yet ready for our world. A submissive too eager to please a dominant can get into trouble quickly in my world."

"So I passed?"

"One test."

"There are others?"

"Many others. Wait until he puts a dog collar on you. I can't wait to see how you respond to that test."

Eleanor glared at him. "I'm not going to wear a dog collar."

"He already has one picked out for you."

"Søren?"

"Who else?"

"A dog collar? Are you shitting me?"

"Would I do that? Collars play an important role in our world. It's a sign of ownership. So you should take it as a compliment. And then after you've taken it as a compliment, you can wag your little tail for him."

"He said you were the devil."

"He only says that because he knows how horny I am."

He raised his hand to his head and held up two fingers as horns. Eleanor burst out laughing.

"I like you, Kingsley. I don't want to, but I do."

He brought her hand to his lips and kissed the center of her palm. No finger sniffing this time.

"The feeling, *ma petite,* is entirely mutual."

They arrived as Kingsley's town house, and he escorted her inside.

"Who's this, King?" A stunning Hispanic-looking woman in a tight white dress came down the stairs. She gave Kingsley a quick kiss on the cheek. "Nice uniform," she said to Eleanor. It sounded like a genuine compliment, not sarcasm.

"We're doing an age-play scene tonight. Teacher-student. I'd let you watch but it's her first role-play." Kingsley ran his hand over Eleanor's bottom.

"Next time, maybe?" the woman said, giving her a wink and Kingsley another kiss. "I'll play her sister, and you can punish us both for acting up in class, Mr. King."

The woman strolled away, her hips swaying seductively with every step.

"Age-play?" she asked. "That's a thing?"

"Here everything is a thing," he said. Kingsley gave her another ass pat.

She thought about finding a knife and slicing that roaming, ass-grabbing hand of his off, but the word *sister* reminded her of a question she wanted to ask.

"Can I ask you a weird question?"

"I might not answer it, but you may ask me anything."

"Was it Elizabeth?" she asked as he took her arm and led her up the stairs.

"Elizabeth? What about her?"

"Søren said when he was married to your sister he cheated on her with someone. Your sister caught him and whoever kissing and ran off and that's when..." Eleanor felt weird about bringing this up but she had to know. "Søren didn't tell me who he cheated with, only that he loved her."

"He said he loved her?"

"Something like that. I keep thinking about why he wouldn't tell me who she was. And then he told me about him and Elizabeth when they were kids...and your sister, she came to visit you all at school. It was an all-boys school, but they let her visit. Why?"

"Because she was a relative."

"Right," Eleanor said and waited. Kingsley said nothing more. "I'm asking, was it Elizabeth who Søren cheated on your sister with? They had a fucked-up childhood. They were lonely. Incest or not, I don't care. It's the only answer I can come up with. I mean, what else could have shocked your sister so much she...you know."

"Killed herself?"

"That. I mean, seeing her husband kissing his own sister? That could shock anyone to death."

"It could, *oui*."

"I want to know who he loved enough to cheat on his wife with. I need to know, and I know you know."

"I know," he said.

"But you won't tell me?"

"Not yet," he said with a smile. "Perhaps in time. But I will tell you this, you're on the right track. Now come with me."

Kingsley escorted her to a room at the end of the hall on the second floor.

"Tonight is my friend Blaise's birthday and we're having a little party for her. I thought you should come and see how our sort plays together."

He opened the door and led her inside a kind of sitting room.

"Oh, fuck."

Everywhere Eleanor looked, she saw fire. Tall taper candles, all alight, covered every horizontal surface—tabletops, window ledges—and a few dozen sat on the floor in ornate silver holders. So dazzled by the scene before her, Eleanor hardly noticed the four other people in the room until Kingsley introduced her to them.

First was Blaise, the birthday girl, who wore nothing but a white button-down shirt. Next was Baptiste, dark skinned and handsome, who had some kind of sexy accent—not quite French, but close. Then another man—Sven or something. She'd stopped listening because Blaise now stood naked in the center of the room.

"Shall we?" Kingsley picked up a candle as Blaise lay on the floor on a large wooden board. Everyone in the room followed suit. Soon everyone, herself included, held a candle in their hands.

Blaise raised her arms over her head and smiled up at Kingsley.

"Happy birthday, *ma fille*." He knelt at her side, bent to kiss her and as soon as the kiss broke, he poured candle wax onto the center of her chest.

Blaise winced in agony. Eleanor winced in sympathy. Everyone else laughed and applauded. Music played. Wine flowed. And one by one every guest took their turn dripping candle wax onto Blaise's naked body. Everyone but her.

"Come, *chérie*," Kingsley said, coaxing her forward.

"I don't even know her," Eleanor said in a whisper.

"This will make an excellent introduction." Kingsley inclined his head toward Blaise on the floor. He was daring her to burn Blaise, and she knew it. Kingsley stood on the opposite side of Blaise, smiling at her. "You know you want to."

"Peer pressure? Really, King?"

"We're all doing it," he said, his tone teasing, his eyes serious. And then she knew it wasn't a dare, it was a test. And since she wanted to pass this test, she burned her.

Blaise gasped as hot wax landed on her inner thighs.

Eleanor brought the candle to her mouth and blew the flame out.

Kingsley gave her a wink and she sat off to the side to watch the show. Soon Blaise's wrists were locked with hardening wax to the wooden board and then her ankles. Once her entire body was coated in the wax, Baptiste blew out his candle and inserted it inside Blaise's vagina. Eleanor watched, breathless, as he fucked her with it. Blaise closed her eyes and moaned in pleasure. Kingsley leaned over her body and kissed Baptiste long and deep.

Eleanor stood up and nearly ran to the balcony door. She threw it open, stepped onto the balcony and shut the door behind her.

She stood there in the winter cold, swallowing lungfuls of ice.

"You left too soon," Kingsley said. She'd been panting so hard she hadn't even heard the door open.

"I needed some air."

"Too much?" he asked. "Were you scared of what was happening in there?"

"Not scared."

"Aroused?"

She laughed.

"A little."

"Jealous?" He wrapped his arms around her and pulled her close. As cold as it was, she didn't fight the embrace.

"It did look kind of fun."

"I forget how young you are. We'll play this game again when you're ready."

"You kissed a man."

Kingsley gave her a quizzical look.

"I did. I like kissing women *and* men. And fucking them. Shocked?"

"I wasn't expecting that."

"For your sake, I will give you this advice—start expecting the unexpected. There are more things in heaven and earth than are dreamed of in your philosophy, *chérie*."

"I'll keep that in mind."

"Come. I'll take you home."

He kissed her on both cheeks again before wrapping an arm around her shoulders and escorting her into the house.

She got her coat and Kingsley walked her to the Rolls-Royce waiting out front.

"I think I'll go home the usual way," she said, staring at the car. "If that's okay with you."

Kingsley raised his chin and studied her.

"Worried you'll fail the Rolls-Royce test this time?" he asked. She blushed as he put the fear she hadn't even admitted to herself into words.

"I like walking," she said.

"Walk away, then." Kingsley chucked her under the chin in an infuriatingly fatherly manner. "For your sake and mine."

He gave her the quickest kiss on the lips and she growled. *Walk away,* she told herself. *Keep walking away and don't look back.*

After a few blocks, her head cleared, her heart settled. Being around Kingsley and his friends was dangerous to her sanity and her virginity.

Eleanor neared the subway entrance but paused when she heard someone call out her name.

She turned around and saw a man standing on the sidewalk ten feet behind her. She couldn't process the sight of him, the reality of him, the existence of him.

But there he was. And for the first time that night she felt true fear.

24

Eleanor

"DAD?"

"Have you missed me, baby?" Her father stood with his hands in the pockets of his long coat, a baseball cap pulled low over his eyes.

"No," she said. "What the hell are you doing out of jail?"

"Shock probation."

"Right," she said, crossing her arms over her chest. She considered running for it. The subway entrance waited twenty feet behind her. "Good for you, then. I gotta go."

She turned her back on him.

"I thought it was only Kingsley Edge you were spreading for," her father shouted after her. "But now I know it's the priest, too."

Eleanor's heart stopped. She slowly turned around.

"What are you talking about?" She kept her voice neutral, trying not to betray her fear.

"I found a business card in your coat. Edge Enterprises.

There's only one reason a man like Kingsley Edge would give you the time of day, and that reason's between your legs."

"You're disgusting."

"I'm right, though," he said. "I tried to figure out how a nobody like you would even meet Edge. Not much reason for him to hang out in Nowhere, Connecticut, right? I asked around and found out he's got this brother-in-law who stops by the house sometimes. A priest. A priest from Wakefield fucking Connecticut."

"Dad, look," Eleanor began, "it's not what you think. I'm not sleeping with—"

"Save it. I have all the proof I need. Want to see? Pictures in my car. Nice one of you and your priest in a black BMW. Where were you two going anyway? Romantic weekend away together?" Her father laughed as if he'd made the most hilarious joke.

"It was a funeral. He wanted me to hang out with his sister, who's my age. He was worried about her, and he thought she would talk to me since he wouldn't talk to him."

"You think the bishop will buy that excuse when I tell him one of his priests is fucking my underage daughter? Can't wait to tell your mother what's going on with you two."

"What do you want?" Eleanor knew her father didn't give a damn who she fucked, what she did.

"I want you to come with me right now."

"Why?"

"We're going to go to my place and have a talk. I'm leaving town and I think you should come with me."

"I'm not going anywhere with you."

"You aren't? Then I guess I'll have to send all these pictures of you and Edge, you and your priest, to the police and your mother and your principal and the bishop. The newspapers, too. 'Priest seduces teenage girl and shares her with his criminal brother-in-law' would make a great headline."

"Show me the pictures," she said.

"They're in the car."

He walked over to an old beat-up Honda and opened the passenger door. He waited.

The last thing she wanted to do was get in that car. No, the last thing she wanted to happen was Søren getting in trouble because of her. She walked to the car and sat in the passenger seat. Her father slammed the door so hard she flinched. He got in the driver's side and turned the engine on.

"Show me the pics," she demanded.

"They're at my place."

"You said they were in the car."

Her father started the engine and swung into the street. He turned the next corner as if trying to get her away as fast as possible from Kingsley's house.

"You should thank me," her father said as he sped down a side street. "You don't want to get mixed up with Edge. I've heard stories about that French fucker. Well, I suppose you know. You're fucking him."

"I'm not fucking him. We're friends."

"Friends? Is he your babysitter, too? That why he picked you up from school?"

"You're sick. Spying on your own kid." Eleanor shook with terror and fury. She'd been right. Someone *had* been in the church eavesdropping on her and Søren.

"Watching my own kid. Not spying. And it's a good thing I did, too. I go away for a year and you end up spreading for some sick piece-of-shit molester priest."

"My priest is the best man alive," she said. Before her eyes her entire world ended—Søren's name in the newspapers, transfer, defrocking, excommunication, and it was all her fault. "He's been a better father to me than you ever were. You got me into trouble. He's the one who got me out."

"Yeah, and we both know how you're paying him back."

"Pull over. I'm getting out."

"No, you're not, little girl. You're getting out of town with me."

"I said, pull over," she shouted, reaching for the wheel.

He slammed his elbow into her stomach so hard it knocked the air out of her lungs. She coughed hard and reached for the wheel again. Her father pushed back and Eleanor twisted around, scrambling out of his grasp.

"Sit down, you little bitch," he ordered. He reached for her neck and Eleanor took a deep breath. She closed her eyes, kicked out and smashed in her father's face with her boots. Blood erupted from his nose and the car swerved wildly in the street.

Eleanor threw open the car door and ran for it. She ran as hard and as fast as she could until she found a taxi and flagged it down. She gave the driver Kingsley's address and begged him to hurry. A few minutes later she threw some bills at the driver and raced up the stairs and burst through the door of the town house and found Kingsley standing in the foyer loading a clip into a gun.

"Elle, what the fuck happened to you?" He looked both relieved and furious.

"My dad… He got out of prison. He made me get in his car. What are you doing with that gun?"

"Killing your father." He shoved the gun into some kind of holster under his coat. He grabbed her by the wrist and pulled her to him. Starting at her thighs, he ran his hands all over her.

"Are you hurt?" he asked.

"No, I don't—"

He held up his hand. His palm was covered in blood.

"Jesus," she breathed.

"Scratch on your neck."

"Dad tried to choke me," she said. He must have scratched her, too.

"Come with me, right now," Kingsley said and took her upstairs to the third floor.

"Why were you going to kill my dad?" she asked as Kingsley threw open a door to a room she'd never seen. It looked like some kind of fancy office. He sat her down hard in a chair and left her there for a few seconds before returning with a first-aid kit. Kingsley knelt in front of her chair, opened the kit and told her to tilt her head to the side.

"You didn't answer my question," she said. Her heart still pounded painfully in her chest; her lungs burned from the running and the panic. "Why were you going after my dad?"

"Because of this." Kingsley dug something out of his pocket and handed it to her.

With an alcohol swab, Kingsley cleaned the cut on her neck as she read the note.

A hundred grand or your girlfriend's body will be at the bottom of the Hudson by tomorrow morning.

Included was an address and a picture.

"Oh, my God," she said, her stomach turning. "This is my sophomore-year school picture. I sent it to him in a birthday card."

She held the photograph in her shaking hand.

"He was going to kill me?" she asked. Her father had tried so hard to get her in the car. And she'd been stupid enough to get in with him.

"He might have. He might have been testing to see if I'd pay him off. I don't care. He threatened you."

"He said he has pictures of me and Søren together. He's going to send them to my mom and the bishop and maybe even the newspaper."

Kingsley sat back.

"I was afraid something like this would happen," he said.

"What are we going to do?"

"Sit. Stay," he said, standing up. "Don't leave this room."

"Okay." She gave Kingsley a blank stare. He laid his hand gently on the side of her face. "Thank you."

That seemed to surprise him. With his hand still on her face he sighed heavily and seemed to make a decision.

"King Louis XIII of France lost his father when he was nine years old," Kingsley began, his face a mask of seriousness. "Too young to rule, his mother Marie de' Medici acted as his regent. She should have ruled until he was eighteen. You see, the law said sixteen-year-old Louis was not old enough to reign. But his mother fucked the country over, so Louis had no choice. Louis exiled his mother and executed her lover, executed her followers and restored order. He took the throne, and all of Paris rejoiced. Some children have the luxury of waiting for eighteen candles on their birthday cake to become adults. The rest of us grow up when we are left no other choice."

Eleanor heard the meaning behind Kingsley's words.

"If my father tries to hurt Søren, I'll kill him with my bare hands."

Eleanor waited alone, trying to calm herself. She prayed quietly in her own mind, prayed Kingsley could help her, would help her.

A few minutes passed, then half an hour. Eleanor stared at the strange Art Deco clock hanging on the wall behind the desk until her eyes ached. This room must be Kingsley's private office. Large wooden filing cabinets with locks on them lined one wall. A black phone—rotary style, like something out of an old detective movie—sat on the desk. She wanted to use it to call Søren, but something told her that would be a bad idea. Something told her Søren shouldn't be involved in what she and Kingsley did tonight.

Finally Kingsley returned to the office and took a seat behind the desk.

"What's happening?" she asked him.

"First, your father lied to you. He's not on shock probation. He turned state's evidence and started naming names to get out of prison early. Some of his old friends have put a large price on his head."

"That explains why he wanted money from you."

"He's likely going to run tonight. Probably try to cross the border and get to Canada."

"Do you think he's going to tell on me and Søren?"

"Yes," Kingsley said. "If only to punish you for choosing us over him."

"What do we do?"

"I have someone who could help your father leave the country. He's going to call me in five minutes. If you want him to do this, then answer the phone and tell him everything you know about your father's whereabouts—where you last saw him, where he last lived. I promise this man will be able to find him. Or..."

"Or?"

"Or when the phone rings, you can let it ring. And the men who want to find your father will find him. And they will find him before morning."

"Why are you doing this for me?" Eleanor asked, stunned by Kingsley's offer of help for her father.

"You belong to *le prêtre.* I protect his property like my own. Your father harmed you. I would like to see him punished.

But that is your decision, not mine. The phone will ring soon. Make your choice."

"What do you mean?" Eleanor asked.

"Sam is off work tonight. I have no one to answer my phone for me. And I never answer my office phone—only my secretary does. When it rings, you answer it. If you want to play my secretary, that is."

They looked at each other across the desk and said nothing. She heard ticking and looked at the clock.

One minute passed.

Her father had threatened to kill her if Kingsley didn't pay him a hundred grand.

Two minutes passed.

Her father had abandoned her after she got arrested, run and let her take the fall for him.

Three minutes passed.

Her father had slapped her in the face, tried to run off with her, tried to choke her and even now the wound still bled.

Four minutes passed.

Her father had threatened to ruin Søren's life.

Five minutes passed.

The phone rang.

"I don't answer this phone," Kingsley repeated. "Either my secretary answers it or we let it ring."

The phone rang a second time.

"You can ask the person on the other end of the line to help your father," he reminded her.

Eleanor tore her eyes from the phone and met Kingsley's steady gaze.

"The only father in my life is a priest. And I'm not your secretary."

The phone stopped ringing.

25

Nora

"AND BY THE NEXT MORNING, I WAS FREE," NORA SAID. She looked over at Nico and shrugged. "Getting himself killed was the nicest thing my father ever did for me."

"How so?" Nico asked. She sat up in bed, the blanket pulled to her chest. Nico still lay on his side, his hand resting on her thigh under her nightgown.

"After I was born, my mom took out a life insurance policy for her and Dad. Dad turns up dead and—voilà—I have money for college."

"Who killed him?"

"Never found out. He had mob ties. He fucked around with the wrong bad guys one too many times. I tried to feel bad about it, knowing I had a chance to help him and didn't take it. But I couldn't. The world was better off without him."

"You were better off without him." Nico sat up and took her hand in his. He kissed the back of it. "My father's more interesting than I thought he was."

Nora laughed and twined her fingers into Nico's.

"*Interesting* is the word for it. Interesting, complicated, dangerous. When he came to Manhattan after leaving France, he was only twenty-eight. First thing he did was find the most dangerous mafia figure in town and do a favor for him. Smart move. Kingsley was under the boss's protection for the rest of his life. Which is a good thing, because Kingsley had a bad habit of pissing off very important people."

"I should be grateful he's still alive," Nico said. "Although I might never look at him the same way again. Lose his watch in you?"

"That devil."

"He is," Nico said. "A gentleman always takes his watch off first."

Nora's stomach quivered at Nico's words. She liked his definition of gentleman much better than simply a guy who held the door open for you.

"It could be worse. One night with my client Sheridan, I almost lost my necklace inside her."

Nora laughed at his look of wide-eyed wonder.

"Tiny girl," Nora said. "She must be hollow."

Nico turned his head into the pillow and burst into laughter—deep, warm, luxurious laughter.

"If you and Kingsley are alike, why is it so much easier to love you than him?" Nico asked, turning his face to her.

"Because, unlike Kingsley, I didn't seduce your mother."

"Don't forget he disappeared after getting her pregnant with me," Nico added. "And you worry he's going to judge us for this night?"

"It's not that," Nora said. "He might not even be that angry. I doubt he'll even be surprised. But I owe him a lot. He's been more family to me than my actual family. And then you come along...."

"What is it, Nora? Tell me the truth."

Nora looked away from Nico and into the fire.

"I wrote a fantasy novel once," she said, watching the flames dance as they died. "Those were my favorite when I was a kid. Unicorns, magic, dragons. A few years ago I took a stab at writing one. I let Zach read it. He thinks it needs some work."

"Not good?"

"He liked it. But, said Zach in his stuffy British editor voice, I broke the cardinal rule of writing fantasy. You see, if there's magic in your world, every time the magician uses it, he must pay a price. I've never forgotten those words from Zach—*magic isn't free.* I was drowning tonight in loneliness and grief and I thought I would go crazy out here. I wished for you and there you were, everything I needed. Like magic."

"Why me?"

"Because the only man who you've ever considered your father just died. You're on the same path I am, only a few feet ahead. If I follow you, maybe I won't get lost. I'm so scared of getting lost."

Nico touched her face. His fingers came away wet with tears. Nora had built her life around certain beliefs, certain truths, and now she found herself questioning everything.

"What was the price you paid to have me here?"

Nora swallowed the lump in her throat.

"I can't go back," she whispered.

"Back where?" Nico wrapped both hands around hers.

"Kingsley's bed."

Nora stared into Nico's eyes. She wanted him to see the truth in her words.

"You should know that not only do Kingsley and I have history, we have recent history."

"How recent?" Nico asked.

"The last time was the night before I flew to France to find you."

If that hurt to hear, Nico's eyes did not betray it. She must have known somehow that once she met Nico she could never be intimate with Kingsley again. They'd had one last dark and beautiful night together. And now…never again.

"And while Kingsley may not seem like a father to you—yet—in his eyes, and in his heart, you are his son. He'll never touch me again."

"Never touch you again? Because he'll be angry?"

"No. Because he loves you."

"Is this why you didn't want to let me in?"

Nora looked back into the dying fire.

"Kingsley has secrets that he shares with very few people. You can count the number on one hand, and I was one of them. Not anymore." She hadn't merely been Kingsley's lover, she'd been his domme as well those nights he'd needed pain. She'd also carried his child once, if only briefly—not that she could tell Nico. In time she would, but not yet.

"You paid a high price to let me in."

"Very high. Kingsley and I have made a habit of hurting each other for twenty years the way only two people who are like family to each other can. But even if Kingsley would want me again, I couldn't do that to you—be with you and then go back to him. This night means too much to me. You mean too much to me."

Nico raised her hand and held it to his chest.

"You're grieving," Nico said. "So I won't ask you to make any decisions. I will only say that if it were my decision, you would stay with me."

"And what? Marry you? Have your babies? That's not who I am. I'm selfish like that."

Nico scoffed. "Selfish is the name the jealous give to the free. I'm free, too."

"You are, aren't you?"

"I am. And if I wanted marriage, children, why would I chase women with children my age? I have a little sister now. Why would I need any other heirs?"

Nora leaned forward and rested her head on the center of his chest. He kissed her hair.

"Don't make any decisions yet," Nico said, caressing her back. "But know this—you will always be welcome in my home and in my bed. And I won't make you pay any price."

Tucking her head into the crook of his shoulder and neck, she breathed his scent, quieted her heart.

"But you aren't the one who sends the bills."

Reluctantly Nora pulled away from Nico's embrace. She'd rarely, if ever, felt this weak around a man. Grief had brought her to this point. She'd rarely known such deep sadness. Her loss had left her lost. Loss? Such a misnomer. Nothing was lost. Something was taken. She felt robbed, like someone had broken into her life and stolen her valuables. It wasn't a loss. It was a theft. And she knew she would never get it back.

Nico crawled out of bed and walked to the fireplace. He threw a log onto the ebbing flames and stoked the fire back to life. He worked quickly and efficiently, wasting neither time nor effort. Since he was a child, he'd told her once, he'd worked in the vineyards. School all day. Work all evening. Sleep all night. The result of such a life—intelligence, strength and a clear conscience.

He came back to the bed and slid in next to her. Gathering her in his arms, he pulled her to him, pressing her back to his chest and dragging the covers over both of them.

"What happened after your father died?" Nico asked, perhaps sensing she couldn't and wouldn't talk about their future anymore.

"Like I said, I got into NYU. I had a future and the money to pay for it. And then the moment I'd been waiting for happened."

"What was that?"

"I turned eighteen. I got my driver's license finally. And Søren and Kingsley started training me. Kingsley took me to my first BDSM club—a little one a friend of his ran. It wasn't like coming home. It was better than that—like when you go to a new city and feel like 'yes, I could live here the rest of my life,' and you mentally start packing your bags."

"I know that feeling," he said and she saw something flicker in his eyes. Was he packing her bags for her so she could stay with him?

"Good feeling," she said, trying not to fall under Nico's spell. "I was so eager to join that world. And yet, there I was, still a virgin."

"Tell me. I want to know what you were like when you were a virginal teenager."

"I was a teenager but never virginal. Even when I was a virgin."

"When did you lose your virginity?"

"I was twenty. Barely twenty. And you?"

"Fifteen. She was thirty-six."

Nora pursed her lips. "That sounds familiar."

"Hard to believe someone with your passion waiting for so long. Was it worth the wait?"

"It was," she said, her mind falling far back into the past. "But he was right to make me wait that long, as much as I wanted him sooner. I understand that now."

"What do you understand?"

"I was ready for sex long before my first time. But I wasn't ready for him, for what he would want from me."

"And that was?"

"Everything. I had a lot to learn before we became lovers. And Søren had some interesting teaching methods."

Nico raised an eyebrow, arched it high. She wished she had a ruler with her. Wonder who could do that eyebrow arch better—Kingsley or Nico?

"Case in point—my first training dinner with Søren the night I got my collar."

"What happened?"

"Well, we were at Kingsley's."

"A good start."

"Dinner was served."

"Keep going."

"And I was bare-ass naked."

26

Eleanor

A DATE.

A real date.

A normal date.

Dinner. Dressing up. Making out. Finally at age eighteen, Eleanor was going on the first real date of her life.

With her priest.

Okay, maybe it wasn't a normal date, after all. But she had a new dress—a short white strappy number—and they would have Kingsley's town house all to themselves since the king was not in residence this week. Close enough to a real date. Søren even promised he wouldn't wear his collar tonight, but the suit she loved on him so much. After he'd made the promise he said something cryptic that had her pondering his words all day long. *Only one of us will be in a collar tonight. I promise it won't be me.*

Kingsley's dining room was illuminated by dozens of candles and the flickering light from the fireplace. Søren was there. Food was there. And yet all she could see was the white box that sat by her plate.

As she stared at the box, Søren came up behind her, kissed the back of her neck, and pulled down the zipper on her dress.

"Whoa, what's going on? We're not eating?"

"You are."

"And you're taking my dress off because…?"

"I want you naked," he said, as if that was the most obvious answer in the world, so obvious she shouldn't have even asked the question.

"This is a naked dinner?"

"For you, Little One. I'll keep my clothes on."

Søren started to pull the straps of her dress down and Eleanor stiffened. He paused.

"Something wrong?"

"No. Nothing. Except you're making me eat dinner completely naked."

"Does that make you uncomfortable?"

"Incredibly uncomfortable."

"Understandable," he said and started sliding the straps of her dress down again.

"But we're doing it anyway?"

"Eleanor," Søren said, turning her to face him. "Tonight is a special night for us. You're old enough now to begin learning what I expect from you if we're going to be together. This is how it will be if you belong to me. I will own you. It's not a metaphor or romantic hyperbole. It's a statement of fact. I should be able to take your clothes off you at any time and whenever I please. Taking off your clothes should require as little explanation or planning as taking off my own collar. I do it when it pleases me to do it and for no other reason."

"Yes, sir." She clenched her hands into nervous fists as she stood in the center of the candlelit dining room and let Søren undress her. She felt ridiculous standing completely naked with her hair piled on her head in a fancy updo and high heels on her feet. Søren didn't touch her other than to slide her panties down her legs. He laid her dress and underwear over the back of the fainting couch that sat near the fireplace.

He pulled her chair out for her and she sat down, wincing as her bare skin connected with the cool wood.

Søren picked up the white box and put it in her hands.

"What is it?" she asked, eyeing the elegant black-and-white wrapping.

"Open it."

She carefully removed the black ribbon and tore off the white paper. She lifted the lid and stared at the object in the box. So Kingsley hadn't been kidding, hadn't been exaggerating, hadn't been trying to piss her off last year during their first Rolls-Royce ride together.

"Like it?" Søren asked.

Eleanor answered with only one word.

"Woof."

Søren laughed and picked up the white leather collar and unbuckled it.

"A dog collar?"

"A slave collar. You belong to me always, no matter where we are or what we are doing. But when I put the collar on you, you'll know that you must give me your complete obedience and your undivided attention. You will call me 'sir' while in your collar and nothing else."

"It's white." She looked up at him.

"I wonder why."

"You know, wearing a dog collar…slave collar," she corrected, "is a little humiliating."

"And that is why I want you to wear it."

She gazed at the collar in his hands.

"Is your collar humiliating, sir?"

"Yes," he said simply. That hadn't been the answer she expected, but she understood it. He wrapped the collar around her neck and fastened it into place with a small silver lock.

"Don't worry, I have the key," he said. "The only key."

"Good."

"Too tight?"

She swallowed easily, breathed easily.

"No."

Søren took a seat in the chair at her side. "You're smiling, Little One."

"I'm totally naked and wearing a dog collar, sir. It was either laugh or cry."

"Both would have been acceptable. How does it make you feel?"

"I don't know." She looked up at him. She smiled, yes, but it was through tears. "I can't tell if I'm happy or miserable."

"An appropriate reaction," he said, lightly tapping her under the chin.

Turning to her meal, she reached for her fork, but Søren snapped his fingers. She stopped and slowly placed her hand back in her lap.

"You do nothing without my permission."

"Yes, sir."

He picked up a strawberry, red and wet, and brought it to her lips.

"Eat," he ordered.

She parted her lips and let him lay the strawberry on her tongue. Her cheeks ached from its sweetness. She swallowed it because she knew he wanted her to.

"Are you comfortable?" he asked, now serving her a spoonful of the soup, some sort of miracle in a bowl. And yet it might have been ashes on her tongue for as much as she enjoyed it.

"Not uncomfortable. Weird. I feel weird."

"You'll have to elaborate."

"I feel..." She paused and looked at her own naked body. She had her legs firmly pressed together, her stomach pulled in tight. She'd positioned her arms to cover her breasts as much as she could. "Very aware of my own body."

"Exposed?"

"That."

"I have seen you naked before," he reminded her.

"That was different. We were on a bed in the dark and doing stuff."

"Doing stuff? You can do better than that. What were we doing?"

"We were..." She exhaled, feeling strangely tongue-tied. "We were kissing and touching and you used your fingers to make me come twice and you came on me and it was amazing."

"Where did I touch you?" Søren gave her another spoonful of soup. She couldn't believe he was feeding her.

Eleanor's feet went numb and her hands trembled.

"You're seriously trying to embarrass the hell out of me, aren't you, sir?" She added the *sir* quickly at the end.

"I am. But also you need to be comfortable talking to me about anything. If you believe you're mature enough to do the acts, you need to be mature enough to talk about them. So tell me, where did I touch you?"

She closed her eyes to remember that night with him in his childhood bedroom. But also so she wouldn't have to look at him while she answered his humiliating questions.

"You kissed me on the mouth and on my neck and shoulders. You kissed my breasts and my nipples. Um..."

"I have to say it amuses me that a young woman with your notoriously foul mouth is struggling so much to say words like *breasts*."

"You're laughing at me."

"I am. And you're blushing and beautiful, and I'm thoroughly enjoying the show. Continue."

"Am I allowed to use slang terms, sir?"

"Not tonight. You have to be clinical and precise. You called Kingsley a cocksucker to his face the night he beat you at blackjack. But tonight I have to wonder if you can use the word *penis* in a sentence without fainting."

"Next time I play blackjack with King I'm calling him a penis. There. Happy, sir?"

"Of course I'm happy. You're here, naked and obeying my every order despite the fact you're nervous and mortified. It's intoxicating to see you so uncomfortable."

"You are totally getting off on making me miserable, aren't you, sir?"

"Yes."

"I hate feeling like this."

"Like what?"

"Awkward. Scared. No, that's not it."

"Vulnerable."

"I hate it," she repeated.

"I've noticed. You rarely let yourself be vulnerable. Your brashness and boldness, your brutal honesty, keeps people at bay. But now here you are, stripped of your defenses. It's quite becoming. So please continue. Where else did I touch you? And do open your eyes."

Eleanor reluctantly obeyed. She took two seconds to mentally drown Søren in the soup bowl before answering.

"You touched my shoulders, chest, breasts, back, ass, I mean bottom, derriere, whatever the official term is. And my hips and thighs. You put a finger inside me."

Søren coughed.

"You touched my clitoris and put a finger inside my vagina," she said, enunciating each word as nervous sweat beaded under her arms. "And I loved it."

"I did, too. Where did you touch me?"

Eleanor groaned and dropped her head onto the table.

"Eleanor, you're eighteen years old. If you want to be treated like an adult you must act like one. Sit up straight and answer the question."

She sat up and straightened her spine like an iron rod.

"I kissed you on the mouth and the neck and shoulders and chest. I think that's all."

"It is. In the future, I will allow you more access to my body."

"Thank you, sir."

"Where did you touch me?" He reached into his water glass and pulled out an ice cube. He placed it at the top of her spine and she gasped at the shock of the cold.

"I touched your face and your neck and your shoulders and your chest and back and penis, and there, I said it. Are you done torturing me yet?"

"No."

"A girl can dream."

He traced the length of her spine with the ice cube from the nape of her neck to the small of her back. She gripped the arms of the chair and tried not to squirm.

"I want to talk about pain with you tonight," he said as the ice cube melted against her skin. "Does this hurt?"

"A little. It makes all my muscles contract."

"That's your body's way of trying to protect itself from the cold. I'm using my bare hands. The ice hurts me, too."

"Kingsley said dominants and sadists use floggers and canes and stuff so they don't hurt themselves while inflicting pain."

"That's part of it. There is another part." He lifted the ice cube off her skin and put the remnant of it in her mouth. She swallowed it.

"What's the other part, sir?"

He fed her another bite of soup. He seemed uninterested in his own dinner.

"People have an instinctive trust of authority figures. It's almost a cliché. Women are attracted to men in uniform. Boys grow up and marry women who remind them of their mothers. We fantasize about our teachers, our doctors—"

"Our priests?" She grinned at him.

"Even priests." He took another ice cube out of the glass. This time he ran it down her neck and over her chest. Goose bumps exploded all over her body.

"Do you see me as an authority figure?"

"Yes, sir. Obviously."

"What sort?"

She bit her bottom lip out of simple nervousness. Søren rubbed his thumb over her mouth to remind her not to do that. Dumb girls. She'd never forget that talk.

"It won't make me uncomfortable if you say you see me as a father figure. I'm addressed as 'Father' daily by people twice my age."

"People would say it was weird to be in love with someone who's like a father to you."

"Why do we care what those people think?"

A good question. She had an even better answer for it.

"We don't."

"Do you enjoy submitting to my authority?"

"I do. It's embarrassing right now. But I trust you. I know you're not going to rape me or kill me. Just humiliate me by making me eat dinner naked and forcing me to talk about your penis. Sir."

"This is only the beginning, Little One. There will be other, greater humiliations. And we aren't even close to playing with real pain yet."

"I want to do everything with you, anything you want to do, sir."

Søren leaned in and kissed her. She loved these nights when they were together at Kingsley's and could be together without fear and without judgment from the outside world.

"Go stand by the fireplace," Søren ordered. "Warm up."

"I'm fine, I promise."

"I gave you an order."

Eleanor stood up and, feeling ridiculous in her high heels and collar, went to the fireplace. Søren picked up the wineglass and brought it over.

"Feel better?"

"Yes," she admitted without shame. "I thought that ice cube might kill me for a second there, sir."

"So how does the fire make you feel?"

"Warm. Grateful. Relieved."

"Relieved? Grateful? If you hadn't been cold to start with, how would the fire make you feel?"

"Warmer, I guess."

"So it would be only a physical sensation, not an emotional reaction?"

"Right."

"If you were in pain and then suddenly the pain stopped and you experienced pleasure, what would you feel?"

"Pleasure, of course. And relief. And gratitude. Happiness."

"So again, an emotional reaction instead of simply a physical reaction?"

"Yeah, that. Is that what S&M does?"

"Precisely that. Instead of the simple pleasures of vanilla sex, S&M adds the emotional and psychological component. Fear. Humiliation. Trust. Longing. Desire. Relief. Gratitude. Also, a young woman like yourself who feared her father and didn't respect or love him can explore those feelings with a father figure she trusts and loves and has a healthy fear of."

"Sounds like good therapy. With orgasms."

"I won't even charge you by the hour." He dipped his head and kissed her again. She heard a clink as he sat the wineglass on the mantel and sighed as he wrapped both arms around her.

He ran his hands up and down her naked back, cupped her bottom.

Taking her hand, he led her to the fainting couch. He sat down first and he pointed at the floor. She knelt at his feet and rested her head in his lap. He tickled the back of her shoulders with his fingertips.

"Now that I'm collared, can we...you know?" She made a hand gesture.

"Use your words, Eleanor."

"Fuck."

"No," he said. "Not yet. I know it's not the answer you want, but I have my reasons for waiting. Sex was created by God and He made it pleasurable. But He also made it complicated. I've had intercourse with two people in my life, Eleanor. Two. And I will feel a lifelong bond with these people. I won't make that bond with you until I'm certain you're ready for it."

"Do you think you should only have sex with someone you're in love with?"

"Complicated question. Sex between women and men is especially complicated. There's always the risk of conceiving. I would never tell anyone else who they should or should not be intimate with. For my own part, I choose not to do it except with someone I can imagine having a connection with for the rest of my life."

"I want that with you, forever," she said.

"I don't need to make love to you to want to be bonded to you forever. I have felt that connection since the day we met."

She rose off the floor and Søren took her into his arms. She lay across his lap, her head on his chest, his arms around her.

"I'll wait for you," she said. "Always. I want you to be proud that you own me, sir."

Søren tilted her chin up and kissed her.

"I already am proud to own you, Little One. As this proves." He touched the collar on her neck.

"Why am I wearing this? It doesn't seem like you."

"It's a symbol," he said. "A symbol others in our world will understand. You belong to me. This is a visual reminder of that."

"I love belonging to you."

"And this makes it official." He kissed her on the soft skin under her collar. "So we should celebrate it."

"Celebrate? How?"

"Like this..." Søren kissed her and as he did, he pushed her onto her back, his hand lightly on her throat, his mouth devouring her lips. A kiss from Søren alone could bring her body to life with need. He kissed her possessively, obsessively, as if staking a claim on her body every time their lips touched.

He pulled back and pushed her thighs open. He took her hand and put it between her legs. He waited, an expectant look on his face.

"You're going to sit there and watch, sir?"

"I may lend a hand. If you're good."

"One question—am I doing this while you watch because it turns you on or because it's humiliating?"

"They are one and the same to me."

She took a deep breath and spread her thighs wider. If she had to put on a show, might as well make it a good one. And she knew Søren wanted her, so why not make his waiting for her hurt him as much as it hurt her?

With both hands between her legs, she opened her vagina and pushed one finger inside herself. For some reason doing this while Søren watched embarrassed her less than sitting at the table and eating dinner. It made perfect sense to be naked while doing something sexual. Being naked while having dinner felt awkward and embarrassing. Being naked and touching herself? Not a problem.

"Show-off," Søren said as she caressed her wet inner lips.

She trailed her finger up to her clitoris and started to rub it. Closing her eyes, she sank into her fantasy world where she and Søren would need a telescope to see the lines they'd crossed so far behind them. He'd warned her he would have to hurt her before he could be aroused enough to fuck her. Fine. Good. She longed for the day she could be flogged and caned and treated like sexual property, like a body to be used by Søren and for Søren. She reminded herself that even though she would be the one having the orgasm, she did this for him, for his pleasure. It made it much less embarrassing to do things under orders. She had no choice.

Søren pushed a finger into her and found that soft spot an inch inside her that made her stomach tighten and her back melt into the sofa. He made tight circles inside her that left her groaning in the back of her throat.

Eleanor continued to rub her clitoris as Søren slipped a second finger inside her. As she started to pant, he began to thrust his fingers in and out of her slowly, scraping the front wall of her vagina with his fingertips. She felt everything as he moved inside her. Her toes curled and her thighs shivered. Her hips tightened and her back arched. Her stomach fluttered and her clitoris throbbed. Her chest heaved and her nipples hardened.

"You can come whenever you like."

"I don't want to come, sir."

"Why not?"

"So you'll keep touching me."

Søren softly laughed.

"Pick a number between one and five."

"What am I picking?"

"I can't tell you that. No, I can, but I won't."

"Then how do I know what to pick?"

"You won't."

"Then five."

"I should have guessed. Come for me, Little One."

She took a deep breath and focused on her own pleasure, on the thrumming of her clitoris against her fingers and the pressure building in her stomach. She rode the wave of pleasure to the top and crashed into it at full speed. Her inner muscles clenched around Søren's fingers inside her and buried deep. As she panted, he pulled out of her and dragged her to him.

"That was one," he said.

"One what?" She collapsed against his chest, spent and sleepy.

"You picked five. One down, four to go."

Her eyes flew wide-open.

"Five orgasms?"

He kissed the tip of her nose as he slid his hand down her stomach and between her legs again.

"Of course, next time I make you pick, you could be picking how many hours I'll tease you before I let you come." He gripped the back of her neck roughly; his tone grew forceful, dominating and cold. She loved it.

"You're a sadist."

"I am."

"I'll always pick the biggest number even if I don't know what I'm picking," she said, panting.

"And that, Little One, is why I love you."

"I love you, too. Even if you do torture me and make me wait and beg for you, sir."

"But will you always?" he asked, his voice suddenly serious and somber.

She touched her collar around her neck. She'd almost forgotten about it. In less than an hour it already seemed like a part of her, a second skin.

"I will love you forever. I'll wait as long as I have to for you, sir."

"What if I make you wait one more year?"

"I'll wait."

"Two more years?"

"I'll wait."

"What if you find someone else?"

"Not interested," she promised. "If you can't have sex without pain, I don't want it, either. And I don't want anybody but you."

"Are you sure of that?"

She leaned her head against his chest.

"Completely," she said and meant it. There was no man for her but Søren, now or ever. "You really think some other guy is going to try to steal me from you?"

Ridiculous idea. If she'd said no to Kingsley in the back of his Rolls-Royce, who on earth could ever tempt her to stray from Søren? No one, that's who.

"Eleanor," Søren said, kissing her on the forehead, "I'm absolutely certain of it."

27

Eleanor

"'TWO ROADS DIVERGED IN A WOOD, AND I...I TOOK the one less traveled by, and that has made all the difference.'" Dr. Edwards closed her book with a wistful sigh, and Eleanor fought the urge to bang her head against the wall. Sophomore American literature and they were reading the same poem she read freshman year of high school? Weren't there a few billion other poems out there they could be dissecting other than "The Road Not Taken," otherwise known as the only poem anyone remembered from high school?

"First thoughts on the poem?" Dr. Edwards asked.

A girl in the front row raised her hand—Rachel Something.

"I love this poem," she said. "It's about how you have to choose the path other people don't take. Be a leader, not a follower."

Eleanor felt her IQ dropping.

"Very good. Anyone else?"

A freshman raised his hand and parroted back almost the same interpretation. Guy walking in the woods. Sees two paths. He picks the road that fewer people had taken and that makes him a hero, blah, blah, blah. Eleanor mentally picked up a baseball bat and slammed it into the back of that freshman's head.

"Great thoughts. Other first impressions?"

"Yeah," Eleanor said. "You're all idiots."

The room went silent. Dr. Edwards's dark eyes widened. She raised her chin and stared Eleanor down.

"You need to have a very good argument to back up a statement like that."

"I have a great argument. Read the poem."

"I read the poem, and I agree with them."

"Then there is no hope left for humanity." Eleanor sank into her seat with a sigh. At the age of nineteen, she had come to the realization that unless she was in the same room as Søren, Kingsley and Sam, she could count on being surrounded by idiots.

"Care to tell us what your interpretation of the poem is then, Elle?"

"Sure. Why not?" She held up her book and pointed at a line. "Did anyone happen to read something in the poem other than the last stanza? Lines nine and ten—'Though as for that the passing there had worn them both about the same.' Anyone else see that part? One wasn't *less* traveled by. They were traveled the same."

"Then why does the narrator call one less traveled by in the last stanza?" demanded Dr. Edwards. "Can you explain that?"

"I can." A male voice piped up from the other side of the room. Eleanor turned her head and looked back at the guy who sat in the farthest corner of the room. She'd seen him before but never paid any attention to him. He had black hair with streaks of bright red through it, an eyebrow ring, black punk nail polish and tattoos on his hands.

"You can, Wyatt?" Dr. Edwards asked. "Tell us, then. Nice to hear you speaking in class."

"I'm with Elle here. I can't keep my mouth shut around so much stupidity."

Wyatt. So that was his name. Seemed to fit him. Weird name. Weird guy.

"What do you find so stupid?" Dr. Edwards sounded less irritated with Wyatt than she'd sounded with her. Dr. Edwards always gave the boys in the class more attention than the girls. But in this case, Eleanor couldn't blame her. Now that she looked at Wyatt she noticed for the first time how attractive he was. Piercings, tattoos, spiked punk hair and he read poetry and called people stupid to their faces? Her kind of guy.

"It's obvious. This poem is in two parts. The first four stanzas are about the actual event. The fifth stanza is the speaker telling us how he will narrate the event in the future. And he's an unreliable narrator. Like Elle says, in lines nine and ten he says the roads are the same. Neither one of them is more or less traveled. But in the last stanza he says that in the future when he's talking about this moment, he'll lie and say one of them was less traveled than the other. As a young man he made a totally arbitrary choice—left road or right road—and in the future he'll make it sound like the choice wasn't arbitrary. He'll give it meaning that it didn't have in the moment. He's not a hero. He's an old man telling lies to the younger generation."

"There is no road less traveled," Elle chimed in. "It's convenient fiction to explain why he went right instead of left. We have to believe the choices we made were for a reason if we want our life to have meaning. This poem isn't inspiring. It's creepy and depressing."

"Right," Wyatt said. "That's why I like it."

Eleanor looked back and smiled at him, mouthing a thank-you. He gave her a nonchalant no-big-thing shrug.

When class finally ended, Eleanor grabbed her backpack off the floor and stuffed her book into it. She saw feet facing her feet. A note with her name on it appeared before her face. She looked up and saw Wyatt standing in front of her.

"It's a very important note," he said. "Life altering. Read at your own risk."

"You're kind of weird, Wyatt. You know that, right?"

"Should you be flirting with me, Elle? This is the first time we've talked, and I'm very shy and girls scare me. I'm probably still a virgin."

She arched an eyebrow at him. She'd been practicing that in her mirror.

"Probably? You don't know if you're still a virgin or not?"

"I didn't ask myself if I was or not. It's a really personal question, and I don't know myself well enough to bring it up."

"I'm going to open the note now."

"I wish you'd reconsider," Wyatt said.

"I might need it for evidence in my criminal case against you."

"Good point. Open it."

She unfolded the paper.

"This is a shark, Wyatt. This is a drawing of a shark." She held up the note.

"What? You don't like sharks? What kind of person doesn't like sharks?"

"I'm not saying I don't like sharks. I'm saying I don't know why you gave me a picture of a shark."

"The shark asked me to."

"Why did the shark ask you to give me a picture of it?"

"Because he thinks you're beautiful, brilliant and he wants your phone number."

Eleanor studied the shark. It was about as well rendered a shark as she could have drawn. For Wyatt's sake she hoped he wasn't an art major. Still, it was a cute shark with impressively large fins. He'd even given the shark a red Mohawk.

She folded the paper back up and handed it to Wyatt.

"Please tell the shark I'm sorry. I'm not available." It shocked her how hard she had to work to force those words out.

Wyatt's eyes clouded over for a split second, and she saw the hurt and disappointment behind the adorable mask of male arrogance.

"Can you and the shark maybe be friends?"

"I've never been friends with a shark before. Will he bite me?"

"If you ask nicely."

"Worth a shot. Shark lunch?"

"Shark lunch."

They talked all the way to the cafeteria in Weinstein about how they couldn't believe Dr. Edwards had been that obtuse about "The Road Not Taken" by Robert Frost.

"Here's what I think," Wyatt said as he finished off his lunch of a cheeseburger and fries, some of the only safe food in the cafeteria. "I think if you know more about a subject than your professor, you get to take their Ph.D. from them. Education should be like heavyweight boxing, but with Ph.D.s instead of belts."

"So which one of us gets Edwards's Ph.D.? I think Dr. Schreiber has a nice ring to it."

"It does. You can have it because you spoke up first."

"Yeah, but you gave the better argument."

"You can have the Ph.D. if you'll play doctor with me, Dr. Schreiber."

"Did the shark forget to tell you I'm not available?"

"He told me, but he didn't have many details so I'm not sure I can trust him as a source. Boyfriend?"

"Sort of."

"Does he go here?"

"Nope. He's in Europe right now defending his dissertation."

"Older man, huh? I see how it is."

"You see, huh?"

"Not even a shark can compete with an older man for a college girl. That's like bringing a stealth bomber to a knife fight."

"It gets worse."

Wyatt winced dramatically.

"How much worse? Is he rich?"

"He's gorgeous. It's obscene how gorgeous he is. But he's not rich. Not anymore. Went the low road, real job, not taking Dad's money."

"Poor by choice. God, I hate this guy. Tell me more."

"Are you a masochist?"

He pointed at his eyebrow ring and the tattoos on his hands.

"I'll take that as a yes," Eleanor said. "What do your tattoos say?"

"They're in German. The right hand says—"

Before he could finish she grabbed his hand and yanked it across the table.

"Es war einmal," she read. "Once there was..."

He handed over his left hand and she read aloud, "*Und wenn sie nicht gestorben sind, dann leben sie noch heute.* And if they haven't died, they are still living."

"You know German?" Wyatt said, seeming to be in no hurry to take his hands away from her.

"German grandparents. You have the beginning and ending lines of German fairy tales tattooed on your hands."

"Is that what those are? I walked into the shop and told them to give me whatever the special of the day was. That's weird that tattoo parlors have those, right? I thought it was weird. You got any ink?"

"Not yet. I want to get the Jabberwocky tattooed on my back."

"Jabberwocky? Better than a goddamn butterfly. Why him?"

"Jabberwocky's my sa—" She stopped herself before she finished saying "safe word." When she'd turned eighteen, Søren had instructed her to choose one. But that wasn't a conversation she needed to have. "My spirit guide. You know, totem or whatever. So you like fairy tales?"

"Grimm's fairy tales, the real ones. Not those Disney ones. The real stories."

"The real fairy tales are incredibly violent," Eleanor reminded him. She not only knew Grimm's fairy tales, but she'd also read them in the original German. "In the original *Cinderella* the wicked stepsisters cut off their toes and heels to fit into the glass slipper."

"I know. It's not the Grimm's version, but in the original French *Sleeping Beauty,* the sleeping princess doesn't get kissed by the prince—"

"She gets raped. Small price to pay."

Wyatt gaped at her.

"Rape is a small price to pay? Did you say that out loud in this school?" He glanced around wildly as if checking for spies and/or women's studies majors.

"*Sleeping Beauty* has the same theme as the creation myth," Eleanor said. "Adam and Eve in the Garden of Eden so young and innocent. If they eat the forbidden fruit, they'll have knowledge of good and evil. But they'll also lose paradise. They give up paradise for knowledge without even knowing what that knowledge is. Sleeping Beauty loses her innocence in exchange for waking. Otherwise she'd live in a dreamland forever."

"She didn't consent to getting raped awake," Wyatt reminded her.

"Adam and Eve didn't know what they would win or what they would lose until they'd both won and lost it. It's like that poem we read. The guy doesn't know what the meaning is of the road he took until he got to the end of it. You choose first, then you find out what you've chosen after. Every choice has a price. Sometimes we don't know what it is until after we've paid it."

Wyatt leaned forward and stared at her from across the table.

"Don't take this the wrong way, Elle, but you should be a writer."

"I am a writer."

He nodded knowingly and tapped the table a few times as if in deep thought.

"Wyatt?"

"Give me a sec. I'm trying to figure out how to bring down a stealth bomber with a knife."

"Don't even try it. Do you write?"

"Yeah, but don't tell anybody. Writing's like masturbating. Everyone does it but no one likes to admit to it."

"I admit to it."

"Writing or masturbating?"

"Both." Eleanor waggled her eyebrows at him before realizing that she was now in full-blown flirtation mode. She had to shut this down and fast.

"So what do you write?" she asked, trying to get onto a safer topic than sex.

"Mostly poetry about death and the meaninglessness of life and how you make decisions when you're young that are arbitrary, but when you're older you have to pretend like they meant something."

"Holy shit. You're Robert Frost, aren't you?"

"Shh..." Wyatt hushed her as if she'd leaked a state secret. "Keep your voice down. I don't want to get mobbed by the poetry groupies, which have never existed in the history of the world ever."

"You're ridiculous."

"And you're beautiful and you speak German and you write and I want to move into your dorm room and sleep in your dirty clothes hamper."

Eleanor stared blankly at him.

"The last part about the clothes hamper was too much, wasn't it?" he asked.

"Only because I don't have a dirty clothes hamper."

"One date. All I ask. Your stealth bomber is in Europe. He'll never find out. He's too busy being smart and pissing me off by existing. We get dinner, we talk. I'll show you my poetry. You'll call the suicide prevention hotline on me. It'll be amazing."

"You are really determined, aren't you?"

"You told Dr. Edwards she was an idiot. I want to make love to your brain. Like Marvin Gaye–style."

"Just dinner?"

"Just dinner."

"You won't try anything?"

"I will try everything."

"You'll take no for an answer?"

"Yes. I mean no. I mean yes, I'll take no for an answer. Wait. What's the question?"

"If you ask me to have sex with you, I'll say no," Eleanor said, giving him a death stare.

"If you ask me to have sex with you, I'll say yes."

"I'm serious, Wyatt. No sex."

"Agreed, sex is off the table."

"So we can't have sex," she said.

"No, we can have it. Just not on the table. That's gross, Elle. People gotta eat here."

Eleanor sighed. She regretted this date already.

"My stealth bomber comes home in a week."

"Then you're safe from the shark in my pants."

"Does your pants shark also have a red Mohawk?" she asked as she gathered her things and stood up.

Wyatt leaned back in his chair and put his arms behind his head.

"What can I say, beautiful? The curtains match the rug."

That night Eleanor and Wyatt had a quick dinner of cheap and unhealthy Chinese food in Chinatown and then went for a walk through SoHo. Eleanor had a feeling Wyatt suggested the walk because a new February snow had begun to fall and the city looked unbearably romantic. She hated—and there was no better word for it than *hated*—how much fun she and Wyatt were having. She laughed so hard her stomach ached. Wyatt adored everything about her. She'd worn knee-high boots over her jeans and he told her she looked ferocious in them. He loved the way she wore her hair in a messy bun at the nape of her neck. He said she looked like a sexy Virginia Woolf minus the suicidal ideations. Conversation proved difficult only when Wyatt asked her about her past and her stealth-bomber boyfriend. She'd rather not talk about her dead father and her brush with the law. And she couldn't talk about the priest she'd been in love with since age fifteen.

"Nothing? I get nothing about Stealth Bomber? Not even a name?"

"I don't want you stalking and killing him."

"That's fair. I can see me doing that. How old is he? If he's getting his Ph.D. he has to be at least, what? Twenty-six? Twenty-seven?"

"He's thirtysomething."

"I knew I hated that TV show for a reason. Call the hotline right now." Wyatt collapsed dramatically against a light pole and stared up at the lamp. "I'm going to hang myself from this thing."

"You're so full of shit." She grabbed him by the front of his coat, put his arm in her arm and force marched him down the street. "Let's talk about something else."

"Can we talk about your lips?"

"They're lips."

"I bet they taste like strawberries and poetry."

"What does poetry taste like?"

"I don't know. But I'd love to find out."

Wyatt stopped walking and stood in the light under a streetlamp. The snow whirled like a dervish around him.

"I walked right into that line," she said. "I'm smarter than that. I don't fall for lines."

"You want to fall for it. Fall for it, Elle."

She stood outside the circle of light. Wyatt pulled his hand out of his pocket and crooked a finger at her.

Søren was across the ocean and Wyatt stood there right in front of her surrounded by light and snow. And he had a smile on his face and tattoos on his hands of German fairy tales. He loved writing so much he'd inked words into his very skin. That alone deserved a kiss. But only one.

She stepped into the light.

The kiss started soft and careful, as if he feared shattering the moment by touching too much of it at once. She gripped the front of his distressed leather jacket and pulled him closer. The kiss deepened and Wyatt slipped his tongue between her lips and wound his fingers through her hair. The kiss went on a long time, longer than she should have let it go on. It went on long enough she almost forgot who she belonged to, almost forgot about the white collar with the lock in the back and the man who gave it to her. Wyatt kissed nothing like Søren did. Wyatt explored with his kisses. Søren conquered with his.

The snow fell all around them and yet she didn't smell winter.

She broke away and took a step back.

Wyatt took a deep breath and the air turned white around him.

"Damn," he said. "I was wrong."

"About what?"

"You don't taste like poetry. Poetry tastes like you."

And at that Eleanor knew he had her.

So it began. Since she'd told Wyatt sex was off the table, he didn't even ask. He didn't do anything but kiss her every chance he had their first five days together. She made sure to give him a lot of chances. He met her after class and they did homework together. They ate breakfast, lunch and dinner together. They went to a party together. They hung out in his dorm room with a couple of his friends and watched TV together. They fought over the popcorn so vociferously Wyatt's two friends got up and left, saying they couldn't watch TV with so much sexual tension in the room as it interfered with the reception. With the room to themselves they made out for two hours on Wyatt's bed. He lay on top of her and she slipped her hands under the back of his T-shirt. She loved the way his skin felt, so soft and smooth. He didn't have Søren's lean muscle mass or his height. She and Wyatt were far more evenly matched than she and Søren. He felt like an equal, a friend. But then he started to lift her shirt and all feelings of friendliness jumped out the fourth-floor window to their deaths.

"Wyatt..."

"Please?"

One *please* and she gave up the fight.

"Okay."

Wyatt pulled off her shirt. He unhooked her bra and slowly slid it off her arms.

He stared at her naked breasts, and she lay there letting him look at her. She waited for him to say something, expected him to say something. Instead he put his mouth to better use. He brought his lips down onto her right nipple and gently sucked. As he kissed her nipples, licked and teased them, she watched him and grew more and more aroused. She dug her fingers into his hair as she felt this overwhelming feeling of tenderness for him. He seemed so young to her, so innocent. She wanted to hold him to her breasts, keep him safe, protect him. He should be naked and underneath her while she teased his body the way he teased hers. With him on top of her, she couldn't help but push her hips into his. He pushed back and soon Eleanor felt her climax building. She shuddered in his arms as a wave of pleasure crashed over her and through her.

"Did that happen?" Wyatt asked, holding himself up over her.

"Did what happen?" She decided to play innocent.

"Did you come?"

"I take the Fifth."

"Elle..." Wyatt gave her a serious, almost pleading look.

"Yes, I did." She laid her hand on the side of his face.

"That was the sexiest thing that has ever happened to me." Wyatt pressed his forehead to hers.

She grinned and kissed him quick. "It happened to me more than you."

"It happened to us. With us. I like saying *us.* Can I say it some more?"

"Wyatt, he's back in three days." She dreaded the conversation she and Søren would have about Wyatt, but not telling him seemed unthinkable.

"I don't care about him. I care about us. We weren't even having sex and you came underneath me. It was so fucking sexy, and I'm about to come from talking about it."

"You can come if you want."

"Do you want me to?"

"You're asking my permission?"

"You're the woman. You make the sex rules."

She grinned up at him. She made the sex rules? She kind of liked the sound of that.

"You can. I want you to."

"Yes, ma'am." He brought his mouth down to hers again and kissed her with a roughness that shocked her. She wrapped a leg around his back and pushed her breasts into his chest. He moaned in the back of his throat as he ground his pelvis into hers. She turned her head to give him access to her neck. The sight of his tattooed hand and forearms against the sheets made her question her "sex off the table" rule. Right now she wanted him—on the table or off.

Wyatt's breathing grew ragged as he moved against her. God, she wanted to push him onto his back right now and hold him down. She'd love to pin those tattooed forearms to the bed. She'd work her hips against him, bring him close to coming and then stop…bring him close to coming again and then stop again.... She'd torture him like that until he begged her to let him come. And maybe if he begged enough, she'd let him.

Instead she held him as his body trembled from his own orgasm before going still. He lay on top of her, barely moving, only lightly kissing her neck as he caught his breath.

"I am going to fall in love with you," Wyatt whispered. "Right...now."

He closed his eyes and she said nothing. What was there to say?

She shimmied out of her jeans. With him in nothing but his boxers and her in nothing but her panties and his Smashing Pumpkins T-shirt, they spooned in his bed and slept together. She'd known Søren for almost four years, and she'd never slept in his arms. She'd been with Wyatt five days and she'd fallen asleep in his arms and woken up still wrapped up in them. She'd felt so cherished and so wanted and so... normal—for once—that it killed her to leave his arms and his bed. Since she was fifteen she'd felt Søren's love for her like a blessing. That morning in Wyatt's bed was the first time loving a priest felt like a burden.

That Friday evening she went to Kingsley's like always. She and Søren would stake out the music room and Søren would talk to her about various aspects of S&M she needed to understand. He also made her write for him. He wanted to know what she most desired when she imagined them as lovers. Those were her favorite homework assignments he'd given her—writing out sexually explicit fantasies of erotic bondage and torture. She loved their Friday-night training sessions, counting down the minutes until she could be with him again. But Søren had been in Rome for three weeks now. She came to Kingsley's tonight simply to be alone with her thoughts, her fears, her terrifying feelings for Wyatt.

Wyatt had asked her to go out with him that night, but she'd lied and said she had to work. Some sort of dinner party was happening in Kingsley's dining room. Eleanor avoided it, hiding out in the music room. She sat near the piano, hoping to feel closer to Søren. It didn't work. From her backpack. she pulled Søren's most recent letter to her.

My Little One,

I wish you could be here with me. I strolled through the Galleria Borghese today and tried to imagine all the inappropriate remarks you would make about the statues in their various states of undress. It's a special kind of torture to be without you among great beauty. I've seen the statues before and marveled at them. What I missed today was seeing you seeing them. This city is old and tired, but it would become young again in your eyes. I don't know if we could ever come to Rome together, although I dream of such a day. I have friends here. I seem to bump into them wherever I go. The city is crawling with priests. After a feast day, sometimes literally.

I hope your classes are going well. I'm sorry I had to be gone so long. I think of you every day, every night. I hope you aren't too lonely and that Kingsley is behaving himself in my absence.

I passed some graffiti today I knew you'd find amusing—*cloro al clero.* You see it painted near Vatican City. It means "poison the clergy" but please don't let it give you any ideas.

My trip here has been successful. I left you as Rev. Marcus Stearns, SJ. I'll return to you Rev. Dr. Marcus Stearns, SJ. You are under orders never to call me Reverend, Doctor or Marcus. You may call me Father

Stearns at church, Sir in your collar and Søren when I'm inside you.

I'm spending the evening with several Jesuits I went to seminary with. I should go now. Soon I'll be home to you. Home, in case you were wondering, is not Denmark nor New York nor Wakefield nor any city, state or country. I'm home when I'm with you.

Jeg elsker dig. (Yes, I know how much it turns you on when I speak Danish.)

The letter was signed with an ornate *S* with a slash through it, Søren's private signature. As she looked up from the letter she saw Kingsley watching from the doorway to the music room.

"What's his name, Elle?" Kingsley asked from the doorway.

"Who?"

Kingsley walked over to her and pulled the collar of her shirt down. She knew he touched the slight red mark Wyatt had left on her chest from last night's kisses.

"Tell me everything right now."

"Kingsley, I'm in trouble."

"Pregnant?"

"Worse."

"What's worse than pregnant?"

She brushed tears off her face with the back of her hand and took a deep breath.

"I think I'm in love."

28

Eleanor

KINGSLEY TOOK THE NEWS BETTER THAN SHE EXpected. He listened and asked no questions, not even when she finished her tale.

"He's in love with me, King. I never expected anyone other than Søren would ever fall in love with me. He must be a masochist," Eleanor said with a grim and mirthless laugh. "I guess anyone in love with me would have to be a masochist."

Kingsley laughed behind his tumbler of Scotch.

"You said it, not me. But I doubt he is one. Or even a submissive."

"Then why does he want to do everything I tell him to do?"

"Because he is a vanilla teenage boy desperate to please, desperate to keep you. A male submissive submits out of desire, not desperation. And a man in love with a woman in love with another man is the secondmost desperate creature on earth."

"What's the first?"

"A man in love with a man in love with another woman."

Eleanor laughed. Kingsley didn't.

"I didn't know I could feel this way. It's not like I love Søren any less. I feel like I have this second heart I didn't know was there until I met Wyatt. I didn't know you could do that, could care about two people that much at the same time."

"Welcome to polyamory." Kingsley sat his drink down.

"Polyamory?"

"*Poly* means multi. *Amory* means love. It's common in our world, having more than one lover. I don't mean lover in the sexual sense alone. I mean loving two people."

"Sounds like a nightmare."

"Wasn't it Oscar Wilde who said there were two great tragedies in life—getting what you want and not getting what you want? Polyamory is the tragedy of getting everything you want all at the same time. Still, anything's better than monogamy, *oui?*"

"I feel…horrible." She buried her face in her hands before looking up to stare at the piano. "But I can't stop. Every day I tell myself, 'Okay, I'll break it off with Wyatt today.' And every day, I don't. We fooled around last night. We slept together, even. I've never done that with any guy before—slept in the same bed. No sex, but I wanted to. I wanted to tie Wyatt down and make him beg for it…." She exhaled through her nose. "Shit, did I say that out loud?"

Kingsley only grinned.

"You did."

"Sorry."

"Don't be sorry. No one in this room can judge you. I've fucked two different people today. And likely a third before the night is over."

"That should help me feel less horrible, but it doesn't. A little jealous, though." She tried to smile.

"This should make you feel less horrible. He knew this would happen. I would say he wanted it to."

"Søren wanted me to fall for someone else?"

"You think he is making you wait so long for him for no other reason than to torture you?"

"Well, yeah."

"It's part of it." Kingsley sat back and threw his long booted legs up on the back of the sofa and crossed his ankles. "But the truth is he loves you. And he's a Catholic priest. And he can't marry you. And he can't give you children. And he can't hold your hand while you walk through Washington Square Park and kiss you under a streetlamp in the snow where all the world can see you. And if that's something you want, he wants you to have it. Sex will seal you to him. You spend a night in his bed and you will never want to leave it. If you are going to get out, you need to do it now before it's too late."

"I want them both."

"If *le prêtre* would allow that, would your boy allow it?"

She shook her head.

"No. He'd hate that. The first day he wanted to know everything about Søren. Now he flinches if I even mention him."

"Then you have a choice to make. But make it soon and make it clean."

"Make it clean?"

Kingsley sat his drink on the side table and, with adroit fingers, quickly unbuttoned his white shirt. He pulled the fabric to the side to bare a large scar that looked recently healed.

"Bullet wound," he said. "Nearly killed me. Not the shot, however. The bullet shattered on a rib. They had to dig out thirty pieces of silver. You want to shoot someone? Have the decency to make it clean. In and out, straight through. No hope."

"No hope? That's brutal, King."

"You say he's an aspiring writer. Break him, then." Kingsley sipped his Scotch and laughed to himself. "It'll be good for his art."

He started to button his shirt, but Eleanor stopped him with a hand on his chest. She pressed her hand against the scar tissue. He didn't seem surprised when she touched his chest. Not surprised and not at all displeased.

"This nun at my school always said Hell was the absence of hope," Eleanor said, tracing the hard line of the scar. She couldn't imagine how much pain Kingsley had suffered, how he'd even survived such a wound. But it was beautiful in a way, this scar of his. She almost wanted to kiss it.

Kingsley covered her hand with his.

"Then your nun was never in love with someone she couldn't have. If you care about this boy at all, give him no hope."

He raised his hand and traced her bottom lip with his thumb.

"I know you, Elle," Kingsley said, his voice so low it lulled her in closer to him, so close they could have kissed if one of them dared to do it. "I know what you are. You will never be content with a boy like that. He will be a game and you will play him and you will tire of the game and him. You need so much more than such a boy can give you. I know this because I'm the same way."

He looked into her eyes and Eleanor looked into his. She could almost imagine their lips meeting… She could rip off his shirt, yank his pants open. He'd look beautiful on his back underneath her, her hands on his wrists, his cock buried inside her as she rode him into the couch.

Wait. What the fuck was she thinking?

Eleanor pulled back and sat on the opposite end of the

couch from Kingsley. He continued to stare at her, a smug smile on his lips as if he'd read her thoughts. He didn't bother buttoning his shirt.

Kingsley took another swig of his Scotch, then handed it to her. She stared into the murky liquid before taking a deep drink of it. She coughed only once as the liquor burned its way down her throat.

"I'm fucked, King."

"Not yet. But the night is still young."

"What should I do?"

"What do you want to do?"

"Fuck them both." She laughed mirthlessly. "I know what I don't want to do. I don't want to hurt Wyatt. I don't want to hurt Søren."

"A nice dream, but this is life, the real world. You will hurt them. They will hurt you."

"Wyatt…he's my age, you know?" She stared down into the Scotch at the bottom of Kingsley's glass in her hand. "He's an NYU student. We can go places together, be seen together. We're both writers. We make sense. Søren and I? We don't make sense. At least to no one but us."

Kingsley traced the wet rim of his glass with his fingertip.

"Elle…I wish you could have known him back when he was a teenager."

"What was he like?"

"Old. He was older then than he is now. An old soul, as they say." Kingsley chuckled at what must have been a good memory. "*Mon Dieu,* you'd never met anyone more arrogant, haughty, pompous and condescending. Everyone at the school hated that blond shit. Everyone but the priests."

Eleanor burst into laughter.

"I can totally picture that. Why was he such a prick back then?"

"We're all shits when we're teenagers. God knows I was, but for him, I think it was this fear of his. He thought he'd been tainted by his father, his past. Better to be hated than loved. Love lets people in. He wanted no one near him. He's better now. Being a priest…he's more open with his affections. Being with you…" Kingsley paused as if the next words didn't want to come. "Being with you makes him better. Happy. Less troubled. My God, he's almost…" Kingsley shook his head. "Almost *fun*."

Kingsley said the word with exaggerated horror.

Eleanor laughed. "He wasn't fun as a teenager?" She gave Kingsley his Scotch back. If she kept it she might drink it all and then some.

"In a different way," he answered, and Kingsley smiled his secret sort of smile before the smile died. "No, he was not *fun* then. He was cold and closed off, dangerous and nearly impossible to get close to. It nearly killed me getting close to him, but in the end the reward was worth the price."

"If I left him…" She faced Kingsley and stared into his dark eyes. "What would happen?"

Kingsley twirled the remaining Scotch and ice around the bottom of his glass.

"You have only seen him by day, and by day we see only light and shadow. But if you left him, the night would come. And then we would all see the darkness."

"What's the darkness like?"

"I will say only this—when *le prêtre* is in the right mood, he can make even the devil afraid to turn his back."

Kingsley downed the last of his drink. Eleanor buried her face in her hands again.

"I hate my life tonight," Eleanor said as his words slipped in through the hairline fractures in her heart and widened them.

"Elle, I once stood at the same crossroads you stand at

now. I have never regretted walking the darker path. The view is better down here. And I am many things, but I am never bored."

"I don't want Søren to ever leave the priesthood, but if we get caught, if he gets in trouble… I wish I could I see the future."

"What's his last name, this young man of yours?"

"Why? You gonna make a file on him?" She knew all about Kingsley's files he kept on anyone who interested him.

"Peut-être," he admitted without shame. Maybe.

"It's Sutherlin. Wyatt James Sutherlin. Want his birth date and blood type, too?"

Kingsley chuckled. "I can find that out myself. Wyatt Sutherlin…Eleanor Sutherlin… It has a nice ring to it, no?"

She sighed heavily. Absurd to think of someone like her getting married, having kids, doing the wife-and-mother thing. She sat in the music room of the most notorious house in the city talking to the most notorious kinkster in the city about the priest she loved.

"My high school best friend, well, my only friend, Jordan, is getting married next summer. She's a sophomore at Anna Maria and she's already engaged. She can't wait to have babies. She called me last week. I couldn't even talk to her. How do I talk to someone like that? I thought…" She stopped and laughed sheepishly. "I thought about asking you to pay her a visit. Seduce her, I mean. She saw you once and it was the only time she ever made a sex joke. She's going down the marriage-and-kids path at eighteen, and I want to stop her."

"I could stop her," he said without any arrogance in his tone. He simply stated a fact. "Would you like me to?"

She shook her head.

"Husband, kids—that's what Jordan wants."

"And you?"

"I want more than that."

"Then you have your answer, Eleanor Sutherlin."

"You call me that again and I'll slap you into the next century."

"Now, *ma belle Elle,* you are speaking my language."

Eleanor kissed Kingsley good-night on both cheeks and threw on her coat.

The temperature had dropped, so she decided to spring for a cab. While scanning the street in search of a yellow, she heard someone calling her name.

"Wyatt?" She turned around and faced Wyatt with shock. "What the hell are you doing here?"

He clutched a bouquet of flowers in his hand, half-dead from the cold.

"You said you had to work tonight," he said without a smile on his face. She couldn't remember seeing him without a smile on his face. "I wanted to surprise you at work with flowers. I didn't know which bookstore you worked at so I followed you. I know that's creepy, but I thought you'd forgive me since all I wanted to do was bring you flowers."

"You've been waiting out here for two hours?"

"The things we do for love, right?" He raised his hands and laughed at himself. "I kind of liked the mystery-girl vibe you have. You don't talk about your past, your parents. I don't even know the name of this guy you're supposedly in love with. It's kind of hot, this whole secrecy thing you've got going. But secrets are one thing. You lied to me."

"I did lie," she admitted. "I'm not at work, obviously. I was visiting a friend."

"A fucking rich friend from the looks of it."

"He's also *his* friend. I didn't want to hurt your feelings."

"Well, they're hurt. No big deal. They'll get unhurt. Eventually. Same way as I'll get unfrozen."

"Eventually?"

"Right. Can we maybe go somewhere and talk—"

"Wyatt, I can't see you anymore." Eleanor let the words rip fast and hard, like tearing off a bandage.

"Am I suddenly invisible?"

She rubbed her forehead.

"You have to stop being so cute and funny, okay?" she said. "He comes back in three days. I can't do this anymore, play this game with you."

"It's not a game. I'm in love with you."

"And I'm in love with him."

"You can't be. He's in his thirties. You're nineteen. I mean, what could you have in common with someone that old? What could you two even talk about?"

"He's brilliant and funny and fascinating, and I'll never reach the end of the mystery of him."

"Guys that age love younger girls. You're easy prey for them. They can impress you by just being older."

"I am not easy prey, okay? I'm not some sheep being eaten by a big bad wolf. He speaks eighteen languages. He's six foot four. He's stunningly beautiful and yes, I'm using the word *beautiful.* He rides a motorcycle and he lives this life like you can't believe and he brought me into it. These parties I've seen, you can't imagine it. And the people? Rich and powerful people like you wouldn't believe. And, Wyatt, none of that matters. What matters is that he loves me and there is nothing he wouldn't do for me. He loves me so much that if I wanted to be with you more than him, he'd let me be with you. He loves me and he knows me, and I am a more interesting person when I'm with him than when I am without him. Without him I'm just an NYU English major with a part-time job and too much homework."

"That's all I am, too."

"Yeah. Exactly."

The words hung in the air between them, hovering like a poison cloud. She knew she'd crossed a line, pushed the knife in too deep. As much as she adored Wyatt, he could never compete with a man like Søren. First of all, Søren was a man and Wyatt was only a nineteen-year-old boy.

"You know what you're doing, Elle?" Wyatt said. "You're living in Wonderland. This guy is older and speaks all these languages and lives this crazy life. It's different, it's weird, it's the Mad Kingdom down the rabbit hole. It's fun for a while, but you still have to go home eventually. You can't live there forever, Alice."

"I'm not Alice." She didn't know what she was—White Rabbit, White Queen or Jabberwocky—but she knew one thing perfectly well. She was no stranger to Wonderland. She was born there.

"This is crazy, you and him."

"What can I say? We're all mad here."

"Elle…" Wyatt ran his hands through his red hair. She did love his punk red dye job. *Be brutal,* Kingsley had said. *Make it clean.* She threw a lock on her heart and put a bullet through her compassion.

"Let me ask you a question, Wyatt. You ever flog a woman?" She took a step forward.

"What? Flog? No way."

"Cane her?"

"No."

"You know how to use a single-tail?"

"I don't even know what that is."

"Got a St. Andrew's Cross in your bedroom?"

"A what?"

"I am not what you think I am," she said. "You are in love with someone who doesn't exist."

"You're kind of freaking me out here," Wyatt said, his eyes wide and scared.

"I haven't even begun to freak you out yet."

"Elle?" Wyatt's voice went quiet and solemn. "What can he give you that I can't? Seriously. I want to know the answer."

She turned her back on him and walked toward the waiting taxi.

"Everything."

Alone in the back of the darkened cab, she let the tears fall. No more. She'd never let herself care about anyone else other than Søren again for the rest of her life. It hurt too much. In the privacy of her mind and in the midst of her sadness, she made herself a promise she knew she would keep. No more vanilla guys ever. She couldn't do this, couldn't straddle the line between two worlds anymore. It hurt too much. Hurt Wyatt, hurt her. It could hurt Søren, would have hurt Søren had he known. And he would know. She'd have to tell him.

She paid the driver and trudged through the sooty snow back to her dorm. She pulled one of her roommate's wine coolers out of their little fridge and drank it faster than she should have. She heard noises from across the hall—the unmistakable sound of a party.

Eleanor sat on her bed with another drink in her hand. Was there anything in the world more pathetic than a lovesick girl sitting in her dorm room getting drunk by herself? *No* was the answer to that question. She shouldn't be drinking alone while thinking about how much she'd miss being Wyatt's girlfriend, how much she'd miss sitting with him at lunch and dinner, talking about books and poetry and the profs they loved and hated. She shouldn't be drinking alone and thinking about how good it felt to lie underneath him last night naked from the waist up as he kissed her breasts and nipples. She shouldn't be drinking alone while thinking about how erotic it felt simply to sleep in his bed with his arm around her all night long. He made her want things, Wyatt did. Things completely different from the things Søren made her want. She wanted to strip Wyatt naked, tie him up, bite him, kiss him, suck him, make him beg her for more. Maybe she'd give him more. Maybe she wouldn't. Maybe she'd get an ice cube and torture him with it. God dammit, where did these fantasies come from? She was a submissive, Søren's property. She couldn't imagine topping Søren. It was ludicrous to even think about it. So why did she want to do it so much? Why was that all she could think about when she and Wyatt were alone together? Didn't matter. A fantasy. She'd forget about it by morning.

She set her wine cooler bottle on the bedside table and stared at it.

Drinking alone was definitely the worst idea ever. She decided to pour the bottle down the drain.

Before she reached the sink, what sounded like a dozen fists pounded on the door.

"Party in the corner suite!" came a cacophony of voices both male and female. They moved onto the next door, banged again and repeated the call.

Typical Friday-night invitation.

Eleanor stared at the bottle in her hand. This morning as she'd tried to leave Wyatt's bed, he'd woken up, pulled her against him and whispered, "I'll wait as long as you want, but you have to know I'm dying to be inside you."

His words and the feel of his erection against her back had left her aching with need all day.

Friday night. A terrible idea to drink alone.

She took a drink and headed to the corner suite.

Why not drink with everybody else?

29

Eleanor

BLEACH. SHE SMELLED BLEACH. THAT'S WHAT THAT was. The acrid scent wrinkled Eleanor's nose as she struggled to open her eyes. Why bleach? And…disinfectant?

"Eleanor? Are you awake?"

"No," she answered.

"Eleanor, I'm Lisa. Can you open your eyes for me?"

"No. But I can open them for me."

She opened her eyes. Bright lights everywhere. Bright lights, white tile, white sheets and lab coats. She closed them immediately.

"Do you know where you are?" the woman, Lisa, asked.

"Hell?"

"You're in the hospital, Eleanor. Your friend thought you had alcohol poisoning."

"Did I?"

"Yes."

"Bummer."

At some point last night she'd decided not to drink alone,

but to drink with everybody else. Drinking had been her first mistake. The company she'd chosen had been her second.

Eleanor tried to sit up but Lisa stopped her with a gentle hand on her arm.

"You've got a saline IV in your arm. You're dehydrated. Try not to move."

"Are you a doctor?"

"No, I'm not. I'm with the rape crisis center. They called me."

"Why?"

"The young lady who called 911 said she found a boy on top of you."

"I'm gonna kill Katie."

"Katie?"

"My freshman-year roommate. Women's studies major. She's the one who called, right?"

"I believe so, yes."

"Sean and I were making out. Katie overreacted. She's trained to overreact."

"Sean who?"

"Sean, the drunk guy. I pulled him on top of me because we were both drunk off our asses and wanted to make out. I fell asleep in the middle of it. As drunk as he was he probably didn't even notice. I think I puked on him."

"Eleanor, many victims go through a denial stage—"

"Oh, my God." Eleanor lowered her voice as her own words caused her brain to vibrate against her skull. "I am hungover. I am exhausted. I am dehydrated, and I need a ten-hour shower. And last night I was stupid. But I am not now, nor have I ever been, a victim of anything or anyone but my own bad decisions, okay? Now, I'm sure somebody got raped in this town last night. How about you go help her?"

"Eleanor," Lisa said with an annoyingly soothing voice. "Please let me help you."

"You can help me. I'm going to give you a phone number. I need you to call it."

"I can do that, Eleanor. Am I calling your mom?"

"A woman named Sam will answer the phone. Ask for Kingsley. Tell him what hospital I'm at. Tell him I was brought in for alcohol-induced stupidity and, for God's sake, tell him to please come get me."

Eleanor closed her eyes and willed herself back to sleep. When she woke up again, she had a much firmer grasp on consciousness. She turned her head and saw a woman, about forty years old, sitting in the chair next to her making rapid notes onto some sort of form.

"Are you Lisa or did I dream that?"

"I'm Lisa. Can I get you anything?"

"Did you call that number?"

"Yes."

"Good."

"Do you want to talk about what happened to you, Eleanor?"

"I got shit-faced and passed out. I woke up puking."

"Would you consent to a rape exam?"

"I must be speaking a foreign language. No means no, you know? No, I didn't get raped. But do the test if it'll shut you up finally."

That didn't seem to be the answer Lisa wanted or expected. Still, two nurses and a female doctor came in her room only minutes later.

The exam was over and done in a few minutes. She'd never had a pelvic exam before but knew what was involved. The speculum didn't hurt, although it made her stomach feel weird. In ten minutes, she had her clothes on again.

"They'll run some tests on the swabs they took, but they didn't see any evidence of trauma. In fact, your hymen—"

"Is intact. And so is my brain."

"It's still possible… We'll wait for the test results."

"Can I go now?" Her head ached, her body ached, her heart ached.

"We'll get your discharge papers. There is someone waiting to see you."

"Is it a superhot French guy in Hessian boots?"

"Um, no. This man is a priest. But if you don't—"

"Let him in. Right now. Please. And you can go."

"Of course." Lisa gave her a kind, sympathetic look that Eleanor wanted to rip off her face.

She left the room and seconds later Søren pushed open the door. Before she could even speak Søren had her wrapped in his arms.

He wore his collar and clerics and she'd never in her life been so grateful to be in love with a priest. The clergy were more welcome in a hospital than any other place on earth.

She rejoiced in his arms around her, rejoiced in his chest that she rested her head against, rejoiced in that scent of him, clean as a midnight in winter.

"You're back early," she whispered through tears.

"I wanted to surprise you."

"Any reason?"

"I never need a reason to come back to you."

She looked up at him.

"I guess I ruined the surprise."

He brushed tears off her face.

"Never, Little One. Never."

He kissed her forehead, and she clung to him even tighter.

"I was at Kingsley's when the hospital called. They said you had alcohol poisoning."

She winced at the abject concern in his voice. Judgment, anger…that she expected. The kindness hurt worse than a beating would have.

"I got stupid drunk last night for stupid reasons and it led to stupid behavior."

"If it helps, the last time Kingsley and I drank together we both ended up on the roof of the rectory. For the life of me I can't remember how we got down again."

Eleanor laughed and winced simultaneously.

"Mine's a little worse. I made out with some guy I barely know. He was as drunk as me."

"As I."

"Right. I passed out while we were making out. I woke up puking. A friend of mine called the hospital. They didn't even have to pump my stomach I'd puked so much."

"Are you certain nothing else happened?" He kept his voice and tone neutral. "You can tell me anything, Eleanor."

Eleanor smiled. Søren would make a much better rape crisis center counselor than what's-her-name.

"Completely. Other than me being an idiot."

"You are not an idiot, young lady, and I never want to hear you say anything like that ever again."

"I am. Hear me out. I did something while you were gone. I met this guy in my American lit class. He… I don't know. He gave me a shark. And then he wanted to have lunch with me, and it was just lunch. Then lunch was dinner and dinner was a walk in the snow and then we kissed and kissed some more. And I…I liked him so much." Her stomach clenched in grief. "It was only six days we were together so I don't even know why I'm so upset about it. We didn't even have sex. I broke up with him last night. That's why I got shit-faced."

She looked up at Søren, expecting to see anger on his face.

Instead he merely smiled as if he'd been expecting this all along. Of course he had been.

"Six days? God created the universe in six days. It might have been a short relationship, but that doesn't mean you can't mourn its loss."

"I'm done mourning," she said, reaching up and touching his face. She loved his skin, the slight hint of stubble on his chin that seemed so masculine and erotic to her.

"Are you making me wait so long for you so this would happen? I mean, so I would find someone else and fall for him?"

Søren exhaled heavily before answering.

"Yes."

"Why?" she asked although she thought she knew the answer already.

"Because, Little One, our choices mean nothing until we're given more than one of them."

"I choose you. It took me a few days, but I did choose you."

"I knew you would. But *you* didn't know if you would choose me. Adam and Eve could have remained in paradise for eternity had there been no apple to tempt them. And their obedience would have been meaningless because obedience would have been the only choice."

"You knew I would pick you."

"I did."

"You're an arrogant bastard, aren't you?"

"I know my strengths. You..." He cupped her chin. "You are one of my strengths, my greatest strength."

"I won't let you down again."

"You never have. Now, shall we go before someone asks me for last rites?"

"Yeah, we'd better jet. You're a hot property in this place."

"The car is waiting outside. We'll spend the weekend at

Kingsley's. Father O'Neil had planned to take over my Masses through Monday."

"Can we do something first before we go to Kingsley's? It'll be quick."

"Anything."

Eleanor gave him her request and Søren turned his head and stared out the window as he considered it.

"I'm not sure that would be appropriate given our relationship," he said at last.

"It's you or no one else."

Søren paused before answering.

"Very well, then."

He pulled a small leather case from his jacket pocket and unzipped it. From it he unfurled a purple stole that he kissed before draping it around his neck. He sat back in the chair and looked away to give her privacy.

Eleanor closed her eyes, took a deep breath and began to speak.

"Forgive me, Father, for I have sinned." She crossed herself and began to confess. She confessed everything she'd kept in her heart her entire life. She didn't bother with her venial sins—lust, lies and self-pity. Instead she told Søren about the phone call she didn't answer that left her father on his own to face the consequences of his choices. She told him about hurting Wyatt and worse, loving Wyatt. She confessed to using a guy last night out of despair. She confessed to everything.

She poured her sins into Søren's hands, and then, like magic, he made them disappear. But it wasn't magic and she knew her sins weren't gone, only forgiven, and for that she was grateful. She didn't want her sins gone. She'd miss them too much.

After her confession and absolution, Eleanor's soul felt clean again. All she needed now was for the outside to match the inside.

At Kingsley's, he gave her the guest room with the largest bathroom. She stripped out of her clothes, stepped into the shower and let the heat and the water wash away the last of her regret, the last of her grief and the last of her pain. She shaved her legs and scrubbed herself down with a loofah, wanting to scrape away the top layer of skin that felt tainted by the drinking and the sadness and the pain she'd caused. After an hour she turned off the taps and stepped out of the shower into a plush white towel held open by Søren.

"I thought you were never getting out." He wrapped the towel tight around her and she laughed as he swaddled her.

"Were you in the bathroom the whole time, you creeper?"

"Only the last fifteen *hours* of your shower. I thought you might have washed down the drain."

He'd changed from his clerics into normal clothes—jeans and a long-sleeved black T-shirt. He had the sleeves pulled up enough that she could see his wrists and forearms. Muscular forearms and large, manly adult hands. No playful tattoos or punk nail polish for him. His hands were serious and dignified—all work and no play. And now those hands toweled the water out of her hair, swiped droplets off her face. She imagined they were a normal couple in their own house. But they weren't a normal couple and never would be and whether the world understood or not, that was what she loved about them.

Søren picked her up off her feet and sat her on the bathroom counter.

"You're really drying me off?"

"And dressing you in your pajamas and putting you to bed."

"Do I get a bedtime story, too?"

"If you want one."

She grinned at the thought of Søren reading her a bedtime story. Could life get any weirder? Any better? As Søren dried her hair, her face, even her legs and feet, the residue of the past week with Wyatt evaporated. She'd adored Wyatt, yes, but now that Søren had come back she saw Wyatt as nothing but a detour, temporary and unexpected. Søren was the path she'd chosen. In his presence she remembered why she'd picked him and why she would never wander off that path again.

"Sam provided the pajamas," Søren said, holding up a little white nightgown. "She picked them out for you."

"I want to make out with her."

"Later. You're mine now."

She stepped into the white shorty bottoms that Søren dragged up her legs and pulled on the camisole top.

"You know, the last time anybody helped me get ready for bed, I was eight and was getting over the flu." Eleanor remembered her mom bathing her tired body and putting her into pajamas. She'd been so limp, so tired then, helpless from the illness that her mother had rocked in her arms like she was still a baby.

Now Eleanor felt tired, tired and happy. And clean, so clean in Søren's presence. Clean and safe. She wasn't helpless anymore, wasn't weak. Out of pleasure and love alone she submitted to his ministrations and let herself become as dependent as a child.

He helped her off the bathroom counter and followed her into the bedroom. She turned down the covers and started to crawl inside, but froze when she felt an impossibly strong hand on the back of her neck.

"Don't move," Søren ordered.

"What—"

She yelped as his hand made loud and brutal contact with her barely covered bottom.

"That was for drinking too much last night."

He smacked her bottom again, this time twice as hard.

"And that was for Wyatt."

Eleanor dug her fingers into the sheets and braced herself. The next smack hurt worse than the previous two combined. She gasped from the pain.

"And that was simply for the fun of it. Now you may get into bed."

"Ow." Eleanor finally managed to get a word out. She collapsed onto her side and pulled the covers over her. She looked up at Søren, who seemed to be fighting off a smile. "I can't believe you spanked me."

Søren grinned at her. "I can."

He bent and kissed her, one of his conquering kisses that made her feel like a newly discovered world waiting for him to plant his flag in her.

He slid his hand under the covers, down her body and between her legs. Over top of her pajama bottoms, he teased her clitoris until she panted into his mouth. She raised her hips, hungry for more, and he pushed the fabric aside to slide one finger into her.

"Would you like to come?" he asked.

"Yes, please."

He kissed her again as he rubbed her clitoris with his thumb. She dug her fingers into the sheets as he edged her closer and closer to climax. She shut her eyes as the pressure built and her temperature rose. And then without warning, Søren pulled his hand away from her.

Her eyes flew open and she looked up at him.

"You're killing me," she said.

He gave her a smile so wicked she almost came from that alone.

"I asked you if you wanted to come. I didn't say I would let you."

"Fucking sadist."

"I'm glad you're starting to realize this. Want your bedtime story now?"

"No, I want an orgasm."

"Good. I'll find the book. But first..." Søren knelt at the side of the bed, and Eleanor rose up on her elbows.

"What are you doing down there? Praying?"

"Digging. Here we go." He pulled some kind of briefcase from under the bed and unlatched it.

"What is that?"

"Kingsley keeps his guest rooms well supplied." He pulled two lengths of rope from the case, shut it and slid it back under the bed. "I have to leave the room for a few minutes, and I'm not sure I trust you with yourself."

"You think I'll furiously masturbate the second your back is turned?"

"Yes."

"You're probably right about that."

Søren took her wrists in his hands. They felt so small and delicate in his grip. He wrapped the rope around both her wrists several times, tying them together before looping the rope around the bedpost and securing it. In awe she watched his expert fingers, how easily he knotted the rope.

"Now stay there."

"Stay here?" she called out as he left the room. "I'm tied to the damn bed. Where would I go?"

Søren didn't answer.

"I hate you!" she called out even louder. This time he answered.

"One hundred twenty-seven," he called back.

As soon as Søren left the room she decided she had to get out of these damn ropes. If she had two minutes she could give herself the orgasm he'd denied her. Her whole body still pulsed with need. Maybe if she twisted her hands, turned this way, dislocated her shoulder and twisted her body around...

"Good, you're still here." Søren came back into the room carrying a book in his hand.

"I wonder why." She pulled her knees to her chest and fumed. "You are the most evil man on earth."

"I am, yes. Would you like to hear your bedtime story now?"

"I would like to punch you in the face."

"It's Lewis Carroll. I found this in an antique bookstore in Rome."

"I hate it. I want to set it on fire."

"It's *Through the Looking-Glass*. I know how partial you are to the Jabberwocky."

"You are the Jabberwocky, you monster."

"It's a long book. Get comfortable. I'll read."

"And I'll murder you in my mind."

Eleanor entertained a few dozen violent fantasies of retribution on Søren. He'd spanked her, aroused her, denied her an orgasm and then tied her to the bed so she couldn't touch herself. And now he blithely ignored her fury as he flipped open the pages of the book and began to read.

"'One thing was certain,'" he began, "'that the WHITE kitten had had nothing to do with it—it was the black kitten's fault entirely.'"

Trapped, Eleanor could do nothing but lie there and listen as Søren read the story to her. Soon she'd lost herself in the story, in the moment, in the ludicrous pleasure of being almost twenty and having a bedtime story read to her. She forgot about the ropes on her wrists and the need in her stomach. After an hour she even forgot she'd planned to kill Søren with a pickax the second he untied her.

He read to her until Eleanor yawned and her eyelids fluttered. She wanted to stay awake and keep listening but she fought a losing battle against her need to sleep. Søren closed the book and sat it on the bedside table.

"Are you asleep, Little One?" Søren asked.

She felt him untying her hands. Once free of the ropes he gently chafed her wrists.

"Almost, sir."

Søren gathered her in his arms and she fell against his chest.

"I love that book." She sighed.

"I know you do. It's one of my favorites, too."

"I love you, too, sir. Even when I want to kill you with a pickax."

"That is all I can ask." He bent and kissed her on the forehead, the cheek. "Before you sleep, there's one thing we need to talk about."

"If it's not about us having sex, I'm going to sleep right now."

"Then wake up."

Eleanor's eyes flew open and she sat up straight.

"When? How soon? Tonight?"

"When I decide, I will tell you." She had the face-punching fantasy again. Of course he would decide when. "But you'll be twenty soon. Not a teenager anymore. You'll need to be ready."

"I'll go to the school clinic and go on birth control."

"Good girl."

Eleanor grinned at the irony of a Catholic priest telling her to start birth control.

"You really are the weirdest priest on earth."

"Little One," Søren said, "you don't even know the half of it."

She should have expected that.

"Now go to sleep," he ordered. "You need sleep to recover from what you've been through."

"Will you stay with me until I fall asleep?"

"That I can do," he said and sat on the bed, his back against the headboard. She lowered her head and rested it on his stomach. Never before had she felt so loved, so adored, so special and so cherished as she did at this moment. She'd spent the past week dating Wyatt. She'd spent last night fooling around with a stranger. Søren had not only forgiven her, but he'd also absolved and then punished her in ways even sexier than sex. This morning she'd woken up in a hospital bed. Tonight she would fall asleep in Søren's arms, the slow steady rhythm of his heart beating against her ear.

"Will you tell me another bedtime story?" she asked.

"I can. What story would you like?"

"A love story."

"I think I can provide that." He wrapped both arms around her and gently rubbed her back.

"Once upon a time," he began, "there was a beautiful girl named Eleanor who had secrets she wanted to keep. Eleanor had pulled her sleeves down over her hands. She was ashamed of the burns on her wrist and feared someone would see them and judge her for them. Then the time came for this girl to take communion. As she reached for the cup, her sleeve slipped back, and her priest saw what she was."

"What was she?" Eleanor asked.

Søren kissed her on the top of her head and whispered. "She was mine."

30

Eleanor

SOMETHING TICKLED ELEANOR'S NOSE. SHE SWIPED at it without opening her eyes. She flipped over in bed and pressed into her pillow. Her pillow didn't feel like her pillow, however. Instead of soft, it felt hard. Very hard.

"Bonne anniversaire," a voice whispered in her ear.

Her eyes flew open and Eleanor sat up in bed. Kingsley lay stretched out on his side next to her on her narrow dorm bed, a white rose in his fingers. He tickled her nose with it again and she batted it away.

"King, what the fuck? How did you get in here?"

She pulled the covers up to her chest. She'd gone to bed in a tank top and panties and nothing else.

"Your roommate let me in."

"Great. So my old roommate sees me getting kissed and calls the rape squad. My new roommate sends you an engraved invitation to jump in bed with me while I'm unconscious."

"It wasn't engraved."

"What time is it?"

"Seven."

"Seven? You're up at seven in the morning?"

"Up? I haven't been to bed yet. Not for sleeping anyway."

"Nice." She grabbed a ponytail holder off her nightstand and tried to tame her hair. "Are you going to tell me what you're doing here?"

"I brought gifts."

"Gifts?"

"Oui." Kingsley pointed to a chair piled high with gifts.

"All for me?"

"Pour toi."

As Eleanor reached out for the boxes, Kingsley grabbed her and pulled her across his lap. In shock she screamed and squirmed. Kingsley subdued her quickly and spanked her.

"This is the best part of birthdays. Stop fighting me, brat."

The word *brat* made her freeze immediately. She wasn't sure why except she had the sinking feeling she liked being called *brat* by Kingsley. As soon as her struggle ceased, he gave her twenty vicious swats to the bottom.

"Twenty," Kingsley said and gave her the last and hardest spank. She yelped and her bedroom door flew open. April, her buxom R.A., looked like she'd just crawled out of bed. She had nothing on but a bathrobe barely closed over her breasts.

"Elle, you okay? I heard screaming."

Eleanor got up on her hands and knees.

"She's fine," Kingsley said, pulling Eleanor back down onto his lap. "Birthday spankings."

April looked hard at Kingsley and ran a hand through her disheveled hair.

"It's my birthday, too," April said to Kingsley.

"April, get out," Eleanor ordered.

"I'm out." April closed the door behind her.

"Are you done?" Eleanor looked over her shoulder at Kingsley.

"Non." He spanked her one more time. "One to grow on."

"I hate you almost as much as I hate Søren."

"You won't hate me after you open your *cadeaux*."

Wincing, she sat back on her bed with the presents in her lap. Sitting in class all day was going to be a challenge.

"Are these from you?" She sorted through the boxes of varying size. The smallest one intrigued her most.

"Three from me. One from Sam."

"Sam?" Eleanor couldn't help but grin. "Sam got me a present?"

"She did. You can open that one first." He picked up a small flat box wrapped in pink paper with a black ribbon. She untied the ribbon and opened the lid.

"Oh, my God..." She held a leather journal in her hand and a fancy fountain pen.

"Sam read one of your stories. She says you should write more."

"Tell her to watch out. I might write about you and Sam someday."

"A good story. Open that one."

She tore off the wrapping and found nothing but tissue paper inside the box. She kept digging until she found an envelope all the way at the bottom.

Inside the envelope she found a stack of hundred-dollar bills.

"Kingsley. I don't want your money."

"It's a birthday gift."

"How much is this?"

"Five thousand dollars."

Eleanor glared at him.

"What am I supposed to do with this?"

"Shop. You need a new wardrobe."

"My clothes are fine."

"Your clothes are fine for school. Your clothes are fine for the vanilla world. Your clothes are not fine for the world you're about to enter. Sam will take you shopping tomorrow at a few authorized locations." He gave her a meaningful look. "Only buy white. We have a dress code."

"I don't like taking money I didn't earn. I only took Dad's insurance money because Søren ordered me to."

"You are the collared property of the most revered man in my world, in our world. I'm feared. I'm respected. He is worshipped. All of the Underground is waiting to make your acquaintance. Do you understand that?"

"No."

"You will."

"King, what's happening here?" She looked down at the money in her hand. She always refused money and gifts and even rides from Kingsley. She wouldn't step foot in his Rolls-Royce unless Kingsley or Søren were with her. The last thing she ever wanted was for Søren to think she only loved him for his connections.

Kingsley rolled off her pillow and leaned back on his hands. He looked almost normal today in his jeans and black T-shirt pulled taut over his strong, broad chest. A leather jacket lay draped over the back of her desk chair. He looked too old to be a student but not old enough to be a professor. Her bitchy airhead roommate Brandi-Ann had probably soaked her panties at the sight of him and told him he could have his way with her.

"You're not a little girl anymore. You're not even a teen-ager anymore. What do you think is happening?"

She looked down at the money, at Kingsley in her bed. First Lady of the Underground?

"It's going to happen soon, isn't it? Like really soon? Me and Søren?"

Kingsley only gave her an enigmatic smile.

"Open the last box."

She picked up the smallest box and removed the lid. Inside on a blanket of black silk lay a single silver key.

"What's the key to?"

Kingsley scooted close to her and put his mouth at her ear. She hated when he got this close to her, hated how much she liked it.

"It's the key to the kingdom."

"Which kingdom?"

"Mine."

"What do I do with it?"

"You'll find out."

Kingsley crawled off her bed and pulled on his jacket.

"The car is picking you up today at three," he said, and when she attempted to object he raised his hand to silence her. "You're the collared submissive of the most venerated man in the Underground. He owns you now. Your opinion is no longer the overriding factor in the decisions that affect you. Sam will pick you up tomorrow. You will do what you are told and you will like it. *Tu comprends?*"

Eleanor glared at him through narrowed eyes.

"Je comprend."

"Your French is improving. Now let's work on your attitude."

"King, you're like the big brother I never had. And never wanted."

Kingsley opened her bedroom door.

"Don't worry, *chérie,*" he said in his most infuriating French accent, "someday you'll have me. We both know you already want me."

"I don't want this money." She held up the envelope. "I didn't earn it."

"No," he agreed almost solemnly. "But believe me, in his bed, you will."

She tossed a pillow at his retreating back and he slammed the door behind him. Kingsley might have a point about her being an unsubmissive submissive. Not that she'd admit that to him. She collapsed back into bed and tried not to think about the money, the key and the shopping trip. How much more would her life change once she and Søren were lovers and a real couple?

Her alarm went off at 8:30 a.m. and Eleanor dragged herself out of bed. She didn't have her first class until ten o'clock, but she had to take her birth control pill at the same time every day. As soon as Søren had declared he couldn't wait much longer, she'd gone into planning mode—planning not to get knocked up. She focused on that aspect of going on birth control, the "I am not going to get pregnant" part. If she thought about the "Søren is never going to have children" part she might have had second thoughts.

She managed to give psych class at least half her attention even with her ass still smarting from Kingsley's spankings. They were studying the Stanford prison experiments—the infamous study where Philip Zimbardo created a fake prison in the basement of a classroom building and filled it with volunteer guards and volunteer prisoners. Fascinating how quickly people took on the roles that they were assigned. Even in a fake prison, it took only one day for the guards to start abusing the prisoners and the prisoners to sink into rebellion or depression. The guards and prisoners internalized their roles so quickly that they had to call off the experiment after only six days. Some of the guards, heretofore normal university students, turned into sadists with the prisoners. The word *sadist* had gotten her attention.

She wondered if stuff like this happened in the BDSM community that Kingsley ruled. Did the dominants dominate because they'd taken on that role? Did the submissives submit for the same reason? Which came first? The submissive or the submission? Maybe she would write her term paper on role-play in BDSM. What if someone put a flogger in her hand, pointed her at a submissive and was told to discipline her? She would, of course. And she'd enjoy it, although she knew she was a submissive, not a dominant. Had to be a submissive, right? She loved sitting at Søren's feet, obeying his orders, getting disciplined by him, and dreamed of the night when he'd beat her the first time. Still…if someone did put a flogger in her hand, she wouldn't complain.

The Rolls-Royce pulled up in front of her dorm promptly at three. She'd hoped to find Søren waiting for her, or at least Kingsley. Sam, even? A night with Sam would make a grand birthday. But only a note and a box waited for her in the backseat.

The tag on the box read Open Me.

She opened the box and pulled out a stopwatch.

A stopwatch?

She picked up the note. On the envelope it said, *Do not open until you are sitting in Q31.*

What the absolute fuck? Q31?

She tucked the watch into her coat pocket. The car dropped her in front of a concert hall. Concert hall?

She found seat Q31 in the balcony. She sat and pulled the stopwatch and the note from her pocket. Down on the stage, an orchestra tuned up while the conductor flipped through some sheet music. Wincing at the discord coming from the stage, she opened the note and started to read.

Happy birthday, Little One. I have two gifts for you on this most blessed of days. First, look down onto the stage. This is one of the orchestras I play with when they need a pianist. In exchange for my services, they've kindly agreed to play a specifically chosen piece for you on your birthday.

The piece will begin as soon as the orchestra is tuned. When the conductor raises his baton, start the stopwatch. Listen to the music, but pay attention to the watch. My first gift to you is this—shortly after the five-minute mark (five minutes and eight seconds if the orchestra stays in time) you will know what I felt the moment I saw you the first time. I'm not as gifted as you at expressing my feelings with words. Perhaps the music will say what I can't.

I will give you my second present soon.

I love you, Eleanor.

She read through the note one more time before picking up the stopwatch. She slid out of her seat and knelt at the balcony railing.

The discordant sound of tuning died away. The conductor tapped his music stand.

He raised his arms.

She hit the start button.

The music began.

First came the initial blast of sound. She hadn't expected such a powerful beginning. Then all went quiet again. The sounds danced a little, skipped down steps and back up again. One long note lingered in the air before it rolled down the steps after the other notes. The piece started to dance again. Sometimes playful, sometimes somber.

A high note, it floated above her head. Quiet... How could an orchestra of so many people sound so quiet?

And then she heard it. The hint of a familiar melody. Where had she heard it before? A hymn. This was a hymn. Wasn't it? It didn't matter. She kept listening.

At two minutes and fifty seconds, the melody came again, whispering over the floor like a secret the composer wanted to keep. She strained her ears to hear more.

It grew louder then, but only a little louder as another section picked up the melody and carried it to her. She accepted it with open arms.

Her hands shook and her toes tightened in her shoes. The music backed up like a river dammed around her.

At five minutes and seven seconds the world turned into music. It erupted around her, went off like a bomb that showered joy and happiness all around her. Tears ran down her face as sounds more beautiful than she'd ever heard in her life wrapped around her and lifted her like hands to the very roof of the concert hall and higher and higher until for one brief second she looked into the eyes of God.

She sensed footsteps behind her but she ignored them. The music had her now and wouldn't let go. The melody disappeared and came back with a vengeance. She couldn't get enough of it. No alcohol had ever intoxicated her so much. How did musicians stand it? How did they stop themselves and put down their instruments long enough to eat or drink or sleep? If she could make sounds like this, her hands would never leave her instrument. She would play until her fingers bled. She would make noise like this until they locked her away.

The piece hit a final swelling note that left her aching for something...not something, *somewhere,* before it died. The conductor lowered his arms, turned and looked up at the balcony.

The applause of one humbled young woman filled the hall.

"Thank you," she called out to the orchestra.

"Happy birthday," the conductor replied.

She turned around and saw Søren sitting behind her.

"If only Beethoven had written a piano part for his Ninth Symphony, my life would be complete," he said with a wistful sigh. The symphony started a new piece now, beautiful but less arresting. She turned the stopwatch off and rested her chin on Søren's knee.

"That was Beethoven?"

"The Ninth Symphony, Fourth Movement. Otherwise known as the 'Ode to Joy.'"

"No piano part?"

"I believe Beethoven simply felt the other instruments would be overpowered by the piano. It's a large instrument. Some people find it intimidating."

He winked at her and Eleanor laughed, grinning up at him.

"It was the most beautiful thing I've ever heard. I think I saw God. He smiled at me."

"I never appreciated the Ninth Symphony until I met you, Eleanor. When I saw you I heard it for the first time coming from inside my own heart. I was seventeen when I first dreamed of you. Kingsley and I were talking, fantasizing about the perfect woman. Green eyes and black hair or black eyes and green hair, we didn't care, as long as she was wilder than the both of us together. Only a dream…and then you."

"Mom asked me once what it would take for me to believe in God. I told her if I could meet one person who seemed like he was created in God's image, I would start believing. And then you."

They stared at each other as if they were two people who'd

met in a dream and upon waking found they still saw each other.

"They say there are no atheists in foxholes. I can't imagine there are many of them in symphonies. God created Beethoven and Beethoven created this.... You can hear hints of the melody in a much earlier work called the 'Choral Fantasy.' He dreamed of it long before he wrote it. Even the angels bend their ears to earth when the 'Ode to Joy' is performed. When you hear music so beautiful it gives you chills, those are angel wings brushing against you."

"I have chills now," she whispered.

"Angels have haloes and wings. We have free will and Beethoven."

"I think we got the better deal."

Søren smiled into the distance.

"Beethoven was deaf when he composed this piece. He couldn't hear his own masterpiece anywhere but in his own head. But we are all deaf in a way. Life is a symphony composed by God, played by us with preludes, themes, movements, passages...and wrong notes, so many wrong notes. Heaven is where we get to hear the music played perfectly for the first time."

"I think life is a book," Eleanor said. "God writes it. We're His characters. He knows what happens on the next page, but we don't. Heaven is where we get to read the book cover to cover and see how it all makes sense."

Søren cupped the back of Eleanor's neck and she rose up on her knees to meet his lips.

"No one down there can see us up here, can they?" she whispered after the kiss.

"Even if they could, I don't care today. Happy birthday, Little One."

"Thank you, sir. Now, I believe you said something about two presents?" She batted her eyelashes at him.

"I do have a second gift for you. Pick a number between one and five."

"Oh, I love this game. Five, five, five," she said.

"Are you sure about that?" His gray eyes twinkled mischievously at her.

"I told you, I'll always pick the biggest number. I'm greedy."

"Very well. Five it is."

Søren reached into his jacket pocket and pulled out five white envelopes, each of them with a number on the front, the numbers one through five.

"There are five dates on cards inside the envelope."

"Dates for what?"

"Our first night together."

Eleanor looked at him then back at the cards.

"You mean—"

"Open the card."

With trembling fingers she picked up the card marked with a five. She resisted the urge to rip right into it. She could do this. She could be calm. From inside the envelope she pulled a piece of paper.

"And the winner is..." she said, opening the note.

"Holy Thursday," Søren said. "Less than three weeks away."

Eleanor stared at the words and forced herself to breathe. She'd been in love with Søren for four years and now in front of her was the day written in ink.

"I can't wait." She pressed the card to her heart. He cupped her face and she grinned up at him. This was happiness—simply being with him.

"I should go. I'm needed back in Wakefield."

"Yeah, I have swim practice. I should go to that."

"Eleanor, about that."

"What?"

He said nothing and he didn't have to. From the look on his face, she understood.

"Okay. I'll quit the team."

"I wish it could be another way."

"This is how it is. I'll tell them today." If she and Søren were going to be lovers, she'd have to spend the rest of her life learning how to hide her bruises and welts. No way to hide bruises in a swimsuit. She knew there'd be a price to pay. This was a small one.

"Jeg elsker dig, min lille en."

Søren kissed her again.

"I'll see you soon," he promised. "You should open the other cards and see what your options were."

"Sadist," she said, smiling against his lips.

Søren left her alone in the balcony with the four remaining unopened cards. She shouldn't open them. She knew she shouldn't. They were the roads not taken, so why even given them a second thought?

Fuck that, she wanted to know.

She opened envelope number one and nearly swore aloud as she read the one word written on it.

Tonight.

If she'd picked number one, she would have lost her virginity on her birthday.

God damn her and her greediness. Maybe card number two would have said Easter or some day after Holy Thursday.

"What the—"

Card number two also said *Tonight.*

Card number three? *Tonight.*

And card number four? Eleanor ripped the envelope open.

"Motherfucking priest."

31

Eleanor

ON THE EVENING OF HOLY THURSDAY, ELEANOR stopped by her old house in Wakefield but didn't go inside. After Eleanor started college, her mother had gotten an apartment in Westport closer to her job and put the Wakefield house on the market. Now it sat empty, abandoned, alone. Her mom had picked Wakefield because of its proximity to its good Catholic schools. Eleanor wondered if her mother regretted going through all that trouble. Her mom assumed Eleanor had turned into a godless heathen at her liberal arts school—the sort of girl who slept around and drank and never went to church. She was no saint, but she'd made it to twenty still a virgin. And God knows she loved the Catholic Church—at least one part of it—with all her heart.

Although she hated it then, now she was grateful that her mother had made her go to church. Otherwise she wouldn't have met Søren, and through Søren she'd found her way to God.

She wondered about who might buy the house someday.

Whoever it was, she hoped God took as good care of them as He had of her. Four years ago she'd sat in a police station thinking her life had ended at age fifteen. Now all she saw before her were endless beautiful possibilities.

A thousand times as a teenager she'd walked from her house to Sacred Heart. She could have driven to the church or asked Kingsley to drive her. But she wanted to walk tonight like she had so many times before. She would have walked all the way from New York if she had to. She would have walked barefoot on broken glass.

At the rectory she paused outside the door and removed her shoes. No one told her to, and she had no idea why she did it.

On bare and silent feet, she slipped in the side door and once inside the house she heard music. Piano music. She'd never heard the piece before but it spoke to her, whispered to her, beckoned her farther in. She found Søren at the piano, his fingers gliding across the keys, waltzing in the shadows cast by a single candle. She sat next to him on the bench, her back to the keyboard, and rested her head against his shoulder. He played until the end of the piece before lifting his fingers off the keys and letting the notes hang in the air. He closed the fallboard and looked at her.

"More Beethoven?" she asked.

"The Moonlight Sonata. I can't complain Beethoven didn't write a piano part for his Ninth Symphony. He did give us pianists the Moonlight Sonata as a consolation prize."

"It's beautiful."

"So are you."

Eleanor took a deep breath.

"Can I ask you a question?"

"Of course, Little One."

"Are you as nervous as I am?"

He exhaled heavily. "I haven't done this since I was eighteen years old."

"So you are nervous?"

"Not at all."

"Me, neither," she said and meant it.

Søren dipped his head and her lips trembled against his. She hadn't lied. She didn't feel a moment's nervousness. Only peace and desire as if this moment had been waiting outside her door her entire life and at last she could let it in.

She reached behind her head and pulled out the pencil she'd used to hold her hair back in a loose knot. Søren smiled at the pencil lying on her palm.

"You're so certain you're going to pass this test tonight?" he asked her. She laid the pencil on the piano by the candle, thrilled Søren remembered their long-ago talk about how she'd take only a pencil to the tests she'd knew she'd ace.

"I plan on blowing the curve."

They kissed again, kissed through their smiles.

"Stay," Søren said as he pulled away from her.

She waited on the piano bench as ordered. From now until the end of time this would be her life—Søren giving orders and her taking them. She would wait when he said wait and where he said wait and she would not move until he told her she could move.

Søren returned to the living room carrying a large ivory basin, a glass pitcher of water and a small white towel.

Her heart caught in her throat when Søren knelt on the floor in front of her.

"Søren, please don't—"

"It's Holy Thursday. This is what priests do on Holy Thursday."

"Why?"

"Because Christ washed his disciples' feet on the night of the Last Supper."

She'd struggled with what to wear tonight, struggled until she remembered it wouldn't matter. If she'd shown up in torn rags, Søren would still love her, still want her. And she'd be naked any moment anyway. She'd dressed in jeans and a sweater. Underneath she wore white lingerie that Kingsley had paid for and Sam had picked out. As weird as it was to get lingerie from Kingsley and Sam, she couldn't fault their taste. Even if it was weird, she liked that. Life would be weird from now on. She was the mistress of a Catholic priest who was the best friend of the king of an S&M empire. Life was weird and wonderful and all she could say to it was Amen, Amen.

So be it.

Søren took her right foot in his hand and she shivered at the gentle touch. As he poured warm water over her feet, she sighed from the heat. So this was love? She tucked this feeling in her heart and hid it there. Someday she would write about this moment. She would write a book about a girl who fell in love with a god and then, to her complete surprise, discovered the god loved her back. Since he couldn't be a man she would be a goddess and leave the mortal world behind for him.

He poured the water over her left foot and dried both her feet with the towel. Not even kneeling at her feet diminished Søren in her eyes. His long eyelashes cast shadows on his cheeks. One mutinous strand of hair wanted to fall over his forehead. She pushed it back and Søren pressed his cheek into her hand. As much as she railed and fought against waiting this long, she now understood why it had been for the best. They met each other as equals tonight. Her submission meant more because she chose it freely instead of letting the law or their age difference or anything in the world impose it on her.

Søren stood up and took her in his arms. He lifted her off

the piano bench and carried her upstairs. She'd never been in his bedroom before, and it didn't disappoint. It seemed a sacred space to her, the room where Søren slept. The white sheets covered the bed like a new-fallen snow. The dark wood of the four-poster bed appeared to her like the trunks of trees—strong and eternal. She felt like a virgin sacrifice brought to an ancient forest. Blood must be spilled for the gods to be appeased. She offered her own blood tonight and would pour it like wine on snow.

A glass of red wine sat by the bed. Søren raised it and drank from the glass. He handed it to her.

"Drink. It will relax you."

She drank as ordered.

"I will be as careful as I can be tonight."

"The more pain I feel, the more you enjoy it, yes?"

Søren opened a box on the bedside table and pulled her white collar from it. He stepped behind her as she kept drinking the wine.

"Yes. But I can still enjoy myself without torturing you."

"You don't have to be careful with me, sir." She inhaled as he locked the collar around her neck. She breathed into its grip.

"You are my most precious possession. I will guard you with my life."

He took the glass from her hand and sat it on the table again. She stared at it, taking her eyes from it only when Søren sat on the side of the bed facing her.

Without a word, he ordered her to remove her clothes. She could do that now, read his wants and desires without requiring his words. He'd trained her well, trained her for this night. And so she obeyed without hesitation, pulling her sweater off and dropping it to the floor. Her jeans she slid off next. She unhooked her bra and stepped out of her panties. It had been like this once upon a time in Eden. A man and a woman in paradise with nothing between each other, nothing between them and God. It had been like this once, and tonight when they made love they would step one foot back into Eden and see what had been lost and what could be found again.

"I want you to hurt me," she said. "As much as you want, sir."

"You say that, but you don't mean it."

"I mean it."

Søren slapped her.

Eleanor started. In openmouthed shock she stared at Søren. She raised a hand to her cheek. It burned.

"Now do you still want me to hurt you as much as I want?" Søren asked. The question wasn't a question but a gauntlet thrown down. *This is me,* Søren was saying. *Take me or leave me.*

She took him.

She held out her hand, and Søren took it. For one second she thought she saw relief in his eyes.

He led her to the bedpost. A large trunk sat at the foot of the bed next to her calves. Søren turned a key and opened the box. Inside it she first saw nothing but more sheets. He lifted the sheets and from underneath them pulled a set of white leather cuffs. He stood and took her right hand. He pressed her palm to the center of his chest as he locked the cuff around her wrist. He did the same to her left wrist. After she could only marvel at the sight of her hands in the cuffs. So this was what love looked like? Now she knew.

"Say your safe word."

"Jabberwocky," she said.

"Good. At any time you can tell me if you need to stop. Tell me what you need and your request will be honored. Say your safe word only when and if you need me to stop everything. You give yourself freely to me. I would never force it on you."

"I know, sir. All I want is to please you tonight."

"You will. You already have. I will flog you first, cane you after. I won't slap you again."

"You can," she said. "I think I liked it, sir."

Søren dropped a kiss on the back of her neck.

"If you're good. I'll tie you to the bedposts after. I want you faceup during sex tonight for the first time. I will give you as much pleasure as I give you pain, perhaps more." He pressed against her back. She felt him unbuttoning his shirt. She pushed back into him, needing his skin against hers.

"What is your favorite sort of pain to inflict, sir?"

"Cutting. Nothing arouses me more than someone who will bleed for me."

"I'll bleed for you, sir."

"On the bed, when I'm inside you, you will, yes. That is enough blood for one night."

Eleanor knew he referred to her virginity. She wanted to give him more. She would give him more.

He pulled a short length of rope from the trunk and weaved it through the buckles on her cuffs. He turned her toward the bedpost and secured her arms high over her head. She stretched out, breathing into the position, feeling exposed from her ankles to her neck. She couldn't move her hands, couldn't run away. Leaving him was no longer a choice. She couldn't if she wanted to. She never wanted to.

Søren ran his hand over her back, touching every inch of skin. No one existed but her and Søren. The world had begun the moment she stepped into his bedroom. It would end when she left it. Everything outside his bedroom door disappeared into nothingness. She didn't miss it at all.

The first blow of the flogger landed between her shoulder

blades. Her back exploded in pain. She almost laughed from the shock of it.

He struck her again. Breath exploded from her lungs. Then again and again the flogger landed, sometimes in the same spot over and over again until tears filled her eyes. She could never guess where the next blow would fall. After fifty she stopped trying to guess. After a hundred she didn't even care. It stung brutally, and her skin burned like fire. More, she wanted. More. Let him burn her to the ground. Let her rise again from the ashes.

The flogging ceased and Søren pressed his chest into her bare back. She cried out as his heat scalded her raw skin.

"Too much?" He slid his hands up her sides and cupped her breasts. He teased her nipples and now she groaned in pleasure. He'd become the master of her body already. Tied up like this she could give herself neither pleasure nor pain, nor any sort of release or relief. All sensation came from him and him alone.

"No, sir."

"You want more pain?"

"I want all the pain you want to give me, sir."

With her arms tied to the bedpost she could only see in front of her. Søren pulled something else from his trunk. She couldn't see it, but she could guess from the sound of the air being sliced in two. When the cane contacted with the back of her thighs, she screamed. She didn't mean to, but the pain pushed the sound out of her. Søren paused as if waiting for her to object, to ask him to stop. If he waited for her to ask him to stop he'd be waiting all night.

He struck her again.

A third time.

A fourth.

She'd never known pain like this pain. She'd never known

strength like the strength she summoned to endure it. And soon she no longer endured it, she enjoyed it. The pain became a game to her. How much could she take? How much could Søren give? He enslaved her with the pain. No one would suffer this willingly, so if she suffered it, it must be because he owned her and could hurt her like this. And yet she'd come here of her own volition. And a single word could stop him. He owned her for the same reason. It made no sense, none at all, and yet her body understood. She knew her body understood because Søren dropped the cane onto the floor and wrapped a hand around her hips. He pressed two fingers into her and sank deep into her wetness. She'd never been this intensely aroused in her life.

With one hand still inside her, Søren reached up and unknotted the ropes. He turned her and pressed her back to the bedpost. With an arm under her left knee, he lifted her leg, opening her up so he could explore inside her more easily. She felt nothing but pleasure as he probed her with two fingers, moving in and out of her slowly. Her wetness eased his passage as he pushed deep into all her hidden places. When he pushed a third finger into her, she winced.

"I know it hurts, Little One," Søren whispered as he kissed her and pushed into the band of tissue at the entrance of her vagina. "Let me do this. It'll be better this way."

"Not with your fingers, please," she begged.

"It will hurt less this way. I'll have more control."

She shook her head.

"Please..." she begged and Søren pressed his forehead to hers. "It's how I dreamed of it. Please..."

"You do beg beautifully."

"I'll beg more if you want me to." She wanted him to break her hymen not with his fingers but when he penetrated her the first time. It had to be that way. She needed it that way.

"You'll beg for mercy when I'm inside you the first time."

"I don't want mercy. I want you."

He kissed her mouth as he lowered her leg to the floor. The entire back of her body from her knees to her shoulders throbbed from the beating. Why did people flee from pain and avoid it like the plague? Yes, it hurt, but so did everything that mattered. Love hurt, life hurt, birth hurt, changing hurt, growing hurt. The dead didn't hurt, only the living. She had never felt so alive.

Søren kissed her again, but only long enough to wet her lips. When Søren gripped the back of her neck, she had an idea of what might be coming next. It didn't surprise her when he forced her onto her knees. She opened his pants and remembered that she'd fantasized about doing this to him since she was fifteen years old. But she wasn't fifteen. She was twenty now. A grown woman. No reason to be nervous. He'd grown hard while beating her and she licked her lips in anticipation. Wrapping her mouth around him, she sucked deep, relishing the taste of him. Søren dug his hand into the back of her neck with bruising strength. From his lips escaped the slightest of groans. The sound of his pleasure emboldened Eleanor. She sucked harder, deeper, licked him from the base to the tip over and over again.

This was what she'd wanted since the day they met. She'd wanted to serve him, to kneel before him, to offer herself to be used by him. Every day he sacrificed himself on the altar of the Catholic Church—gave up his time, his wealth, his freedom. That she could give this one thing to him, the pleasure of using her, and she would give it with all her heart, body and soul.

She winced as Søren dug his fingers even deeper into her skin. She knew she'd have a black bruise from his fingers tomorrow.

"Stop," he ordered and Eleanor sat back on her knees.

Søren cupped her chin and ran his thumb over her lips.

"I think you enjoyed that."

She smiled up at him.

"I live to serve."

"You do now."

With his hand on her chin, he guided her off the floor and back onto her feet.

"Wait by the bed."

Søren left her standing at the bedpost while he pulled the top sheet of the bed down. He took more rope and another set of cuffs and laid them on the bed.

As he prepared the bed, Eleanor stared at the wineglass on the table. She walked to it and drank the last few drops of wine. She took a step back and then another.

When Søren turned back to her she held the glass out in front of her.

"Eleanor?"

She dropped the glass and it shattered on the floor at her feet…her bare feet.

"Eleanor—"

Before he could order her to do otherwise, she took a step forward onto the broken glass.

"You said nothing pleases you more than someone who will bleed for you." She took another step. The glass cut into her heel, into her toes. Søren inhaled sharply as she walked to him—bare feet on shattered glass. She hardly felt a thing. The only sign that glass had cut her were the bloody footprints she left behind her. She looked into Søren's eyes. His pupils had widened hugely and his bare chest moved in shallow pants. She crossed the four feet to the bed.

"If it had been fire, I would have walked through fire," she whispered.

"If it had been fire, I would have carried you through it." He lifted her and laid her in the center of the bed.

She wound her arms around his neck and he dug his fingers deep into her hair, bending her body back, baring her neck. He kissed the hollow of her throat, bit her collarbone and shoulder. With his knees he forced her thighs apart. He grasped her clitoris between his thumb and forefinger and she flinched from the marriage of pain with pleasure. He pried the lips of her vagina wide open and hooked his fingers over her pubic bone, pushing the tips into that soft hollow an inch inside her. Low moans escaped her lips as he took possession of her body. The pain in her feet was long forgotten as her inner muscles pulsed around his fingers. Before she could come, however, he released her from his grasp and pushed her hard and fast onto her back. In seconds he had her wrists and ankles cuffed to the bedposts, and left her lying there as she breathed and waited and wanted. She closed her eyes as he returned to her, a wet cloth in his hand. He wiped blood and glass off her feet, a move so careful and tender she could scarcely believe that he was the same man who moments earlier had nearly ripped her open with his fingers.

You have only seen him by day. She remembered Kingsley's words. *All light and shadow. But the night will come and you will see the darkness.*

So this was the darkness? Then may she live the rest of her life by night.

After binding her to the bed with leather cuffs and black rope, Søren stared down at her helpless body.

"Mine," he said and met her eyes.

"Yours, sir."

When he'd finished binding her, she lay on her back unable to move her legs or her arms. This was how it would be. This was how it would happen. This was the beginning. This was the end.

Søren stripped out of his clothes. She had dreamed of his naked body and now she saw it bathed in moonlight and candlelight and his own light that came from within him. Even naked he still seemed clothed with dignity and strength, and he wore his strength like a shield. With his body, he covered hers. His thighs felt like marble against her thighs. His skin shone like polished gold. His lips tasted as sweet as the wine and she drank deep of him.

"Why did the king tie Esther to the bed?" he asked.

"Because he loved her."

32

Eleanor

SØREN LINGERED AT HER MOUTH. HE KISSED HER AND she returned the kiss with equal and even greater fervency. Their tongues mingled and she drank of the wine on his lips, swallowed the heat of his mouth. Eleanor winced as Søren nipped her bottom lip.

Søren dusted kisses across the sensitive skin of her chest. Under his mouth her heart pounded, her blood throbbed. She ached to touch him but every time she tried to move her hands the bonds held her. Kingsley had warned her about the bondage. Søren needed to stay in control as much as possible. The more helpless she was, the more he would feel compelled to protect her.

She inhaled as Søren licked the tip of her right nipple. He brought his mouth down on her breast and sucked gently as he teased her left nipple with his fingers. Tied down as she was, she couldn't do much but arch her back to offer more of her breasts to him. He moved his mouth to her left nipple. Heat gathered in her breasts and melted through her stomach, settling into her hips. She wanted him inside her. No, not wanted, needed.

"Please, sir..." she begged.

"Please what?" He raised his head and cocked his eyebrow at her as if amused she would even dare beg for anything.

"I want you."

"You have me."

"I want you inside me."

"I'm always inside you, Little One."

Eleanor entertained a brief fantasy of stabbing him in the neck. But then he moved his lips to her mouth again.

"Patience," he whispered against her skin. "I have waited years for this night. I won't rush it."

"Did you really want me from the day we met?"

"So much it scared me."

He ran his fingertips down the center of her body until he rested his palm against her clitoris. It pulsed against his hand.

"I want you to come for me. I need you as wet as possible before I enter you. Understand?"

"Yes, sir." She started to breathe heavier as Søren pressed the heel of his hand in deeper. He dipped two fingers into her vagina before pressing his now wet fingertips against her clitoris. Desire engulfed her as he made tight circles on the swollen knot of flesh.

Her hips rose off the bed and she went still underneath him. Her entire body locked up before exploding with pleasure. Her vagina clenched and released rapidly, fluttering inside her and pressing against nothing. She couldn't wait to come around him, to let him feel her own pleasure on his body.

"Good girl," he said, brushing a lock of hair off her forehead.

He kissed her nipples again as she recovered from her orgasm. He sucked leisurely, lazily, at them as if he intended to spend all night lying between her breasts. She had a vague memory of Wyatt kissing her nipples like this. When he had done it she'd watched him and felt tenderness toward him like a mother to a child. They might have been the same age but she felt so much older than him. But with Søren she felt like the property of a king, like Esther in a harem, captured and conquered. And like Esther, she knew she had conquered the conqueror with the greatest of all powers—love.

Søren kissed the valley between her breasts and his lips traveled down her stomach and over her hips. He nipped her hip bone with his teeth and the moment the pain registered, Søren moved between her thighs. Eleanor stiffened as he licked her, kissed her, made love to her with his mouth.

"Fuck..." she groaned, unable to contain herself. She hadn't expected him to go down on her. He'd said he would pleasure her but this act seemed almost submissive to her as he knelt between her legs. But then he increased the pressure on her clitoris with his tongue and he pushed in two fingers and rubbed that soft hollow on the front wall inside her. He mastered her with his mouth. With his fingers he spread her folds so wide, exposing the entrance to her body. She couldn't hide from him. He saw all of her, all her most secret places. He licked her clitoris again and again, and when she came, she clenched at his lips and fingers.

He rose up and kissed her. She tasted herself on his mouth and couldn't get enough of it. Had she imagined anything so erotic before? His hand traced a line down her body from her collared neck to her thighs. He slid his thumb into her and she winced at the strange sensation. The wince turned into a gasp of pure pain as he pressed down hard against her hymen, not hard enough to tear it but hard enough that tears sprang to her eyes. He inhaled sharply as if he registered her pain inside his own body. He experienced her pain as his pleasure.

Let him hurt her, then, so he could feel the pleasure of it. Let him destroy her so she could be reborn.

The pain passed and Søren settled in between her thighs, the tip of his length pressing against her clitoris. She pushed her hips hard into his, opening herself to him, offering herself to him.

She looked up and saw Søren's eyes were closed. His long, unnaturally dark eyelashes lay against his cheeks. The veins in his strong arms and shoulders quivered as he held himself over her. He started to speak but not in English. It was Danish, his first language. She knew some Danish, enough for her and Søren to tell each other "I need you, I want you" without anyone understanding them. But in her fevered state she could recognize nothing he said, not at first. He murmured the words like a prayer. She raised her head and pressed a kiss against his throat, her most favorite part of his body, the part hidden by his collar. The final words of his prayer she understood.

Jeg elsker dig.

I love you.

"I love you," he said, in his first language, and the words rose like a banner over the bed.

With her eyes half-closed, she felt the world falling asleep around her. She heard music somewhere in the distance, a haunting solo voice almost inhuman in its beauty. Did she hear this? See this? Or did it all come from within herself like a dream half remembered only hours after waking? She buried her head in the hollow between Søren's chin and shoulder. She breathed in and inhaled the scent of snow, new snow, clean and cold. And then she knew the truth.

Søren didn't smell like winter. Winter smelled like Søren.

Jeg elsker dig.

She heard Søren's voice through the mist.

With one thrust, he pushed inside her.

Pain like she'd never imagined rent her in half. Rent her in half, split her in two, burned her like fire, tore her like paper.

Beneath Søren she struggled and cried, her face buried against his chest. He cradled the back of her head as she wept tears of agony and surrender. He didn't pull out of her, didn't apologize. He held himself still, but inside her he pulsed as her vagina stretched and strained to take all of him into her. This was the price she had to pay for the kiss that couldn't be unkissed, for the apple that couldn't be unbitten, for the road she had taken. They had gone too far now. They could no longer go back.

She never wanted to go back.

The pain suffused her entire body. It burned like the hottest fire and if she had the use of her arms she would have tried to push him off her. One word could stop her suffering. She said nothing.

Slowly she emerged from the haze of pain and heard Søren's ragged breathing in her ear, the slightest catch of his breath, the subtlest moan in the back of his throat. Had there ever been a more beautiful sound than this—the sound of the pleasure he took inside her?

Instinct told her to shrink from him, to pull away. But she fought that urge and instead raised her hips again into his. He penetrated her until it seemed as if his entire body filled hers to the breaking point. Each slow, controlled thrust stretched her open wide, tearing the gate that would keep him out of her. She wanted it gone, wanted everything between them gone forever. His hand found her hand and he locked their fingers together as he rose up and pushed in again. She braced for pain but instead felt a deep stab of pleasure. Her eyes flew open at the shock of it, so carnal, so animal. With a cry she pushed her hips into his again and again. A rush of fluid between her thighs eased his passage even more. Blood, perhaps? Her own wetness? It didn't matter. All that mattered was that he impaled her, invaded her, took ownership of her with every controlled yet merciless thrust.

She focused on his face, on the long dark eyelashes resting on his cheeks, on his partly open lips, on his blond hair that she ached to run her fingers through, on the sheen of sweat that covered his forehead, his shoulders and the vein that pulsed visibly in his neck. It must have taken all his strength to hold back and not lose himself inside her. Sixteen years since he'd last done this. His self-control could shatter at any moment. She wanted it to shatter.

Raising her head off the sheets, she kissed his shoulder. She whispered, "You own me."

Søren opened his eyes and gazed down at her.

He thrust so hard into her she stopped breathing. He thrust again just as hard and she exhaled once more. It had to be like this, it had to be brutal. It wasn't enough to take her virginity—he had to obliterate it.

For an eternity she could do nothing but breathe through the pain, breathe it into her and breathe it back out again. But as he moved in her, the pain waned and something else took its place. Something...desire, hunger, greed for more of him. Søren slid a hand between their bodies and kneaded her clitoris, stroking it as she ground her pelvis into his hand. A deep and primal need overtook her. She writhed underneath him, writhed and thrashed. Her inner walls throbbed against him. He pulled out and pushed in again as he teased her clitoris, dragging her close to a climax again.

The moment she saw him the first time all those years ago, she'd felt as if a golden cord had encircled her at the sight of him and tightened with each step toward him. Now she felt the cord again tight around her hips and her heart. As he pressed deeper and deeper into her, she felt the cord lifting her, carrying her higher and higher until her heart scraped the sky. The cord broke at its apex and she crashed to earth. She came apart, crying out as her climax crashed through her. This was it, the moment she had lived for and longed for since she'd first seen him. Communion was theirs at last.

Søren pushed faster against her and with a final thrust that left her gasping, he came inside her, driving into her, pouring into her endlessly as she shuddered around him and shattered beneath him. He lingered inside her after coming, devouring her mouth with his. At last he pulled out and blood and semen rushed out, pooling underneath her.

Once more Søren knelt between her thighs. He lapped at her sore inner lips, at her still throbbing clitoris. She rose up again and crashed once more. When Søren kissed her this time, she tasted blood.

He pushed his fingers into her tender opening. Soon he mounted her again, entered her again, fucked her again. Their first time might have had pretensions of lovemaking. The second time he didn't bother with any of the niceties of civilized sex. He fucked her brutally, unapologetically, fucked her like he would never have another chance to fuck her again this side of heaven and hell, and he would make the most of it even if it killed them both.

After he came a second time inside her, he pulled out and stared down at her naked, bleeding body. Welts and bruises scored her back. Cuts covered her feet. Her vagina felt lacerated from his thrusts. She'd come four times tonight and knew one thing for certain from the look in his eyes.

He'd only begun to hurt her tonight.

The cane came out again. Then the flogger. He unlocked her from the bonds and brought her to her hands and knees and entered her still bleeding body as she steadied herself with one hand on the headboard, one hand digging into the sheets. His hands roamed over her bruised back, her thighs and hips. He grasped her by the back of the neck and held her still as he rammed into her from behind. She felt like property in his hands, owned, possessed and enslaved.

She lost herself in the night, ceased to be Eleanor, ceased to be a person with a mind or a will of her own. She was His and *His* became her only identity. If someone asked her who she was, "I'm His" would be the answer. He pushed four fingers into her, more than she'd ever dreamed she could take. And yet she took them and then him again because he gave her no choice in the matter.

"How much more can you take?" he asked as he pushed her down to her stomach.

"I can take anything you want to give me," she said. The sex and the beatings had sent her into a near-ecstatic state of peace and bliss. The pain had anesthetized her. She barely felt her body anymore. It was as if she floated above the bed. The hardest strikes of the flogger only tickled. The most vicious blow of the cane barely stung. Søren put her on her stomach and pushed into her again. For sixteen years he'd abstained from sex. He seemed determined to make up for lost time all in one night. Let him. Let him fuck her until neither one of them could move anymore. She begged to drink from this cup. She would drink until she choked on the wine of his body and his sadism. She would drink until she drowned in it.

Søren fucked her a fourth time, pausing every few minutes to bite her back and shoulders. Then he knelt on her thighs and struck her with a thin reed cane that left a line of fire on her skin wherever it landed. Never had she dreamed he would beat her while inside her. She should never have doubted his sadism. She would never doubt it again. As he rode her with long, hard thrusts, he spoke to her and told her how proud he was to own her, how she was his most precious possession, how she pleased him more than she could imagine, how he would love her always and never let her go.

By dawn she could take no more from him. By dawn he could give no more to her. He gathered her body, bruised from shoulder to knee, front and back, and held her in his arms.

They didn't speak of what had happened between them. What could they have said to each other? He had shown her his soul. She had given him her heart. They had joined their bodies and an immutable bond now sealed them together. And nothing could break them apart because nothing could break them.

When she awoke the next morning, the sun had joined them in bed.

Eleanor flinched as she stretched against the sheets. The bottoms of her feet throbbed. No doubt she still had shards of glass embedded in her skin. Her shoulders and back ached as if she'd been stretched on a rack. Her breasts and nipples were sore and swollen. Inside she was bruised and raw. She couldn't recall ever being in this much pain.

It was the best morning of her life.

Søren opened his eyes and gazed at her like he was trying to remember where he'd seen her before. She kissed him. He kissed her back.

"So now what?" she asked.

Søren smiled and something in that smile told her she was in the biggest trouble of her life.

"Everything."

33

Nora

NORA OPENED HER EYES AND ACROSS FROM HER IN the bed was Nico, not Søren. And she was glad to see him there, glad enough she smiled.

"Is that the end of the story?" Nico asked. She could see his eyelids were heavy, as heavy as her heart.

"The story never ends. It's only the storyteller who grows too tired to keep telling it."

"What happened next?"

"Kingsley came for me at Søren's house. He came right into Søren's bedroom and carried me to the car. I spent a week at his house recovering from that one night. Your father..." She paused and conjured the memory. She could still feel it all the way to her feet. "He put me on his bed and sat at my feet and with a pair of tweezers cleaned the shards of glass out of my skin. He said some poor bastard had to pick the shrapnel out of his chest once. This was his way of returning the kindness to the universe."

"What happened with you and your mother?"

"She did it." Nora rolled her eyes. "She joined a convent. When I was in college she went back to school. The order she wanted to join—the Sisters of Saint Monica—required the postulants to have a bachelor's degree and no debt. Took her four years, but she got there. She took her first vows when I was twenty-four."

"Were you happy for her?"

"No," Nora admitted. "We weren't even speaking then. I moved back in with her after college to try to mend the rift. Didn't work. Instead she found out about me and Søren. It was a bad time. I didn't speak to her for three years. So…you should forgive Kingsley and your mother." She poked him in the chest. "Trust me on this. Do it now before it's too late."

"I want to love him," Nico said.

He gave her a tired smile.

"I'll tell you the story of him and Sam and his club, The 8th Circle, one day. Then you'll love him."

"Tell me now."

"No, it's almost dawn."

"My vines need me," he said, reaching for her and pulling her close.

"Do you like being needed?" She settled against his chest, so broad and so warm. "Doesn't it scare you?"

"I like knowing another life depends on me for its being. I like proving it made the right choice to put its faith in me. Does it scare you?"

"Being needed? Yes. Very much. Probably one reason why I decided long ago I didn't want children, not even Søren's. And it's why I've never owned anyone."

"Never?"

She shook her head. "I've had pets—human ones. But that was just play at the club. I never owned anyone the way Søren owned me. It's terrifying to be needed. Being responsible for another human being? For years? Sounds like a prison sentence. I don't even have plants."

"You should try it," he said. "It's not as bad as you think it is. It's not always a prison. Sometimes it's a palace. Subjects need their kings and queens."

He brushed her hair off her shoulder. Nora smiled to herself.

"What?" Nico asked, touching her lips. "What's the smile for?"

"You just reminded me of something I said once—it's nothing." She kissed his fingertips.

"You said you never needed Søren, but he needed you."

"He did, yes. Even after I left him he would call me sometimes and tell me he needed me. I loved him so I went to him."

"Did that feel like a prison sentence to you?"

"No," she confessed, recalling those nights she slipped over to the rectory and gave her body to him. "It felt like a privilege."

"That's what it felt like to me," Nico said. "When you needed me last night? A privilege. An honor."

"What are you saying, Nico?" Nora asked.

"I need you."

He touched her face, her lips.

"I need you," he said again. "You're everything I ever dreamed of in one woman. My Rosanella. Beautiful, graceful, intelligent, fearless, and yet you trembled in my arms during the storm and then you drank me from a wineglass. You owned me last night with everything you did to me and everything you let me do to you. No one on this earth deserves to have everything they desire. No one is entitled to have what he wants. But if I were to have what I wanted, I would need you to give it to me. Because it's you, Mistress Nora."

Nora couldn't look at Nico. Hearing him call her Mistress Nora was like hearing Søren call her "Little One" for the first time, like learning her real name. After she'd told Nico who his father was, he'd asked her for Kingsley's last name. "Nicholas Boissonneault," he'd said, his eyes shining with unshed tears as he tried out his new name. It hurt to learn who he was. It hurt her, too, but for a different reason.

"Go to sleep, my love." She kissed him on the forehead. "It's an order. You have a long drive back."

"What will you do?"

"I don't know yet," she said. "But I'll be okay. I always am."

Nico's eyelashes fluttered and in minutes his breathing settled into the deep rhythms of sleep. She gazed down at him, at this beautiful young man in her bed with callouses on his hands from the hard work he did every day. She'd never loved a man with calloused hands before. She had callouses, however. The callous on her finger from so much writing. The callous on her heart from so much loving.

She dragged herself from the bed and found her nightgown. She pulled a book from her suitcase and took it downstairs with her.

After building up the fire again, she curled into a chair. Carefully so as not to let any papers fall out, she opened her Bible.

More and more lately she found herself turning to this book for comfort and guidance. Queen Esther still enchanted her, as did Ruth and her threshing floor seduction of Boaz. The Psalms brought her solace—"Yea, though I walk through the valley of the shadow of death, I will fear no evil." King David and King Solomon spoke to her from ages past—two adulterers who found their way into the lineage of Christ. And how she loved Isaiah and the words that had become so much more meaningful to her of late—"For unto us a child is born; unto us a son is given."

But it wasn't the words of the Bible that she turned to in this last hour of night. From its pages she pulled a photograph, a child barely a year old with his mother's turquoise eyes and his father's blond hair.

She stared at the photograph of Fionn in her hand. In it her editor, Zach, held his son on his shoulder. The first time she'd held the boy in her own arms, the sudden depth of love she had for him had shaken her like fear. She'd trembled so hard she had to give him back to Grace almost immediately.

"If anyone ever tries to hurt that boy I will burn their world down," she'd said to Zach. "But please never ask me to babysit."

Zach had laughed and pulled her into a tender embrace, not caring that his wife stood five feet away watching and rolling her eyes at the both of them. They were long past jealousy and shared only joy among them all.

"Born to be a soldier, not a politician," Zach had teased her, then kissed her quick on the lips.

"What do you mean?" she'd asked.

Zach had looked into her eyes and smiled.

"Love the risk, hate the responsibility."

She hadn't argued. Zach knew her all too well by now.

Nora studied the boy in the photograph. She'd shown the picture to Nico once after showing him a picture of his newly acquired half sister Céleste.

"My godson," she'd said with pride.

"He doesn't take after his father," Nico had said, noting Zach's black hair and Fionn's blond locks.

"He does actually," she'd said with a secret smile. "So let's pray he gets his personality from his mother."

She needed to look at Fionn's picture right now. That little face of his with those wide, watching eyes consoled her more than any words of any song or psalm or prayer could right now. Death had come to her house and stolen a precious thing from her. But life had won this round. Fionn was her victory banner.

Knowing that he lived, that a new generation had already come into the world to fill the shoes of the lost, Nora could now look at the silver box on the mantel without denial or fear or regret. One death. One life. And so it would go until death died.

Nora closed her Bible, held it to her chest and for a while she dozed in the chair. She woke a few hours later, shivering from cold. Her fire had died again. She set her Bible aside and returned upstairs.

Standing by the bed, she watched Nico sleeping. What did vintners on the Mediterranean Sea dream of—the wine or the water? Did he dream of her? She'd never met a man like Nico, a man at complete and utter peace with himself. He loved older women, sexual submission, his wine and his work. He made no apologies and offered no explanations for any of it. He had never battled with demons. He'd never wrestled with angels. He stood upon the earth immune to hell's seductions, untroubled by heaven's demands.

Nico should have hated her, after all. Only last year the man he knew as his father had died. And when she'd come bearing the news another man had sired him, it was, as he said, like losing his beloved father a second time.

But he didn't hate her, although he'd grieved and she'd grieved with him. Instead he'd thanked her for telling her the truth about his birth and the half sister he loved the moment he learned her name. It comforted Nico to know that another man had tempted his mother, seduced her even, but she'd chosen her husband in the end. Kingsley had been grateful to Nora, as well. He'd wanted children as long as he could remember and soon after being blessed with a daughter, he learned he had a son.

"Thank you for my son," Kingsley had said when she'd told him of Nico, told him she'd met his son and the young man was everything a father could wish for and more. Kingsley's voice, usually so suave and measured, had been hoarse with his gratitude and grief for the lost years. "Thank you for finding him."

Thank you for finding him. She heard those words even now in her ears. She had searched for him and sought for him and found him, and now here he was before her in the bed they'd shared. And in a few hours he would leave her.

Nora reached out and touched Nico's lips. Nico, who she and no one else had found.

"Finders keepers..."

Nico stirred in his sleep. His eyes opened. She knelt by his shoulder and lowered her nightgown to her waist. Leaning over him she brought her breast to his mouth. He latched on to her nipple and she sighed as the pleasure rose up in her and pushed back the sadness. The dead felt nothing. That she could feel the scrape of his teeth, the heat of his breath on her skin, the gentle tug of his mouth, was all the proof she needed that she lived.

She shifted to give him her other breast as his hands roamed over her arms and down her back. Nico dragged her closer and grasped the fabric of her gown, pulling it up and off her completely. For the first time she was naked with him, completely and utterly naked.

"I need you," she said into his ear.

"Then take me."

She took him in her hand and guided him inside her. With her hands on his chest, she rode him. He gripped her hips as her inner muscles clamped onto his thick inches that penetrated to her core.

She leaned in and kissed him on the mouth, spiraling her hips to work him deeper into her. She stayed low over him, her hands braced on either side of his head, pushing against him until he gasped and arched underneath her.

Nora lightly gripped his bare neck, not to hurt him or even hold him, but simply to touch the most vulnerable part of him at his most defenseless. Her nipples grazed his chest as she moved on him, grinding her clitoris into the base of his shaft and forcefully clenching herself around him. When she couldn't hold back anymore, she came. Her vagina fluttered with deep contractions as Nico exhaled her name. He came then, too, pouring into her, filling her with his wet heat.

Panting, Nora collapsed onto Nico's chest. He held her close, held her tight. She should have been at peace now, but she wasn't. It wasn't enough to fuck him or let him fuck her. She wanted to possess him—every part of him. She wanted to own his heart, his body, his cock, his semen, his soul, even his life. But she couldn't ask that of him, could she?

"You have to go soon, don't you?" Nora asked, once they'd both caught their breaths.

"It's a long drive back, but I'll stay until you tell me to go."

She never wanted to tell him he could go. But she knew his vines waited for him and she cared about him too much to keep him from the land and the work that was his raison d'être.

"I think I'm ready now," she said.

"I'll come with you," he whispered. He knew what she needed and offered first, saving her the indignity of having to ask for it.

They rose from bed and bathed together. Nico put on yesterday's clothes—he'd brought no others with him. She wore a simple white skirt and sweater.

Nico took the urn off the fireplace mantel and put it in her hands. He held the door open for her and side by side they walked the stone path toward the lake. The sun had risen and God had given them a perfect spring morning—cloudless and cold.

They reached the water's edge and Nora stood so that the lake lapped at her toes.

"I prepared a speech on the plane ride over," she told Nico. "Seems stupid now. I tried to say it yesterday and could only get one word out."

"Say it now. I want to hear it."

She swallowed and nodded. Then she began.

"Søren..." She paused and let the pain claw at her. The dead felt no pleasure, but they felt no pain, either. Pain, too, was proof of life. "Søren isn't here. I know you wouldn't want him here so I didn't ask him to come with me."

She stopped again, breathed again.

"You should take that as a sign of how much I love you, that I didn't ask him to come with me."

Another breath.

"You never should have hated him. I think I hated you a little because of how much you hated him. But that was unfair of me, and I'm sorry. After all, you're the reason we're together. If you hadn't made me go to church that day, practically tricked me into going to church that day, I would never have met him. But you know what's funny about you and him?"

Nora closed her eyes. A tear escaped and dropped into the water at her feet.

"I still remember on the way to church that morning, you asked a question. You said, 'All I ever wanted was a daughter who loves God, goes to church, respects her priest and maybe even respects her mother a little. You think that's too much to ask?' Well, Mom, I go to church every Sunday. Did you know that? And I not only respect my priest, I love him with all my heart. And I do respect my mother, too. More than a little. She put up with me for thirty-six years. I think you probably qualify for sainthood at this point."

Nico stepped forward and with his bare hands wiped the tears off her face.

She looked into his pale green eyes.

"She thanked me, you know," Nora said. "The mother superior of her order called me two weeks ago and said, 'Come now if you want to see your mother this side of heaven.' I left immediately. Got there just in time. She was already going in and out of consciousness. But she woke up enough to recognize me. That's when she thanked me."

"For what? For coming?"

"For being a bad daughter," Nora said, laughing. "Mom smoked until I was eleven years old. She caught me trying to smoke one of her cigarettes. That's when she quit. That might have given her a few extra years, quitting. By the time they found the cancer, it had spread all over her. She didn't even have any symptoms. Only a cough."

"Be grateful you had those few hours. My father dropped dead in the fields."

"What would you say to him if you could say anything?" she asked.

"Blood might be thicker than water, but wine is thicker than blood," Nico said.

It was over a cup of communion wine that she'd first looked into her Father's eyes.

"That is it," she said.

She turned back to the water before her—the expanse of

lake so clear and blue and cold. She wished the water weren't so cold.

"A nun for a mother. A priest for a lover. Søren, *now* I can hear God laughing at me."

"He's laughing at me, too," Nico said. They both knew why.

"I wish we could have found a way to be friends," she said as if her mother could hear her. "I wish we could have known each other better. But you never told me your story. I wish you had listened to mine. If you'd heard the story I told Nico last night you would know that Søren was the best thing that ever happened to me, that he wasn't the monster you wanted to believe he was. I am glad I left him, though, ten years ago. At least you and I got to spend a little time together."

She stopped once more to breathe. Why was it so hard to breathe?

"You probably thought I was angry at you all this time," Nora continued. "And that's why I stayed away from you. But the truth was I wasn't angry. I'd worked so hard to become another person and the minute we were together, I was Ellie, your disappointment of a daughter again. I hope the view is good from where you are right now, and you can look down and see that my life is beautiful and rich and full of the love of generous and noble people and that my days are filled with work that is fulfilling and worthwhile and my nights are even better and none of your business."

Nico laughed softly next to her. She wished she could take his hand, but the box weighed her down. She would let it weigh her down no longer.

"I hope you see, too, that I do love you, and I did love you all this time, even when we were apart. And I will see you again someday, because even though your heart led you down a different road than mine, we will eventually reach the same destination."

She knelt at the water and opened the silver box that contained her mother's precious ashes.

Gingerly she lowered the box into the water and let it sink to the bottom. The ashes of Margaret Delores Kohl, of Sister Mary John, of Nora's mother, rose up and spread through the water like a pale cloud.

"I love you, Momma."

It took everything she had to say, but she said it and she said it smiling.

She unclasped the saint medal she'd worn for a week now.

"Every saint medal I own Søren gave me. Every one but this one."

"Who is it?" Nico asked.

"Saint Monica. My mother wore it all her life. Monica, patron saint of mothers of disappointing children."

"Is that why she wore it? She thought you were a disappointment?"

"Monica was also patron saint of women in abusive relationships."

"You said she thought Søren abused you. Is that why she wore it?"

"No." Nora looked Nico in the eyes. She remembered her father slapping her, shoving her, choking her. "She gave it to me before she went into the coma and told me something I never knew, but should have. Father Greg gave it to her two months after she got married. Only he knew the truth. She wore it because of my father. That's why she'd hoped for a miscarriage. Not so she could become a nun, but so she wouldn't have to marry my father who beat her. It wasn't that she didn't want me. She didn't want him. And all this time I thought she regretted having me...."

With a shaking hand, Nora reached out over the water and let the necklace go.

But before it could break the surface of the lake, Nico caught it.

She looked at him in surprise.

"I never told you this, but you were my nightmare," Nico said to her, clutching the medal in his fingers. "I counted ten men my mother had affairs with. Those were the ten I saw. I know there were others. I also knew I looked nothing like my father. I knew someday someone would tell me the truth, the truth I didn't want to know. And that person was you. Even if this medal feels like a weight, don't let it go. Your nightmare might turn into your best dream someday."

Nico turned his hand and showed her a tarnished gold band that he wore around it.

"My father's wedding ring," Nico said.

He took her wrist and poured the silver chain and pendant into her palm.

"If you stood outside the circle that is Søren and me and our love for each other, you would see me sleeping with dozens of other men in the past twenty years. You would see him loving someone else, another man who Søren loves as much as he loves me. It makes no sense to anyone outside our circle. But step inside it and you'll find nothing but love there. You don't know what secrets your parents kept from you. You don't know what their marriage was. If your father didn't judge her, didn't hate her, you shouldn't, either."

Nico nodded and put his arm around her. They walked away from the water, away from the ashes, away from her grief, away from her past.

"You're leaving now," she said once they reached the cottage. "I feel bad for keeping you up all night. It's a long drive on little sleep."

"I'll be thinking of you all the way home. You'll keep me awake."

"Thank you for listening to me. I needed to talk last night."

They held each other for a long time. She felt Nico's body trembling under her hands.

"Are you laughing?" she asked him.

"Trying not to," he said. "I'm laughing at Kingsley for giving you Sutherlin as a last name."

"I told that asshole if he called me Eleanor Sutherlin again I'd slap him into the next century. When I became a dominatrix and needed a new name, he pulled that out of his memory banks."

"What did you do?" he asked, as they walked to his car.

"I slapped him into the next century."

Nico grinned at her.

"What happened to your Wyatt? Did you keep in touch with him?"

"No," Nora said, her smile fading. "We looked good on paper, Wyatt and I did. And Søren and I made no sense at all. But here it is, almost twenty years later and Søren and I are still together, still in love. And Wyatt..."

"What about him?"

Nora swallowed hard. "Four years after we graduated, they found him dead in his apartment in Chelsea."

Nico's eyes widened.

"Turns out Wyatt had bipolar disorder. Explained how he had so much energy he could talk circles around me, which takes either talent or a manic episode. A college friend of mine told me. Apparently they changed his meds and he..." She paused and tried to imagine her life had she stayed with Wyatt. Would they have married? Could she have helped him? Would she have been a widow at age twenty-six? "They published his poetry after he died. He was good."

"Nora," Nico said. "So much lost."

"So much found." She took his face in her hands and kissed him. "Do you believe in God?"

"I'm a grape farmer. My whole life I've watched water turn into wine. Of course I believe in God."

She took a deep shuddering breath and looked up at Nico. Last night had meant something to her, meant so much that she couldn't bear to sully it with a secret.

"Ten years ago I got pregnant. It was Kingsley's. I didn't have the baby. I should have told you this months ago, should have told you before you even kissed me. I'm telling you now. I don't regret my choice, but all this time I haven't been able to shake the feeling I was supposed to have Kingsley's child. When I learned about you that feeling finally went away."

Nico only stared at her a moment, and then he did something she never expected he would do. He kissed her on the forehead.

"It went away, because I am Kingsley's child," he said. "And you had me, Mistress Nora, and you will always have me."

"Nico..."

"Kingsley is my father. Søren is your 'Father.' We were meant to find each other. And that is my theology."

"I appreciate your theology," she whispered.

He kissed her then, a final kiss, a goodbye kiss. The worst kind of kiss.

After the kiss, Nico didn't speak. He turned away, got into his car and drove off. He didn't look back when he left her, and she watched him until he disappeared from view.

Nora returned to the cottage, crawled into bed and slept the day away. When she awoke it was nearly night in the Black Forest but still evening in America. She found her phone and walked with it until she picked up a signal.

It rang only once before he answered.

"Eleanor?"

"God, I've missed you."

"Where are you?" Søren asked, sounding more relieved than she'd ever heard him.

"Bavaria," she said. "I'm in the Black Forest."

"Bavaria? It's been two weeks and no one's heard a word from you. What are you doing—"

"Mom died."

On the other end of the line she heard nothing but stunned silence.

"It was lung cancer," she said, as if it mattered. It didn't.

"Little One, I'm so sorry."

"She only had days or hours, they didn't know. That's why I left so fast. I had to be there before she was gone."

"Were you?"

"She was lucid for a day before lapsing into a coma for four days. I held her hand while she died." Nora closed her eyes. Her mother had clung to life with terrifying tenacity. On the fourth night of the watch, Eleanor had fallen asleep bedside, holding her mother's hand. Her mother's hand was warm when Eleanor fell asleep. By the time she woke up five hours later, it was cold. "She wouldn't have wanted me leaning on you for comfort. She wouldn't have wanted you there, even for me. Out of respect for her…"

"I understand," he said. "I know how she felt about me. And I was always grateful that she kept our secret even though she hated me."

"I owed her because of that. Before she died, she said she wanted her ashes spread here in the Black Forest. This was her favorite place as a little girl."

"How are you, Eleanor?" Søren asked, and she heard the concern in his voice from an ocean away. "Tell me the truth."

"We're all orphans now—you, me, Kingsley," she said, and she didn't know why. "I wonder what that means."

"It means we must love each other even more because all we have is each other."

"I'm sorry I missed our anniversary, sir."

She broke on the *sir* and cried into the phone.

"You shouldn't be alone right now," Søren said. "I hate that you're alone."

"I'm okay, I promise."

"When's your flight home?" he asked.

"I don't have one. I bought a one-way ticket."

Søren went silent on the other end.

"Eleanor," he finally said, "you are coming back, aren't you?"

"I'm coming back. I always come back to you. Eventually. And you know how much trouble I get into in Europe anyway. Better get out before I do something I regret."

"I don't think you've ever regretted anything you've ever done in your entire life, Little One. And that is why I love you so much."

"Will you love me if I stay here a little while longer?"

"What's keeping you in Germany?"

"Nothing," she said truthfully. "Nothing at all."

"Is something keeping you in France?"

Although his words were as neutral as his tone, she knew that he knew. He might not know she and Nico had spent the night together, but he knew what they were to each other. She could hide nothing in her heart from Søren.

"It is beautiful there," she said.

"You've been through so much in the past few months. Take all the time you need. But know I will miss you every moment until you come home to me."

"I love you, sir."

"I love you, too, Little One. And you should know, your mother loved you, too. She told me that in the days before I became the enemy. She told me how much she loved you."

"I miss her, Søren. I didn't think I would miss her this much."

"You miss her so much because you lost her twenty years ago, and only now are you letting yourself grieve."

"She turned her back on me the night you sent me away."

"I came back for you."

"She didn't," Nora said.

"That was her loss, and my eternal gain."

Nora didn't speak. And into the silent void of her pain, Søren prayed aloud over the phone.

"'Therefore once for all this short command is given to you—*love and do what you will.* If you keep silent, keep silent by love, if you speak, speak by love, if you correct, correct by love, if you pardon, pardon by love—let love be rooted in you, and from the root nothing but good can grow.'"

"Amen," Nora said. "That's beautiful. Whose prayer is that?"

"Saint Augustine's."

Eleanor smiled. "Monica's sinner son."

"Monica's *sainted* son," Søren said, ever the pedant, ever the priest.

Nora told Søren she loved him one more time before hanging up and walking back to the cottage.

She hadn't slept well for two weeks. Now she surrendered to her exhaustion and slept through the night. When she woke up, she knew exactly what do with her mother's Saint Monica medal.

In no hurry whatsoever, Nora cleaned up last night's mess in the cottage. The cottage had treated her well, given her and

Nico sanctuary—she would return the kindness. She packed and dressed and put her things in the car.

She drove all day, leaving Bavaria far behind her. Her mother had been born in Germany and Germany was part of Nora's ancestry, her past. Now she looked to the future.

At dusk she finally passed through Marseille. At nightfall she stood in front of a French country house that stood on dusty soil in the midst of rolling acres of grape vines.

She knocked on the door.

"Sanctuary?" she said to Nico when he opened the door.

He narrowed his eyes at her.

"If I let you in, I'll put you to work."

"I'll earn my keep."

"Not in the vineyards. I want stories."

"Stories I have. And it's you I want."

He took a step back and let her in the door. He dragged her into his arms and brought her to his bed. They made love in a frenzy and when the frenzy passed, Nora pulled the Saint Monica medal from her bag and clasped it around Nico's neck. The silver shone against his skin like moonlight on water.

"There are three eternal truths about me you have to know, Nico," she said. "I love Søren. I belong to Søren. And I will go back to Søren."

"Wine and women should always be allowed to breathe. You own me. I would never try to own you."

"I've never owned anyone before." She touched the medal where it hung next to his heart. "I've done everything else, but never that."

"I'm honored to be your first." Nico kissed her to make it official. If a promise couldn't be sealed with a kiss, it wasn't a promise worth making.

She stretched out on top of him, her head on his shoulder and his arm around her, not to keep her but simply to hold her.

"Where's my story?" Nico asked.

"Which one do you want? I have so many stories..."

"Tell me the one that you said would make me love Kingsley."

"That's a fun story. It involves a lesbian bartender in a three-piece suit, your father in a corset and high heels and a televangelist with a dirty secret."

Nico's chest rumbled with his laugh.

"Tell me," he said. "Tell me all your stories."

"This is the story they told me. And now I'm telling it to you."

She settled in closer to Nico, as close as she could get. She would return home to America and to Søren eventually, but now this was her home—Nico's bed, Nico's body, Nico's heart. Søren owned her and Kingsley. Kingsley owned Juliette. And now that she owned Nico it was as if the final tumbler had turned and the one locked door in her life opened. Time to walk through it.

She took a breath and began her tale.

"Once there lived a King without a kingdom..."

* * * * *